Jackie Collins brings the <s> sexy world of superstardom alive. Her phenomenally successful novels have made her as famous as the movers and shakers, power-brokers and super-stars she writes about with an insider's knowledge. With 200 million copies of her books sold in more than forty countries, Jackie Collins is one of the world's top-selling writers. In a series of sensational bestsellers, she has blown the lid off Hollywood life and loves. 'It's all true,' she says. 'I write about real people in disguise. If anything, my characters are toned down – the real thing is much more bizarre.'

There have been many imitators, but only Jackie Collins can tell you what *really* goes on in the fastest lane of all. From Beverly Hills bedrooms to a raunchy prowl along the streets of Hollywood. From glittering rock parties and concerts to stretch limos and the mansions of the power-brokers – Jackie Collins chronicles the *real* truth.

# JACKIE COLLINS

# The Stud

# &

# L.A. Connections

PAN BOOKS

*The Stud* first published 1969 by W. H. Allen.
First published in paperback 1970 by Mayflower Books.
First published by Pan Books 1984.
*L.A. Connections* first published 1999 by Macmillan.
First published in paperback by Pan Books 1999.

This omnibus first published 2007 by Pan Books
an imprint of Pan Macmillan Ltd
Pan Macmillan, 20 New Wharf Road, London N1 9RR
Basingstoke and Oxford
Associated companies throughout the world
www.panmacmillan.com

ISBN 978-0-330-45204-5

1 3 5 7 9 8 6 4 2

A cip catalogue record for this book is available from
the British Library.

Printed and bound in Great Britain by
Mackays of Chatham plc, Chatham, Kent

# The Stud

# 1

## TONY

## LONDON 1969

There is something very exciting about the beginning of the evening—well, the beginning of my evening, usually about ten-thirty, eleven o'clock. Every night at 'Hobo' is like a party—a great party where everyone knows and likes everyone else.

They start coming in slowly. First the ones that want to be sure of a good table, then the watchers. Usually this whole group is stacked neatly out of the way on the wrong side of the room, or if they are really rough, in the back room. We've got a closed membership, but a few manage to find their way in. Then everyone sits around waiting for the swingers, and about twelve-thirty, one o'clock, they start arriving. Golden-haired girls in cowboy outfits, Indian gear, boots, backless topless see-through dresses. The wilder the better. Their escorts varying from the long-haired mob of rock groups to the latest young actors. Elegant young debs in full evening dress, with chinless-wonder escorts. The older society group. The rich Greeks. The even richer Arabs. An odd movie star—an odd M.P. or visiting senator. Anybody famous who's in town. Young writers, dress designers, photographers, models. They all come to look and be looked at, and to see their friends. It's like a building excitement—reaching a breathless climax at around two a.m. when the room is so jammed you couldn't get anyone else in except maybe Frank Sinatra or Mick Jagger.

It seems ridiculous that six months ago they would hand me a couple of quid and wouldn't recognise me if we passed in the street. Now they can't wait to grab hold of me—'Dahling'—kiss—kiss—kiss—'Who's here tonight?' Sly grab if the boy-friend or husband isn't looking. 'Please don't give us a lousy table like last time'—affectionate squeeze and promising look. Then husband or boy-friend steps forward—firm handshake, few

5

masculine chummy words, and I hand them over to Franco, swinging head-waiter supreme, who whisks them off to whatever table their position rates. The watchers on one side of the room, the doers on the other. All very neat, the duds with the bread tucked firmly away in the back room.

Yeah, I'm very popular now, everyone wants to know. Funny thing, isn't it? I'm the same guy, talk in the same voice, the clothes are a little more expensive but that's about the only difference. You wouldn't believe it though, the ladies practically fight to climb in the sack with me. You would think I was doing them a big favour, and listen, the way things have been going I think I am!

I tell you it's a great life if you don't weaken.

I suppose you're wondering how this all came about, how a guy like me, Tony Shwartsburg from somewhere near the Elephant and Castle, turned into Tony Blake—man about town, friend of the stars, host at the most 'in' discothèque, 'Hobo'. I have exchanged confidences such as 'Where can we get some pot?' and 'Got any birds?' with some of the most famous in the land. 'Tony can arrange anything' is a well-known catch phrase around town.

Well, to begin with I had the same useless tough life as most of the kids in my neighbourhood—fighting in the back streets, watching in on the fights at home. My parents, Sadie and Sam, were a nice old Jewish couple who hated each other. Sam couldn't care less about me, but to Sadie the sun shone out of my left ear. 'Learn a trade like your cousin Leon,' she would say, 'let the family be proud of you.' I got laid at thirteen, just before I got barmitzvahed. If the family knew they'd sure as old harry be proud of me. It was all good clean fun. The girl, she was a few years older than me, gave me the crabs, and I spent about six months alternatively trying to get rid of them and passing them on to any girl who got lucky! Eventually I passed them on to the wrong girl and everyone found out. Sadie had hysterics and Sam patted me on the back and bought me some ointment.

At sixteen I got caught pinching petrol from a car. It was a good racket while it lasted. You hosed it out into a can, and sold it back to the garage where it had probably come from in the first place! Anyway, they shoved me on probation and that was the end of my criminal tendencies.

I got a variety of jobs, delivering papers, sweeping up in a factory, usher in the local cinema—I got fired from that when the manager found me making it with a bird in the back row of the stalls. It was his best usherette and he was screwing her at the same time, so he was a bit choked. Unfortunately I knocked her up and there was a family scandal, but seeing the manager wanted her back, as good usherettes were hard to come by, he paid for her to get unknocked up and everything was all right.

By this time Sadie and Sam were getting a bit fed up with me, and who could blame them? Sam stopped screaming at Sadie and started on me. It was a good job someone thought of Uncle Bernie.

Uncle Bernie was the success of the family. He owned two delicatessens and had sort of cut himself off from the rest of his clan. Anyway Sadie felt that as she was his only sister he owed her a favour, and she dragged me down to his place in Great Portland Street and insisted he gave me a job. He wasn't too thrilled at the prospect, but knowing he wasn't going to get rid of Sadie any other way, he agreed.

He had a daughter, Muriel, a big strapping girl with lots of thick black hair—everywhere—you name a place, Muriel had thick black hair there. She wasn't bad apart from that, a bit sexy looking. Big tits and a thin crooked nose. I suppose I shouldn't have, I mean she was my cousin and all, but one day the opportunity arose, and if the opportunity arises who am I to put it down? Of course Uncle Bernie found out and there ended my career in a delicatessen. It was all too much for Sadie, and even Sam wasn't pleased about it.

Life at the Elephant was becoming a drag anyway, and having got as far as Great Portland Street, I thought why not go a bit further. I got a job as a dishwasher at the Savoy, and a room in Camden Town. Life was great. I entered my twenties a happy man.

I met a girl, Evie, a pretty curly-haired blonde, she was a

7

hostess at a clip joint. She fixed me up with a job as a waiter and I discovered the world of tips. It was great, taught me a lot about people. Taught me the right way to milk a pound from a drunk whose intention was to leave nothing.

I was making twenty quid a week. I branched out to striped Italian suits and pointed shoes, then dated girls with a bit more class, hairdressers, shop assistants and all that group. Not bad, I felt like a king! Visited the Elephant on Sundays, and handed Sadie a fiver. Of course she never took it, she always came out with a speech about how I should save my money, settle down, look for a nice Jewish girl and get married, be like cousin Leon—in my opinion a real schmuck.

I left the clip joint and started as a busboy in a high-class restaurant, not so much bread but a road to better things. And the better things were all around me. The birds that came into the place Beautiful! Furs, jewellery, expensive smells.

From there I became a waiter in another high-class place and I became involved with Penny, daughter of the owner. Penny was something else. Red hair, she was very neat, small and compact. I suppose I fell in love with her. Couldn't make it, that was probably why. Looking back on it now, I reckon she was undersexed, but at the time it bothered me a lot. She was the first girl that I had wanted and couldn't have.

I don't want to sound conceited, but imagine a taller Tony Curtis with a touch of Michael Caine and Kris Kristofferson.

Anyway Penny and I wanted to get married. Her father of course was furious, but she got round him and since he didn't want his daughter marrying a waiter he opened a new place and put me in charge—sort of a de luxe head-waiter.

It all started there. That's where I first saw Fontaine.

Of course everyone's heard of Fontaine Khaled, she's sort of like a national institution, though not so old—around thirty-five I would say, even now I still don't know the truth.

Fontaine looks very haughty upper-class English. Beautiful, of course, with chiselled cut bones (by nature or cosmetic surgery no one knows), a fine parchment skin, an angular boney body which lends itself to fancy clothes, and long blonde hair worn pulled back.

When I first saw her I couldn't take my eyes off. Here was a lady. Sounds corny I know, but there was no mistaking the fact. She had been a world famous photographic model, and had retired to marry Benjamin Al Khaled, billionaire. She was always in the papers, jetting here there and everywhere, showing us around her house in Acapulco, her castle in Spain, her town house in London or penthouse in New York.

I read the columns a lot. In my business it's always good to know who's who, so as soon as she came in I knew it was her. She was with three men and two women all of the same social scene but not in the same class as her. I led them to their table personally, a thing I had stopped doing when I took over the place. I even referred to her by name just to let her know I was around. But she didn't give me a glance. So much for the instant impact of Tony Blake.

There was no Benjamin Al Khaled with her, and I didn't think she was anyone's date, very square the fellows with her, typical no balls types, with loud public school voices.

She was wearing what I thought was a rabbit coat, but later I discovered during a course of intensified education that it was chinchilla. I thought I was pretty hip then, but I didn't even know a Gucci handbag from a Marks & Sparks.

I hovered around the table a lot, but not so much as a look.

I eavesdropped, 'St Moritz is becoming a terrible bore'—'Did you know Jamie broke his leg in Tibet?'—'Do you *believe* St Laurent this year?'

Pretty dull snatches of conversation came my way.

The one that paid the bill left a nothing tip.

Two nights later she was back, this time with her husband. He was much older than her. They were with another old guy. She threw me a brief smile on her way in, which startled me, and after that they came in a lot whenever they weren't flying round the world.

Penny was causing me problems. Since her father had promoted me, so to speak, I was having a fair amount of success. Customers liked me, I remembered their names, saw their food was just right, and became casually friendly with some of them.

The place developed a good reputation, people were disappointed if I wasn't there. They liked to be greeted by name and made to feel important.

Penny's father realised I was good for the joint and I realised Penny was no good for me. It was not a good situation. She started to get very narky and jealous, accusing me of all sorts of things, which were true. Well, I don't know if she thought I was jerking off or what, but I certainly wasn't getting any action from her. I moved to a small one-roomed flat off the Edgware Road and she caught me there one day with a red-haired croupier—female of course!

What tears and scenes! She even offered me her virginity but, by that time, I didn't even fancy it. So we parted bad friends.

Needless to say it was a matter of time before her father and I also parted company. I had my eyes wide open for another job. By that time I had had the waiter bit, I wanted to move up in the world, progress. The ideal situation would be to get my own little place, but for that one needed bread, and who had any?

I cast my eyes around and one memorable night they met squarely with Fontaine's. It was one of those looks, her cool aquamarine eyes clashed straight on with my moody dark stare (many's the bird who's told me I've got a moody dark stare) and that was it. We both knew something had to give.

She went to the powder-room shortly after and I was waiting when she came out.

'Tony,' she said, she had a deep very English clipped accent, 'you're wasting yourself here—why don't you drop by and see me tomorrow, I have an idea that maybe you can help me with.' She handed me a small hand-engraved card with her address and added, 'About three o'clock will be fine.'

I nodded dumbly, to tell you the truth I was knocked out by the whole thing.

I must have changed my outfit ten times the next day—was a casual look best or should I go for the slightly formal Italian gear? I finally settled for a pale lilac shirt with a stiff white collar, and a black silk suit.

I arrived half-an-hour early at this knockout pad she had in

Belgravia. It was too much! I found out it was an ex-embassy. They even had a swimming pool.

A butler settled me down in what I suppose was the living-room, but it turned out to be a mere waiting-room. It was all expensive with crazy carved furniture and jazzy old pictures on the wall. Some of them were rather sexy—there was one with three birds and one guy that was a bit strong, but just when I was studying it a bit closer Fontaine came in 'Are you interested in art, Tony?' she asked.

She looked great in a long sort of silk robe and her hair all loose.

Man, I can still remember how nervous I was. This was real class.

'Let's go in the study,' she said. 'Would you care for a drink?'

I asked for a sherry, I figured it was the thing to have.

'You don't look like a sherry man to me,' she said, her eyes cool and amused.

I started to get excited there and then, and in the tight black trousers I was wearing, this was no joke. I approached her warily, she didn't back away, in fact she came towards me. I put my arms around her, she was tall, I could feel her bones through the thin robe. She fastened her arms about my neck and pulled my mouth on to hers.

It was some kiss, she was like a hungry animal pushing and probing with her tongue, biting and sighing. I think I can safely say I gave back as good as I got.

'Let's go upstairs,' she said at last, and added, 'It's all right, Benjamin is away.'

I followed her to a small elevator and we pressed closely together as it started up. She unzipped my trousers and rubbed me with her long talented fingers. Man, I was ready to shoot off there and then!

Suddenly the elevator stopped and she shrugged off her robe.

I stared at her lean body. She had tiny breasts with pale extended nipples. 'Are we there?' I asked foolishly.

'No, but we soon can be,' she replied pulling at my trousers.

The elevator was small, gave you a touch of the claustrophobia, but she managed to get me down to my bare skin.

11

I must say in all my dealings with birds I've never had one behave like *this*.

'Tony, you come up to all my expectations,' she muttered. 'Sit down, I'll show you how to do it in a lift.'

Oh man! What an experience!

Thinking back I didn't get a chance to do much because she did everything. Of course I rose to the occasion magnificently. I was out of my depth and knew it. I just let her have her way, I wasn't going to blow this set-up.

She dug her nails deep into my back and twisted her long white legs around me. She didn't moan or cry out. She muttered, 'Screw me you bastard, keep it hard.'

Well, I'd never had any problem doing *that*.

Afterwards she was all calm and businesslike. She stood up and put her robe on. She waited for me to struggle into my clothes, then the elevator took us back to the study.

I was destroyed. I flopped into a chair. She rang a bell, and the butler appeared with tea.

She chatted away in her high-class tinkly voice and who would have thought that half-an-hour earlier she'd been frothing and raving about in the elevator.

'I want to open a discothèque,' she said. 'Something different, something chic, somewhere to go that's fun—something mad and exclusive.'

'Yes?' I was all interest. Here came my big chance.

'You could manage something like that, couldn't you?'

She chatted on about how there was nowhere to go that was chic. 'All these places now are filled with scruffy little nothings—don't you think this town needs something different—somewhere for grown-ups like Paris has, or Rome?'

Her line of chat killed me. Somewhere for grown-ups yet! However I nodded seriously. I was looking for an out from the restaurant—this could be it.

'You start looking for premises, Tony,' she said, 'money's no problem. My husband will finance the whole thing. We'll pay you a good salary and five per cent of the profits. How's that? Of course you'll be running the whole show, does it appeal to you?'

12

Did it appeal to me? You bet your ass it appealed to me.

She stood up, smoothing her robe down. 'I have to get dressed now. Start looking and keep in touch.' She turned at the door. 'Oh, Tony, in the lift, that was nice, very nice, let's do it again soon.' Then in the same cool voice she added. 'The butler will show you out.'

It was all too much. This was a real cool lady and a raver to boot. I had a feeling I'd fallen in the right direction.

I set to work, started getting up early in the mornings and hanging around the estate agents, saw a lot of lousy joints. I had a feeling for what she wanted (ha ha) and I kept right on looking until I found it. It was a rooftop restaurant that had gone bust—bad neighbourhood everyone said, impossible to park—but baby, you get the right doorman and nowhere's impossible. To me, it was just right. Not too big, not too small. Different because instead of creeping down to some cellar you went up and you had windows and a view. I called Fontaine right away, and she came gliding over with a chauffeur in a Silver Cloud Rolls. She loved it too. We were in business.

We had tea at Fortnums. I hadn't seen her since the day at her house. She was wearing a silver mink coat and hat, and everyone turned to take another look.

She stared at me with those cool eyes and I knew the look. 'Benjamin's home,' she said, 'but I have another place.'

'Well, let's go,' I said, gulping down dainty tea sandwiches and feeling pretty good.

She dismissed the chauffeur and we took a cab to a small apartment building in Chelsea. It was one room luxury, a big bed covered in white fur, rugs, mirrors everywhere, louvred shutters to remove the daylight and red-tinged lights. A few erotic pictures on the wall, a lot of dirty books in a built-in bookcase next to the bed.

'This is my whore's room,' she said with a small tight smile. I didn't know what to say, I'd never met anyone like her before. She took off her clothes and stretched out on the bed. I fumbled with mine, I mean, well, I was embarrassed!

I finally got them off and started some action. She just lay there very stiff, smiling slightly. Very different from the last time. It was rather exciting really, took me off guard so to speak. I mean, I was expecting it to be like the last time.

It didn't take me long before I was through—wowee! I rolled off her and studied our bodies in the mirrored ceiling.

She said very slowly, 'Tony—how would you like to learn to be a good lover?'

I sat up on one elbow and stared at her. Was she kidding? I mean I was all there you know, I'd never been lacking in *that* department.

As it happens, looking back on it now, I suppose she did teach me a lot. Little tricks she'd picked up in Beirut, Tangier, South America. You name it, she knew it. She was a great teacher, very detailed. I grew to look forward to our little classes more than anything. Of course I was knocking off another bird on the side. Fontaine didn't know about it, but it was useful, gave me a chance to do my homework so I'd be in good shape for Fontaine.

Lana was a stripper, a bit of a scrubber but a knockout when it came to practising my lessons. In fact, she added a few ideas of her own. She had the best pair of knockers around, a big full juicy bird. I mean Fontaine was very classy and all that jazz, but a bit lacking in the tits and ass department. A man likes his steak rare, but he needs his bread and potatoes too.

Life was really good. I left the restaurant and started organising the new place. Interior decorators, waiters to find, members' lists, ordering stock. There were a million and one things to do.

Fontaine chose the name, 'Hobo'. It was good, although Benjamin offered the suggestion of calling it 'Fontaine's'. She said that would be tasteless and vulgar. She was right, she was usually right.

And so eventually we opened. Big party, lots of publicity, all the right people. They all came, they always turn out in bulk for anything free. Fontaine personally supervised the guest list and I think that's what started the whole thing off, her guest list. It was such a wild mixture—from rock groups to movie stars to high society to hookers (international ones of course!). It was great. It

14

all just happened, and within a few weeks 'Hobo' was *the* place and all of a sudden I was *the* person to know.

It's wild really, I still sort of expect the bubble to burst. But here I am, Tony Blake—ex-nothing, ex-waiter, now great host, lover and friend of the stars.

Great me!

# 2

## FONTAINE

I have always enjoyed waking late and breakfasting in bed. Benjamin says it's because bed is my favourite place. He's right actually. He gets up at the unearthly hour of seven a.m., so I lie awake with my eyes closed and listen to him cough and belch and fart! Delightful! Benjamin Al Khaled in the mornings—I wonder what the society gossip columns would make of an exclusive like that! I've begged him for separate bedrooms but that's one thing he won't surrender to. He likes his nightly ashes hauled, and maybe in the middle of the night too if he feels like it. So the communal bedroom stays. It's worth it, he's very very rich. Even I don't know how many millions. He's sixty-one years old and randy as hell.

Bed is delicious. I can lie here and think and relax and not have to do anything. At eleven my maid wakes me. She brings breakfast and the papers, runs my bath and lays out the clothes I tell her to. I can have anything I want. Benjamin will give me anything except actual cash.

We have been married for five years and both of us were married before. His ex-wife is a bitch. Plain and dreary with two hulking great children by him—Alexandra and Ben junior. My ex-husband is somewhere in California now, basking in the sun on the money that Benjamin had to pay him to agree to a divorce. Paul was always lazy. When we were married he never did a stroke of work, just lived off my hard-earned modelling money. He was rather beautiful though, and very virile. It was a shame to have to divorce him, but I was bored with modelling, and one doesn't grow any younger, and there was Benjamin offering me a title and all that divine money. Well, really, I had no choice.

Being married to Benjamin is rather like a part-time job. He works so hard and travels so much that I hardly ever see him. That's why he said I could do the discothèque, somewhere for me to go, 'a little interest' as he calls it. 'Little interest' indeed. It's making a fortune! Benjamin would have a fit if he knew, he hates me to have any money of my own. He thinks it would make me independent of him. Isn't that silly? As if I would be independent of all his millions.

Benjamin thinks I'm faithful to him. He told me. He thinks that if I'm well looked after at home I won't want any more. For a man of sixty-one he's really very naïve, especially since he's away half the time. As if I could be satisfied with that withered old thing!

Fortunately I have arranged my life rather well, and I have occasional exciting affairs. In London the current one is Tony. He's really rather divine. Very obvious looking, but tremendously sexual. Tall and strong, he has a body rippling with hidden muscles, and a black hairy chest which is *very* exciting. His face is an open invitation to bed. What an innocent he was when I got hold of him, and look at him now. Of course, basically he'll always be a head-waiter, but I think I've improved him beyond recognition.

The first time was a disaster. Of course he had an animal charm, a sexy walk, but that was about all. In bed he had a marvellous body, but he had no skill. For someone so well endowed it was a shame. I thought to myself, he is very attractive in a basic way. If he appeals to me he will probably appeal to lots of women. That's why I decided to use him in the discothèque. I needed someone, and as it turned out he's just the right person. Of course I know he's having an affair with everyone in sight now, including my best friend Vanessa. He thinks I don't suspect. Isn't that silly?

I mean I don't mind, but of course I must pretend not to know, pretend a little touch of jealousy, otherwise his manly pride would be hurt. Vanessa and I laugh about it, 'Tony the stud' we call him. It's great fun comparing notes. He thinks he's the best lover in the world. He's not bad, but if he wasn't so well endowed he would be disastrous. Poor conceited Tony.

I'll never forget the first time he came to see me at my house. The clothes he had on—unbelievable! A cheap black silk suit with trousers so tight his pecker shone through like a beacon! I decided I had to take a look. Benjamin was away, so I took him in my lift and enjoyed him there. Well, I mean to say there is nothing more dreary than always doing it on a bed. When I got his clothes off I thought 'Not bad', but after it was all over I knew there was a lot to teach him.

The best lover I ever had was this great big black zulu. I was doing a swimsuit lay-out for one of the glossies deep in the heart of nowhere—and we took a break for a cigarette and he grabbed me behind a tree and gave it to me quickly. Delicious! I'll never forget it, his timing was perfect, he brought me to the most beautiful climax ever! Unfortunately we moved to a new location the next day and I never saw him again. I often think about him, usually when Benjamin is sprawled on top of me huffing and puffing.

Vanessa says Tony is awed by me! Can you imagine! I suppose it's being married to a billionaire and everything. Rather useful, brings people to their knees, lots of respect and all that. Fame, money and titles that's all people really care about.

I don't want children. What for? They ruin your figure, give you a lot of boring trouble, and then leave you. I don't need children, I don't have what I suppose is called the maternal instinct. Personally, I like being free. My God, my mother never gained any advantages by having me. A woman should be strong, I've seen too many marriages fail because the wife was weak. Vanessa has three children and she never sees them. They live with their nanny on the fourth floor and she never goes up there. They might as well be in Siberia. Isn't that silly? She doesn't look too bad, a bit saggy. Saved by that pretty pretty face. One day I'm going to tell Tony I know about him and Vanessa. He'll have a fit! He thinks he's being so clever. He's like a little boy, hates being found out. I don't care, as long as he's got enough left for me he can do what he likes. He's really an idiot, a sexy idiot stud! It's that lower class mentality of his, he'll never change. He's useful though, definitely worth keeping on the leash. And so eager to learn. Always asking me where by bag came from, and what perfumes was I wearing, and who made my clothes.

Think I'll give him a call, pop in before the hairdresser . . .

# 3

## TONY

Tonight's going to be good. Two big parties in town and everyone will be coming along after. Fontaine nearly caught me today. Fast asleep in bed with this bird—Janet something or other, and her ladyship phones. 'I'm coming over.' Charming! Wake up Janet, she complains, horrible whiney voice, long sloppy black hair, ugh! I must have been well stoned. She struggles complaining into a dress hardly long enough to cover her ass, nice ass. I shove her out the front door, five minutes later Fontaine comes wafting in. I hardly had time to hide the sheets!

Sometimes she's like a witch, very cold. 'I have to go to the hairdresser,' she announces, stepping out of her Rhavis skirt, Gucci shoes and Dior stockings.

At times I hate her, I'm not a machine. She remains standing with her suit jacket still on, her hair hidden in a mink turban. She leans obscenely against the wall. She wants it standing up. I think of her husband. Poor guy, he's working his ass off while she's handing out the action. Never trust a woman that's what I always say. She looks like a high fashion model top half and a dirty photograph bottom half. The thought excites me and I manage to accommodate her. Oh man, I can imagine the scene if she'd caught me this morning!

She dresses briskly, her legs are getting thinner, she diets too much. 'I'll see you tonight,' she says zipping up her skirt, 'keep my table for seven—we have a French diplomat and his wife with us.' Then she was gone, leaving a cloud of Hermes 'Caleche'.

It was a good thing when it started. Fontaine Khaled and all that jazz. But she's kinky, she's definitely kinky and I don't want to be used the way she uses me. Her whore's room and her strange preferences.

What about her old man? He must be a right idiot. Now I've got all the crumpet I want. High class crumpet galore. But she's got me by the balls, 'Hobo' is hers, if I want out of screwing her then I'm out, period. It's not really fair, I built the whole place up, worked my ass off until five every morning, and all I get is peanuts compared to what the joint is making—and I've yet to see my share of the profits. I have no contract, nothing. I just work for her. She's a pretty cool bitch—a pretty clever bitch.

'Franco, bring me a scotch.' Franco's a great head-waiter. Probably I could grab him if I left here and opened up somewhere else. But with what? I've got no bread. People have offered to back me in a new place—women—it would be the same scene all over again. I was casting my eye around for a guy to promote a new joint, one of the rich Greeks would do. Got one in mind, but I'll have to play it cool, make it seem like his idea.

'Hallo, Tony darling.' This bird threw her arms round me, I swear I'd never seen her before.

'How are you?' I said beaming with pleasure, winking. The well-known Blake charm churned forth.

'I'm fine, this is Chicky and this is Robin and this is Henry.' Three nonentities strained forward to give me greetings. The evening was starting.

There are certain regulars who always congregate at the top table. It's called the top table 'cos it's at the top of the room in the best position for seeing everything, and it's where I sit, *when* I sit, which is about twice a night. I always make sure it's available for any visiting celebrities in case there's nowhere else. The regulars

19

can always be shuffled around. If I have a date she sits there. Oh, I'm allowed to have dates as long as it's not the same girl too often. After all, they just sit there by themselves all night.

The regulars are all guys, a varied selection, my friends. There's Sammy—small, wiry, dark-haired. A hat manufacturer —crumpet mad—always chatting up different birds. Likes them tall. I should really get him and Fontaine together, but she thinks he's revolting and he says she's a rich old bag. Any female over twenty is an old bag to him. Sammy's a sweet guy, but a lot of people don't understand him.

Then there's Franklin, quiet, young, good-looking and shy. Sits there drinking Coca-Cola all night. We all reckon he's a virgin.

Next Hal—an American promoter, constantly stoned, a wow with rich old widows. Fortyish, attractive if you like the Dean Martin type. He has a big heart, every bit of honest bread he makes he sends to his kid brother in New Jersey and that's the only thing he doesn't brag about.

Lastly, Massey, a singer. Good-looking in a black is beautiful way. Great dancer.

When there's nothing better to do and if none of us have dates, we sit there and discuss the talent. 'I'd like to screw that!' is a constant cry from our table.

Fontaine hates them all. 'Why do you always have that motley group around?' she questions. But they pay, so there's nothing she can do.

They all suspect about Fontaine and me, but no one actually knows. I like the regulars, they're a good group of guys.

Franklin came in first tonight. With a girl, surprise, surprise. His father is a big guy in the film business. The bird he was with was definitely too hot for him, probably thought he'd put in a good word with dad. She had those pouty lips and jaded eyes that all would-be movie stars have. Too much screwing and not enough fresh air! Franklin was treating her like a lady, all proper and polite. He's a nice kid, but a schmuck. Treat them rough if you want to lay them. She had lots of long thick reddish hair and she gave me the well-known come on look.

'Janine James—Tony Blake,' Franklin said, 'Janine's over here doing a film.'

'Hi,' she simpered.

Ugh, sometimes American broads turn me off, that horrible nasal twang. I gave her my angry knowing stare, that usually gets them. She responded with what I took to be a sexy look. Poor Franklin, he didn't have a chance with this one.

The next of the regulars to bounce in was Sammy, friendly, Cockney, pussy-crazy Sammy. As luck would have it he had no date, and he immediately launched into a line of chat with Janine. Franklin sat silently, I could see it was going to be one of those nights.

Fontaine's usual table was next to ours. I had explained to her a hundred times that she couldn't have the top table because it was the only table that could be made easily available in an emergency. This bugged her, but she settled for the next best. After all, she certainly wasn't there every night. Maybe six nights in a row then not at all for two or three weeks while she was on her travels. The places she went made me dizzy. Benjamin had his own private jet which was useful. She never came in with less than five or six people. She had this girl-friend Vanessa, blonde, pretty, a bit plump, but with huge bouncy knockers. Married to the son of the owner of a very famous chain store. Worth a fortune. Got three kids. Vanessa was a mess. She idolised Fontaine and copied her faithfully. It was only fair that I should knock her off. She practically begged me. I went to her house one afternoon while hubby was at the office and the kids were out with nanny. I don't think she knows about me and Fontaine, anyway she promised she wouldn't tell anybody about us. I hope to God she doesn't. It's all very risky. Anyway she's a lousy lay, but these unbelievable tits! I could just stay playing with them for hours, they smother you, all big and soft, very mumsy. Vanessa is usually in Fontaine's group with or without hubby who isn't bad—a lot better than Benjamin. I hear he's got a girl tucked away in a neat little flat. In my business you get to hear most things.

Fontaine and party made the grand entrance about one-thirty. She was covered in white mink to the ground. Her hair was piled high and secured with the gleam of diamonds. Husband was by her side, shorter than her and fat. She looked fantastic. Who would have thought that in the morning she had been leaning against my bedroom wall with her pubics on show! I had an insane desire to shout out—'I've had that!' but instead I went into the whole greeting routine. All the kisses and nice to see you's and all that bullshit.

Vanessa and hubby were naturally present. She looked her usual pretty mess. Whispy hair, boobies flopping in a chiffon dress. I gave her an unseen tweak on the nipple when I kissed her cheek. She blushed, I shook hands with hubby. 'How's Veronica?' I was tempted to say, Veronica was his girl-friend.

They had an elderly French couple with them, another youngish man and this girl. She stood back from the others and was quite obviously embarrassed by all the loud greetings. She was plainly dressed in comparison, a simple wool dress slightly too long and a single strand of pearls. She had long shining auburn hair pulled straight back and secured with a plain pearl slide. Very little makeup, in fact she wasn't that pretty—but there was something about her that gave me a jolt I could feel right in the pit of my stomach. She had these wide brown very innocent eyes, they stared at me with slight contempt. She certainly wasn't some little ding-a-ling obsessed by who to lay next, or how short her shirt could get. She was quite young, about seventeen or eighteen. All in the space of seconds I knew that I had to have this one. This one was special.

They were all sitting down. Wasn't anyone going to introduce me? Fontaine was busy ordering champagne, her cool aquamarine eyes darting around to see who was in. She waved at a few people and then Vanessa's husband took her off to dance. If there's one thing Fontaine's lousy at, it's dancing. It's good to know there is at least one thing she can't do. She's got no rhythm, sort of jerks around like a skinny puppet.

I smiled at the guy with the auburn-haired girl and extended my hand, 'I'm Tony Blake,' I said, very friendly like.

The girl didn't even glance at me, she stared off into the middle distance, looking bored. The guy was a creep. Square suit, short back and sides, a real nothing.

22

Benjamin joined in, 'Oh, Tony—don't you know Peter Lincoln Smith?'

The name rang a bell. I had met his father several times. He owned half of London.

'And this is my daughter Alexandra,' Benjamin finished proudly, 'just arrived home from Switzerland today.'

His daughter Alexandra! My mouth must have hung open for at least five minutes. His daughter!

She threw me a sulky 'How do you do.'

The French couple butted in then, and I had to chat to them. It seemed their daughter came in all the time and they had heard lots about me. I knew their daughter, ugly little blonde nympho who wore Paco Rabanne dresses and thought she was the knock-out of all times. I hadn't actually been there, but Sammy had, and his verdict was thumbs down.

Benjamin was now urging the creep to dance with Alexandra. She was blushing and saying she didn't want to dance. Peter Lincoln Smith was caught in the middle and didn't know what to do, to please Daddy or daughter. Daddy won, and a reluctant Alexandra was led off to the dance floor. There were hints of a great body. The dress wasn't showing anything, but it was there, hidden underneath.

I didn't know what to do, I was caught up with this girl, don't know why. I hadn't even spoken to her, she was probably a spoilt rich bitch. I fancied her like crazy, man, this was going to be tricky, dare I take the risk?

Fontaine came back to the table, breathless and slightly hot in all that white mink. The whole room had seen it, so she slipped it off, revealing a black body-moulding backless sheath. She certainly knew how to show herself off.

I took myself back to the regulars' table and ordered a stiff scotch. Massey had arrived with a thin angular model girl called Suki. Her hair was cropped close to her head, her skirt close to her ass and she wore a weird white makeup with huge clown-like eyes.

Massey was his usual cool self. 'Hey, man,' he said sitting down beside Sammy, 'what's the action tonight?'

'Same old action, everything's swinging,' I replied.

He was wearing a white suit, very smart. I thought I might get myself a white suit.

I spied Alexandra on the dance floor. Amongst all the movers she stood quietly holding her boy-friend at arms' length doing a sort of nothing shuffle.

I grabbed Suki and took her off to dance edging my way near to Alexandra. The only reaction she gave was a slightly incredulous look at Suki. Shit! What could I do to make the rich bitch notice me?

Suki was a very stylised dancer, religiously studied every new step, and wouldn't be caught dead doing anything that was out. She and Massey made a great couple. Me—I did a sort of wild shake and that was it.

'I bet this is different from Switzerland,' I yelled above the din of the music, an inane grin on my face.

Alexandra just ignored me. Either that or she didn't hear me.

Suki said, 'What?'

'Nothing,' I muttered, dragging her back to the table.

An Italian actress, Carla Cassoni, was making an entrance, surrounded by three attentive men.

'Wowee,' Sammy whistled through his teeth, 'How about that?!'

She was beautiful, black hair, olive skin, a body edging on being plump, but ending up merely voluptuous. Her new movie had just opened in town. Something about a peasant girl who gets raped by an army—I could understand the army!

I hurried over to give greetings, shaking hands warmly, meeting crystal-clear green eyes, a throaty accented voice. Ordinarily I would have become Charlie Charm, dancing attendance, but tonight my mind was elsewhere. I saw she got a good table, and left her with the three guys.

Miss Rich Bitch was sitting at her table. Peter was being led off to dance by Fontaine. I nipped in quickly, Vanessa was dancing with her husband and Benjamin was talking to the French couple. I sat down next to Alexandra and we both stared off into space. She was drinking plain orange juice. 'How do you like it?' I asked.

'How do I like what?' her voice was soft and very precise.

'The club,' I waved an expansive arm around.

'Very nice,' she said, stifling a yawn. I noticed her nails were cut short and painted a buff colour. Most of the girls or women I knew had either long red talons, or short chipped bitten ones.

'Would you like to dance?'

'No thank you.'

No thank you indeed! Most girls would give their false eyelashes to dance with me! We sat there with nothing else to say until Fontaine and Peter returned.

The club was filling to capacity. The music was getting louder and louder. Time to take off the records and put on the group. Time to circulate around some tables, give them the chat. Time to give the waiters a blast.

I got up, silly little cow, she wasn't even that pretty, and man, like I could have the prettiest. I grabbed my scotch, gulped it down and wandered around the joint. People liked me to sit down at their table, it showed they were really 'in'. I tell you this is such a phoney business; maybe that's why I dug Alexandra sitting there so bored and unimpressed.

I joined the table of the Italian star. She was with her 'Producer'—fat—good-looking, didn't speak a word of English; an English actor, and his stunt-man boy-friend. Carla Cassoni was very lovely, with this incredibly throaty accent. The producer kept a firm hand on her thigh, but she winked at me and flirted, safe in the knowledge that he didn't understand one word.

'You are very attractive,' she purred, 'such a lovely body, but no money huh? It ees beeg shame,' she laughed a deep sexy chuckle. She was a smart cookie.

I asked her to dance, she shook her head, 'Ee is veree jealous,' she indicated the producer, ''ee don't like me to dance with other man.'

Nobody wanted to dance with me, it just wasn't my night.

Suddenly Franco rushed over, stared bug-eyed at Carla and whispered something in my ear. It seemed some black chick had come in wearing a topless dress, and what was he to do? Should he ask her to cover up, or what? He pointed her out, she had just sat down, and the top of her dress which was all fringe, parted as she moved, revealing firm dark brown breasts. It was tantalising, now you see them, now you don't. The guy she was with was old, suited, obviously out on a jaunt. She was a wild chick called Molly Mandy—part-time dress designer. What the hell, there was no law against topless dresses. I told Franco to leave her be. A few people had noticed and a lot of staring was going on; then she got up to dance and the staring really began. The old guy didn't care, he got up there with her, proud as punch. She started on a slow shake, titties hardly moving, then suddenly she started to go and the fringe swung and the titties swung, and baby *she* swung.

Everyone stopped dancing and made a hand-clapping circle round them. The guys all loved it, some of the birds looked a bit choked. I saw Fontaine rush over to the side of the dance floor with Vanessa to get a better look. It was a wild scene. Then the Greeks joined in, threw some glasses to start it off, then a couple of them shouldered the old guy out of the way and started dancing with Molly. One of their girl-friends, not to be outdone, ripped off her blouse unhooked her bra and joined the scene. Everyone cheered.

The time had come to stop it otherwise we'd get the police. Charming! I pushed my way through the crowd just a little too late. One of the mad Greek shipowners had grabbed hold of a brown tit and the old guy attempted to punch him and ended up flat on his back.

A lot of screaming started, but Franco had his waiters in there so fast, and the old guy was carried out, and the Greeks were persuaded back to their table, and Molly sat down at our table saying 'Shit, man, what's all the fuss?'

It was action like this that made 'Hobo' the only place in town.

I glanced over to Fontaine's table, she was just sitting down, laughing. Alexandra and escort had gone, probably left during all the confusion. Just as well.

'Hey, Molly baby, don't come here like that again,' I said.

She smiled at me, rows of white pearly teeth plus a few gold fillings. 'What's the matter, Tony sweetheart, don't you like my boobies?' She shook her shoulders and the fringe parted giving me an eyeful.

'You know I like them—but not in here, you'll cause a riot, come on, I'll take you back to find your boy-friend.'

She made a face, 'Man, that old fart's out cold, I feel like fun tonight.'

I was getting irritated, what did she expect—to tag on to me? I didn't even fancy her—I looked to Sammy, but he was busy chatting up Janine.

I took a grip on her arm and led her to the reception area, the old guy was laid out in the office at the back. He was just coming to when we got there.

'I'll arrange a cab, you take him home,' I hissed at her.

She pouted, 'O.K., but maybe I'll come back, isn't it about time you and I had a scene?'

I gave her a shove towards the old trout and got out of there. I think it was the gold fillings that turned me off.

Fontaine summoned me with the imperial wave when I was back inside. I knew the gesture well—she raised one long thin arm high and sort of clicked her fingers at me. Charming! Sort of a—come here serf!

I went. After all she was the boss.

'Tell us about it,' she said, excitement gleaming in her eyes. The others all leaned forward too, anxious to hear the story. 'Who was that pathetic little man with her?' Fontaine went on, 'I mean, really, they made a ridiculous couple.' She gave me a sharp kick under the table, her signal that she wanted me to ask her to dance.

I obliged. I hated dancing with her, talk about looking ridiculous. Is there anything more ridiculous than an elegant-looking lady jumping and squirming around like a seventeen-year-old? Especially when she's got no sense of rhythm. I gave my secret signal to Flowers—the disc jockey, to put on a slow record. He launched into a medley of Tony Bennett, making a face, he was strictly a Motown man.

Fontaine held me tight. 'Did you touch her?' she asked licking silver-coated lips.

'Did I touch who?'

'Oh, you know who, she looked straight out of the jungle!'

I ignored that. Fontaine had a poor opinion of anyone who

27

wasn't in her set, she was also very bigoted, and was for ever trying to get me to get rid of the black waiters and Flowers. In bed one time she had gone on about how they made her feel uncomfortable, and then she had got very excited and given me a few scratches on my back I'll probably have for ever. I can't imagine anyone making Fontaine uncomfortable.

I would never get rid of Flowers, he's the best D.J. in town. A tall thin black guy with freak out hair and pale blue eyes. Usually stoned out of his mind. But he can feel a room like I can feel a woman.

Fontaine was dancing very close. I glanced over at her husband. He was talking with the French couple.

'Hello, Tone,' a girl greeted me. She was dancing alongside us. I smiled at her. .

Fontaine dug me in the ribs and said with an amused smile, 'You love it don't you, all these little dollies after you?'

I must admit I did love it.

Wouldn't you?

# 4

## FONTAINE

I arrived at Tony's shortly after phoning him. A horrible little scrubber with long black hair came yawning out of his apartment. I waited a few minutes before ringing the bell, it would never do to let him know that I knew all about his little 'affaires'. One would think he would show a degree of taste, but no, he would sleep with anything, studs usually do.

He greeted me with a kiss. What a sloppy habit, I have a great distaste for kissing, especially when his mouth has the lingering odour of someone else.

Immediately he started fumbling with my clothes, and getting my skirt off, he pinned me to the wall.

I must admire him, he's never at a loss. He took me like that, quite exciting, though only momentarily of course.

The awful thing about Tony is that he's a terrible bore. He has nothing even remotely intelligent to say. After sex I really have to get away from him.

I dressed again and told him I was late for the hairdresser. Of course I wasn't, so I popped in to visit Vanessa.

Vanessa reminds me of a big blonde jersey cow. Placid, slow, always churning children forth. What on earth Tony can see in her I really can't imagine. Probably that big mother earth bosom.

In my position it's difficult to acquire friends, I mean it's got to be someone on the same social level, otherwise they're just absurdly jealous. All my friends from before became impossible after I married Benjamin. Each new mink coat or diamond ring was greeted with tight little smiles, they just couldn't stand it. Vanessa of course has no need to worry, I suppose her husband is nearly as rich as mine, although to look at her you would never guess.

I love having beautiful clothes and jewels and being envied and stared at. I suppose I always knew that I was destined for this kind of life.

I was a very plain child with a very plain mother and a bastard of a father who made mother's life a misery. Felicity Brown of Bournemouth. I grew up very quietly, went to the best girls' school, decided I would like to be a vet, and knew nothing about sex except what the other girls whispered. All nice little English girls want to be vets, it's part of our tradition—well it was then anyway. At sixteen I was allowed on my first outing with a young man, none of this 'raped at thirteen' business in my past. He was nineteen, the local doctor's son and a nice quiet boy. We got along fine, held hands, had a few furtive kisses and decided to get married. I was a good chaste Bournemouth virgin engaged to be married, with a sweet marquesette ring, and stars in my dull little eyes. We decided, along with the help of our middle-class parents, that we would marry when he was twenty-one and I was eighteen.

My future was cut out and planned. He went off to finish his medical studies and I enrolled in all sorts of activities, such as sewing and cookery classes. I really didn't know any other boys and I thought I loved Mark. What a situation! I had no idea what love was all about.

At cookery class I met a girl called Marcia. She was pregnant and unmarried and people whispered about her. My mother called her 'fast' and 'shocking', and my father said it was a disgrace she was allowed to join the cookery class. But join she did, and she was the first breath of fresh air I had encountered in all my nearly seventeen years.

We became friendly and I told her about Mark and my plans.

'What's he like in bed?', she asked.

I looked at her blankly.

'Oh, no,' she started to laugh, 'don't tell me you haven't?'

I had to admit that I hadn't, what's more I wasn't going to because it wasn't what nice girls did, was it?

This made her laugh even more, and then she got very serious and said, 'How on earth can you marry someone if you don't know if you like each other in bed. It's very important, you *must* do it.'

Of course she was no walking advertisement for sex, with her belly swollen out and no visible husband, but I did think she was right, I *should* try it.

I waited anxiously for Mark to come home on holiday, half excited, half terrified at what I planned to do.

He was allowed to borrow his father's car and we went to a film and he held my hand and afterwards we went to one of the big hotels for dinner.

It's very difficult when you're a nice quiet virgin suggesting that your equally nice quiet fiancé make love to you, especially when he's never attempted anything along those lines.

I said, 'Let's drive down to the beach, it's such a lovely night.'

'Oh, Felicity, I'm tired.'

'Please, Mark.' I was quite determined to get the beastly deed done.

'All right,' he reluctantly agreed.

We parked somewhere along the front and sat there, he made no movement towards me.

After a few moments of silence, I said, 'Mark, if we're going to get married don't you think we should get to know each other?'

'What are you talking about, Felicity?' he replied crossly.

I moved closer to him, 'You know what I mean.'

He was genuinely shocked and pushed me away, 'If I want that type of girl there's plenty around.'

I was very excited by this time, the first moment in my life I had been sexually excited, and Mark—the man in my life, was pushing me away. I was furious.

He drove me home in silence and I refused to ever see him again.

The next night, still determined to find out what sex was all about, I went to a local coffee bar, and there met a tall leather-jacketed boy called Ted. I had seen Ted before around town, and I decided that he would do to initiate me into the mysteries of life. We started to talk and when he invited me for a walk I accepted readily.

We strolled along making our way towards the beach, and then he grabbed me, kissed me, pushed his hands up my skirt, and we both fell down on the sand. I was ready for him without any preliminaries. He forced his way into me and the pain was exquisite and I clung to him and begged him for more, and as he was finished and went limp I wouldn't let him go. He was trying to get away and I was hanging on to him. It was wonderful. We fought silently and he called me a bitch and said I was hurting him! *Me* hurting *him*, that was a delightful statement.

A new Felicity Brown had emerged. I loved it! I tried everyone and everything. A whole new life had opened up for me and soon Bournemouth wasn't big enough and I left for London. My father by this time was pleased to see me go. My mother shed a few tears I think.

I arrived in London, tall, skinny, with mousy hair, but plenty to offer. And by the time I was twenty-two I was Fontaine—top model. Beautiful—a few changes here and there, blonde, a girl with London at her feet.

I was making lots of money and lots of men, and then I met my first husband, Paul. He was very attractive. Lean and lazy with smoky green eyes and a beautiful body. He was a sometimes male model, sometimes actor, but mostly enjoyed living off some lady. He was divine in bed. His gymnastics nearly matched up to mine. He was the first man who really satisfied me and saw I stayed satisfied.

So one day we got married amidst a blaze of flashbulbs, and he sat back while I worked, and life went on. He gambled, drank, and was unfaithful, but we stayed together, because I suppose I must have loved him.

Everyone told me I was mad but there was still a little bit of Felicity Brown left in me somewhere, and I wanted my marriage to work.

At twenty-nine I looked in the mirror and took stock. I had been a top model for seven years and that's a long time to have been at the top in any profession. How much longer could it last? Paul used up all my money, soon I would be thirty, and how many more magazine covers lay ahead?

Also I was exhausted. Modelling is not an easy job as people seem to think, it's back-breaking work, a constant grind of hairdressers, make-ups, blinding hot lights, and anatomically impossible poses.

I certainly wasn't faithful to Paul any more, after six months of marriage we both agreed it was ridiculous to confine ourselves to each other. As a matter of fact, we had rather a lot of fun with 'group parties'. Very interesting.

I finally decided Paul was a luxury that would have to go and I cast my eyes around for someone more substantial to take his place.

I met Benjamin in St Moritz. I was doing a fur show there for one day and he was with his unbelievably dreary wife and two ghastly children. We met in a group and I knew who he was. We managed a few words alone, 'Can I see you in London?' he asked. He reached a little past my shoulder in height. I gave him my phone number.

It took exactly five weeks for him to offer to divorce his wife. I played my game very carefully, I gave him everything but, and I had him mad for it. There's a ghastly expression Tony uses—'I'm hot for you, baby,' and that just about sums up how Benjamin felt.

It was no problem getting rid of Paul. Benjamin paid, and he took. Benjamin's wife was also easy. She agreed to divorce him with no argument. Of course she got a fortune and also the children. We have never spoken, but I am obliged to see Ben Junior and Alexandra sometimes. They are really very dreary. Young Ben is twenty and an even shorter version of his father. Alexandra is just plain, no sparkle, like her mother I suppose.

So that's my story. Benjamin and I got married, once more in a blaze of flashbulbs, and we honeymooned on a new yacht he bought for the occasion.

He buys me whatever I want, I have my occasional stud and I'm happy—I suppose.

Whatever happened to Felicity Brown?

Vanessa was not dressed when I arrived. Her big breasts were flopping about in a blue dressing-gown and she was eating toast and honey and reading a gossip column.

It's very important in our circle to see your name quite often in print. If Vanessa hadn't been very rich she would have been a real slut. I knew that Leonard, her husband, was keeping some tramp in a flat, but I hadn't told Vanessa, what was the point?

We greeted each other warmly, and I ordered a champagne cocktail from their Filipino houseboy and sat down and relaxed.

'What's new darling?' Vanessa yawned.

I slipped off my jacket, 'Nothing much, just had a little session with the stud.'

We both laughed. 'Was he in good running form today?' Vanessa asked with more than a touch of interest.

I have a feeling she has a secret crush on Tony, offhand as she may try to be.

'Yes,' I replied, 'when is he ever not?'

Vanessa was a bit bored at that, she had to wait for Tony to approach her, *I* had a far different kind of relationship with him.

The houseboy brought my cocktail. It was cold and delicious. A good champagne cocktail really sets you up for the day.

'What are you wearing tonight?' I asked.

Vanessa shrugged, 'I haven't really thought.'

Hadn't really thought indeed, I planned my outfits months ahead. No wonder she always looked such a mess.

We chatted a while longer and then I went off to the hairdresser.

Alexandra arrived at our house fresh from Switzerland at seven. She dislikes me and I can't stand her, but of course Benjamin fails to see this. She looked as dull and plain as ever. It always amazes me how in this day and age a girl can look so utterly dowdy. Her hair scraped back, no makeup, uninteresting little wool dress. She's seventeen and yet manages to look years older.

Benjamin greeted her warmly. She's polite to him, but I'm sure she hates him for deserting 'Mummy'. He has a huge trust fund for her when she's twenty-one. She sipped an orange juice, and soon the others arrived—thank God!

I wore my new full-length white mink, and Vanessa loved it. I have no doubt she will shortly appear in a bad copy, she copies everything I have, but invariably it just doesn't suit her to wear my style, we are completely different types.

Dinner at 'Annabels' was fun. Lots of friends there. It was a terrible bore having Alexandra along, she was always looking at me with a sort of disdainful half smile. I wish she would stick with Mummy in the country instead of bothering us. Now she's talking of sharing a flat in London with a girlfriend, and Benjamin is insisting she come and live with us. How dare he! Thank God she's declining the invitation. Stupid child is starting a job as a secretary. What's the point with all her money?

Dinner lingered on. I danced with the old French goat who held me too tight and breathed garlic in my face. Delightful! I danced with Leonard, he's not bad although Vanessa's description of his activities in bed are very dull indeed. He probably saves it all up for his little popsie on the side. It's quite amazing how the most unimaginative of husbands can turn into a real Casanova in someone else's bed.

We finally set off for 'Hobo'. I simply love it there. Such a marvellous mixture of people, always something going on. And Tony, well, Tony at work is a real sight. Absolutely everyone's best friend!

I must admit, it's when I like him best. He's king of the whole place, everyone wants him at their table, all the women want him.

He has a very sexy animal walk, almost as though he has a hidden erection. I wish he had as much confidence in bed, after all I've taught him his tastes are still a little on the suburban side, he can't seem to project any originality. To be a good lover you need a constant source of inspiration.

Of course his friends are unbelievable. They gather at his table like a clutch of male rejects. What a motley group!

The records are fabulous, so loud you can't even hear yourself think. I love dancing. The whole room is staring at my coat—one little dance in it won't be too hot. Let them all get a good look before I slip out of it.

Alexandra sits like a ton of bricks. I really can't stand her. Benjamin is so proud, he thinks she's so lovely. And as for the little bore he has fixed her up with, why his father's got more life in him than he has. Actually, he's just right for Alexandra, two dreary non-personalities together!

Oh no, he's not going to ask me to dance. Yes he is. Oh, how awful. Rich men's sons are all the same. Real smug little bores. This one's probably about the same age as Tony—only he's got about as much sex appeal as a flea. It's no use rubbing yourself up against me, sweetheart, you just haven't got what it takes.

'Let's sit down, Peter dear, it's so hot.'

He looked disappointed. I'd be disappointed if I had to go back and sit with Alexandra. Why, she wouldn't even dance with him. I must say, I love to dance. So lovely and uninhibited, Tony can't wait to dance with me and show me off to the whole room.

There was some sort of commotion going on at the dance floor.

'It's some black girl completely nude!' Vanessa said excitedly. We both jumped up and rushed over. Mustn't miss a good show.

After, Vanessa and I went back to our table. 'You didn't say goodbye to Alexandra,' Benjamin said crossly.

'I didn't even know she was going,' I replied, delighted she had left.

'She had a headache,' then relenting he added, 'Perhaps you'll phone her tomorrow.' He squeezed my leg under the table. His hands were sweaty. He had grey hair, bald in patches, like moth-eaten fur.

Tony was coming back in the room and I called him over. He looked very sexy tonight, God, those trousers he was wearing didn't leave much to the imagination!

He asked me to dance. Slow music was playing and he held me very tight.

'Aren't you being a little obvious?' I said indicating Benjamin, but he just held me tighter and I felt him and I wished we could do it there and then in front of everyone. Oh what bliss! But tonight is impossible. Benjamin is in town and *he* will probably want to do it. What an utter bore! Sex with Benjamin is so utterly dreary. I like young strong bodies, not old tired ones. He huffed and he puffed like he would never quite finish the show. Dear Benjamin was so monotonously the same in bed, he was unlovely and un-interesting.

Fortunately he was quick.

We left 'Hobo' soon after and once in the privacy of our bedroom I flopped on the bed exhausted. What a day!

Benjamin announced he had to leave for Paris the next after-noon. Did I want to come? Well, I wanted to come, but not to Paris. I decided I might pop over to New York to our flat for a few days. I adored the shops over there and I supposed I should visit Ray. He is an adorable looking hairdresser whom Benjamin has set up in his own salon there. I haven't spent time with Ray for ages. A few days with him might be fun.

Benjamin was pulling at my dress. He knew I hated that, I got up quickly and he backed away. Oh, poor old Benjamin, I'd frightened him. He was always frightened I'd say no—but of course I never did.

I peeled off the dress and hung it up carefully, then I lay flat on the bed, the way he liked me to and waited for him.

I closed my eyes and thought about Tony and Ray and Paul and it wasn't too bad. In fact, if he wasn't so goddamned fast it might not be bad at all.

He washed himself after, a habit that drives me to distraction. I took off my makeup and put on my sleep mask. He was reading now. Oh, for separate bedrooms. What à joy!

# 5

## TONY

Sammy said, 'Watcha dancing with that old bag for?'

Sammy Schmuck! What did he know about class.

'I mean I know she owns the place but—'

'I think she's fantastic,' Janine interrupted, 'really fantastic, did you see that coat she had on?'

'What's a coat if there's nothing but skin and bone underneath?' Sammy chuckled at his own joke. 'Now that Italian number's not bad, nice pair of boobies.'

I should remark that Sammy has no conversation except about women. We have all heard clinical descriptions of every bird he's ever laid.

'Come on, darling, I'll do you a favour,' Sammy dragged Janine off to the packed dance floor.

Franklin looked miserable. 'Listen, long face,' I said, 'that's not for you, let Sammy have her, she's a pig.'

Massey said, 'I've got a beautiful little bird for you, Suki's sister—wouldn't she be great for Franklin?'

Suki nodded wide clown-like eyes. 'She's only fifteen but lovely.'

I had heard it all before. Everyone was always fixing Franklin up, but nothing ever worked out. He was too shy to make it with a bird. To get Franklin laid was one of our group projects. He would sit and listen to all our chat about women and agree with us when we told him he should blow his cherry, but nothing ever happened.

The evening was at its peak.

The place was so jammed that some tables' occupants had to take it in shifts to dance because there wasn't room for them all to sit down at the same time. It was always dodgy dancing at this time anyway. For one thing the tiny dance floor was so jam-packed you couldn't move, and for another you took a risk of losing your seat altogether.

I looked around with satisfaction. It was one of the more star-packed nights. There was a good sprinkling of top talent from most professions.

'The Must', current top rock group were all present. Long hair, tighter than tight clothes. They were nice boys, stoned out of their heads, but harmless, with their flaxen-haired girl-friends who all looked the same. It's a funny thing how in the rock world it's important to all to be on the same wavelength—you know—the long hair bit. They all look like out of the same mould. They try to be different from everyone else and bingo—there you go—all the same.

More people were crowding in. I got up and did the greeting bit. I wandered round a few tables having a scotch here and a scotch there. The world was starting to buzz. I could fancy something cuddly. Fontaine had left me with a sour taste in my mouth. As a matter of fact, I could fancy Vanessa, but that was impossible, there she was with hubby. I must remember to give her a ring, sneak in while nanny and the kidlets are out!

I kept on thinking of Miss Rich Bitch—she was so sort of different from other birds, she had this kind of aura of class. I wondered if I'd see her again. Probably not, she looked like she hated it here.

Flowers grabbed hold of me—'Got to see you, man,' his eyes were distorted and nervous. He was flying on pot, probably needed more bread, that was always his problem. He was living

38

with Tina, our Swedish receptionist. What a couple they made—he, dark and wild, she, white and quiet. There was a song there somewhere!

I lent him five pounds, listened to his bullshit about how grateful he was, and made a mental note to get it back from his next week's salary—otherwise I'd never see it again.

Miss Italian Movie Star and party were leaving—'Bye, Bye, Tonee,' she purred slowly through pearly white teeth, 'not long before we shall meet again huh?'

I loved her voice, it was a real turn on. 'Yeah,' I gave her the sincere stare. All the Italian waiters were going mad, hovering around to get a closer look. 'S'long, Tony, old boy,' the actor said. 'Bye, Tone,' the stunt-man said. They all wanted to know me, be my friend. The Italian producer muttered some Italian, gave me a dirty look, gripped Carla by the arm and they were gone. Good. I quickly had Franco put a visiting senator and party at their table.

So the evening reached its peak, and slowly around two-thirty it started to thin out, and by three-thirty only super swingers and odd-balls were left. Franklin said he was going and Janine said she wanted to stay, and they argued quietly and then he left.

I caught him at the door. 'Listen, kid, we'll get you a date with Suki's sister. O.K.?' He shrugged. A waiter came at him with his check and I grabbed it. 'The cokes are on me tonight,' I said.

'Thanks, Tony.'

Back at the table Janine seemed to fancy me, and in spite of Sammy's frantic efforts she didn't want to know. She asked me to dance, and tossed the sad starlet's mane of red hair, and wriggled the sad starlet's curvy body, and the accent twanged.

We ended up in my flat. I just don't like going home alone.

I was loaded and she didn't stop talking. I heard all about the movie she was doing, some bit part in a B film no doubt, and how Franklin was very sweet but such a baby, and how she loved London, and 'Hobo' was such a wild place, and just as I got it in, she said, 'Can I have a free membership?' So I gave it to her.

That's life.

# 6

## ALEXANDRA

It's simply terrific to be home.

Madelaine and I flew back together. Her father and brother met us at the airport. Michael, her brother, is super. Of course I've known him for ages, we were all children together, but lately he has become *so* attractive.

I daren't tell Maddy what I think of him because she wouldn't understand. I mean him being her brother and everything she most likely sees him in a different light. We always discuss boys together, not that there was too much chance in Switzerland, our school was run like a convent. However, Maddy had this huge crush on the school gardener. I used to unlock the hall window at night and she would sneak out to meet him. We'd probably have both been expelled if we'd been found out. Anyway, she had a lovely time, he was quite old—about thirty, and they used to neck and once she let him take her sweater off *and* her bra. But she said he went a bit berserk after that and used to try all sorts of things, so she didn't meet him any more. It was just as well because I didn't think he was much at all. Rather dour really.

On our last vacation we went with Maddy's parents to Monte Carlo and I met a gorgeous boy who sort of looked after our beach. He was so brown. He took Maddy and me dancing one night and kissed me goodnight. It was awful, he stuck his tongue in my mouth!

Anyway, here we are out of school at last. It's like a wonderful dream. No more school!

Madelaine and I have a plan. She's going to work on her parents and I'm going to work on my mother and we're going to share a flat. In London!! In Chelsea!! We decided Chelsea was the best place, sort of swinging and everything. We'll both get jobs and have a terrific time. After all, I've been seventeen two whole months now. I'm practically old. And nothing exciting has ever happened to me—nothing!

We went back to Maddy's house, it's in Virginia Water, and she's always lived there, with both parents. My parents are divorced. My father went off with an awful woman who lured him away from Mummy. I think it was really selfish of him. We were all so happy before, and my mother is great fun. Very sensible. I wish she wasn't so sensible, then perhaps she would have held on to him. I must admit that Daddy's new wife is quite glamorous. She hates me, I can tell. Not that I care because I can't *stand* her, and fortunately I don't have to see them very much, only on occasions like tonight when I'm on my way home from school.

Maddy's father's going to drive me into town tonight for an evening out with Daddy and Fontaine, and then tomorrow morning I'm getting the train down to Mummy's. We live in a house near Newmarket, Mummy, my brother and me. We moved after the divorce because although Daddy would have let us stay in our old house it was too big, and anyway I don't think Mummy was very happy there any more.

Our new house is splendid, and has stables, I have my own horse. We have a swimming pool, although of course it's never warm enough to swim in. But somehow it's not the same. Anyway, the last year I've been in Switzerland and before that boarding school, so I really haven't spent that much time there. I'm sure Mummy will let me come to London, she's so understanding, and I'll be with Maddy so I don't see how she can object.

'What are you wearing tonight?' Maddy came into her room wrapped in a towel. She always took ages in the bath. I had been waiting to get in the bathroom for half-an-hour.

'I'm not going to dress up,' I replied. Actually I didn't have anything to dress up in if I'd wanted to, 'cos we mostly lived in sweaters and skirts in Switzerland. Both Madelaine and I had to get ourselves kitted out, our clothes were awful and old-fashioned.

'I don't blame you,' Maddy said, 'I certainly wouldn't get dressed up for *her* either.'

We both shared a mutual loathing for Fontaine, although of course Maddy had never met her, but knew all about her from me.

I bathed, brushed my hair, and put on the cleanest dress I could find.

Maddy supplied some makeup. I didn't put on much, because quite frankly, I wasn't very good at it. I needed practice.

'Have a glorious time,' Maddy said when I was ready, 'see you later.' I was coming back to stay the night.

I went downstairs to find Mr Newcombe. He was going to a business dinner in London. He really is a nice father, I liked him awfully, and I wished *my* father was like him.

Oh good! Michael's coming too. He's very good-looking, tall, with lovely longish hair. He lives in London. I'm sure when Maddy and I get our flat in town we'll see lots of him. Anyway, I hope so.

He sat in the front of the car with his father, and I was in the back, so there wasn't much chance for talking on the way.

My father lives in a big house in Belgravia. Mummy says it's in very bad taste. It has a lot of white statues balanced about outside, and inside it's huge and not at all comfortable. There is even an awful indoor swimming pool which is in a sort of glass room, all dark and depressing, with hundreds of vines and plants growing around it. It's creepy. I loathe it.

I said goodbye to Mr Newcombe. Michael smiled at me.

I said, 'See you soon.'

Maybe he likes me too. Maddy was always talking about how he has heaps of girl-friends, maybe I could be one of them or *the* one.

I mused on this as the butler let me in, and took my coat.

Fontaine came bearing down on me. 'Alexandra darling, how wonderful to see you.' She kissed me on the cheek. I knew she was only doing it for Daddy's sake.

He hugged me. He seems to have grown shorter and older. Suddenly I felt a warmth towards him and I hugged him back. Oh, if only he'd stayed with Mummy! Everyone knew Fontaine just loved him for his money.

'We're going to have a lovely evening,' my father said.' How was school? Tell me all about it.'

We sat together on the sofa, and I wanted to cry because he did look so old and tired. I had seen him four months before and he had looked fine, but now—oh my goodness, what had she done to him?

'Are you well, Daddy?'

'Of course I'm well. Working very hard but that's what I like. I was never one for sitting about.' He glanced over at Fontaine, but she was taking no notice of us. She was sipping champagne, and reading a fashion magazine. 'How's your mother?'

'I haven't been home yet, but I spoke to her tonight and she sounds fine. She said she just got a letter from Ben and he's having a marvellous time.'

My brother Ben was at a University in America.

'Wonderful woman your mother, very strong . . .' He tailed off.

I could still remember the day Mummy told us he was leaving. She hadn't cried or anything, but I knew he was breaking her heart. My mother is a pretty woman, about fifty. When she was young she had been gorgeous. In their wedding photos she was petite, with golden curling hair and a dimpled face. I knew that she had married my father long before he was rich.

'I'll give Mummy your love,' I said, and wondered if that was the right thing to say. But it was all right because he just smiled, and patted me on the knee.

'I'm going to come and live in London,' I blurted out, 'I'm going to share a flat with Madelaine and get a job.'

'When did you decide all this?'

'Maddy and I have been thinking about it for ages. Actually it's not all set yet, but I've written off for three jobs and I've got interviews next week, and Maddy's got two flats to see. Don't you think it's a good idea?'

My father frowned. 'But if you want to come to London you can live here, you don't need to get a job. Fontaine and I would be more than delighted to have you here.'

'No, Daddy, you don't understand. I want to be independent and free. I'm eighteen now and I know at twenty-one I'll have heaps of money from my Trust. Well that's why I want to keep myself, sort of support myself for a few years. I don't just want to be a rich man's daughter. I want to think for myself and work for myself and then at twenty-one I'll be able to accept the responsibility of my money. I don't want to "come out" and be a deb. I want a few years as just an ordinary girl.'

There! I'd said it. The speech I'd prepared for my mother.

Father beamed, 'That's my girl,' he said, 'that's my little girl. But I could help you find a nice job, you could take your choice.'

'*No*, Daddy.'

Some more people arrived, and my father joined Fontaine in greeting them.

'Alexandra, I want you to meet Peter Lincoln Smith. He's kindly agreed to escort you this evening.'

My face burned. *Kindly* agreed to escort me! Oh, my father was *so* embarrassing. I didn't want to be fixed up, it was so awful and old-fashioned, and my father hadn't even mentioned it to me.

Peter Lincoln Smith had a mean thin mouth and a limp handshake. I didn't like him, and I don't think he liked me.

There were two other couples, much older people. We had a long, dull dinner at 'Annabel's'. I wished I was with Michael, then it would have been wonderful.

Fontaine never stopped talking all night. I really don't know how my father can stand her, she's so loud.

Afterwards they all wanted to go to a discothèque and Peter and I had to go too. I don't think we had exchanged more than six words all evening.

I felt embarrassed trailing in behind Fontaine. Everyone stared. It was awful. At one point the manager sat down and tried to be nice to me, for Daddy's sake I suppose. He asked me to dance and I said no. Honestly people are such phonies. Just because of my father they think they have to be nice to me. Well, they jolly well don't.

I felt very tired. It had been a long day and I had the ride back to Virginia Water. I asked Peter if he'd mind putting me in a taxi.

There was some commotion on the dance floor and Fontaine had rushed over to see what it was. So I said goodnight to Daddy and thankfully left.

Peter had a red M.G. which he had driven me to the club in.

'I'll run you home,' he said.

'Oh no, it's much too far and much too late.' I didn't want to face another hour of Peter's company.

'Nonsense,' he said, suddenly linking his arm in mine. 'No traffic at this time of night, won't take long.'

So I was stuck. I climbed in and we set off in silence.

Peter drove fast and I leaned back in the seat. I soon fell asleep. I must have slept for ages, because when I awoke we were parked in a country lane and Peter was kissing me.

I didn't know what to do, he had taken me by surprise and I didn't want to offend him. After all, he had driven me all this way. So I sat quietly while he kissed me, waiting for the right moment to push him away.

Oh no! Suddenly I felt his hand on my breast. Well, I certainly wasn't going to just sit there now. I moved his hand away, 'Please stop that, Peter,' I said firmly.

But he didn't, and soon I found myself really struggling.

His hands were everywhere. 'Don't fight me,' he said, as I managed to push his hands away again, 'just lie back and enjoy it.'

I hated him! He had one hand up my skirt now, and I swung my arm at his head with all the force I could muster.

He stopped at once, clutching his mouth where my blow had landed. 'You little bitch!' he exclaimed in surprise.

Well honestly! I couldn't wait to tell Madelaine.

I jumped out of the car and ran off into the night. It was awfully dark, it wasn't a main road at all, and I had no idea where I was. Men are really disgusting, all they think about is one thing.

Suddenly I heard a car. It was Peter's, headlights full on, he was coming to find me. Maybe he wanted to rape and murder me! I mean things like that *do* happen, you read about it all the time. On second thoughts perhaps he was scared I would tell Daddy and wanted to take me home.

I didn't know what to do. Should I duck down and hide, and hope he wouldn't see me. Or should I climb in his car and demand he take me home.

It was cold and spitting with rain. I was completely lost. I stood quietly by the side of the road, with dignity I hoped. The car stopped beside me and Peter leaned over from the driving seat and flung open the door.

'It's all right, I'm not going to rape you,' he said as though reading my thoughts. 'Get in.'

I climbed into the car. The least he could do was apologise.

As it happened we were only about five minutes from Maddy's house and we both maintained a stony silence on the short drive. I climbed out as soon as he stopped the car. 'Goodnight,' I said coldly.

'Goodbye cock-teaser!' he yelled, and drove away.

Oh! Oh! I was *so* furious.


# 7


## TONY


A week has passed. I saw four movies, had dinner at Trader Vic's, lost twenty-five pounds at roulette—bought three new shirts and got laid every night.

Fontaine has gone, taken off on one of her trips. She never tells me she's going, just buzzes off. I suppose she thinks it's good to keep me in suspense.

Janine has sort of moved herself in and I can't seem to get rid of her. 'The Twang' as I call her, seems to think she's here to stay. She comes to the club every night and sits with the gang and then she comes home with me and rushes off to the studio a few hours later, then she's back at seven—just about when I'm getting up. She's not a bad bird after all, very accommodating. But she'll have to go. I haven't had a chance to call Sadie this week.

It's Saturday, big bright Saturday, busiest night of the week. It's eight p.m. and I'm seriously thinking of getting up. 'The Twang' is still asleep. Well, I mean she's knocking herself out, poor little bird. Not so little, she's built like a brick shithouse.

I would like a new flat. This pad I have now is very small. When Fontaine gets back we're going to have a serious talk about money. I need more, I deserve more. Every night except Sunday from ten p.m. till four a.m. is no joke.

I think I shall wear the black silk turtle neck and new black slacks tonight. That's where all my bread goes—on gear. Well, I like to look smart, keep up an image. It's important in my business, no use looking like one of those long hairs—dirty and all that. I reckon I've got a good look and I'm going to stick with it.

I mean I don't have short hair—not by any means. It sort of curls around the back of my collar—just right.

If I'm lucky, I can get out of here before 'The Twang' wakes up.

I wasn't lucky. She caught me at the door. 'Babee,' she squealed, 'wait for me, where are we going?'

Oh shit! that meant she expected me to buy her dinner.

I waited while she wriggled her starlet's body into a too-tight white dress and back-combed her hair and put on her eyelashes. She was definitely becoming a drag.

I called Sammy, he had a date, so we joined up with him at a little Italian bistro and dined royally on spaghetti and meatballs.

Sammy's date was fifteen if she was a day. He had picked her up at a bus stop. One of Sammy's habits was to cruise the streets in his secondhand E-type looking for likely birds. He never copped out, always came up with something. I guess they liked secondhand E-types. One of his favourite stories was of how he followed a bus from Baker Street to the Elephant and Castle because he fancied some little darling on it, and according to him he made it at the end of the ride!

One of these days he was going to get himself into a lot of trouble. Some tough father was going to ram a fist down his stupid throat. Anyway, until that day came, he was happy.

After dinner we went to the club. I liked to get there early on a Saturday. It was too soon for anyone to be in, Flowers was playing a few far out sounds. Franco was screaming in Italian at his waiters, Tina was polishing her nails.

47

'The Twang' and the fifteen-year-old went off to the ladies' room where they stayed at least half-an-hour.

'What do birds do to their faces that takes so long?' Sammy said, "Ere, what's with you and this American bit, going a bit strong, isn't it?'

'Sammy, Sammy, you know me better than that. As a matter of fact I wondered if you wouldn't mind stepping in.'

Sammy shook his head sadly. 'She had her chance, anyway she's a bit old for me.'

Janine was all of twenty-five.

To tell the truth, I felt rather bad about Franklin, I knew he was choked about her latching on to me. I wish I could talk her into showing him the ropes—in other words, get him in the sack with her. He was a great-looking kid, some lucky girl was in for a thrill. I mean he'd been saving it up for a long time.

They started to come in. As usual, the ones who weren't too sure of a good table first. It always reminded me of a show. The audience files quietly in, sits down and waits, then here come the performers. Yelling greetings, kissing everyone, wearing maxis, minis, caftans, flowers, bells, you name it, they wear it. The beautiful people. An assorted group of high frequency talent, and every one of them my friend.

On Saturday you get the 'one night out a week' group too. Dressed to kill, they make a lot of uncool noise and most of the regular clientele send them up. However, they have the money and run up the really big bills, so you have to put up with them.

Here comes a group of them now. Hymie Verne Blatt, dress manufacturer, and his heavily jewelled wife Ethel Verne Blatt, with Jack Davidsonly, coat manufacturer, and even more heavily jewelled wife Bessie Davidsonly. What a group! Every time the wives went away, which was often, Hymie and Jack would appear with au pair ding-a-lings—proud as punch.

Meanwhile, from what I heard, Ethel and Bessie were making it with a couple of Spanish beach boys in Majorca!

However, tonight they were all a happy family. Neither couple had ever been known to appear anywhere alone, there were always the four of them, or the two guys or the two wives. Did they fuck together? We all wondered.

What a greeting I got when I went over to their table! You would think I was their closest dearest friend. These were the same four people who wouldn't look at me sideways when I was a waiter, many's the time I've seasoned their salad.

'Who's coming in tonight, Tony doll?' Ethel asked anxiously, she was the blonde one, Bessie was dark, they obviously thought they were a hot team together, appealing to all types.

I gave her a kiss on the cheek, standard procedure, 'You'll see, you'll see.' I had four types of greeting routines. Big stars I didn't know, firm handshake, sexy look. Big stars I did know, kiss kiss. Ding-a-lings and swingers (female or male) hug and a kiss. Everyone else a kiss on the cheek.

The evening was starting to swing. It was going to be a good one. On a Saturday night we could do with a hundred more tables and fill them all. Who would have thought that people would fight and struggle to get into a hot smoky crowded atmosphere with deafening music, but they did and loved it.

Franklin arrived girl-less and sad-faced. He sat and stared at 'The Twang'.

Hal arrived with an American widow to whom he was showing the sights of London. What an operator! Always dressed to kill in the best Savile Row had to offer, hand-made shoes, Turnbull and Asser shirts, and a lot of gold from his fillings to his cufflinks.

Meanwhile he was flat on the heels of his ass, busted out, broke. His last fifty pounds had gone to the kid brother in New Jersey.

He lived in the best hotels, promoting here, promoting there, and there was always some rich old bag to bail him out. This one tonight was a real horror. From the blue-rinsed hair to the sagging body. Oh boy, Hal certainly had to work somewhere along the line, and I didn't envy him.

Franco was patting me on the shoulder, we were reaching jamming up point and there were only a few emergency tables left. Someone at reception was asking for me. Shit! He knew I never went out front on a Saturday night. Too embarrassing turning people away. He muttered something about friends of Benjamin Khaled's. Well, they could go screw. No room, not on a Saturday baby.

On second thoughts, maybe I should give them the bad news

myself—people never said they were friends of Benjamin's, it was always—'Fontaine insisted we come by'—and then they would be shocked when they got a bill.

I went out front, there were two young guys, a sandy-haired girl, and another one talking to Tina.

'I'm sorry,' I said, 'but we just don't have a table—you know it's—'

My stomach did a somersault. It was Alexandra. She gazed at me with wide brown eyes and tentatively smiled. She had a gorgeous smile.

'Hello, do you remember me?' she said softly.

Did I remember her—ha!

'Of course I do.' What should I call her? Alexandra? Miss Khaled? What?

She said, 'Couldn't you squeeze us in somewhere? Daddy said it would be all right.'

As if I would turn her away, even without the threat of 'Daddy'. She looked different, prettier. Her auburn hair was loose, kept off her face with a green head band, and she wore a matching green sweater and tweedy slacks. Nothing flashy but she looked great.

'I'm sure we'll find room for you. How many? Four?'

She nodded, well pleased, and attached herself to the arm of one of the fellows. I hated him.

It was then I had a sudden flash of inspiration and decided to jam them all on to my table. What a great idea!

I led them in and told Sammy, etc., to move over. They all looked choked. The table was crowded as it was. But I managed to get the four of them seated. Then I offered them a drink and was shocked when Alexandra agreed to have wine with the other three. I had sort of imagined that she didn't drink.

They chatted amongst themselves while I hovered by the table. Sammy pantomimed a face at me as much as to say—what the hell is this?

I really don't know why I had flipped for this girl, but I had, and this time I wasn't going to let her get away.

I studied the schmuck she was with. Casually dressed, slightly long hair, much too good-looking in a boyish way. He had an arm around her and was tapping her shoulder in time to the music. This was certainly no creepy little Peter Lincoln Smith. This was probably the boy-friend. Well, we would soon find out.

'The Twang' suddenly yelled at me across the table, 'Can we dance, sweetie?'

I froze her with a grim look. Stupid loud-mouth. Got to get rid of her. 'Franklin, dance with Janine,' I said pleasantly. Silently I said —For Christ's sake give her a grope and get her interested in you.

They went off to dance. That was a start. I sat down. I stuck out my hand to Alexandra's boy-friend, forcing him to take his arm from around her. 'Tony Burg, glad to see you.'

Alexandra said, 'Oh, I'm sorry—this is Michael Newcombe'— then she indicated the other two, 'Michael's sister Madelaine, and Jonathan Roberts.'

We all shook hands.

'Super of you to squeeze us in,' Madelaine said, 'we didn't believe Alex when she said she could get us in. Michael's been trying to come here for ages!'

That made Michael out to be a right idiot.

'I hope you like it,' I said. 'Saturday night's a real killer.'

Sammy leaned over, his cockney accent cutting the air, ''Ere— take a look at that.'

We all turned to see Massey and Suki come in. She was wearing the shortest dress ever, split under the arms to below the waist at the side. It was a good job she was flat-chested. Even then, it was some dress. What with her huge made-up clown eyes, her mannish haircut and white face, she looked like she was in fancy dress.

Massey was cool as ever. 'Hey, man.'

They squashed down at the table and I could see Michael giving Suki a stare. Good. I performed introductions and soon everyone was talking.

Alexandra had one of those classless beautifully spoken voices. She really was a knockout, and she was nice. She wasn't a stupid little rich bitch as I had thought. Her friends of course were a bit on the square side, hadn't been around much I reckoned. From the conversation I gathered that Madelaine and Alexandra had been at a finishing school in Switzerland together.

51

Michael hadn't taken his eyes off Suki and I could see Alexandra getting a bit edgy. What an idiot he was to stare at a freak like Suki with a girl like Alexandra by his side. Still it was just as well, what did he know, he was your typical well-educated student type. I willed him to ask sweet little Suki to dance. Sweet little Suki indeed. She was your typical bony angular model girl, all legs and no tits. Massey and she had been going together for a few months on and off, and though they both appeared regularly with other dates, they had a nice scene going.

Bingo. Michael, the jerk, was asking her to dance. I thought for a second the dumb face was going to refuse, but no, she couldn't resist the opportunity of wriggling her backside. She got up. Michael got up. Alexandra frowned.

Madelaine looked embarrassed and started to chatter loudly. I grabbed my opportunity like a sinking diver, 'Come and see round the club,' I said directly to Alexandra.

'Super,' Madelaine replied.

Alexandra shook her head, 'I think I'll stay here.'

I glared at Madelaine who had got up, and then to cap it all Jonathan asked Alexandra to dance and off they went.

Have you ever been choked?

I caught Franco's eye. I said to Madelaine. 'We'll have to take a rain-check, I'm wanted out front.'

Tina was patiently turning people away. She smiled at me, she looked tired and pale. I guess it was no joke living with Flowers, he probably never quietened down.

'How's it going?' I gave her a pat.

'Fine, Mr Blake.' She brushed a lock of blonde hair off her forehead.

I felt sorry for her. 'Go home early tonight, you look tired— I'll get Franco to bring one of the boys out front.'

'Oh, thank you, Mr Blake, I don't feel too good . . .'

I went back inside and hovered by the dance floor. Alexandra was making an attempt to move. She wasn't very good at it. I studied her body partly visible through the folds of clothes. A nice full bosom, slim waist, small hips and long legs.

Was she or wasn't she? Did she or didn't she? I had a hard on to find out.

Madelaine was dancing with Sammy, and his teen-age wonder was nowhere to be seen. Probably back in the ladies' room.

Franklin and 'The Twang' were sitting down.

'Hi, Tony,' a girl I knew on her way back from dancing. She was very pretty. She squeezed my arm, 'When am I going to see you?'

I honestly couldn't remember if we'd made it or not. Some nights I was so loaded I wouldn't have known who it was wriggling about underneath me.

She was with a well-known singer, Steve Scott. One of the new breed, trying to project the sexy Englishman image and not doing a bad job. She was a dancer, a swinger, I did remember her. Her name was Carolyn something or other. I went over and sat with them and bought them a drink.

'Want to come to a party tomorrow?' Steve asked. 'My place, all you need is a bottle and a bird.'

'Yeah,' I was half catching glimpses of Alexandra dancing through the throng.

'You must come, it will be great,' Carolyn said. She jotted down Steve's address which I absentmindedly stuck in my pocket. Who needed parties on a Sunday anyway?

Flowers was launching into some slow soul sounds and when I glimpsed Alexandra again she was clutched in the schmuck she was dancing with's arms. Well, Flowers could forget that. I rushed over to him and made him change mid record to something fast. Automatically Alexandra and partner jerked apart. I noticed happily that Suki and Michael didn't.

Massey noticed too: 'Think I've lost her,' he joked when I sat down. 'Always knew she'd go off with the first white cat that came on strong.'

Now—how about Massey and 'The Twang'? No—she didn't like spades unless they were stars, and he didn't like busty chicks. Oh well . . .

Alexandra was coming back to the table. She looked flushed. 'It looks like we've been deserted, Jonathan,' she said with a wry grin to schmucko. I took her arm which she politely but immediately pulled away.

Oh God, her skin felt like velvet.

'Listen, I want to make you (should I add the rest of the sentence) a member. Let's go to the office.'

'Now?' she looked surprised. 'It's very nice of you but I don't think' . . .

I didn't let her finish, 'You've got to be a member, it will only take a minute and then you can come here anytime without having to go through the whole bit.'

'O.K.,' she got up. 'Come on Jonathan.'

He got up too and fast thinking I said, 'You stay here, otherwise the table will jam up and there will be nowhere for you to sit when we get back.'

He sat down. I had her.

This time I took a firm grip on her arm and propelled her through the crush. She was looking over to the dance floor to see Michael and Suki. I got her out to reception and then down one flight of stairs to the office. It was quite dark and only the faintest sounds of music reached us. I unlocked the door and switched on the light. It was a bare room with filing cabinets, a desk and a couple of chairs, very unromantic.

She stretched and yawned, her breasts taut against her sweater.

I had a mad urge to grab her, strip her clothes off and make violent love to her. This little bird had really got under my skin. But it would never do to rush things. To get her out of my system I had to have her, and to have her I had to play it cool.

I lit a nervous cigarette and she sat down, tapped impatient buff nails on the desk and said, 'Who's that awful girl Michael's dancing with?'

I sang a few off key lines of an old song 'Jealousy'.

She glared at me. 'I'm not jealous I can assure you,' she stuck her chin out, a gesture I immediately loved. 'But she's just ghastly. Who is she?'

'Some dopy model. Is Michael your boy-friend?'

'Oh no,' she flushed. 'Actually, we've known each other ages,

54

him being Madelaine's brother and everything, but this is the first time we've been out together.'

The scene became clear, schoolgirl crush, fancied him since she was a little girl bit. Well, we would soon get rid of him.

I found a membership form and doodled on it with a chewed pencil that was on the desk. She looked at me expectantly, wide brown eyes, beautiful eyes.

'What's your address?' I asked. You know, this bird made me nervous.

'I wonder if I should give you Mummy's address,' she mused aloud, 'I shall probably be there every weekend and it is my proper address.'

I didn't want Mummy's address. I wanted her improper address.

She licked her lips, they were very full and shiny with some kind of lip gloss, very sexy. 'No, perhaps I should give you my address here although I don't know how permanent it will be.'

Was she a virgin? No, impossible. There are no virgins left over the age of fourteen in London, even Sammy hasn't come across one yet.

'Madelaine and I are sharing a flat,' she said, rather proudly. 'Can Madelaine be a member too? The address is 14 Dundee Court, Chelsea.'

Chelsea yet! What did she want to go and set herself up amongst all that mob for? Oh well, at least she was in London and not living either with Mummy or Daddy. 'Phone number?' I asked, silently rehearsing what I would say the first time I phoned.

She gave me the number and I said, 'That's great, we'll send you the card this week and then I expect to see lots of you.'

She blushed. There are actually girls that still know how to blush.

'I doubt it,' she said standing up. 'I start my job on Monday, and I have to be there by nine every day.'

'Nine in the morning?' My voice was incredulous. Nine in the morning was ridiculous.

She smiled, 'That's right, I'm a secretary.'

Was I going mad, or was there a definite note of pride in her voice?

A secretary indeed! Could this possibly be Benjamin Khaled's daughter? I was choked, but so what, I still fancied her even if she didn't have any money. The old bastard, making her work. Fontaine was clad from head to toe in mink, and this poor little bird had to go out to work. What a game.

Still it was just as well, if she'd had money everyone would have thought I was after that.

She was at the door, anxious to get back to see what Michael was up to, no doubt. I stayed sitting at the desk like an idiot.

'Shall we go back?' she said politely.

Didn't she realise I fancied her? Couldn't she tell? She treated me like I was nobody special. I mean, I don't want to sound big-headed but I do run the place and everybody likes me. And I do have a good look, and she should bloody well pay me *some* attention. Running after some little long-haired student, the girl was mad.

We went upstairs and Tina gave me a knowing smile.

At the table Sammy said loud-voiced as ever, "Ere, where you bin?'

And then 'The Twang' had the nerve to say, 'Tony babee, you're neglecting me, let's dance.'

That was the end of her. She had gone far enough. She could pack her false eyelashes and hank of hair and go.

Alexandra said, a trifle irritably, 'Is Michael still dancing?'

Madelaine nodded and looked embarrassed. I seized the opportunity and grabbing Alexandra before she could sit down said, 'If you can't beat 'em, join 'em,' and I whipped her off to the dance floor.

I vaguely heard 'The Twang' shrieking in astonishment, 'Sonofabitch!'

Alexandra let me hold her at a discreet arm's length to the beat of 'Jimmy Mack'. I signalled Flowers to put on some slow sounds and she said, 'Your girl-friend's furious.'

'My girl-friend.' I looked amazed. 'I've never seen her before tonight.'

She smiled, that insane innocent smile, and I pulled her a little closer as Flowers switched to 'Groovin' and she struggled a bit but I had her in a tight grip and I wasn't letting go. She smelt of clean hair and toothpaste. I could feel her full breasts against me and her narrow waist was firm against my hands. She felt every bit as good as I'd expected her to.

'Isn't that Steve Scott?' she asked suddenly. He and Carolyn were wrapped casually around each other close by.

'Yeah – why? You like him?'

'Oh yes,' she was like a little schoolgirl, 'I always buy all his records, I think he's a terrific singer.'

Any second I expected her to produce an autograph book. She was a real sweet innocent.

Suddenly I had a great idea, 'I'll tell you what I'll do for you since you're so nice.'

She looked at me with those big brown eyes.

'How would you like to go to a party at Steve Scott's house tomorrow?'

'Really? You mean I'd actually meet him?'

'Sure, I'll take you. How's that?'

She pondered a bit, 'Have you been invited?'

Oh, this girl was too much! I nodded seriously. 'Of course. We'll go, O.K.?'

'Can Madelaine come?'

Fuck bloody Madelaine, I was getting good and fed up with her. 'That might be a bit tricky, but we'll go anyway.'

She made a snap decision, 'All right, but I can't stay out late.'

Had I made a wise move? Steve's parties were always a bit of an orgy. Well, that was O.K. We could always leave and go somewhere else—a nice romantic little restaurant, or my place, my sumptuous gaff off the Edgware Road. I kept on meaning to move, but who had the bread.

Flowers gave me a freaky look as we danced by, 'Man, who is the disc jockey tonight?' he muttered, rolling mad eyeballs. Sometimes he got very temperamental. He would go on kicks of playing far out sounds that nobody knew and then when he was told to play something a little more 'in' he would sulk for days. At other times he was so stoned he didn't even know what he was playing. But when he was good, forget it. He could make the room move like nobody else. He was great.

Alexandra said, 'What shall I wear?'

All birds are for ever asking that question and you know they already have the whole outfit planned.

'Nothing dressy, whatever you fancy.'

Perhaps she would fancy something with a long back zip that I could get her out of in next to no time.

I must say I had been neglecting the club since Alexandra had arrived, but it suddenly came to my notice that a great struggle was going on in the corner, and all I could see was the backs of three waiters and a worried-looking Franco. Alexandra felt so good I didn't want to let her go, but there was always tomorrow. Business was business. I gave her a gentle push in the direction of our table, 'Be a good girl and go sit down. I sense a little trouble.'

Stewart Wade, bum drunken actor, was sitting on the floor screaming four-letter words at the waiters while they answered angrily back in Italian. They were trying to pick him up and he was landing a drunken punch anywhere he could.

'What's the trouble?' I asked Franco.

He waved his arms around excitedly. 'The punk, 'ee no wanna pay 'ees bill, 'ee broke one of my boys' noses, 'ee say 'ee never pay bill anywhere.'

I pushed through the waiters.

'Come on, Stew, baby,' I said, 'let's not cause a scene. On your feet.'

'Ah, Tony,' he had one of those booming Shakespearean voices. 'Tell your frigging morons to leave me alone.'

'Come on, sweetheart, let's go and talk about it outside.'

'I want to stay here.' He sat there, all two hundred pounds of him with a childish drunken smile. 'Fuck the lot of you,' he shouted gleefully. 'I'm Stewart Wade, *the* Stewart Wade, I never pay, so fuck you.'

The waiters were muttering angrily amongst themselves.

'Pick him up and throw him out,' I said. I'd had enough. Customers like him we didn't need.

Happy in their work, the four waiters grabbed him by the legs and arms and proceeded to carry him out bodily while he bellowed—'I'll get the frigging police,' and then he passed out cold. A large scrubber in a micro-mini with legs like a football player scurried out after him.

Franco and I looked at each other and shrugged. You get used to anything in our business.

Back at our table Michael and Suki had finally returned. Alexandra was saying she wanted to go, and so were Madelaine and Jonathan, but Michael was saying nothing, just looking a bit glassy-eyed in Suki's direction as she studied her face in a Mary Quant make-up box.

'I say, could we get the bill?' Jonathan asked.

'That's all right,' I looked at Alexandra who was looking at Michael, 'it's on me.'

'Oh, that's awfully nice of you,' Madelaine said. She wasn't bad in a debby sort of way. A suitable room-mate for Alexandra, not flighty, a bit plain and plump.

They all got up and exchanged goodbyes around the table. I walked them out front. I managed to pull Alexandra to the side, 'I'll pick you up around eight p.m.'

'Oh fine.' She looked like she had forgotten all about it.

They piled into the lift and left. The last glimpse I got of her she was staring accusingly at Michael. She opened her mouth to say something, but the lift doors closed.

I stretched in anticipation of the following night. I would soon have her forgetting all about Michael.

It was two a.m., peak time. Flowers came strolling out, the group had just gone. 'Just going round the corner, man,' he said. Off to get high, at least he had enough sense not to smoke in the club.

Hal appeared with his blue-rinsed bag. I had to admire him, he certainly had a lot of style. 'We're going to play a little chemmy,' he announced giving me the wink. That meant *he* was going to play a little chemmy with *her* money. He was a mad gambler and sometimes won a bundle which he would immediately blow on new gear.

She smiled at me, rows of nicotine-stained teeth, 'I just love your little old club, honey.'

Hal said, 'Mamie's got a girl-friend coming in next week if you want to make up a foursome.'

A girl-friend yet! She was about sixty! I shook my head seriously, 'I'm engaged.'

'Oh, what a shame, honey, she would have loved you.'

He was a bum. He knew I didn't go for the rich old widow scene, yet he never gave up, he was always trying to recruit me.

'You and I as a team, Tony, we'd destroy them,' he would say.

Fontaine was enough for me, thank you. I could just about make it with her, although it was becoming more and more difficult.

Fontaine—I had forgotten about her what with her being away and all. But I glumly supposed she would be back soon. How would she feel about me and Alexandra? I pondered on this fact and decided she wouldn't like it at all. It was a tricky situation. If I had any sense I wouldn't go near Miss Alexandra Al Khaled with a barge-pole. But I had flipped for her, she had really knocked me out. So let's face it, I wasn't playing it too smart, but so what? Fontaine would never find out, and Alexandra and I could have a fast affaire, then bye-bye. 'Schmuck,' a little voice kept saying in my ear, but I ignored it.

'Well, baby, I guess you and I can call it quits,' a furious voice said. It was 'The Twang', all quivering, sexy five foot five of her.

I wanted to say, 'Yes, you're right,' but Alexandra had put me in the mood, and 'The Twang' was there and ready, and there didn't seem to be much else available stock around. One more night with her wouldn't be too much of a hardship. I patted her sexy bum, 'Customers, my lovely, I've got to be nice to the paying people.' She pouted, and I put my arm around her, 'Let's dance.'

# 8

## ALEXANDRA

What a week! It has rushed by, and *so* much has happened. Maddy and I are sitting here in our *own* flat, in *Chelsea*! And on Monday I start a *job*! And tonight I've got a date with Michael!! I feel *so* lucky. Mummy was first class about the whole thing. She gave me money and came to town to look at the flat with Maddy and me before we took it. We had lunch at Fortnum & Mason, and she bought us a tea-set and some cutlery.

Maddy and I have thoroughly discussed the Peter Lincoln Smith incident and we came to the conclusion that he behaved like a pig. Maddy said I should tell Daddy. But I don't think so.

We have both made up our minds that with the right boy sex would be all right. Actually we have both decided that we *should* sort of—well you know—*sleep* with the right male. Being a virgin is definitely out of date.

I have secretly decided that Michael and I should have an affair. Maddy and I discussed birth control for hours. Maddy says we should find a nice old doctor to prescribe us the pill. It certainly sounds a lot easier than all the other undignified methods. I mean they all seem so *complicated*.

Between us our sexual experience is very limited. I have been kissed by three boys, including Peter, and Maddy about the same, although, of course, she has been sort of semi-stripped when the school gardener got her bra and sweater off. We talked about that a lot. Maddy said she felt all sort of weak-kneed, and he had kissed her there, and sucked on her nipples like a baby. But then he had been angry when she wouldn't let him go any further.

Maddy has small breasts. Mine are bigger. I feel all embarrassed when I think of Michael looking at them.

'I wonder what Jonathan Roberts is like,' Madelaine suddenly said. 'Isn't it funny that Michael wants to be your date.

Maybe I'll have you as a sister-in-law!' she giggled.

I blushed. 'Don't be so silly. He's just being nice to us I expect because we don't know anyone in London.'

'Huh! Michael's never been nice to me before. In fact, he's very selfish. *I* think he's after your body, your pure white virgin skin.'

Honestly, Madelaine could be infuriating at times.

Michael had telephoned the day before and said that he and a friend of his were going to take us out. Maddy had answered the phone and I was trying to listen. 'Do you want to go?' she had whispered to me.

'Yes,' I whispered back. 'Of course I do.'

So it was settled, much to my delight, and they were picking us up at eight.

Michael had instructed his sister that we were to wear something casual. I had rushed down the Kings Road and found a Jaeger shop where I got some green tweed slacks and a matching sweater. There were lots of other shops with incredible clothes in the windows, but Mummy had always said, 'Buy quality' and I knew Jaeger was quality.

Michael and his friend Jonathan were half-an-hour late. I felt sure they had forgotten all about us.

Jonathan seemed quite nice, and Madelaine looked pleased.

Michael said, 'Well, girls, we're going to show you the town.' He looked terrific in a yellow roll-neck sweater and black trousers. Honestly, he is *so* good-looking!

We all piled into Jonathan's Mini, Maddy and me in the back. They took us to a very small cellar restaurant, jammed with people, and we sat at a corner table, scrubbed pine with a black candle in a glass holder. *Very* romantic, but rather noisy.

I was sitting opposite Michael and he leaned across and said, 'You don't look too bad tonight. London suits you.'

Oh, what a wonderful evening!

We drank red wine and ate chicken casserole. Madelaine got on awfully well with Jonathan, and Michael was really nice to me. In fact, the best thing was when he said to me at the end of the meal, 'You know—for a girl you're quite intelligent.'

It was past twelve when we left, and Michael held my hand. I felt marvellous.

'What shall we do now?' Jonathan said to Michael, 'Want to pop into "Judie's" and have a dance?'

'Can't stand that place, it's always filled with such a grim crew.'

'How about "Hobo"?' I ventured. It hadn't been much fun for me before, but with Michael it would be different.

'I'm not a member,' he said, 'and they're very sticky about letting non-members in.'

'That's all right,' I said, 'my father sort of has money in the place. I'm sure we'll get in.'

'Not on A Saturday night,' Jonathan said, "Hobo's" the hottest place in town.'

'I'm *sure* it will be all right,' I felt rather proud of the fact that they all seemed to think the place was so exclusive. I tried to remember the name of the manager. Tony something—Beard, Bird—I wasn't quite sure.

'Look, if Alex says it's O.K., let's go,' Madelaine said.

'It will be a wasted trip,' Jonathan said, 'that place is impossible. You've got to be Marlon Brando at least.'

'Come on, Marlon,' Michael said with a grin, squeezing my hand. 'Show us the impossible!'

By this time I was a bit nervous. What if I couldn't get us in? I wished I hadn't said anything.

Outside the club cars were double parked all down the street. Jonathan dropped us and we waited outside while he went off to park.

A beautiful girl arrived in a black sports car. She left it smack in the middle of the road and strode into the club. Michael turned to stare at her. I felt a pang of jealousy.

Soon Jonathan got back and we all marched in, me at the front.

'Yes?' a blonde girl behind a desk questioned.

'Er, we're friends of 'er—Benjamin Khaled. He said it would be all right.'

'Did you book?' she asked.

'Well no, but—'

'I'm sorry,' she shrugged, 'if you didn't book I can't help you.'

'I told you,' Jonathan jeered. 'Come on, let's go.'

'Just a minute,' I said, determined not to be embarrassed. 'Is Mr Bird here?'

'Mr Who?' the girl behind the desk said.

'Mr Tony Beard.'

'Oh, you mean Mr Blake.' She pressed a buzzer on the desk and a waiter appeared. 'Luigi, tell Mr Blake—*if he's here*—that there's some people who say they're friends of Mr Khaleds.' The girl smiled at me sympathetically. 'Saturday night you *must* book,' she said, 'and also a member has to sign you in. If I were you I'd talk to Mr Khaled.'

I heard a voice behind me say, 'I'm sorry, but we don't have a table.'

I turned quickly. It was the Manager. I smiled, 'Hello, do you remember me?' Oh thank goodness, he's smiling back.

'Of course I do,' he said.

'Couldn't you just squeeze us in somewhere? Daddy said it would be all right.'

I waited with a tense smile. How awful if he turned us away! But it was all right. He said he would find room for us somewhere. I grinned triumphantly. We followed him in.

What a terrific place it is, with the loud music and frantic dancers. How super to be here with Michael.

We were crowded on to an already full table and I was jammed next to Michael. He took my hand and said slowly, 'Very, very good.'

It was all great until some awful girl appeared and started ogling Michael, and then he danced with her practically all night.

It was just too bad. The only good thing that happened was that I saw Steve Scott—in the flesh!! And Tony Blake invited me to a party at Steve Scott's house!

I was very quiet on the drive back to our flat, and then Jonathan parked the car and he and Maddy started talking in low voices. I was trapped in the back seat with Michael.

He said, 'Well, little Alex, we'll have to do this again.'

Little Alex! I was furious!

'Maddy,' I said in a loud voice, 'we've been invited to a party at

Steve Scott's tomorrow night. Tony Blake's going to take us.'

She squealed. 'Oh, marvie! How did you manage that?'

Michael said, 'You can't go out with Tony Blake.'

'Why not?' I asked, my heart fluttering.

'You just can't,' he said. 'Two little kids like you, he'll eat you for dinner!'

Honestly! 'Come on, Mads, let's go'. How dare he call us kids. 'Thank you for dinner,' I added, and then rushed into our entrance, not even waiting for Maddy.

Tears sting my eyes.

I think I am in love!

# 9

## FONTAINE

New York is cold. The people in the streets and shops are boring. They all seem to discover you're English and to them this means instant friendship, they think they can chat to you for hours about their dreary grandma in Scunthorpe. Today a perfect stranger came up to me in 'Bendels', and demanded in a deep Southern drawl where had I got my dinky chinchilla. Why, she practically ripped it off my back with her eyes. However, they *are* chic, the very rich women.

Ray has become the darling of the society set. They all pop into him for their comb-outs. Actually, he's become a bit effeminate, I'm shocked! He who was always so virile. Maybe it's my imagination, but I'm not usually wrong about these things. He hasn't even approached me about going to bed together. Success has definitely gone to his head. I shall have to talk to Benjamin about him, take the salon away or something.

After a week here I find myself thinking about Tony. A week of

65

nothing sexually, only a short two-hour affaire with the husband of a friend of mine. Nothing special, rather boring actually.

It would be rather amusing to have Tony come over for a few days. Show the sexy animal off. I could tell Benjamin I wanted him to see New York, to find out what he thinks about opening 'Hobo' here. Tony would love it. I could buy him some clothes, show him the city.

Yes, I shall call Benjamin tonight and have him arrange the whole thing. Tony could be here by Monday and we can fly back the following weekend together.

I dressed carefully. Lunch with Sarah at '21', wife of the man I'd had the two-hour affaire with. I knew she wanted to tell me about her latest lover. The gossip around town said he was a Chinese waiter. Well Sarah has always been kinky, so I wasn't surprised.

Sarah would adore Tony. She's a very well educated society matron in her thirties, thin and beautiful, we used to model together. She married a Texan oil millionaire, then a Californian property millionaire, and now Allen, attractive unsuccessful writer. She has loads of money and Allen spends it well. They both have affaires and neither seems to mind. Actually she would be rather pleased if I told her about Allen and me. He wasn't very good though, a disappointment.

Sarah looked divine. If ever I decided to turn lesbian she would be my choice. Thin slavic face, jet black hair dramatically plastered down with a centre parting. She wore yellow, this year's Dior. I was a little more avant garde in Yves Saint Laurent.

We started with champagne cocktails and ordered melon and steak. Life is a permanent diet.

'Tell me all,' I demanded.

She smiled dreamily, 'Fontaine, my darling, if you haven't tried the mysteries of the East you haven't lived.'

I smiled back, 'I like my men a little—shall we say taller?'

She giggled, 'It's the quality not the quantity.'

'Give me quantity, to hell with quality!'

It was a pleasant lunch, I always enjoyed being with Sarah. We are alike in many ways.

Later I called Benjamin, 'Darling, I've got a marvellous idea.

What about a "Hobo" here? Yes, here in New York. Can you arrange to have Tony Blake sent over for a few days? Now, immediately, tomorrow if possible. You're wonderful, of course I miss you. Yes, darling, have your secretary call me back with the details. Yes, of course I'll be home soon. I love you too, 'bye.'

Poor old Benjamin. He really believed I loved him. I mean how could he? Didn't he ever look at himself?

Oh well, a party at the Sidwells tonight. Better dazzle them with the new Courrèges. Soon I would be dazzling them all with Tony. Quelle fun!

# 10

## TONY

It's four o'clock in the afternoon and there's no getting rid of 'The Twang'. It's her day of rest and she's making the most of it. Fast asleep like a lump of clay, unmade-up face hidden beneath a tangle of hair. In the daylight it's orange and quite revolting, she says it photographs fantastically. She's very ambitious. I'm also ambitious, ambitious to get her out of my bed and on her way.

I gave her a gentle tap on the shoulder, she snuggled down in the bed and snored softly. Oh man, the only thing that was going to wake her was something I didn't feel like giving her this morning.

I went in the bathroom and had a wash. She slept on. I made coffee and turned the telly up loud. She didn't stir. I gave her a shove. She sighed and stretched out tarantula arms. I ignored them. She opened sleep-filled eyes and said, 'C'mon back to bed, baby.'

Really, she and Sammy would have been great together.

'Get up, Janine,' I said, 'my mother's coming to visit.'

'Your mother,' her eyes snapped wide open and she sat up revealing full orange-tipped boobs fresh out of the centre spread in *Playboy*.

'Yeah, my mother, she takes it into her head once a year to come—today's the day.'

'Oh shit,' Janine twanged and got up.

She was built. Although without makeup her face was puffy and washed out. It's amazing what makeup can do for a girl.

She stomped into the bathroom and closed the door. I congratulated myself on the mother bit, and tidied up. I could go out, get something to eat and then get ready to pick up Alexandra. I wanted the pad to be in good shape in case she wished to view it.

Janine emerged an hour later, face in place, figure in sweater and too short skirt. Her kind of figure didn't go with mini-mini's. She was playing it cool, trying to look like she didn't care too much. I had gathered her things together in case she hadn't twigged.

She smiled at me coolly, 'Bye, sweetheart,' she said, 'see you around.' And exit 'The Twang'.

I phoned Sammy.

'What a night,' he moaned, 'the little raver wouldn't leave me alone.'

'You want to grab something to eat?' I asked him.

'Yeah, pick me up.'

I pulled on old gear, and drove over his place five minutes away. I was driving some decrepit old car that a girl-friend had left with me to look after while she did a dancing tour of the Far East. I wondered if Sammy could be conned into lending me his E-type for tonight. Very sexy the E-type, a low slung roaring phallic symbol.

Sammy looked terrible, still in his dressing-gown, unshaven and seedy eyed. 'I'm giving up the young ones,' he announced, 'too much bloody energy.'

We went to a little salt beef hangout nearby and I listened to the tale of Miss fifteen-year-old's sexy acrobatics.

'And to top it all,' Sammy concluded, 'she pinched a fiver from beside the bed when she left. Liberty!'

By this time it was half past six and I wanted to get home and changed for Alexandra. 'What are you doing tonight, Samuel?' I asked.

'Going to bed, I'm knocked out.'

'Can I borrow your car?'

'What for? You've got the mini.'

'Oh, come on, Sammy, I've got an important date, I can't take her in that.'

'Who is it?' Sammy was like a nosey old woman.

I kept my voice casual. 'You know, the bird from last night, Alexandra.'

'She's not your style,' Sammy said in surprise. 'You like flashier models than that.'

'I like her,' I said shortly. 'Can I borrow it?'

'Sure, only I've got to 'ave it by eight tomorrow morning.'

He tossed me the keys and I gave him the keys of the mini. He was all right Sammy was.

At home the phone was ringing and under my door was a telegram. I picked up the receiver and flipped open the buff coloured envelope.

'Mr Blake?' a crisp efficient bird's voice. 'This is Alice, Benjamin Khaled's secretary, I've been trying to get you all day but your line's been out of order.'

I always take the phone off the hook when I'm asleep.

'Yeah,' I said. Maybe Fontaine had had an accident.

'Mr Khaled requires that you fly to New York to investigate the suitability of opening a "Hobo" there.'

'What?' I was stunned.

'Mrs Khaled suggests you leave immediately, I actually had you booked on the eight p.m. flight, but I shouldn't think you'll make that now. Of course if you rushed—'

I interrupted, 'I can't go tonight, death in the family you know,' I always have been an exaggerated liar.

'Oh,' the crisp voice paused. 'Well, how about seven-forty-five tomorrow morning?'

What the hell was this? What was all the urgency? Of course I would love to see New York, but what was the panic? I scanned the wire quickly.

*'Need you here. Benjamin will explain. Make it fast. Fontaine.'*

'How long am I supposed to go for?' I asked Alice.

'A few days I believe. Is the seven-forty-five all right?'

'Yes, that's O.K.'

'Fine, a car will pick you up at six a.m., everything will be taken care of this end, a car will meet you on arrival. Bon voyage!' Alice's crisp voice hung up.

I sat back a bit stunned. New York. I'd always wanted to go there. What about visas and everything? I thought it took months. What should I take? 'Hobo' in New York. What a scene *that* would be!

. There was no time to waste, I didn't want to be late for Alexandra. I'm off to New York in the morning—sounded good.

I sorted out some things to take, counted my money, only twenty quid, well I supposed Fontaine would take care of that. Then I dressed. Best-casual clobber. Groomed the barnet. I was ready.

Alexandra and Madelaine lived in a big grim block of flats. I rang the bell of No. 14 and waited. I was shocked when Madelaine's brother Michael answered. He was unconcerned at seeing me, and invited me into an old-fashioned large living room. Madelaine bounced in next, dressed in a flouncy blue dress, she said, 'Is it going to be all right for me to come too?'

I looked sad. 'Sorry, darling, absolutely not. I warned Alex.'

'Oh,' Madelaine's bounce sagged a bit, but she lit a cigarette and choked. Then she brightened. 'Well, Alex can tell me about it anyway.' She wasn't a bad little bird, certainly understanding.

Michael offered me a drink. He acted like he lived there. Then, enter Alexandra. She looked lovely in one of those Victorian-type dresses with frills everywhere, her hair was tied back and she really looked so young and pretty. I was knocked out.

Michael said, 'You've got everything but the kitchen stove on.'

She glared at him and replied, 'Better than wearing the minimum.'

Rather clever I thought. I said, 'You look great,' and she smiled triumphantly at Michael.

I was getting fed up with the whole thing between her and the idiot, so I quickly downed the weak scotch he had given me and said, 'Come on, we can't be late.'

Then followed a whole explanation about why Madelaine couldn't come too. I was in trouble if Steve Scott blew his big mouth off about open house.

Finally we got out of there and she admired Sammy's E-type, I forgot to mention it wasn't mine, I mean why confuse things? And then we were off.

It suddenly struck me we were much too early to go to the party. I mean nine-thirty would be the earliest we could appear, and then we'd probably be the first anyway.

A nice cosy drink somewhere was the thing. I decided the rooftop bar at the Hilton was suitably romantic. London shimmering and shining below us was a good scene. Or maybe I should destroy her with one of those wild drinks at Trader Vic's.

She was sitting demurely, the ribbon tying back her hair gave her a real little girl look. To tell the truth, I was worried about taking her to Steve's. His parties got very wild, plenty of booze and birds and everyone turning on. I don't go for the pot scene myself—cannot see what all the fuss is about—it doesn't do anything for me. Just give me a few scotches and I'm all right. Of course, in my business, to certain people, I have to pretend I turn on—otherwise they would think I wasn't cool, and you've got to keep a hip image going. Fontaine and friends smoke occasionally. It's like a gang of children having naughty fun. They think they are so decadent. I have found that the really cool pot smokers just get on with it and don't make a whole group scene. Hal was always high, but he never discussed it.

'It's a shame Madelaine couldn't come,' Alexadra said.

'Yeah, sorry about that. Listen, I thought we'd grab a fast drink, we're early for the party.'

'Oh, what time does it start?' She fiddled with a few of her Victorian frills.

'About nine. Is the Hilton O.K. for you?'

She nodded. 'I've never been there.'

I was amazed, I'd never met anyone who hadn't been in the Hilton.

I took her to the rooftop bar. If she'd never been there this was something she had to see. The view was a knockout.

I could see she couldn't decide what to drink so I ordered her a champagne cocktail and I had a double scotch and coke. We attacked the nuts and she giggled a bit and said. 'What a super place!'

'Have you really never been here?' I was still surprised.

'No,' she shook her head. 'Actually I haven't spent very much time in London at all, Mummy hates it, so we never came. But now I've finished school I wanted to come so much and Mummy simply had to agree to let me share a flat with Madelaine—you see Madelaine's mother and mine are best friends.'

'What about your father?' I asked.

'Oh, Daddy,' she shrugged. 'Well, since he married that awful woman we haven't really spent much time with him,' she stopped, then rushed on, 'I suppose I shouldn't call her an awful woman, but she is.'

If she had stuck her tongue out and added—so there—I wouldn't have been surprised.

I wondered what Alexandra would have said if she'd known about the affair Fontaine and I were having.

She sipped her champagne cocktail and I gulped my scotch. Her dress didn't reveal any flesh at all, even her arms were covered and the skirt wasn't particularly short.

As if she sensed me thinking this she said, 'Now that I'm in London I must shorten my skirts. I feel like an old frump. In Switzerland we had to wear a regulation skirt length and that was that.'

'You don't need your skirt any shorter,' I said quickly. Quite frankly, I was fed up to the teeth with all the birds around practically exposing their knicks. On a clear night in the club you could see for ever. I didn't want Alexandra joining the ranks of the ass flashers. Really a very short skirt only looks good on a seventeen-year-old flat-chested girl with great legs (thin) and how many of those are there around? Not many I can tell you.

Alexandra finished her drink, 'What time can we go to the party?' she asked brightly.

72

I glanced at my watch—one of Fontaine's very few presents—Roman numerals, black croc strap. It was nearly nine, so I figured it would be all right.

Just as I asked for the check, a loud voice yelled, 'Tony, honey pie,' and arms were thrown around me. It was Molly Mandy. Just what I needed. She was wearing a multi-coloured jersey dress cut out everywhere, and as I tried to disentangle myself from her I noticed Alexandra's look of —well—amazement I guess.

Molly finished her greeting, flashed very white teeth in a friendly smile at Alexandra, winked, said, 'Have a ball,' laughed, and swung off back to her escort, a soberly dressed old man, her speciality. God knows where she found them and God knows why they wanted to be seen out with her.

'Who's that?' Alexandra asked breathlessly.

'Just a girl that comes into the club, a dress designer. Come on.'

I took hold of her hand, she went a bit stiff, but didn't pull away. We set off for the elevator. Oh, if Fontaine could see me now.

I thought I had better cover my tracks. 'Listen, you know your father might not approve of my taking you out. I work for him in a roundabout way and he might not like it, so I think it's best not to mention it. Right?'

'All right,' she replied, a bit surprised.

'I'd like to see you a lot more,' I added quickly. 'What do you think?'

I was making a right berk of myself. Never acted so stupid with a girl. The right way to go about it with someone you like is at the end of the evening to mumble casually, 'I'll call you' and then don't call for two weeks. That always gets them going. But I thought this girl was wonderful and sweet and warm and I wanted her to know how I felt. We were outside. 'Party time,' I said, and helped her into the car.

I was right, we were too early. Steve lounged to the door in his underpants and a sweater.

'Come on in,' he said. 'Just finished boffing, where's your bottle?'

I'd forgotten he'd said to bring a bottle.

Carolyn appeared wrapping a pink dressing-gown around her.

73

She had nothing underneath and I noticed the firmness of her small breasts and I remembered the night we'd had together. She was a right raver.

'Tony, you're so bloody cheap,' she said, 'no bottle indeed, I suppose you forgot.' She smiled at Alexandra. 'Hi, I'm Carolyn.'

Alexandra smiled back and I noticed her eyes wandering to Steve's crotch. I started a slow burn.

'Make yourselves at home,' Steve said. 'We're going to dress. Answer the door if it rings.'

'He's terrific,' Alexandra whispered when he'd gone.

'Yes, I could see you liked him,' I replied drily, but it was lost on her.

I fixed her a vodka, all I could find. She made a face, but sipped it all the same. I couldn't see any food. Steve was the one that was cheap.

Soon the mob started to arrive. All the familiar faces. What a small town London really is. I spread the word I was off to New York to open a joint. Everyone was suitably impressed. Steve's parties were O.K. when they started, it was only after a couple of hours that they went to rack and ruin.

Alexandra seemed quite happy sitting with her vodka (third one, I aimed to get her smashed).

Steve said to me. 'Who's the pussy cat?'

Dirty bastard—I hadn't thought she would be his type. He was chatting her a bit and I was choked. I didn't leave her side, and then who should walk in but 'The Twang'.

'Ooh, Tony, is that your mother?' she asked in her loud nasal voice. I could have killed her. 'You're a lousy sonofabitch,' she said in a lower voice, 'I could take my choice, you know—I don't need you.'

Well, why didn't she leave me alone then?

I figured it was time to go. I didn't want Alexandra involved in the scene that was starting.

'Come on,' I said, 'the time has come to find food.'

'I feel awful,' she said, 'sort of buzzy.'

I got her up and she leaned on me. I realised she was loaded, my fault.

74

Janine said, 'Bye-bye, lover boy.' She really had a big mouth.

Outside the cold air hit Alexandra like a ton of bricks. She clung to my jacket and said, 'I feel sick.' Then she was sick, narrowly missing my jacket by inches. Then she started to cry and I felt like the world's worst shit.

'Please take me home,' she moaned.

So much for an evening of fun.

I got her in the car and she huddled miserably on her seat, 'I'm so embarrassed,' she said weakly. 'I've never done anything like that before.'

'Don't worry about it,' I said, 'it happens to everybody. You just had a little bit over the odds, you'll soon feel better.'

'I'm so sorry.' She really was in a state.

'I'll tell you what, we'll go back to my place and I'll fix you some eggs and you can rest up a bit.'

She made a face, 'I couldn't eat, ugh! I just want to crawl into bed and hide.'

Didn't she realise that's just what I had in mind? 'Well, how about some coffee then, nice strong black coffee?'

She nodded and I headed the phallic E-type in the direction of my pad. I switched the car radio on, a touch of Aretha Franklin at her most soulful—very nice. Things were looking up.

We arrived and Alexandra said. 'Where are we?'

'My place, going to make you some nice hot coffee.'

'Oh, Tony, I'm being such a bother. I can make coffee, you don't have to go to all this trouble. Just drop me home, and I'll be off your hands.'

Was she very smart or genuinely an innocent?

I got out of the car and helped her out. 'It's no bother.'

She looked pale, but being sick had obviously done her good. We stood by the car.

'I'd rather go home,' she said, 'I'd feel much happier.'

'Don't be silly,' I was determined to get her to my flat, 'you'll feel better after some coffee.'

'No, really, Tony, I must go home.' She started to climb back into the car.

Well, I couldn't stand there arguing all night. Mummy had

probably warned her about going to big bad men's apartments, and Mummy was dead right. I got into the car too.

She smiled at me, 'You're being very kind.'

How could I resist those liquid brown eyes? I took her home, saw her to the front door. Shook her hand (her idea, not mine), kissed her on the cheek (my idea), said goodbye and promised to phone her as soon as I got back from New York.

'Super,' she said, and was inside her flat with the door closed in my face quick as a flash. Charming!

But she was a lovely little bird, and I could wait.


# 11


## ALEXANDRA


Madelaine and I discussed it. I was forced to tell her how I felt about Michael, because I had to tell someone, and since she was his sister and my best friend perhaps she could help.

She roared with laughter when she heard. 'Soppy old Michael! You're joking, I hope.' But then she could see that I wasn't, and she got very serious and said. 'Alex, he's terrible with girls. He just wants them for one thing and then drops them.'

I didn't see how Maddy could know that. After all, she had been away at school with me for most of the year. Anyway if he wanted one thing he could have it.

We sat up late on Saturday night talking and Maddy came to the conclusion that the best thing to do was make him jealous. 'I think he quite likes you,' she said, 'only I don't think he looks on you as a potential girl-friend. After all, you've known each other since we were all kids together.'

'He still thinks I am a kid,' I said miserably, 'he said so.'

'We've just got to make him realise how gorgeous and desirable you are.' Maddy's eyes were gleaming, she loved organising things. 'Tomorrow night, when Tony comes to fetch us—we'll get Michael to be here. and you'll sweep past him looking absolutely fantastic and sort of act very cold and off-hand with him.'

'How do I look absolutely fantastic? I haven't got anything to wear.'

We went through my wardrobe and the only thing remotely glamorous I possessed was a frilly terylene dressing-gown.

'You can wear that!' Maddy exclaimed. 'Put a belt around it and no one will know.'

I tried it on, and with shoes and a belt it really did look quite good. So I decided I would wear that and we finally got to bed at three a.m. I was exhausted.

Maddy phoned Michael the next morning. Actually it was about twelve o'clock as we both overslept.

'We're in frightful trouble,' she wailed, 'we've blown a fuse and I can't work the television, and the stopper's jammed in the bath.'

'Christ!' Michael complained. I was listening on the extension. 'All right, I'll come over when I get up.'

'We've got to pop out now, Do you think you could make it about seven?'

'Seven. Where the bloody hell are you going?'

'We have to go and see Alex's father. Is seven O.K., then?'

'Yes, I suppose so, but I can't take you for dinner if that's what you're getting at. I've got a date.'

'That's O.K.,' Maddy said sweetly, and hung up giggling. 'All fixed,' she declared. 'Now you've got to really devastate him.'

We spent the afternoon in preparation. I washed my hair and Maddy set it. I washed the dressing-gown and Maddy ironed it. It was fun having a flat of our own. We had bacon sandwiches for lunch, and pears and cream for tea washed down with heaps of Coca-Cola. What a thrill to be able to do anything you want!

When Michael arrived I was shut in the bedroom with my hair in rollers trying to do a proper makeup. My hand shook and I smudged the eyeliner, so I had to take it all off and start again.

Maddy was ready. She had promised to keep Michael busy until Tony arrived. I wasn't supposed to come out of the bedroom until

Tony got there, then I was supposed to just glide out and practically ignore Michael.

I was only just ready by eight. I heard the doorbell and counted a slow sixty as arranged (it felt like six thousand and sixty!). I then walked casually (my heart was beating so loud I was surprised no one mentioned it!) into the living room. Michael was sprawled in a chair.

'I can't come,' Madelaine wailed, 'Tony said he tried to get me invited too, but it's just not possible.'

'What a shame.' I didn't really want to go without Madelaine, especially now.

'Sorry, girls,' Tony said, 'just one of those things. Come on, we can't be late.'

I looked at Michael. Was he just going to let me walk out of here with a comparative stranger to a wild pop star's party and not say anything? Apparently he was.

'Goodbye,' I said.

Madelaine smiled half-heartedly, and Michael said, 'Don't forget to get his autograph!'

Tony had a very nice car. Actually he was being sweet to me. I wonder why he's bothering. Because of Daddy. I suppose. Lots of people are nice to me because of Daddy, him being so rich and everything. Mummy always says. 'Having money doesn't make you any better than the next person.' I think she's right.

Tony said, 'We'll go to the Hilton for a drink first.'

It was rather fun and I drank champagne.

Tony seemed awfully popular. He joked with the barman and kept on saying hello to people. He made me feel very comfortable and he was funny. I wished Michael could be as nice as him.

I suppose a lot of girls would consider him good-looking. He has lovely black curly hair, but he's really not my type, and I'm sure I'm not his!

'What time can we go to the party?' I asked.

The champagne had made me feel good and I was determined to forget about Michael and have a terrific time.

When we left, Tony held my hand and said that Daddy might not approve of his taking me out and would I please not tell him.

Well, that confused me. I mean I had thought that *was* the reason for his taking me out—to sort of get in Daddy's good books. 'All right,' I said.

Steve Scott's party was fantastic. We were the first ones there and he answered the front door practically naked. Then he and his girl-friend went off to dress and Tony gave me a drink, I don't know what it was but it tasted vile. I swallowed it down, anyway.

. Tony stayed by my side most of the evening and I felt so sort of light-headed and witty. I felt I could talk to anyone, I even knew exactly what I would say to Michael if he was there.

Steve Scott was wonderful. Once, when Tony was fetching me another drink, he sat on the arm of my chair and said, 'I bet you've never had it.'

'Had what?' I replied.

'Oh baby,' he laughed, 'I could show you a thing or two. You and I could really fly.'

Then Tony came back, and Steve said. 'Who's the pussy cat?'

Tony said, 'Hands off, lover boy.'

Then Tony's girl-friend appeared and started yelling at him, and I drank some more of my drink, it was about my fifth, and Steve said, 'What's your phone number, sweetheart? Little girls like you are far too rare.'

So I gave him my phone number, and Tony came back and said we should go. Just when the party was getting to be fun. I couldn't wait to tell Madelaine that Steve Scott had asked for my number!

As soon as I stood up I felt horribly sick.

Tony put his arm around me and helped me outside, and then—talk about being embarrassed—I *was* sick and could have died! Why didn't the pavement just open up and swallow me!

'Please take me home,' I begged, hardly daring to look at him.

He kept on talking about going for coffee and food. Ugh! I couldn't face food. Really I couldn't face anything, I just wanted to get home and into bed.

He drove somewhere and stopped the car.

'Where are we?' I asked.

'My place, I'm going to make you some nice hot coffee.'

He got me out of the car and I got back in and insisted it was too much trouble and I *had* to go home.

He was very nice about it. I don't expect he really wanted to be bothered making me coffee anyway. After all, he was off on a trip to America the next day and probably had to get up early.

Oh, the relief of saying goodnight to Tony, dashing into our flat, and throwing up again.

He was probably glad to be rid of me, anyway.


# 12


## FONTAINE


The thought of struggling along some crowded freeway with a talkative chauffeur is an utter bore.

I did want to see Tony, and although I hadn't planned to go to the airport, I suddenly decided it might be fun. So I cancelled lunch with friends, managed to sit through the boring drive to Kennedy International, and here comes Tony now. I can see him through the glass standing in line for Customs. He has a cheap suitcase—nothing worse, a give-away immediately. I must take him into Gucci.

He does look attractive, rather white in the daylight, he has an eerie night-club pallor which makes an exciting contrast to his jet black hair. What a shame he's not a bit more intelligent, though if he was he wouldn't be wasting his life in a discothèque.

Poor Tony. Poor stud. What will happen to him when his hard body and curly hair are gone? Who will want him then?

At last he's through Customs and hurrying towards me smiling. He's not subtle, I can see he's going to kiss me, so I fend him off with a handshake—stupid boy, there are always photographers lurking.

'How was your trip?'

'Great,' he yawned, exhibiting his tonsils to America. 'Saw a movie, boozed a bit, what's this all about anyway?'

I shrugged, 'Just an idea of mine.' It was best not to tell him I wanted to see him, it would go to his head and he would become impossible.

'Have you got a location or what?'

'Oh no, we're not that advanced, I thought I would hear your opinions and see what you think. We can visit all the competition and you can decide if it would be a good idea.'

He laughed, he had good strong white teeth, 'You mean all the panic was just for me to look around?'

'Yes, actually it was, I thought you would be thrilled to see New York.'

'Yeah—but did I have to leave like a shot out of a gun?'

'Really Tony, I'm surprised at you, you wanted to come while I was still here, didn't you?'

We were in the car by this time and I told the chauffeur to go to my apartment. Alice had arranged a room for Tony at a hotel, but he could damn well accommodate me before going there.

I laid my hand lightly over his, 'How's "Hobo"? Have any of my friends been in?'

Tony shook his head. He didn't look as delighted with this trip as I had thought he would be. He was probably tired from the journey.

'What about Vanessa and Leonard?'

'Haven't seen them.'

'Not even her?'

He looked at me, guilty as hell, probably been screwing the life out of her.

Oh well, *I* had him now.

I certainly wasn't going to force the conversation, let him be uncommunicative and sulky.

I leaned back in the car and closed my eyes. Tony Blake should be kissing my feet. I found him. If it wasn't for me he'd still be a waiter, bowing and scraping all over the place, full of phoney smiles and running for a tip. The trouble with people is that they never appreciate what you do for them. Tony probably thought he would still have been successful without me.

I mean, *really*, 'Hobo' was *my* idea. I could have taken any one of hundreds of good-looking studs, and each one of them would have been as popular as Tony.

'This is wild!'

Oh goody, the great oaf was finally talking. We were entering the city and he was window gazing at the tall buildings, rushing people and general din. Big dirty New York, the city of fairy tales and garbage cans, society balls and riots. You can get anything or do anything here, as long as you have the money of course.

'I thought I'd take you to my apartment first, and then the chauffeur will take you to your hotel. I've got all sorts of exciting things planned for tonight.'

'Great,' his voice lacked enthusiasm. Tony was definitely not himself.

Benjamin had done rather well for me in the Big City. I suppose you could say I have one of the best apartments in town. Of course Tony's eyes fell out as soon as he saw it. It's one of my favourite homes, small—only three bedrooms—but with this marvellous four-sided terrace which goes all around, alive with rose bushes, winter flowers, and an adorable lemon tree. Very pretty. Adamo—our Vietnamese man, takes care of it. He bowed us in and produced martinis.

'Lunch is laid out in the blue room, Madam,' he spoke like an English butler, perfect. All my friends were trying to steal him, but he liked working for Benjamin and me, after all, we are hardly ever here.

'Fine Adamo, you may go, I'll buzz if I need you.'

'Very good, Madam.'

He lived in the basement of the building, very convenient, easy to summon and easy to get rid of.

Tony was prowling around. 'This is fabulous,' he said, 'I've never seen anything like it, this view is the end.'

'How about this view?' I unbuttoned my dress.

One thing I'll say for Tony—he knows his part—and tired or not, he'll play.

We embraced very slowly and then he pushed me to the floor and took off the rest of my clothes.

'Welcome to New York,' I whispered.

He *was* a stud.

# 13

## TONY

I don't think I've ever met a girl like Alexandra before. She's so sort of innocent and girlish and pretty and soft. She looks great. Clean and tidy and young, I really like her, I really do. Even the thought of New York doesn't turn me on too much and Fontaine doesn't turn me on at all any more. In view of the close relationship involved I'd be much better off to avoid Fontaine completely. (Impossible) My only chance is to get away from 'Hobo' and open up on my own. But there's that old problem—money.

I fancy the hostess wriggling up and down the aisle in a tight skirt. I bet she's got something waiting for *her* in New York. Sammy says he's made it on a plane, on a night trip to the South of France. According to him, he had it off with the hostess in the loo—bit crowded I bet.

'Can I get you anything?' She smiled at me, ignoring the old lady in the seat beside me.

'Yeah—but I don't think it's on the menu.'

She giggled, getting the message immediately. These air-hostesses weren't slow.

'Do you wish to see the movie?' She smoothed down her tight skirt.

'Any other suggestions?'

Another giggle. 'Well, some of the passengers come and sit at the back if they have already seen the film.'

There's no doubt about it, I'm irresistible to women! 'I'll come and sit at the back then.'

'Good.' Another smile, and then wiping it off, she leaned across to the old lady and said briskly, 'If you care to see the film there will be a slight charge!' I got a whiff of perfume—cheap but sexy.

We had only been in the air an hour, but I reckoned I was going to be all right.

After a decent interval of three minutes I followed Miss Tight Skirt to the back of the plane. She was busy with another girl getting tin foil trays of cold roast beef, congealed potato salad and hard-boiled eggs that had seen better days.

'Need any help?' I asked, trying to squeeze into the tiny kitchen.

'Sorry, you're not allowed in here.' She smiled to take away the sting. 'You can sit in any of the back row seats if you like. I'll be free when the movie starts.'

The other girl grinned at me too, she had a suntan and freckles. It looks like being a jolly afternoon.

I sat down near the window, viewed the grey expanse of sky and sea, and fell asleep.

I was woken up by Miss Tight Skirt sitting beside me. I kept on thinking of Sammy's experience. 'Ever done a night flight to Nice?' I asked casually.

'Why yes, as a matter of fact I used to be on that run.'

Oh no, it couldn't be true!

The movie was on and the plane was pretty dark. We were sitting on the inside two seats of a three-seater, and there was no one across the aisle.

'What's happening?' I asked.

'Anything you like,' she replied.

I mean, it had to be the same girl.

I thought of Alexandra so sweet and innocent. I guess I wouldn't be being unfaithful, because nothing had happened with her—yet. I put a hand on the hostess's knee.

'Oh come on,' she said, 'you can do better than that.' She pulled a big regulation rug across us. 'Shirley will warn us if anyone comes back to go to the loo.'

What a scene! Under the rug I fought my hand up the tight skirt. She wriggled down in the seat helping me. She had nothing on underneath, making things very easy she was! I unhooked her bra under her prim blouse, her breasts were small but nice, I wished I could see them but there we were all huddled up under the rug.

She unzipped my trousers and with a deft movement twisted herself towards me, and then I was up up and away!

'What about the pilot and stewards?' I asked. She was wriggling and squirming at a good pace.

'It's all right, they're all boozing up front,' she gasped.

Charming, the pilots were boozing up front, and the hostess was screwing at the back. I wouldn't travel on *this* airline again!

'Quick, someone's coming,' a whispered voice said. It was Shirley, and how right she was!

Oh boy—fun at twenty-six thousand feet, I was hardly finished when Tight Skirt pulled out and all in one movement was standing, smoothing her skirt down, and smiling at the passenger who was on his way to the loo.

'Everything all right, sir?'

He nodded. 'Er, I'd like a whisky and soda, is that possible?'

She winked at me, destroyed under the blanket. 'Everything's possible on this airline, sir.'

She deftly hooked her bra as he carried on to the john. 'I don't know your name,' she said to me, 'but I hope you'll fly with us again.'

I went back to my seat, there seemed no point in hanging around.

The old lady smiled and nodded to me.. 'Lovely trip,' she said.

'It certainly was!'

'I beg your pardon?'

'Nothing.' I slouched down in my seat and watched the end of a silent Doris Day movie. A silent Doris Day is better than a talkative one. Man, I was tired, I fell off to sleep until Tight Skirt appeared pushing my shoulder and saying, 'Fasten your seat belt, please, we're coming in to land.'

She had freshened up and added a jacket and matching cap. Very smart and efficient.

I yawned and inspected the view. New York was spread out beneath me. What a sight! I wondered what Alexandra was doing now. Poor little chick getting sick like that. I scribbled her a fast postcard conveniently supplied along with a paper bag to throw up in.

'Dear A. Dull flight. Had any good vodka lately? See you soon—Tony.'

On the way out I handed it to Tight Skirt to post.

'What are you doing tonight?' I asked, more for conversation than anything else.

She gave me a wide grin, 'Going on the town with my fiancé, he's the pilot you know.'

Charming!

I went through Immigration and Customs. An emergency visa had been waiting for me at London airport, along with a vaccination. Money can buy anything.

Fontaine was there to meet me, wrapped in mink, shod in crocodile I was surprised, I didn't think airports were her scene. I forced a smile and set off in her direction. Everyone was taking a second look, she was that kind of woman.

She wanted me to kiss her, she offered that elegant chiselled face, but I wasn't going to fall for that with everybody looking our way. Benjamin could be having her followed or anything and I wasn't going to be the patsy. We shook hands and chatted about the journey. I was dying to find out what this trip was all about, but she was giving nothing away.

We rode in silent luxury to her apartment. She kept on questioning me about who had been in, but that was all.

What a great apartment! Huge and very modern on the top floor of the tallest building I've ever seen, surrounded by a wild garden with a not-to-be believed oriental butler dressed in flowing robes with an English accent. Too much!

It was the usual scene. Servant bowing and scraping, serving drinks and then vanishing. This one backed out of the apartment with such an inane grin on his face that I thought he would trip over his robe.

It was the same old Fontaine. He had hardly closed the front door when she was stripping off her clothes and making a grab for me.

'On the floor,' she whispered.

Oh no, after last night, and the trip, and her relationship to Alexandra, I didn't know if I could make it. But strength will tell, and I managed to do my best. I felt like a heel but what could I do? Alexandra wouldn't forgive me for this, but what *could* I do?

My mind was going in sixteen different directions, all the opposite way from the lady under me. *That awful woman* as Alex described her. And she *was* an awful woman. She had dazzled me at first with all her glamour and fame, but now I saw right through her. A social nymphomaniac, that's what she was.

'You're out of practice, Tony,' her voice was cold and edgy. I finished before she was ready, and she was choked. Little did she know she was lucky to get anything at all, what with the scene on the plane.

'Yeah, well what do you expect with you away and everything?'

'Oh, please, Tony, let's not play the innocent virgin with each other.' She shifted about on the floor, 'Finish the job for God's sake.'

I obliged.

This really is a wild city. Great hotel, fantastic T.V. in the room with lots of channels. Since the chauffeur brought me here two hours ago I've changed stations ten times. Take your choice—quiz show, old English movie, cowboys and Indians. It's all too much! And about room service, great! Club sandwiches I've only dreamed about. I've ordered three times already.

This is the life. I lay on a king-sized bed after a shower watching a blonde chick in a plastic raincoat announce the weather on T.V. Fontaine was picking me up at seven, I had an hour yet.

I wanted to phone A. But Benjamin would be paying the bill and I didn't want him checking through and finding phone calls to his daughter.

I tell you married women disgust me, they're all out for a piece of action away from their husbands. There's hardly one married woman I know that I couldn't truthfully say I could have if I wanted. It makes a man think twice about getting married.

What was I thinking about marriage for anyway? It's not for me, not after all the things I've seen. If I ever did get married it would be to Alexandra. My lovely lovely Alexandra. And she had no money, so where would that be going?

Not that I minded about her having no money—I mean I did think it was a bit strong on Benjamin's part—but I had no money either, so I couldn't even think about getting married. Alexandra Blake. Hmm—not too lyrical but nice, very nice. I imagined Sadie and Sam's faces if I married a girl that wasn't—'a nice Jewish girl'. They would go mad, but so what, I was a big boy now.

The time had come to get dressed. Fontaine had plans for the evening's entertainment—she had reeled off a list of things we were going to do that made me dizzy. We were to start off with a cocktail party, and then go to some friends apartment, and then to dinner, and then a round of discothèques, and then there were a couple of other parties we might attend.

I chose my suit carefully, this would be the first time I had been out with Fontaine socially. I guess under normal circumstances I would be flattered, but things were different now, it all seemed a bit of a drag. It had been quite a day.

I decided on a pale lilac shirt from Turnbull and Asser, hand-made, of course. Actually it had been made for Hal, but he didn't like the colour, so I bought it from him. We took the same size in shirts which was useful. He had some great gear which he got fed up with in a hurry—then I would buy it from him at half the original price. He made bread that way 'cos some old dear had probably bought it for him in the first place. Good old Hal. The last of the great promoters!

To go with the shirt I had a toning polka dot tie. The suit was black, with it I wore pearl cuff-links and tie clip, black socks and shoes. Even though I say it myself, I look pretty damn good.

The desk rang to tell me a car was waiting.

Great—New York City, here I come!

# 14

## FONTAINE

After Tony left and the chauffeur returned I went for my massage.
Bliss. Hot sweaty hands pounding and pummelling my white skin.
Then a delicious steam bath, followed by a soft massage with oil of
pine, its odours sinking into my body.

Oh, what luxury, almost as good as sex. Wrapped in pink
towelling I had my hair washed, then lay on a floating pink couch
while it was dried by concealed jets of air.

This is 'M'lady's Parlour', the very latest beauty house, and I
must say, very impressive.

Sarah dragged me here immediately I arrived. 'It's so divine,
darling, you'll come eighteen times.'

It's beauty in an aphrodisiac atmosphere. All the boys here are
queens, it's like a harem with eunuchs preparing you for the
night's fantasy.

Roger did my hair, small petite Roger with a mass of golden
curls and pursed bitchy lips. 'Darling, do you believe what
Clarissa wore to the premiere last night? She looked like a baby
yellow elephant! Ridiculous! My friend says her dress was a Rudi
Genreich, but I can't believe that Rudi would be so wicked!'

I smiled. The good thing about Roger was the fact that one
could relax and listen to all the gossip. His bitcheries could go on
for ever.

He continued, 'Saw a dreadful movie last night, I couldn't
believe the clothes though, terribly now. You'd look divine in
white satin with lots of fox fur. I think I'm going to do your hair
Grecian. Strand it with pearls and things.'

I felt so good from the massage, my body tingled. Oh God, if all
these little twits could see Tony they'd cream themselves!

He was getting a rather attractive quality of self-confidence.
With me he had always been so fawning and adoring. Now he
seemed to treat me in a slightly cooler fashion. Although of course
he was still a boy scout when it came to material things. Why the

way his mouth had popped open when he saw my apartment! The stud prowling around and sniffing the luxury!

Of course, I know eventually he will begin to flap his wings, but I'm sure this trip will cool him down and make him realise exactly who he's mixing with. After all there aren't many women like me around, and however many little affaires he has to indulge in, he'll soon find that out.

Roger did wonders with my hair, only two pieces and it looks marvellous.

'Have a lovely time,' he said, stepping back to admire his work.

I went home and phoned Sarah, we were all to dine together. I hadn't told her about Tony, I had just said a business associate of Benjamin's was joining us. I couldn't wait to see her face!

'What are you wearing?' she asked.

'I haven't decided yet,' I replied, although I was going to wear the black silk backless Cardin.

'Neither have I.' What a liar she was.

'We'll see you about eight, going to pop into the Carlton's party first.'

'What a bore. They're so show business, Allen can't stand them.'

Actually I knew that Sarah and Allen hadn't been invited, as Salamanda Smith, a Hollywood film star, and Allen had been a very hot item indeed the previous summer, and Peter Carlton, whom she had since married, was terribly jealous. Oh, the intricacies of the social set!

'Are the Bells and Sidwells meeting at your place too?'

'Yes, everything's arranged,' Sarah lowered her voice, 'I had a wonderful afternoon. Have you ever tried yoga?'

I didn't want to get involved in one of Sarah's sexual discussions, they always began with a lowered voice.

'Yes, darling, often. See you later.' I hung up.

Tony looked refreshed. He also looked flashy and a bit cheap, but I was prepared to forgive him that. It was the terrible tie he had on that did it, change that and he wouldn't look too bad. I slid the glass down between me and the chauffeur and said, 'Stop at

Saks.' They were still open. I smiled at Tony and said, 'Let's pop in a minute, I want to get you a little something.'

Everyone stared at us. Well, Roger had gone a bit avant garde with my hair, divine for evening but not quite suitable for a flit through Saks. People who say that nobody stares at you in New York are mad. They stare more than anywhere else. Blue-haired mink-stoled ladies with beaded handbags and plastic rhinestone studded shoes are the first to say, 'Oh ma Gawd, lookit her!'

In the men's department I picked out six divine imported ties and made Tony put one on. 'We'll come here tomorrow and do some more shopping.'

The salesman goggled at me and gave Tony the package.

'Didn't you like my tie?' He was surly.

'It was lovely, I just like this one better.' Oh God, don't tell me he was going to sulk. He should be delighted with six new thirty-dollar ties.

The party was a shambles, so many people. Salamanda, floaty in pink chiffon. Tony was impressed. He still got awed by meeting film stars.

She gushed over to us, 'Gee, so great of you to come, Mrs Khaled,' she held the smile for the hovering photographer.

What a dull pretty little face she had, not a bone worth anything in the whole structure. Her puffy eyes surrounded in caked mascara were studying my diamonds.

'Tony Blake, our hostess, Mrs Peter Carlton,' I said.

He beamed, 'I loved your last film,' he said almost stuttering. 'How did you manage so long in the desert?'

Oh God, save me from the film fan!

She blinked, 'Gee, it was O.K. Petey came down on the weekends.'

'All that way?'

'We made it just outside of Vegas—hey,' she started to laugh, 'wacha think, we, made it in the Sahara or somethin'? They wouldn't get lil ole me there, honey.'

I really think Tony is a cretinous bore. I can't imagine why I wanted him here. I left the two of them and looked around. The same old faces, oh God, sometimes *everything* is so boring.

# 15

## TONY

Fontaine is the biggest put-down merchant of all time. Here I am, looking great, feeling great, ready to go, and she gives me one of those tight little smiles of hers and says, 'Tony, darling, we'll simply have to stop and get you a decent tie. You just can't go out like that.' I mean screw her, sitting there with her hair looking like a Carnival Queen. Who does she think she is? She doesn't own me, and pretty soon she's going to find that out.

She dragged me into some store and lumbered me with six of the dreariest ties you could imagine. Imported yet, probably couldn't find a buyer for them in their own country.

I put on the best of the bunch, to keep her happy, and silently fumed. Fontaine was a cow. An old cow. I contemplated telling her to take a running jump, but I had no money to pay the hotel and I'm sure if I did that, no job to return to in good old Blighty.

Fontaine Khaled had me by the short and curlies, and what was worse she bloody well knew it.

We arrived at the party, it was pretty jammed, but everyone turned to take a look at us. Fontaine hadn't bothered to tell me whose party it was, but I soon got the message when Salamanda Smith, *the* Salamanda Smith, came wafting over.

She was a gorgeous bird, curvy and blonde with a pair of bristols that fair knocked your eyes out. I'd just seen her in a wild desert movie, full of sex and sand type thing. She was bowled over by Fontaine, but I could see she had an eye (baby blue) for me, and we got to chatting about her last movie.

She had to go to greet some more people and Fontaine had done a vanish, so there I was on my todd. I scouted around and got hold of a scotch from a white-coated guy who called me 'bud' and was really loaded. Was he a waiter? The way he was acting I wasn't quite sure. But he picked up a tray, belched, and set off in the direction of some guests, so I guessed he was.

He weaved into a fake marble column, and it swayed, but stood its ground, then he staggered with his tray over to some people and hands stretched out like vultures, relieving him of the glasses. He came rolling back in my direction—'S'elluva party,' he mumbled, 'lotsa cooze.' Then he was off again towards Salamanda, and dropping his tray with a loud crash, he grabbed hold of her with one hand, and with the other unzipped his fly and said, 'Get a load of this, honey!'

There was a short silence while she struggled to free herself. Then three guys jumped on the waiter and he disappeared beneath a torrent of blows.

It was a funny scene really. Salamanda took a deep breath, smiled, and the waiter was dragged, blood dripping from his face, out of the room. Great! I counted ten knowing that Fontaine would appear at my side, anxious to hear all.

Fontaine—the last of the great gossips. She was there on the stroke of nine. 'What happened?' her silver-lidded eyes glistened anxiously.

'Just some drunk waiter, nothing exciting.'

'Oh,' she was disappointed, 'is that all?'

Salamanda was now retelling the story to a small group surrounding her, and Fontaine went over. I trailed behind. She was just saying, 'and there was his enormous *thing*! Just staring me in the face!'

Fontaine shot me a dirty look, I'd left out the best bits.

I wished I could phone Alexandra. I looked around for a phone, nobody would notice me making a quick call to London with this group. I strolled out of the door, looked about and found an empty bedroom with a shiny gold bedside model. I grabbed it quick. 'Overseas please—London England—a personal call to Miss Alexandra Khaled—8934434. No, I'll hang on.'

A beautiful girl came into the room, long straight black hair, long straight black body. She looked directly at me, 'You going to Marcellos after?'

'Who's Marcello?'

Her eyes were stony, unsmiling. 'You putting me on?'

'Nope.' I shook my head and winked. 'Who is he? I'm a stranger here.'

'Ah God almighty,' she smoothed down her long black hair. 'Marcellos is a restaurant, man, everyone seems to be going there, I'm looking for someone to take me. You interested?'

I was interested all right, but unavailable. 'I'm with someone. How about another night?'

Her eyes swept over me. 'Yeah, maybe.'

Just then the operator said, 'I'm putting you through now, your party's on the line.'

Then Alexandra's voice, clear and sweet, 'Hello?'

The girl was combing her hair at a mirror.

'Hello, baby, and how are you today?'

'Oh, Tony, how super of you to phone me all the way from America. I'm much better, thank you. I feel such an idiot about last night.'

A warm glow came over me, 'Don't give it another thought. It was my fault for taking you to a lousy party like that. What are you doing?'

'I'm in bed actually.'

I imagined her with brushed shining hair and a fluffy pink nightdress. 'That's the best place to be.' I glanced over at the girl, she was hanging around. I covered the mouthpiece of the phone, 'Write down your number,' I hissed at her. I said back into the phone, 'I miss you.'

I did miss her. The girl wrote Norma and a number on some book matches and threw them at me, then she went out.

There was silence from Alexandra. 'I said I miss you.'

'I know,' her voice was a whisper.

'Well?'

'Well, what?'

'Do you miss me?'

'I don't know. I mean, you've only been gone a day, and after all we don't know each other very well.' She paused. 'Yes, I do miss you.'

My heart did a little skip, 'I'm going to be back soon, then we'll get to know each other really well. Be a good girl.'

'Yes.' She had such a lovely accent.

'See you soon.' I hung up. It was good to be alive. I peered at myself in the mirror. I looked good but wished I had a suntan. Maybe Fontaine would fancy a few days in Florida.

I went back to the party and found Fontaine. She was holding court, her clipped British tones ringing round the room. When she paused for air, she noticed me. 'Oh there you are, we've got to be going.' She wasn't as friendly towards me as she had been. You never know with Fontaine, she blows hot and cold. Maybe she didn't like having me out with her, maybe she thought I wasn't good enough. All right for a fuck, but not for her friends. I scowled. She glared. We left.

In the car she said testily, 'You know, Tony, you shouldn't act so star-struck. I would have thought that by now you would have been used to meeting celebrities.'

*Me—star-struck!* I was choked! That was the *last* thing *I* was.

She tapped talon-like nails on her small gold (real, of course) handbag and added, 'You made a fool of yourself with Salamanda. You acted like a film fan. Don't you realise five years ago she was a stripper, and you—anyone—could have had her for ten dollars.'

I've learnt one lesson in life. Never argue with a woman when she's putting down another woman.

'Yeah, you're right,' I conceded. Who needed an argument?

She softened a bit. 'Just don't forget—you'll probably meet many big stars while you're here. Don't mention their work or anything about it, socially that's just not on.'

Silly cow! I yawned. 'I'd love to go to Florida.'

She ignored me.

We arrived at a big apartment house, and the doorman nearly broke his neck getting her ladyship out of the car.

'These are my dearest friends in New York,' Fontaine said, 'Sarah and Allen Grant, a wonderful couple. Don't embarrass me.'

I mean, what did she think I was going to do—pee on the carpet or something?

We went into a fantastic pad on the ground floor. Big dark, crammed with antiques, stuffed animals and tall plants. Very nice. What a scene you could have here!

95

This lady came to greet us, bony face, pulled back black hair and whiter than white skin. She looked like she was suffering from a touch of malnutrition. She and Fontaine kissed, summing each other's outfits up with their eyes. Then Fontaine said, 'Sarah, I want you to meet Tony, Benjamin sent him over.'

Man, she made me sound like a package! Sarah looked me over. She had wild black eyes that burned right through you. Her lips were thin and painted dark red. I guessed she must be about forty. If you like skeleton thin older chicks she was a knockout. Personally I don't. Her glance jumped between me and Fontaine, and she smiled slightly. 'Well, what a surprise.'

Fontaine smiled too, 'Yes,' she said, and they linked arms and walked over to the bar, leaving me standing there like a right berk.

There were four or five other people sitting about, and a guy got up and came over to me. He had what women's magazines would call a craggy handsome face. He wore a shapeless grey suit, 'Allen Grant,' he said, shaking hands and giving me an amused squint.

'Tony Blake.'

'Come and have a drink.' He took me over to the bar and fixed me a very large scotch on the rocks. He fixed himself an even bigger one and disposed of it in three hefty gulps. Then he made himself another and said, 'Who are you?'

Charming! I mean I love questions like that from a complete stranger. What do you say? The Pope—Gunga Din—'I'm over here for Ben Khaled, looking for—er—properties.'

'Oh. Are you having an affair with the lovely Mrs K. then?'

I mean was I supposed to hit him or what? Fortunately Fontaine came over. 'Allen, you naughty boy, what are you saying?'

She was flirting, a pose of hers that drove me mad.

He laughed. 'Nothing. How are you my sweet?'

'I'm fine.' Their eyes met in the sort of intimacy usually reserved for lovers. They probably were, that would just about be Fontaine's scene, knocking off her best friend's husband. I didn't care. My little Alexandra was tucked up at home in bed, and that's all I cared about.

Sarah took my arm, 'Come, Tony, I want you to meet the others.'

I racked my brain to find out where I'd seen her before. I pride myself on never forgetting a face, and I knew I'd seen this one somewhere. She hadn't been in the club, that I was sure of. She was certainly very striking, although as I said before, not my type at all. Her hand was brittle on my arm, skeleton fingers digging in. Suddenly it struck me where I knew her from. American Vogue three months ago, a big layout of her in Bermuda or somewhere modelling beach exotica. I told you I have a great memory. Sarah Grant—society bigwig—New York City.

'Fontaine never told me about you,' she said in a deep husky voice, 'you're divine.'

Instant lay, better watch out, didn't want to upset her ladyship.

I was then introduced to the others, your average rich couples—neither of the women could hold a candle to Fontaine or Sarah, and the men were balding and moved in a cloud of cigar smoke.

After some boring small talk we left, a convoy of chauffeured cars.

First stop was dinner, an exclusive restaurant off Fifth Avenue, with hothouse plants growing wild, and gold-jacketed waiters. I sat between Fontaine and Sarah, fighting a losing battle to taste my food against the fumes of their respective perfumes.

They both ignored me, making polite small talk around the rest of the table. I couldn't join in as I didn't know who or what they were talking about. I mean are you ready for 'Fleur met Itsy in St Moritz and they had a terrible fight and he ended up with Poopsie at Mooeys.' Allen was the only one who spoke to me. I had a feeling he was as bored as I was.

So this was New York—social circuit number one. You can have it and stick it. I wished I was with Norma at 'Marcellos', wherever that might be.

Dinner dragged on and on and I was getting a bad case of yawning. At last Fontaine said, 'I think we'd better get Tony to "Picketts" before he falls asleep on us.' She shot me a dark look to let me know she was furious about my yawning all night.

'Picketts' was the newest disco to open and make it big. I had heard about it, but all the same it was a shock. The whole interior of the club was like a huge monster's open mouth. Fangs and cobwebs hung from everywhere, and in a transparent tooth hanging like a light fixture from the ceiling, a near-naked female freaked out to the blaring sounds of James Brown. There was an assortment of waitresses dressed in flimsy bits of cobwebs, and lots of glimpses of a tit here, an ass there. Pretty wild, but not what I'd call a cool scene. I mean who needs gimmicks? The customers are supposed to make the fun.

Fontaine made her usual grand entrance, the guy running the joint nearly kissed her feet. He was small, dark and nervous looking. No competition there.

We were sat round a table shaped like a huge withered hand, and a little teeny bopper, happy in her cobweb gear, took our order. Champagne all round and a scotch for me.

'Why fight it,' Allen murmured. 'Why not get used to her habits?'

'I only drink scotch,' I answered.

'Come on, Allen sweetie, let's show 'em.' Fontaine was getting frisky as she dragged Allen off to dance.

'Shall we?' Sarah asked with arched eyebrows, already getting up without waiting for my reply.

I followed her to the dance floor. She was even more embarrassing stiff-assed than Fontaine.

What the hell was I doing here? Six months before I would have given anything to be involved in this scene with these people, in fact I wouldn't have believed it was possible. But now—well, who needed it? I had everything going for me in London, I didn't need this trailing behind Fontaine bag.

We stayed at 'Picketts' an hour, and then on to 'The Flower Mission', a wild mass of psychedelic symbols and freak-out light effects.

By this time the other two couples had dropped out and it was just Fontaine, Sarah, Allen and me against the world. We were all well smashed.

'Have you ever studied yoga?' Sarah asked me, black eyes piercing and probing.

'Er—no.'

'You should. You have a powerful body. I'm sure you would excel at it.'

'Tony,' Fontaine said excitedly, 'Allen's met a man here who can get us some cigarettes,' her voice lowered on the word cigarettes and I knew with a sinking feeling she meant pot. That's all I needed, one of her 'aren't we being wicked' pot-smoking scenes. I just don't dig it, it doesn't do a thing for me except make me go to sleep, and from the way Fontaine is carrying on, me going to sleep is not what she has in mind.

'We'll go to Sarah and Allen's, shall we?' Not so much a question, more a statement.

So we left and chauffeured all the way to the Grant pad.

Once there the two women disappeared and Allen made a beeline for the bar. He wasn't talking, just knocking back a large glass of brandy and looking hollow-eyed.

'What's the action?' I asked helping myself to a drink as he didn't seem to be offering.

'God knows,' he said. 'You're lucky, at least you're not married to yours.'

What did *that* mean?

I glanced at my watch, it was three a.m. I was bushed. I tried to calculate what time it was in London. Five hours difference but I couldn't remember which way.

Sarah came back in first. She had changed into a full-length brocade caftan, and her jet-black hair was combed straight down. She looked vaguely Indian.

Fontaine followed, her hair was still piled high on her head, but she had changed into a long white floating thing, slightly transparent, and I could see the outline of her small naked breasts.

'Allen,' Sarah said. 'why don't you and Tony put on these?' She handed us each a black silk sort of short Japanese kimono.

'Come on,' Allen said resignedly.

I followed him into another room, and he stripped off his clothes and put on the black kimono.

He smiled grimly, 'I know why I'm doing this, how about you?'

I felt well choked about the whole thing, but what the hell, in a way it was rather exciting.

99

I put on the kimono, the silk felt great. I wished it wasn't so short, it just about covered my balls!

We went back inside. Fontaine and Sarah were smoking already, taking long thin-lipped drags. I went to sit beside Fontaine but she motioned me over to Sarah. Oh boy—if the regulars could see me now!

There was some weird Japanese music playing, and Sarah offered me her cigarette. I took a drag. We were sitting on a sofa, and opposite on another sofa were Fontaine and Allen.

I handed the cigarette back to Sarah. She puffed and leaned back blowing little smoke rings to the ceiling.

My turn, this wasn't too bad, I felt a certain numbness creep over me and the music sounded fantastic. I put the cigarette back in her mouth, and she leaned over and put her hands under the kimono. Her fingers felt like burning tongs as they fled around my flesh.

I glanced over at Fontaine. She was lying against the cushions and Allen was peeling the white thing off her. I watched fascinated as her body came into view and he started to kiss her. Her legs were spread and she moaned softly.

Meanwhile Sarah's hands manipulated me. She took off my kimono, and man, I felt great! Then I started to fly and I was pounding into someone and when I looked it was Fontaine and then Sarah and then both of them were all over me. It was a kaleidoscope of faces and, man, for the first time I was really stoned.

# 16

## ALEXANDRA

My first day at McLaughton & Co. was awful. To start off with I was late, unforgivable on one's first day; secondly, I felt dreadful, with what I supposed was my first hangover; and thirdly, according to Madelaine all Michael had said about me the previous evening was, 'What a ridiculous dress'.

I wasn't sure that I liked working. It was awfully dull just sitting at a desk typing. Perhaps I should have let Daddy help me to get an interesting job. I couldn't wait for five o'clock when I could rush home and have a proper chat with Maddy.

Fortunately five o'clock finally came and I took a taxi home. Maddy was lolling about reading magazines, the lucky thing didn't start her job until next week.

'What was it like?' she asked. 'Have you got a super boss who looks at your legs when you take dictation?'

'No, I've got a grumpy old man who doesn't even know what legs are!'

We both laughed. 'What's for dinner?' We had planned to take it in turns to organise meals, and today was Maddy's turn. It was fun actually as we could try out all the recipes we had learnt at school.

'Roast beef and Yorkshire pud, and to start, puréed Avocado pear, and to finish, crème caramel, and we've overspent on our budget and Michael and Jonathan are coming to dinner. I thought you'd be pleased.'

'Oh great! How did you fix that?'

'Easy. I just asked them. My brother's not one to turn down a free meal.'

I was delighted. 'What can I wear?' I wailed. Clothes in London were a great problem. I *had* to go shopping.

'Slacks and a tight sweater. Let him see your bosom, maybe *that* will attract him.'

I suppose my bosom *was* one of my best features.

I didn't have any tight sweaters, so I borrowed one of Maddy's. It *did* look good.

'Wow!' Maddy said. 'Are you wearing a bra?'

'Of course.'

'Take it off. Men find it more exciting if you're not.'

'I can't do that.'

'You want to get him in your evil clutches, don't you?'

I went back in the bedroom, took off my bra. and slipped the sweater back on. You could tell I wasn't wearing one, they bobbed a little when I walked.

Maddy prepared a really gorgeous dinner. Michael and Jonathan devoured every mouthful of the food, then watched T.V.

Michael said, 'How was the party last night?'

'It was very nice, but I got s—'

Before I could finish Maddy blurted out, 'She's got a date with Steve Scott. He's mad about her.'

I blushed. How could she tell such awful lies?

'You really are seeing London,' Michael said grimly, 'moving with the in crowd already, I bet your mother won't be too pleased with the company you're keeping.'

He was insufferable! They watched a bit more television and then left. I decided I hated him.

Madelaine giggled as soon as they were gone. 'It's working,' she said, 'I think he's jealous.'

'He's not, he's *so* sarcastic to me.'

'That's good. At least he's *aware* of you now, you're not a little kid he's known for ages any more. And he couldn't take his eyes off your sweater. You see, he'll ask you out.'

'Yes, I bet.'

We cleared up the mess—one bad thing about not living at home, the washing up! I was really exhausted. What with the hangover, the first day at work, and the dinner. I had a bath, brushed my hair and collapsed into bed. I was soon asleep, and dreaming a really awful dream where I appeared at work stark naked and lots of fingers were typing on my body, then my breasts turned into typewriters, and Michael came and looked at me and turned his back in disgust, and a bell started to jangle louder and louder. I woke up. The telephone was ringing.

Maddy reached it before I did. 'It's for you,' she said sleepily, 'Tony Blake phoning from New York. Do you know it's one-thirty. You certainly made a hit with him.'

I took the phone and Maddy leaned close so she could listen. Why was Tony phoning me?

He was very friendly, wanting to know if I felt better and everything, then he said he missed me, and Maddy hissed, 'Say you miss him too.' So I did.

He said goodbye and I turned to Maddy exasperated, 'What did you want me to say that for?'

She smiled, 'If he's spending all that money phoning you, you may as well be nice to him. I think he likes you, actually I think he's rather divine!'

'You can have him then,' I said crossly, 'I don't miss him, and I wish I hadn't said I did. Honestly, sometimes I think you're mad.'

'You won't think I'm mad when I tell Michael about it, he'll be green if he thinks Tony Blake is after you *and* Steve Scott.'

'Maddy, let's go to sleep.'

'All right, but you'll see, you'll get your man in the end!'

# 17

## TONY

I opened my eyes and I was in my room at the hotel lying on top of the bed with all my gear on. How did I get back?

That bloody bitch Fontaine was a real balls breaker, and her skinny friend—Miss No Tits society bag. All right, so we'd had a big scene and there wasn't a gun at my head, but how could I have done it? What about Alexandra? What about Sadie and Sam, my nice respectable parents? What if they ever knew, could see? I've always had this funny sort of thought that after you die you sit in a room and like watching a movie your whole life plays across the screen and all the people you know get to watch it. Charming! Last night's scene would make lovely viewing. Shit! Making it with Fontaine is one thing, but having a show with her so-called friends is another.

That faggot husband of Sarah's tried to sneak it in while the two women crawled all over me. But I caught him at that little game, thank you very much. I remember Fontaine saying, 'Let him do it, Tony, you'll love it.' Wow, she was *really* stoned. Bitch!

It was two o'clock and I was starving. I had a shower and ordered three eggs and a hamburger from room service. What was I supposed to do? Hang around until her ladyship decided to call me? I viewed television. Maybe I should call the club later. Maybe I should call Alexandra now. What the hell am I doing here anyway? It's a long way from the Elephant and Castle.

I guess I fell asleep again, 'cos when I woke up the T.V. screen was alive with sweaty teenagers and the phone was ringing.

'Yeah?'

'My, my. Aren't we American already!'

I glanced quickly at my watch, five-fifteen, and she was only just calling, 'What's happening?' I asked.

'Well, darling, all sorts of exciting things. Did you enjoy last night?'

'No.'

Her voice went very cold. 'Oh—why?'

'It's not my scene, Fontaine, I don't like threesomes or foursomes. What's wrong with normal sex?'

Her laugh was amused, 'Tony, you are *such* a suburbanite. It was fun. If you relaxed it could be a lot more fun.'

'I don't want to do it again, O.K.?'

Her voice was sarcastic. '*Yes sir.*We will not indulge in any more naughty little orgies.'

There was silence. I knew she hated being criticised, but God almighty, somebody had to tell her. It was bad enough screwing around on her husband, but this beat the band.

'What's happening?' I asked.

'I don't want to corrupt you, Tony dear, but I thought you might like to come over for an hour or so, then there's two parties and dinner with Sarah and Allen.'

Oh Christ! I certainly didn't want to face Sarah and Allen again. What were we all supposed to do—discuss positions?

'Look, I don't want to see them. I'll come to the parties with you, then maybe I'll roam around on my own, get the feel of things.'

'Tony, you can be such a bore! All right then, do that. Be here in half-an-hour.' She slammed the phone down.

How did I ever get myself into this?

It was too early to phone the club, but Alexandra should be home. Was it a clever move to risk a phone call? No.

I thought of her pretty wide-eyed face and her soft auburn hair. She was the sort of girl who would still look good in ten or even twenty years. When I got back to London I decided I would take her down to the Elephant and Castle and introduce her to Sadie and Sam. What a shock they'd get to see me with such a lovely girl. They thought I only ever went out with showgirls and 'tarty bits of fluff' as my Ma always said. How many times had they both said to me—find yourself a nice Jewish girl and settle down. So what difference Jewish smooish as long as she was nice. They would love pretty little Alex.

I got dressed. Polo-necked striped silk shirt, one of Hal's best buys, and my Dougie Hayward grey suit. I had to get some money from Fontaine. I was walking around with nothing. It was embarrassing, especially if I was going to take off on my own later.

On top of the T.V. with my comb and cigarettes were several book matches I had picked up at various joints the previous evening. I liked things like that, lay them around the London pad and people knew you had travelled. Scribbled across the front of 'Lorenz—eat in style' was the name Norma and a number.

Norma? I didn't know a Norma. Come to think of it I'd never been to a place called 'Lorenz' either.

Norma, Norma, Norma. Ah yes, the tall lady with the long black hair at the party last night. Rather beautiful, a definite raver, very cool. I dialled the number and a guarded tired voice answered 'Yeah?'

'Is Norma there?'

'Wait a minute, I'll see. Who is it?'

'Tony Blake, but she doesn't know my name, we met at a party we—'

'Hold it, baby, I don't want your life story.'

The guarded voice left me hanging on while I strained to hear the muffled conversation the other end. Then a voice identical to the first one said, 'Yeah?'

'Norma?'

'Yeah?'

'We met at Salamanda Smith's party last night.' Nothing like dropping a name. 'I was on the phone in the bedroom remember?'

'Yeah.'

She was a wild conversationalist. 'I thought I could see you later, like buy you a drink or something.'

'Sounds O.K. I'm having dinner with some guys, you can join us if you like.'

'Some guys' didn't sound too exciting. 'Look, if you're busy maybe another night.'

'Suit yourself. We'll be at "Marcellos" if you change your mind.'

She hung up. Friendly girl, couldn't care less if I came or not.

I didn't even have cab fare, so I walked the few blocks to Fontaine's. She let me in herself, her hair hanging smoothly down her back, her face a mass of white cream, but her eyes fully made up. She wore a thin silk dressing-gown.

'Come in the bedroom, I'm making up. Fix the champagne first, it's in the fridge.'

I went in the fully fitted oak panelled kitchen and opened several cupboards before locating the fridge, which was cleverly disguised as part of the wall.

I opened the champagne and took it in the bedroom. Fontaine was lying on the bed, the silk dressing-gown exposing her from the waist down so that the whole thing looked slightly obscene. She stretched her arms back behind her head.

106

'We won't need glasses,' she whispered, 'just bring the bottle, we'll drink it my way.'

I was excited in spite of myself. She repulsed me, but my body was responding to her.

I took off my suit and shirt, I certainly wasn't spoiling the outfit.

'Come on, Tony,' she said impatiently, 'I'm thirsty.'

When it was all over and the room stunk of champagne I lay on her bed watching her calmly get on with her makeup. I knew I couldn't make it any more. Oh, I could 'make it' in the physical sense, no problem there, but after—well, I get this kind of unclean feeling, this sort of feeling of shame. With other women there's always some affection—something—even if it's just a casual lay. But Fontaine is cold as bloody ice, it's almost as if she's using my body to suit herself. She's a bitch, and I've got to get away from her. Especially now with Alexandra in the picture.

'Can I shower?' I asked.

'Of course, you don't have to ask permission. Use the one in the guest-room.' She was painting her thin lips and didn't look up.

I showered the smell of the champagne off me and the smell of Fontaine, and then I just stood there turning the water on to icy cold. It felt good.

When I got back to London I was going to find someone to back me in a new club. It shouldn't be that difficult, I had a lot of connections, and me in a new club couldn't fail. I mean I'm not being conceited but 'Hobo' would never have made it without me. Maybe the new place could be called 'Tonys', or is that too obvious? I like it myself, sounds good. Find a location, find a backer, and kiss Fontaine Balls Breaker Khaled goodbye.

'Tony, are you ready?'. She walked in wearing black satin and a lot of diamonds. She looked annoyed. 'What the hell are you *doing* in here?'

I got out of the shower quick, skin shrivelled by the cold.

'Come on, for God's sake. I hate hanging around waiting.' She swept out of the room.

I dressed quickly and found her on her terrace smoking.

'Listen, since we'll be splitting up later I'd better have some money,' I said. 'I was rushed over here so quickly I couldn't arrange any.'

'I see.' She looked furious. I knew she hated parting with cash. 'Why on earth didn't you ask Benjamin's secretary?'

'I didn't meet her. The whole thing was arranged by phone.'

She opened her small evening bag and extracted three ten-dollar bills. 'That's all I have,' she said, 'I'll make some arrangements for you tomorrow.'

Charming! Thirty measly dollars to see New York on. That wasn't going to get me very far.

We went to the first party. Held in a restaurant the crush was terrible. I stood by the door watching Fontaine waft around. I drank three scotches.

After half-an-hour she found me, gripped my arm and said, 'We're leaving. Do see if you can be a little more sociable at the next party. Klaus is coming with us.'

Klaus turned out to be a small gay dressmaker, dressed to kill in frills, with rotting teeth and beady eyes. He sat between me and Fontaine in the car, pressing his thigh close to mine.

'Klaus has taken New York by storm with his thirties trouser-suits,' Fontaine remarked.

Well, good for little old beady-eyed Klaus. He may have taken New York by storm, but he was going to get a punch on the nose if he pressed his leg against mine any harder.

The second party was even worse. A party full of queens. Droves of them. Scattered among them were the well-dressed ladies, and a few—very few—normal guys. At least they looked normal.

Klaus said, 'How divine. Everyone's here.'

Fontaine said, 'All the best designers in New York. You'd better stay close to me, Tony, I know how you feel about your precious ass!'

I hated her. So beautiful and elegant and bitchy.

I stayed there about ten minutes, but I was getting so many leers and coy glances I couldn't stand it any longer.

'I'm getting out of here,' I told Fontaine.

She brushed me aside with a cool, 'Bye-Bye,' and I wandered out into the New York night.

It was still early, before nine, and I tried to decide if it was too early to try 'Marcellos'. I was starving, with gnawing pains in my stomach. I walked into a hamburger joint and had three. That felt a lot better. What now? Seek out the wild Norma? There seemed to be nothing else to do. I hopped a cab and told him 'Marcellos', and he knew the place.

From the outside it looked all right. Small red and white awning, few steps down, pretty girl at reception desk. She smiled at me. 'You 'ave reservation, sir?' She was Italian. Should have known it when I saw those great big eyes.

'I thought I'd have a drink.'

'Certainly, sir—downstairs.' She smiled again. I smiled. If Norma didn't show I wondered what time this little darling finished.

Downstairs it was packed. The bar bordered the restaurant and every table was full. I ordered a scotch and looked for Norma.

She was easy to spot with her sleek black hair pulled back into a long plait and her huge horn-rimmed tinted glasses. She was at a table with three guys. I watched them a bit, before going over. She was a very striking girl, her features more Indian than black, her eyes big and soulful.

'Hi there,' she said. She was authoritative, and got a waiter to bring another chair with a snap of her fingers. She nodded round the table: 'Mark—Terry—Davey—this is Tony.' Two of the guys were white, the other a very good-looking black guy with a beard.

'Hi man,' the bearded Davey greeted me.

The whole thing was a very warm scene. I could relax. Norma surveyed me coolly through her tinted lenses. 'Hey, what were you doin' at that *awful* party? What a giant sized drag!'

I nodded, 'Somebody took me.'

'Yeah, somebody took you all right,' she laughed. 'First time in my goddamn life I ever got stood up. Some prize jerk supposed to meet me there, and the sonofabitch never showed!'

'That will teach you to go with stars, girlie,' Davey said, grinning.

'You can bet your ass on that,' Norma agreed. 'Now to beat the band, the sonofabitch's secretary—secretary yet—hasn't even got the balls to call me himself—phones me today and says—quote—Mr Nicholas is *so* sorry he couldn't manage last night. Can I confirm your address as Mr Nicholas wishes to send you a colour television set. Man, I laughed and laughed. Tell Mr Nicholas to take his colour T.Vee and shove it right up his rude white ass, I said.' Everyone laughed. 'That guy is too much,' Norma continued. 'He can only make it with us black girls. He has some kind of hang up, cannot make it with a white lady. Then the poor bastard thinks he has to pay. I've got a little news for him—If I was planning on getting paid, a colour T.Vee wouldn't go anywhere near covering the cost! I should never have balled him, but he's so goddamned beautiful—umm—that body—wowee!!'

Buck Nicholas is a very famous movie actor, mostly appearing in tattered Tee shirts and tight Levi's to show off his equally famous body.

'You know we met before,' Norma said, lifting her glasses, balancing them in her hair and staring at me.

'We did?' I couldn't remember, and I had a good memory.

'Yeah, "Hobo", London. You used to run the joint, all the little girlies creaming themselves over you.'

I was sure I could never forget meeting a girl like Norma.

'Yeah, I still run "Hobo". When was it?'

'Coupla months back—you wouldn't remember me. I was wearing a blonde wig. You came over. I was with Steve Scott.'

Bingo! Could I ever forget her. What a night *that* had been, with every guy in the place fighting to meet her and Steve playing it cool.

'Of course! You look completely different now.'

'Yeah—I use the blonde wig when I want to really knock 'em in the aisles. I was only in London two days, crazy city, I'm going back soon. What are you doing here?'

'We might open up "Hobo". I'm getting the feel of things.'

'Yeah? Great. Talk to Davey, he can *really* show you the town.'

She was right. After dinner (I just drank) Terry and Mark went off, and Norma, Davey and I saw New York. But I mean *really* saw it. We went all over in Davey's silver Porsche, uptown, downtown, Harlem, Chinatown. Norma was a wonderful girl. She talked in her laconic clipped style non-stop, and she danced like a mother, and she laughed a lot and drank a lot, and at six a.m. exhausted, drunk and happy we landed up at her apartment.

'Hey, you're O.K.,' she said laughing, undoing her plaited hair until it hung jet black and straight to her waist.

'You're pretty O.K. yourself,' I replied, putting my arms around her and pulling her close to me.

We were both loaded and both in the same happy mood. She was almost as tall as me, and I'm six one. She had on a clingy orange dress which I helped her out of. Underneath there was gorgeous brown skin and nothing else.

She laughed and moved out of my arms. 'Want a drink?'

'Yeah, great.' I watched her move about the room pouring two scotches and clinking the ice. She had a fantastic body, like a long supple panther.

I felt a little twinge of guilt about Alexandra, but this lady was so *beautiful*! A man can only take so much temptation. She came over to me and held the drink to my lips. I caught hold of one of her wild boobies. She took the drink away from me and put it carefully on a table.

'You want to swing, man—let's swing. I've got an insane bedroom. Only no hang-ups, huh?'

I covered her ass with my hands, 'No hang-ups.'

'O.K., let's go!'

She turned around and I followed her, my hands sticking to her backside, so high and round like a boy's.

Her bedroom was great. Leopardskin walls and a huge circular bed with a giant poster blow-up of Mick Jagger (Mick Jagger?!?) on the ceiling. She pressed a button and Ray Charles singing 'Eleanor Rigby' flooded the room.

I pushed her on to the bed and she stared up at me with amused black cat's eyes as I got undressed. I pinned her shoulders to the bed.

I started to kiss her, and we began to make it, and I could have sworn Mick Jagger's eyes moved!

To me New York will always mean Norma. What a girl!

I left her asleep at eleven the next morning and cabbed it back to my hotel. There was a message for me. 'Please be ready to leave on noon plane for London, Alice Clerk—secretary, for Benjamin Al Khaled. All tickets, etc., to be collected at Kennedy airport information desk.'

Charming! I was on the move again.

# 18

## FONTAINE

Reflecting on the whole thing it was a dreadful mistake. I should have left Tony where he was, he is nothing but an embarrassment here.

From the moment he arrived three days ago he has been gauche, naïve, star-struck, and a bore. Of course there was that one rather fun evening when we all got high, but he had the nerve to lecture me the next day about how I shouldn't involve myself in orgies, and that he certainly wasn't going to do it again. I mean, really, as far as I can remember he enjoyed it more than anyone!

Sarah thinks he's a bore. 'All cock and no brains,' she says. 'Really, Fontaine, find yourself an oriental.'

She is right. The stud is a dismal failure in New York. I have arranged for him to leave on the noon flight and this time I am *not* going to the airport.

Benjamin is flying in anyway. Dear rich, randy Benjamin.

There are a lot of things I need at 'Tiffany's'. Also I have seen a beautiful sable coat. And Saks have some divine Rudi Genreich originals.

Benjamin is arriving at the perfect time.

The phone rang and I waited for Adamo to announce who it was.

'Mr Blake, Madam.'

'Tony darling.' I may as well say goodbye with charm, the poor stud was probably shattered.

'Look, Fontaine, I just received a message that I'm supposed to be leaving.'

'Yes, darling. Well, Benjamin's coming into town, and I think you've seen enough to form some opinions. There's no point in you being away from "Hobo" too long.'

'Yeah, well I suppose you're right. But, Jesus Christ, I mean I'm shuttled around like luggage. Why didn't you mention it last night?'

'Oh, don't be boring, Tony. I didn't know last night. Anyway, do give everyone my love, especially Vanessa. I'm sure you'll see Vanessa.' Oh God, he probably couldn't wait.

'Yeah. I'll see you in London then.'

'Ciaou, sweetie.'

That's got rid of him. Back to his little London dollies. He's so narrow-minded. After all I've taught him he still only likes one position! Stupid boy.

The phone again. 'Mr Grant, Madam.'

'Allen darling.'

'How about meeting today?'

'Where's Sarah?'

'Out. Well? Two o'clock the Plaza?'

'No, that's too late, Benjamin's coming in this afternoon. How about the St Regis at one?'

'Fine, I'll arrange it.'

'Allen.'

'Yes?'

'Bring your imagination.'

He laughed. Dear Allen wasn't so bad, not as equipped as

Tony, but passable. After the little *ménage à quatre* of the other evening, I was really rather fond of him. It would be a pleasant way to pass the day until Benjamin arrived.

# 19

## ALEXANDRA

My second day at McLaughton & Co. was no better than the first. I can understand why girls become models and things, I mean just sitting here typing is worse than school. Mummy said I can take a modelling course if I want to, and if I wasn't so determined to pay my own way I would say yes. I don't suppose I would be a very good model anyway, I'm not thin enough, and my face is not unusual. But I don't think I can stick it at this job.

Maddy was all pleased with herself when I got home. She was a mass of Carmen rollers and face cream. 'I've got a date,' she announced, 'Jonathan phoned to thank me for dinner last night, and would I like to see a flick.'

'Great,' I said with as much enthusiasm as I could muster, 'what about Michael?'

She immediately looked guilty. 'Oh sorry, Alex, Jonathan didn't mention him. But I promise I'll pump him tonight and find out all the gen. You know, what girls he sees and everything like that. It will be very useful to know all those things.'

'Yes, very.' I was acutely miserable.

Madelaine spent the next hour doing herself up and singing and generally being far too cheerful.

'Stay out of the way when Jonathan fetches me,' she said, 'I'll tell him you're at some party.'

'Thanks,' I said, shutting myself in the bedroom with a tin of cold baked beans.

I heard the doorbell and a mumble of voices and then the door slammed, and I was alone. I phoned Mummy. I wished I was at home.

'Why don't you bring some friends down with you this weekend?' Mummy said. 'We could all go riding.'

'Perhaps I will. Can I let you know?'

I decided to invite Michael, whether Maddy thought it was a good idea or not. It was awful being in the flat alone. I suppose this is the bad thing about living away from home. I even felt nervous, sort of kept on hearing funny noises as it got later and darker.

I drew all the curtains, turned on the television and concentrated on a play. Then the phone rang.

'Is Alexandra Khaled there?' A husky mysterious voice.

'This is she.'

'Steve Scott. How are you?'

'Oh—I'm fine. How are you?' I felt myself blushing.

'All right. Sort of movin' along like a good boy. I thought you might want to come out.'

'Now?'

'I sort of thought tomorrow night, like dinner and that bit. You want to?'

'Yes, I'd like to.' Wait until Maddy heard about this!

'All right then, why don't you come round here about nine?'

'I'd love to.'

'See you then.'

'Oh, just a second,' I frantically searched for a pencil and paper. 'Could you please tell me your address.'

He did so, adding, 'Don't dress up,' and was gone.

How terrific! Although I would sooner it was Michael. I couldn't wait to see Maddy's face!

She staggered in looking awful. She reminded me of how I had felt on Sunday night. 'Alex, I think I'm going to be sick!' she announced. 'Too much wine'.

'For goodness sake, make sure it's in the bathroom.'

It was, and like me she felt better afterwards. She lay on top of her bed groaning and I made some tea.

'I think I'm in love,' she murmured between groans.

'What happened?'

'He tried to rape me in his mini. Of course he didn't, I pretended to faint and then he was *so* sweet, he even did my bra up and helped me to the door and kept on asking if I was all right.'

'How far did you go?'

'Far enough,' she replied mysteriously, 'far enough.' And with that she fell into a deep sleep, snoring loudly, with all her clothes on.

I managed to get her shoes and dress off but she was too heavy for me to get her properly undressed, so I pulled some covers over her and left her to her snores.

So much for my exciting news about Steve Scott. It would have to keep until morning.

'Don't look so nervous, I'm not going to eat you.' Those were Steve Scott's opening words as I stood at his front door.

I must admit to being nervous. After all he *is* a star, and *so* dreamy looking. Not conventionally good-looking, but exciting, with his long wild hair, and very bright blue staring eyes.

'Come in then, don't stand there with your mouth hanging open.'

I shut my mouth quickly. I must say he is rather rude. Madelaine and I discussed my date when she blearily opened her eyes this morning. 'Whatever you do you must sleep with him,' she had announced dramatically. 'It's so dull being a virgin, and it would be marvellous for you to be able to say your first man was Steve Scott.'

'What's new, pussycat?' he asked.

'Er—nothing,' I replied. He had on a denim shirt and tight jeans.

'You're a funny little thing,' he said. 'How come you were with the big bad Tony the other night?'

'He works for Daddy,' I stuttered, 'er—what I mean is my father sort of owns "Hobo".' I wished I hadn't said that, I sounded like some awful little rich girl.

'Who's Daddy, then?'

116

I didn't want to start boasting about Daddy. 'Nobody special, just a—er—er—businessman.'

'Oh,' said Steve, studying me with those bright eyes of his. 'What do you do, then? Model or actress?'

'Actually I'm neither, I'm a secretary.' That should stop any ideas he might have about me being rich. I hated people knowing I was rich, it embarrassed me.

'Great! Want to do some typing for me?'

'Yes—if you like.'

He laughed, 'I'm kidding. You know I think you're for real, a baby innocent.'

'I'm eighteen,' I lied.

'You're ancient,' he replied, still laughing. 'Where have you been?'

'I've been at school in Switzerland.'

He took my arm, 'You know for an eighteen-year-old bird you certainly manage to come across like fourteen.'

I was furious and pulled my arm away, but he gripped it again and said, 'Hey, I'm not knocking it, I like it. You don't know how unusual it is. Are you a virgin?'

I blushed.

'You are!' he said accusingly. 'I bet you are.'

How I wished I had never come. How could he ask me questions like that?

'Let's go and get some food,' he said, 'I want to hear all about Daddy and Switzerland and why you're still a virgin at your advanced age.'

He had a big old-fashioned Bentley, brightly polished. Everyone stared at us as we drove along.

Fortunately once we reached the restaurant he was descended on by various friends, and didn't have a chance to question me during dinner.

He drank an awful lot, and the language at our table was incredible. Maddy wouldn't believe it, even the girls swore. I couldn't wait to get away. Perhaps I could just sneak off to the loo and not come back.

'Hey listen, everyone,' Steve suddenly said loudly. 'This girl's a

117

virgin!' And he clapped his hand on my shoulder and everyone stared at me.

Oh floor, please open up and swallow me!

'That's nice for you, Stevie,' one of the girls said, 'makes a change,' and she giggled.

I blushed beetroot. 'I think you're a pig!' I hissed at him. 'Please take me home.'

'It's nothing to be ashamed of,' he said surprised, 'You're probably the only bloody virgin of eighteen in England!'

I gulped my coffee, and was just deciding to get up and leave when who should walk in but Michael, *my* Michael—with that funny-looking girl he had danced with all night at 'Hobo'—Suki something or other. She looked ridiculous in a silver tunic outfit.

She came over to say hello to Steve. Michael walked behind her, saw me and looked amazed.

'Hello, Michael,' I waved gaily, wishing Steve would put his arm around me *now*.

'Hello, Alex,' Michael returned my greeting. I could see he was impressed.

'See you later at "Hobo",' Suki said to Steve, and she and Michael went off to sit at a nearby table for two.

After a while, Steve said, 'So, what do you want to do? My pad? "Hobo"? Or there's a poxy party going on somewhere?'

'I think I'd like to go to "Hobo",' I said, hoping that Michael would follow shortly.

'Let's go then.' He got up, and without even saying goodbye to anyone we left.

In his car he lit a cigarette and offered it to me.

'No, thank you, I don't smoke.'

'That's all right, take a drag, it will put you in good shape.'

I gingerly puffed on the cigarette. It had a funny taste and smelt vile.

'There you go, little girl, you're turning on nicely.'

'I really don't want any more,' I politely handed it back to him. I suppose it was one of those 'funny' cigarettes, I'm not exactly as dumb as he seems to think.

We sat in the car silently while he finished the cigarette.

I know I'm in love with Michael. Here I am sitting next to Steve Scott and *all* I can think of is Michael.

'All right, let's go,' Steve said, more to himself than to me, 'Let us go out into the night and swing, little baby girl.'

I peeked quickly at my watch. It was nearly eleven-thirty. If this was going to be a late night how on earth was I going to get up for work tomorrow? I am one of those people who need masses of sleep.

'Hobo' wasn't very crowded. 'I like getting here early,' Steve said, 'you can feel it build that way.'

Soon we were joined by some of the people who had been with us at the restaurant, and others. I was determined not to get drunk so I stuck to Coca-Cola. I didn't really care how stupid Steve thought I was, I had decided that whatever Maddy said, I wasn't going to bed with him. He was much too personal and rude. I couldn't bear the thought of him seeing me without my clothes on. Honestly, the whole thing was going to be embarrassing enough without someone like him.

I watched the entrance, waiting for Michael, which of course was the only reason I was here.

'Come on, let's dance,' said Steve. 'You *can* dance, can't you?'

'Of course I can!'

On the dance floor after a few minutes he said, 'I thought you said you could dance.'

'I don't know why you wanted to take me out,' I said angrily, 'you've been rude to me all night.'

'Oh come off it, little Miss Virgin, I'm only kidding. Can't you take a joke?'

'I am *not* a virgin, and I *can't* take your sort of hurtful so-called jokes.' With that I went and sat down, surprising, even myself.

He followed me, laughing. 'Them there's fighting words, little girl. Want another coke or shall we go back to my place and see who's right?'

'Another Coca-Cola please.'

At last Suki and Michael came in. She headed straight for Steve. 'Carolyn's downstairs,' she hissed.

'Oh shit!' he said quickly. 'She's supposed to be working

119

tonight. Great!' He turned to me. 'See the trouble you're just about to get me in?'

'Why, what have I done?'

'Carolyn's my girl, she'll go mad if she sees me with another bird. Look, go over and sit with Suki. I'll see if I can get rid of her.'

'But—'

'Go with Suki.'

Honestly!

Suki giggled. 'Carolyn will scratch your eyes out. Come and sit with us.'

So to my complete embarrassment I had to go and sit with Michael and Suki.

Michael said, 'What's going on?' and Suki explained.

He wagged a finger at me, 'You're certainly getting around in your first week in London. How's the job going?'

'Fine.'

The three of us chatted a bit. Michael had his arm around Suki's waist and he kept on giving her little squeezes.

Oh, where was Steve? I didn't want to sit here playing gooseberry to the man I loved.

'Oh look!' Suki suddenly said. 'There's Jan and John, I must go and see them.' And she dashed off.

Michael said, 'Noisy here, isn't it?'

I nodded.

'Well, perhaps I'll take you to a nice quiet little place I know one night, that's if you can fit me into your busy schedule.'

'Oh yes,' I said weakly. 'I could manage tomorrow.'

# 20

## TONY

On the plane back to good old Blighty I made several important decisions.

(1) Get out of 'Hobo' and into something else where I wasn't gripped tightly by the balls by a sex-mad nympho.

(2) Tell Alex how I feel about her (I do love her) and give up other girls.

(3) Save some money if possible, in case I should decide on marriage.

My mind was made up that a place called 'Tony's' would be fantastic. I had a lot of friends, and between them I could raise enough money—I didn't need one big backer. The new place would knock 'Hobo' right out. I could picture it now.

First thing tomorrow I'll be out searching for a suitable location. I think I can swing the whole thing for about ten thousand pounds. Now that shouldn't be hard to raise. If I can only get five people to come up with two thousand each. Sammy must have a couple of grand stashed away and Hal would be able to find it, and Franklin could talk to his old man. It was all going to work out great.

We landed about midnight and I decided to get a cab straight to the club. I only had one suitcase.

What a trip! I'd hardly even had time to take a pee before I was on the plane home again! Still it was good to be back. I would wait until the morning to phone Alexandra, she was probably deep in the land of nod. Poor little kid, having to work at some lousy nine to five job. Maybe one of these days I will marry her, and then she can spend her time looking after me. Oh boy! Mustn't think about her like that. I can feel myself getting horny. I think the high altitude affects me!

I took them all by surprise at the club. 'Flowers' was chatting to his girl-friend at reception—sonofabitch. He jumped up like he had a candle under his ass when he saw me. Franco was nowhere in sight. Inside a waiter was playing the records, and I couldn't see another waiter in the room.

I stormed into the kitchen where it was like an Italian wedding. Franco and the girl cashier were dancing—dancing yet! And the other waiters were slouched around watching. I can't leave the lousy place for a minute.

'Come on everyone,' I screamed. 'What the fucks going on here?'

'Meester Blake!' Franco reeled like a startled rabbit. 'Meester Blake—we wasn't expecting you.'

'Yeah, I can see that. Get back into the room, you lazy slobs. Let's have a little action here, get some drinks moving.'

The waiters milled around in panic and confusion, while Franco started screaming at them in Italian. The cashier slunk back behind her desk.

Franco got rid of all the waiters and turned to me crest fallen, 'Meester Blake, I—'

'Yeah, yeah, I know, Franco, you weren't expecting me.'

I went back inside. Flowers was at his stand, waiters were rushing around looking busy. We were back to normal.

I went over to the regulars' table. Sammy was there, arm around a horrific little black-eyed teeny bopper. 'Tony me boy, wacha doin' back? What happened? Good to see you.'

'Yeah,' I replied. 'Have a drink, Sammy, I'm going to do the rounds, see you in a minute.'

I tell you 'Hobo' knocks spots off all those New York joints. It's got what I call classy flash—excitement—call it what you like, it's got it.

I bought a drink here, a drink there, shook a lot of hands, kissed a lot of faces, pinched a few bottoms. Then, wowee—pow! Alexandra sitting there as calm as you like. Pretty, she was very pretty, like a gorgeous cultured rose amongst a lot of dandelions.

*What the bloody hell is she doing here?*

I shook her hand, trying to keep cool. She smiled at me. She looked tired. She was with Ring-a-ding Suki and that schmucky student type. I sat down.

'Tell us all about New York,' Suki asked. Was she with the student or was Alex?

'How do you feel?' I asked my lovely Alex.

'Fine,' she said brightly. 'You certainly had a short trip.'

'Come on, darlin'—all fixed,' Steve Scott appeared. 'Hey, Tony, you back already?'

'Yeah, baby, I'm back.' We shook hands.

'Well, come on then,' he said to Suki, but Alex got up.

I watched, shocked as he took her by the hand and pulled her off to another table.

*My* Alex with that randy little singer—*my* Alex—*impossible*—there must be some mistake.

'What's she doing with him?' I asked the clown-faced Suki.

She shrugged, 'I don't know, I guess he's on another kick. You know, educated Miss Prim and Proper for a change.'

'You should be so bloody lucky as to be even a tenth as educated as she is,' I said burning. 'What is she—prim and proper because she doesn't screw on sight?'

'What's the matter, Tony, I only said—'

'I don't give a goddamn what you said, Suki. You're not fit to sit at the same table as her.' God, I was so angry. I got up and stormed over to Steve and his table of cronies.

'Tony, sit down, have a drink, tell us about the New York scene.'

I could have smashed his stupid face in.

'Alex, I want to talk to you,' I said, trying to appear casual.

'Yes, Tony?' She questioned me with her wide brown eyes.

'Leave her alone,' Steve said loudly. 'She's mine tonight.'

'You're talking to a lady,' I said grimly, 'and if you don't mind I'd like to speak to her.

Alex got up quickly. She was blushing. I took her out on the terrace and held her very gently by the shoulders.

'Look,' I said quietly, 'you can tell me to mind my own business, but a girl like you shouldn't be out with a shit bag like Steve Scott.'

She brushed her hair back with her hand, 'He is rather awful,' she admitted, much to my great relief.

'Tell him goodbye then, I'll take you home.'

'I can't do that. I mean he *has* given me dinner and everything, I can't be rude.'

'Listen, sweetheart, that animal doesn't even know what rude is.'

'It's nice of you to be so concerned, but honestly I can manage.'

I couldn't stop myself, I grabbed her tightly and kissed her. I pressed my mouth against her lips hard. Her mouth was dry and refused to open, but I pushed my tongue between her teeth and forced her to let me in. I put my hands on her breasts and felt their warmth and roundness through her dress.

She struggled and pushed me away. Her cheeks were flushed. 'Honestly!' She exclaimed, 'I thought you were warning me about Steve.'

'Can I see you tomorrow?' Young schmuck asking for date.

'I'm sorry, Tony, I'm busy.' She smoothed down her dress and looked at me in a funny way, 'I'd better get back inside.'

'Yeah,' I was destroyed, 'I guess you'd better.'

I felt like I'd been kicked in the stomach. First of all I was hot as hell after kissing her and feeling her fantastic body. Secondly, I knew I wasn't about to let Steve frigging Scott take her home.

I followed her inside. She sat down beside Steve and he whispered something to her. Bastard! I was going to fix him. I went over to Suki who was busy feeling up her student boyfriend under the table. God, Massey was well rid of this freak.

'Who did Alexandra come here with?' I asked.

She was mad at me. 'I don't know.'

I exerted a bit of the famous Blake charm. 'Come on, Suki sweetheart, don't be so touchy.'

'She came with Steve— and then Carolyn arrived downstairs looking for him—well, he must have got rid of her because that's when he came back and took Miss Goody Two Shoes off again. Why are you so interested anyway?'

I shrugged. 'She's only a kid, I'm keeping an eye on her.'

'Oooh!' Suki the Freak shrieked with laughter, 'Sir Galahad Blake!'

Michael butted in. 'I expect she can look after herself.'

I glared. Who asked for his ten cents worth?

Anyway I had a plan. I went downstairs to the office and dialled Steve's home. As I thought, Carolyn answered, she had been sent home to wait. I disguised my voice (I could have been a wild actor) 'Your boy-friend's at "Hobo" making it with another girl.' Then I hung up, went upstairs and waited.

Fifteen minutes later Carolyn came storming in, her wild red hair flowing, her eyes mean and narrow.

Steve didn't even see her coming. She gave him a whack across the face that made me wince. 'You lousy sonofabitch,' she screamed, 'what the *fuck* is going on here? Giving me some story about you had to show the head of Gloom Records around. Some fucking head.' She paused and glared at Alex who seemed quite cool and collected. 'It might interest you to know,' she continued, 'that this is my fucking husband you're sitting next to. We got married last week and I wasn't supposed to tell anyone because it might upset his fucking fans. So fuck off.'

Steve practically slid under the table. What a scene! But Carolyn wasn't finished yet, 'I'm three months pregnant too—so stick that up your jumper—you little cow!'

Alexandra had gone visibly pale in the dim of the club. She stood up. 'I'm so sorry,' she said quietly, 'I didn't know,' and with that she made for the exit.

She certainly had class, lots and lots of class.

I caught up with her outside. She was crying. I wanted to wrap her up in my arms and carry her somewhere safe. Silently I handed her my handkerchief and she blew her nose.

I called a cab and we got in. I gave the driver my address. This time I wasn't letting her escape. She didn't say anything until the cab reached my place, and then we went through the same old discussion:

'Oh, Tony, it's simply much too late, I must get home.'

'Just one quick brandy, you need it.'

'I hate brandy.'

'Well, a coffee then.'

'It will keep me awake, please take me home.'

The cab driver sat there, his ugly hawk face listening to every word.

'Look, just five minutes, we'll have a quick coffee, a chat, and then I promise I'll take you right home.'

She sighed. 'All right.'

I paid the cab and he winked and muttered, 'Enjoy the quick coffee, guv.' Lousy dirty old man.

My flat smelt horrible, all the windows had been closed, and something had gone off in the fridge. I let some air in and stuck the kettle on. It was a horrible little pad. I had to move.

Alexandra sat on the sofa and I put on an Astrud Gilberto album. Now that I had her here I didn't know what to do with her.

'This is a nice flat,' she said in her best polite voice. 'Have you lived here long?'

'A few months, it's too small. I want to move, get somewhere nicer.'

We lapsed into silence until the whistle of the kettle boiling. Coffee was a mistake, I should have given her a drink, got her more relaxed.

'How about an Irish coffee?' I asked.

'I've never had that.'

Not that I had any cream or brown sugar or any of that jazz, but I could put a slug of whisky in it, better than plain coffee. 'You'll love it.'

Astrud was singing. 'The Shadow of Your Smile'. If I had been with any other bird by this time we would have been stripped off and hard at it.

'Did you have a nice time in America?' she asked.

'Yeah—great.' I finished the coffees and handed one to her. It tasted good—personally I don't think you need all that sugar and cream shit.

'You know, Alex, I've got a lot of things to tell you.'

She sipped her coffee and stared at a picture of me taken the opening night of 'Hobo'.

'Do you want to go to bed with me, Tony?' she said politely, as if asking what time the next bus home was.

I was stunned. I practically spilt my coffee. 'What?' I stuttered like an idiot.

She was blushing now and biting her lower lip. 'Well, *do* you?'

126

This wasn't exactly the way I had the whole thing planned. I had figured on telling her how I felt, maybe kissing and cuddling her a while. 'Yes, of course I do,' I said lamely. She had really caught me off guard.

'All right then,' she said calmly.

We sat and stared at each other for a bit, and I noticed her hand was shaking as she drank the coffee.

I went to her, took the cup out of her hand and kissed her. This time her lips parted and she gave a little sigh.

I ran my hands around her body, feeling her squirm under my touch. She was wearing a brown woollen dress, high-necked with small buttons down the back. I started to undo them.

'Can we go in the bedroom?' she asked. 'Perhaps I can go in first.'

'Yeah, O.K.' She had me so excited I didn't know where I was at.

'I'll call you when I'm ready.'

She trotted off and left me in a state of shock. Wowee—I had thought she was a little baby innocent. I still loved her though, in spite of the fact that she had obviously—well—been around.

I wondered should I strip off? I wished there was time to take a bath. I felt hot and sweaty from the plane trip.

'I'm ready, Tony,' a little voice called. 'Please don't turn the light on.'

She was in my bed, covers up to her chin.

I took my clothes off clumsily, throwing them on the floor. I kept my pants on and jumped into bed beside her.

She had velvet skin, I swear to God her skin was actual velvet. I could only see her faintly in the darkened room, she had drawn the curtains and wouldn't let me pull the covers off her.

I felt her slowly. Her breasts were very high and full, her waist narrow and her hips curved out, all covered with this wild velvet skin. She lay on her back, her body tense, her hands gripping the covers.

'Relax, baby!' I whispered. 'Take it easy, enjoy it.'

Her body hair was sparse and silky like a fine down, she tightened her thighs when she felt my hand there.

I rolled on top of her and forced the covers out of her grip. She was shivering. I stood up over her and took my pants off. She shut her eyes and I came back on top of her and worked to get her legs apart.

'Tony, I'm a virgin,' she suddenly said after a short silent struggle during which I couldn't shift her legs open.

I felt myself go down like a punctured balloon.

She opened her eyes quickly, 'You don't mind, do you?'

Mind? Mind! I was delighted. Only it put another aspect on everything. She was a virgin, and she wanted to go to bed with me, which could only mean that she must love me.

'You silly kid, of course I don't mind, I think that's wonderful, perfect.'

'Oh good,' I felt her relax.

I rolled off, gathered her in my arms, and held her.

'You see I don't know what I have to do, I don't know how not to have a baby or anything. It's—it's the first time I've ever seen a naked man.'

Well, they say that if you wait long enough, everything comes your way. I felt like a giant! A king!

We lay there for a bit. I was perfectly content just holding her beautiful body. I shut my eyes. I was a bit knocked out by the plane trip and everything.

'Tony, is everything all right? You're not disappointed or anything?'

I opened my eyes quickly. Wow—I was so comfortable and happy that I must have dropped off to sleep for a second.

She had escaped from my arms, and was kneeling on the bed holding a sheet in front of her.

'Of *course* it is, baby. Come back here.'

'I just mean—well, if you are disappointed and you don't want to, well—I quite understand.'

'You're kidding!' I pulled the sheet away from her and she quickly lay down. I kissed her face and stroked her hair and felt her unbelievably perfect breasts. She started to make little soft noises, like a kitten.

I had this funny sort of choking feeling. Christ! I loved this girl *so* much. It wasn't even sex, I wasn't so sure that I wanted to make love to her. She was so pure and innocent, and maybe she should stay that way.

But she wanted me. She wanted to belong to me. She smelt so sweet, like summer flowers.

I was on top of her and showing her what to do. And she was gasping and biting her lower lip and staring at me with those wide brown innocent eyes.

Oh God! I pulled out just in time. It was fantastic! Then she rolled away from me and lay on her stomach.

She was mine.

# 21

## FONTAINE

It is such a relief to be rid of the stud. I have learnt a little lesson, never take people out of their natural surroundings. My God, look at the zoo, all those poor animals locked up in cages neurotic as hell.

In London in charge of 'Hobo', Tony is a man. Here he is nothing.

I spent a very entertaining afternoon with Allen. He has a lot of possibilities, and he *did* bring his imagination! He told me some absolutely shocking stories about himself and Salamanda Smith. *Très risqué*! I shall look at the vapid blonde movie queen with new eyes.

Benjamin has arrived and is showering, cleaning his teeth, and gargling. God know what else. Benjamin is immaculate. He washes his short round body at least three times a day. Whenever we make love he showers first *and* after, an infuriating habit, although very hygienic. He changes his underwear and socks twice a day—sometimes three times. As a businessman Benjamin is a genius. But as a husband he is an infuriating, irritating bore!

Unfortunately only the Body Beautiful can really interest me, that and money of course. Benjamin and I have very little to say to each other. Social gossip doesn't interest him, and financial and business talk drives me to distraction. His children bore me to tears, and he hates discussing my clothes. Actually we are very rarely alone together.

Once he asked me if I would have a child. I told him that at his age it was a ridiculous idea. I don't like children. I find them time-consuming, dirty and noisy. Apart from which, they destroy your figure. Look at Vanessa, big cow-like Vanessa.

Yes, I must say, I am quite happy with my life the way it is. I really have everything.

It's so exciting finding new studs and watching their progress. Tony is a prime example—from waiter to my lover to—well, what exactly is he? A host I suppose one could call him.

There comes a time in every relationship I undertake when a man's body is not enough. I think I have reached that time with Tony. I think he must go. I'll throw him to all the little dollies who may not want him when he's no longer at 'Hobo'.

I must remember to get Benjamin to arrange to have him fired when we get back.

Of course what I really need is a *rich* stud, with all the things that Benjamin has. Then I could divorce Benjamin and *really* be happy.

I don't think I've ever come across a rich stud, they just don't seem to exist. All the men with *real* money and position are old, fat, and desperately boring—like Benjamin. Poor old Benjamin.

'Did you have a nice shower, darling?'

'Yes, very nice. Is my secretary here yet?'

'I don't know, I'll buzz Adamo. I've arranged dinner with Sarah and Allen. He's Sarah's latest husband, a writer, I'm sure you'll like him.'

'You know I can't stand Sarah.'

'Darling,' I went to him and started to pull off his bath towel

130

which was tied round his middle. He looked ridiculous with his white hairy legs peeping out.

He turned away, 'Not now, Fontaine. My secretary should be here.'

Well, well! Independent Benjamin, after any separation he was usually rarin' to go.

Deliberately I stepped out of my negligee and stretched. 'I think I'll have a bath while you're with dear old Miss Clerk. Do you think I'm getting too fat?'

I knew there wasn't an ounce of fat on my entire body. I knew the sight of my body excited old Benjamin like hell.

'No, you're not getting fat.' His beady little eyes flicked over me, and then abruptly he turned away for a second time.

Was he getting senile at last?

I rang Adamo on the intercom. 'Is Mr Khaled's secretary here?'

'Yes, Madam.'

Benjamin was busy getting dressed. 'She's here. You *will* be finished by six, won't you? I promised the Sidwells we would drop by for a drink.'

He grunted. I stretched my naked body, blew him a kiss, and went off into my bathroom.

After all, if the poor old fellow can't get it up, well what can one do?

# 22

## TONY

I can remember when I was a kid seeing all those wild Hollywood movies where there would be some kind of great love scene—and then the hero (usually Gene Kelly) would say goodnight to his girl and rush off into the street singing and dancing it up a storm.

Well that's exactly what I feel like doing now. Man, I feel like Gene Kelly ten times larger than life.

What if I burst into song and dance in the middle of the Kings Road? I'd probably get nicked for being drunk!

I took my little Alexandra home in a cab. She was very quiet after, very lovable, very shy. In fact, she didn't say a word. She dressed in the bathroom while I snatched a quick kip, then she shook me awake and said please could she go home.

I didn't know what to say to her, I was so sort of knocked out by it all. So we both sat quietly in the cab, and then I dropped her off and let the cab go, and here I am in Chelsea. It's three a.m. and now I'm wide awake, starving hungry, and feeling great.

I picked up another taxi and rode over to 'Hobo'. They never learn—this time there was nobody out front.

I raged inside, grabbed a frightened Franco and said, 'Where the hell is Tina?'

'Meester Blake—we wasn't expecting you back.'

'Yeah, baby, you're not telling me anything new.'

'I think Tina no feel good, she go home early.'

'Great Franco—great. So if you let her go home why not put someone else out front?'

'Of course I deed, Meester Blake. Frederico is there.'

'Frederico ain't there.'

Franco looked shocked. 'I keel that Frederico, I told 'im 'undred times to stay out front.'

I felt too good to argue any more. I just had to be there, that was all. Franco was fine when I was around.

Flowers was playing Lou Rawls. The place had that nice relaxed atmosphere at the end of a good night. There were about thirty people left in the room.

Sammy was still sitting with his juvenile wonder. He grabbed me. 'Where you bin? You missed all the excitement. It's a good job I was 'ere, I straightened things out a bit.'

'What happened?'

'That Carolyn's a mad bird. She started picking everything up in sight and throwing it at Steve, and 'e's trying to 'ide under the table, and the f-ing and blinding that was going on is nobody's business! So anyway, I grab a hold of 'er, and then she starts to cry, and 'e goes running out of the club, and then what do you know—the bleedin' newspapers arrive—some joker must 'ave phoned 'em. What a barny!'

I shrugged. I wasn't sorry I'd missed it all, because if I had stayed I'd probably have smashed that half assed pop singer to pieces.

Sammy's bird sat gloomily in the corner chewing on her thumb. 'Can we go?' she whined.

'In a minute, don't be so anxious, I'm going to give it to you.' Sammy replied, winking at me and mouthing—'a raver'!

Sammy was still chasing scrubbers. Why didn't he look around for a nice decent girl?

'Hey, Sammy, while I was in New York I was thinking.'

'Ye gods—'e's thinking yet!'

'No, Sammy, seriously. I've got this great idea for opening a new place.'

'A new place? Watcha want to do that for? What's wrong with 'ere?'

'Well, you know, Sammy, I'm the last one to ever see any bread out of this place, it's making a bomb and I see about tuppence.'

'Yeah? Well, you're a schmuck, aren't you? Watcha want to make yourself a lousy deal for?'

'Because I wasn't in a position to make *any* deal when this joint opened. Anyway—who knew it was going to take off like it did?'

'Yeah, well—why doncha get 'em to pay you some more? You work 'ard enough—*when* you're 'ere, that is.'

'Why let them put *more* money in their pockets? This place is *me*—without me they'd be finished in a couple of weeks.'

'Hold on, boy, you mean a lot to the place, but it still managed very nicely while you were in New York.'

'Aw, come on Sammy, let's go,' said the whiney-voiced scrubber, 'I'm fed up with sitting here all night.'

'Yeah, you go Sammy, I'll talk to you tomorrow.' I could see that I wasn't going to get much out of him.

'Meester Blake,' Franco was at my elbow. 'There ees Meester Ian Thaine outside with a party of ten, they want to come in, but we cannot serve any drinks now and 'ee is screaming 'bout that.'

'O.K., Franco, I'll handle it.'

Ian Thaine was a pain in the neck. He had made a fortune in so-called 'swinging London' gear—clothes, souvenirs, old uniforms, posters. He had 'Thaine' shops everywhere, and he made Sammy look like one of the aristocracy. He was about my age, thin and weedy-looking, out to better himself socially but never making it. I knew he hated me, because he saw me chatting to all-comers—film stars, lords, politicians. It killed him. He wanted to be someone. In fact, the rumour had it that he hired a permanent press agent to try to get his name in the gossip columns alongside the élite. I suppose he was worth a few million at least. He was usually with a motley crowd.

Tonight it was a couple of last season's debs, three members of a scruffy rock group, a once glamorous sexy actress with her nineteen-year-old 'Manager', a bit part actor, and two wide-eyed teeny boppers obviously culled from the streets of Piccadilly.

'Ian, m'boy,' I gave him the brotherly firm sincere handshake.

'Tony,' he sneered at me, 'is that right we can't get a pissing drink?'

'Sorry, Ian, that's right, got to think of our licence.'

'Balls to your licence,' he said peevishly. 'We want drinks.'

I smiled pleasantly, 'You'll just have to go somewhere else then.'

Ian bit on his lower lip, 'Oh, all right, we'll suffer on Coca-Cola then. I can see I'm going to have to open a place of my own in this town before I can get a drink.'

Bingo! Lights flash. Ian Thaine. Why hadn't I thought of him before?

'Come on, Ian,' I put my arm around his shoulder, 'I'll buy you all Coca-Colas myself.'

My mind was working quickly. Ian was perfect for the set-up I had in mind. He would jerk off at the thought of owning a successful joint. All I needed was a little sweet talk. He had the

134

money, plenty of it. We could go fifty-fifty. He to put up all the money, me to put up myself.

'Hey, Ian,' I said, 'I've been thinking . . .'

# 23

## ALEXANDRA

Maddy was asleep. It seems whenever I need her she's huddled in an immovable ball beneath her covers. I gave her a push, but she groaned and vanished under her eiderdown. The most important night of my life, and she doesn't even want to hear about it.

I feel strangely weak at the knees, but studying my face in the mirror I really don't look any different. Perhaps a little more sophisticated?

What an evening! First the terrible time with Steve Scott, then his *wife* appearing. I could have died with embarrassment. And Michael being there witnessing the whole thing. I must have looked such a fool.

Anyway, at least Tony was very nice coming after me and everything. He was so sweet and kind that when we were in the taxi outside his flat I suddenly decided that if I was going to go to bed with someone, *he* would be the perfect person. After all, he's the only one who seems to pay attention to me.

I think he was a bit shocked when I asked him if he wanted to make love to me. *Me* approaching *him*! I don't know how I did it. But I had decided I was going to lose my virginity and I was determined.

Michael likes women of the world. Am I a woman of the world now? It wasn't much fun. I mean I just sort of lay there while Tony climbed on top of me. He was awfully heavy and it hurt. I don't know what all the fuss is about if that's all you do. And it's so messy—ugh! I didn't enjoy it at all. I can't *ever* imagine Mummy and Daddy doing it. Did they? I suppose they must have.

I shook Maddy again, but she refused to budge. I'll never get to sleep until I tell *someone*.

Of course, the most exciting thing is the fact that I have a date with Michael! A date! Just the two of us. He must like me if he wants to take me to a quiet place for dinner.

I don't know how I'm going to face going to work tomorrow.

Oh, Michael, have I done the right thing? I only did it for you.

What if I get pregnant? Tony said he'd been careful but how do I know? What does he think of me? I don't know if I can face him again. Surely it was better in the old days when a man was supposed to want his wife to be a virgin. Now the whole thing has changed, and it's dumb to be a virgin. I feel so confused.

'Maddy, wake up!'


# 24


## TONY


Ian Thaine was easy. I couldn't understand why I hadn't thought of him before. He was craving to be a big man, dying to be friends with everyone, and what better way than to own a club?

I chatted him and he responded like a baby. I'd hardly ever given him the time of day before, because he was an obnoxious sonofabitch, but talking to him I realised just how much he wanted to be liked.

After an exhausting hour of costs and profits and all that jazz we shook hands.

'It's a deal,' Ian said.

Beautiful! He would put up all the money. I would do everything else and get a salary plus forty-nine per cent. I struggled for fifty, but Ian wasn't budging on that.

'We'll call it "Ian's",' he said.

'Yeah,' I muttered. We could argue about that later.

It was all too good to be true. It was late and the waiters were looking mutinous. Ian and party were the only customers left. One of the debs came and plonked herself on Ian's knee. He slid his hand up her skirt. The aged actress was in a tight clinch with her young manager. Nobody looked like budging.

I stood up. 'I think it's bedtime.'

Ian stood up, the ex-deb sliding in a furious heap to the floor. 'Yes, let's go.' Ian was now my friend.

To the waiters' relief the whole party got itself together and we all left.

Downstairs the three rock singers piled into a Ford with the two teeny boppers and roared off. The actress, her manager and the bit part actor got into a taxi. The two ex-debs, Ian and I were left. He was driving a white Lincoln Continental with gold fixtures and maroon upholstery.

'Where's your car?' he asked me.

'Er—in the garage being fixed.'

'I'll drop you then.'

'No, that's O.K., Ian, I can take a cab.'

'I said I'll drop you.' He took me to one side, 'Besides I want you to take Diana with you. You'll like her.' He whispered her speciality.

'Look, Ian, I don't want to get involved.'

He ignored me. I climbed in the back of the car with Diana. She was horsey-faced, tall and skinny. I couldn't have fancied her on the best of nights.

'Where to?' Ian asked.

I told him. How the hell was I going to get out of this? I mean he obviously thought he was doing me a big favour. The best thing was play it by ear.

He dropped me off and Diana clambered out with me.

'See you at my office at three,' Ian said. 'Have a good time.'

Shit! He drove off and Diana and I stood there. 'Where do you live?' I asked her when the car was out of sight.

'With Ian,' she replied slightly surprised. 'Why?'

It looked like I was lumbered. Why was I such a jerk? Why hadn't I just taken Ian to one side and explained? I suppose because I wanted a deal, and if accepting one of his tatty girls was going to please him, well, I guess I would just have to accept her.

'Come on,' I said wearily.

Please forgive me, my wonderful Alexandra, but I'm doing it for us.

# 25

## FONTAINE

Benjamin is not himself. Surly, bad-tempered, and positively rude to Sarah and Allen. I am absolutely furious. I've never seen him like this. Of course I know he's a monster in business, but, with me he has always been placid and polite, and never verbally attacked my friends, which he did quite viciously last night, calling poor Allen 'a lily livered, poor man's Tennessee Williams'. Well, I mean really! I didn't know he'd even read anything of Allen's.

Sarah was livid. I have rarely seen her angry, but last night her eyes were flashing and the words practically spitting from her lips. Needless to say we all parted outside 'Le Club' simply dreadful friends. I haven't spoken to Benjamin since. How dare he think that he can insult me and my friends!

Allen says he knows all about us. What nonsense! How can he possibly know? I'm always very discreet.

On top of everything else we have the added thrill of beastly little Ben junior joining us tonight. Alexandra is bad enough, looking down her nose at me all night, but Ben junior is impossible. Mutual hate abounds.

God knows why Benjamin insists I have to see his children.

They're *his*, not mine. I want no part of them.

What I would actually like to do is go back to London. I expect I am missed there.

I have decided to wait a few weeks before having Benjamin fire Tony. After all, he is different in London and I may as well make use of him until I find another London stud. I must say I feel quite nostalgic about Vanessa and 'Hobo' and all the little intrigues.

Oh God, I suppose I shall have to make peace with Benjamin. Why the hell *I* should make peace I don't know, but I *do* want to buy that sable coat today and it *is* twelve thousand dollars. I'll put on my white mink over nothing and go and wake him.

Benjamin, of course, is already up and at his office. It is noon and he always rises at seven.

Adamo remained impassive at the sight of me wandering around in my coat. Dear Adamo, the perfect servant.

Benjamin wouldn't appreciate me turning up at his office in my mink and nothing else. The erotic secret of being naked underneath is very exciting. But of course Benjamin is much too staid to enjoy it.

I phoned Sarah. 'Darling, I'm sorry, I'm just too upset for words.'

Sarah's voice was acid. 'I'm sorry for *you*, sweetie, *you're* married to him.'

'That's all right, darling. He's full of remorse today. I'm just off to get a new sable.'

'They're more chic in Paris this year.'

Sarah was a bitch, but I could out-bitch anyone. 'Why don't you buy Allen one?'

She laughed coldly. 'You're so amusing, Fonta.ne, maybe I shall.'

We said our goodbyes, and I phoned Benjamin at his office.

'Yes, what is it? I'm busy.'

Oh my god, he was impossible. It crossed my mind to forget the coat and let him beg my forgiveness. But a sable coat *is* worth a slight effort.

'You're not still angry?'

'What is it, Fontaine? I'm busy and can't discuss things now.'

'Well, darling, I need some money.'

'Talk to my secretary, she'll send over what you need.'

'Twenty thousand.'

There was a pause. 'Twenty thousand dollars?'

'Yes, darling, I've seen a gorgeous sable coat, and I have to get a few other bits and pieces.'

'But I just bought you the white mink.'

'I know, darling, but I *need* a new sable.'

'No, Fontaine, we'll talk about it later.'

'What do you mean, no Fontaine?' I was shaking with fury.

'Goodbye,' he hung up on me.

I phoned back at once. 'Mr Khaled is in conference, and can't be disturbed,' an embarrassed secretary said.

'But this is Mrs Khaled.'

'I'm sorry, he said I wasn't to interrupt him for anyone.'

I slammed the receiver down. How dare he! How dare he! He would pay a lot more than a sable coat for this.

# 26

## TONY

I think I'm a right bastard. What I should have done was told Ian Thaine to take his messy little ex-deb home with him and screw the fact that it might louse up our deal. If our deal depended on me knocking off one of his birds, then to hell with it—who needed it?

I did. Who even knew if he was going to come up with the money anyway? So far it was all conversation.

I really felt bad. Diana had gone, I had to force her to go. She was disgusting. And I was disgusting too, laying back and letting her slobber all over me. Well, at least I hadn't touched *her*.

I have definitely decided I'm going to marry little Alex. It's a big decision, I know, but I love her, I truly love her. I think I would kill any bastard that tried to touch her.

The whole situation is very dodgy. I've got to get away from Fontaine and 'Hobo'. Christ, if Alex ever found out about me and Fontaine it would be all over. She's a girl of principles, so sweet and kind, and that body! Wowee! I've never seen such a gorgeous body, so shy, and a virgin. I can hardly believe it, and she's mine, all mine.

I think what I'm going to do is get up, dress, and maybe take little Alex for lunch. Of course, I don't have her office number. I should have asked her last night, but maybe her girlfriend is home.

I dialled their flat, but there was no reply. Shit! I couldn't even remember the name of the firm she worked for. It's twelve o'clock, which means I've got to wait until five-thirty or six before she gets home.

I had to meet with Ian Thaine at three, that would pass the afternoon. Maybe Sammy would fancy a bite of lunch.

I couldn't track Sammy down, but I found Hal and Franklin in our favourite coffee bar, a nice little place where you could sit all day and watch the American tourists go by.

Hal said, 'Listen, baby, I've got a beautiful deal going. You remember Mamie? Well, her old man invested in this film company in Rome before he died, and now the company's going bust and she's putting up a lot more bread and I'm taking over. We're leaving for Rome tomorrow. Beautiful huh? If you're a good boy I'll put you in a movie, you're pretty enough!'

Hal came up with a deal like this every so often, but something always ballsed it up, usually him.

'That's great, Hal, you're going to be a big man.'

'Baby, I'm always a big man.' His smokey eyes surveyed two American ladies struggling with their mink stoles. He was always on the look out. 'So what's new, Tony baby? How was my town?'

'Great, Hal. I had a ball.'

'Yeah, one of these days I'll go back. I'm waiting for my bookie to die! Got to be a success in that city baby, otherwise you're nowhere—but nothing.'

My favourite waitress came scurrying over. 'Morning Mr Blake. Same as usual?'

'Yes, pretty. Make sure the eggs are nice and firm.'

She dimpled a smile at me. 'I see your club made headlines today.'

'What?'

Hal said, 'Yeah, baby, didn't you see it. A load of shit about Steve Scott.'

'Oh,' I patted my waitress on the bottom. It felt like she had nothing on under the flimsy blue skirt and white apron. 'Be a darling and grab me the papers.'

'I'll try, Mr Blake. We're awfully busy just now.'

She returned in two minutes flat with three morning papers. I scanned them quickly. Steve Scott was on the front page of all of them. The headlines screamed about his secret marriage. I read the first one.

'*Steve Scott (23) disclosed at London discothèque "Hobo" last night his secret marriage to actress and dancer Carolyn England (23) some time last week. Steve Scott found fame two years ago when his record "Laurie Baby" shot to the top of the charts. Since then his records have stayed consistently in the Top Ten. He has just finished recording his own Weekly T.V. Show and is due to start work shortly on his first film "MUD". Miss England has appeared countless times on your T.V. screens and was only last year voted "The girl with the longest legs on T.V." The news was broken when Miss England surprised her new husband at "Hobo", where he was enjoying a quiet evening of fun with Alexandra Khaled, eighteen-year-old daughter of billionaire Benjamin Al Khaled. The new Mrs Scott also announced the fact that they are expecting an addition to the family. The Steve Scott fan club hung a black flag from its windows early this morning. Steve Scott has no comment on his surprise marriage.*'

There was a big picture of Carolyn leering sexily in a black fishnet cat-suit, and a small picture of Steve having his shirt ripped off by a band of fans.

I was really choked. Where the hell had they got their information about Alexandra? Why should *her* name be brought up?

142

Lousy newspapers. They all carried more or less the same story.

My poor Alex would be upset if she saw it. Well, it would teach her a lesson for going out with the randy little bastard in the first place.

I attacked my eggs.

'Hello, mind if I sit here?'

It was Suki, dressed for the day in a thigh-length Indian shift and fringed jacket.

Franklin said, 'Where's your sister? You promised to fix me up.'

'Oh yes, sorry, I've been busy. I forgot about it. I'll talk to her.'

I don't understand Franklin. He's a good-looking boy with every opportunity to chat up all the birds at the club, but he never makes a move. Now he's hanging his hopes on Suki's sister.

'If you promised him, do it,' I said. 'Get your sister for tonight.'

'She might be busy,' Suki replied, producing her compact and studying her freaky face. 'Anyone seen Massey lately?'

Under all the piles of weird makeup she was probably quite pretty.

'What do you want to know about Massey for? You've got your little student now,' I said.

'I just wondered if anyone had seen Massey, that's all,' she replied defensively, 'I thought he might be here today.'

I finished my eggs and ordered some cheese-cake. Eating is one of my favourite pastimes, but I never get fat. I stay in great shape. Twenty-five push-ups a day. My stomach's hard as a rock.

Just then who should walk in but Massey. Cool as ever in a white suit and brown polo-neck sweater. He's a great-looking guy.

'Tony,' he clapped me on the shoulder, 'good to have you back. Hello, Suki—Franklin—Hal.' He sat down at our rapidly expanding table.

Suki snapped her compact shut and put it away. 'Mass, can I come back?' she asked.

'No,' he said quietly, 'no, baby, you stick with your little white boy.'

Her clown eyes filled with tears. 'Oh come on, Mass, let me back.'

'I said no, Suki.' And he turned to talk to me about New York.

Suki sat there a few minutes, then with two black tears hovering in her eyes, got up and left.

I ate her open cheese sandwich, which she hadn't touched.

'She thinks she can just come walking back to me when she gets a little bored with her sweet little white boy,' Massey said grimly. 'Well, she can just sweat it out.'

I think Massey was actually jealous.

I hung around until it was time to meet with Ian Thaine, then I walked the short distance to his office.

He sat on a black leather throne in front of a huge antique desk in a red room hung with pictures of himself. His opening words were, 'I told you you'd get a good job done, didn't I? Those little convent-educated bints are the ones.' His face was evil and his eyes thin yellow slits.

'Yeah, well thanks, Ian.'

'It's nothing.'

He then proceeded to give me a full sex summary of the three birds he had living with him, including Diana. Then he unlocked a desk drawer and produced a stack of polaroid pictures of them in various stages of undress. They became obscene. I felt sick to my stomach.

'I took them all,' he said proudly. 'Sometimes I have special parties. Next time I'll see you're invited.'

Here was a man after Fontaine's heart! Was I climbing from the frying pan into the fire? What about getting down to business?

I flicked quickly through the rest of the polaroids and said, 'Very nice, Ian. Now what about contracts and things?'

'Contracts?' he said. 'What's the matter, don't you trust me?'

'Of course I trust you, but if I'm going to start knocking myself out looking for locations, I want to be sure everything's cool—you know, have it down in black and white. Of course as soon as we find somewhere I'll leave "Hobo".'

144

One thing I was sure of. I wasn't going to be Tony Schmuck again. If I had to get involved with this slimy bastard it was all going to be legal, so that when he wanted me to attend any of his parties I could safely say no without getting chucked out. Fontaine unwittingly had taught me to be smart.

'All right,' Ian said, 'I'll have an agreement drawn up. Meanwhile start looking. What about Mrs Khaled?'

I looked at him in surprise. How did he know about me and Fontaine?

'What about her?' I said suspiciously.

'Shall I mention her in the agreement?'

'What for?' Now I was really surprised.

'She's your—er—partner, isn't she? She'll be in it with us, won't she?'

I was speechless.

Ian carried on. 'I'd like to meet her. When can I meet her?'

This was charming. When had I ever mentioned Fontaine?

'She's in New York,' I said vaguely.

'Now there's a beautiful woman,' Ian said admiringly, locking his polaroids away.

I stood up. 'O.K., Ian, I'll wait to hear from you.'

'Yes, I'll have my solicitor draw something up. Shouldn't take long.'

'Fine, I'll start looking.'

We shook hands. I didn't trust him, but as long as he thinks Fontaine is involved he'll probably come up with an agreement and the money. I don't know why he thinks she's my partner, but if it keeps him sweet, let him think it. Why disillusion the poor schmuck before the time came?

I couldn't wait for my little Alex to come home from her office. I wondered what she would want to do tonight. I wasn't going to take her on any wild outings, just a nice quiet dinner somewhere small, and a serious talk about us. Then she was going home to bed early. My darling must get some sleep. I figured I would drop by a few estate agents to pass the rest of the afternoon. May as well start the ball rolling.

# 27

## ALEXANDRA

I don't think I've ever been so embarrassed in my life! Mr McLaughton himself summoned me into his office. I was half-an-hour late this morning, and I suppose this is it.

He was a huge man with bushy eyebrows from under which peered watery red eyes. I don't know why *he* has to fire me, I'd never even seen him before.

'Sit down, Alexandra,' he boomed. 'You don't mind me calling you Alexandra do you?' and he chuckled.

I sat nervously. Daddy was right. I should have taken a job with one of his friends.

'Well, well, well,' Mr McLaughton said, suddenly lapsing into a fit of coughing, 'so we have a celebrity in our midst.'

'A celebrity, sir?' I questioned dimly.

'You are Ben Khaled's daughter are you not?'

How on earth had they found out?

'Yes, sir.'

'You should have told us. Why so secretive?'

I blushed, 'I don't know, sir.'

Honestly, what was I expected to do? Come marching in for the job announcing to all and sundry that my father was Benjamin Khaled?

'I think we can give you a better position than you have,' Mr McLaughton said, beaming. 'I think we can bring you into my office as a junior personal assistant, at an extra five pounds a week. Not that the money matters to you, I'm sure.'

I didn't want to be brought into his office as a junior personal assistant at an extra five pounds a week just because he knew who Daddy was.

'Thank you, sir,' I muttered. I'm weak. I hate to cause scenes. I would have to phone up or get Maddy to phone and say I couldn't work there any more.

'My two daughters are great fans of Steve Scott, you'll have to get them his autograph.'

I looked at him in astonishment, 'Steve Scott . . .' I stammered.

He picked up a newspaper from his desk and waved it at me, 'Pretty girl he married,' he said. 'Is she a friend of yours too?'

I took the newspaper from him and read it quickly. The whole thing became clear. That's how they knew about me. What would Mummy say if she saw this, and Daddy? He would be furious.

'I haven't seen this,' I mumbled.

'Don't forget about the autographs. You can take the rest of the week off if you like, start your new job on Monday heh? Perhaps I can meet your father one night, have a little chat about his talented daughter.' He chuckled again.

'Yes, sir. Thank you.' I fled.

By three o'clock I was home. Madelaine was out. I phoned Mummy. Apparently she hadn't seen the newspapers because she didn't mention anything about the whole mess.

'You are bringing some friends this weekend, aren't you?' she said.

I hadn't even asked Michael yet, I hoped he *would*·come. 'Yes, Mummy, just one.'

'All right, jolly good, darling. See you tomorrow.'

Madelaine came in shortly after, laden with packages. 'I've been shopping.' she announced, 'got myself some terrific gear. What on earth are you doing home?'

We talked while she unwrapped her parcels and tried everything on.

'You must get one of these crochet dresses,' she enthused, 'they're so terrif, and with your figure it will look fabulous! If you like you can borrow mine tonight.'

Maddy had discovered via Jonathan that Suki had been sleeping at their flat, and that even worse she had moved lots of her things in.

'Jonathan's absolutely livid!' Maddy said. 'It's only a tiny flat and her things are everywhere. He says Michael is dotty about her. Sorry, but I'm sure it won't last.'

'Why is he taking *me* out tonight?' I was confused.

She shrugged. 'Search me. I say, when are you seeing Tony again?'

'I don't know. Never I hope.'

'Oh, Alex, he's nice, awfully good-looking. He's your lover anyway, you'll have to see him.'

'I won't.'

We had discussed my losing my virginity from seven a.m. when Maddy finally woke, to eight-thirty, when I had dashed off to the office. Maddy had asked a thousand questions. Did it hurt? Did I love him? Was he enormous? Did I scream? I couldn't really remember any details. I suppose he did have a nice body. Of course I didn't love him, I loved Michael, Michael, Michael, that's all I could think of.

At six o'clock Tony phoned. 'Well, beautiful, how do you feel?'

'Fine, thank you.'

'What time shall I fetch you?'

'Fetch me?' I racked my brains to think if I had made any arrangement with him for tonight, and I was sure I hadn't.

'How about eight o'clock? We'll just have dinner and then I'll bring you straight home.'

'Look, Tony, I'm awfully sorry but I am already going out.'

There was a long pause and then he said, 'You're kidding?'

'No, I've had this arranged for ages.'

There was another long pause and then he said, 'Break it.'

'Break what?'

'Your date, idiot. I'll fetch you at eight.'

'Tony, I can't, it's—'

His voice was suddenly very angry. 'Who are you seeing that's so bloody important?'

I hated people being angry with me. 'I'm sorry, Tony, it's—it's family, I just can't get out of it.'

'Oh, Alex, Alex. What are you doing to me?'

'I'm not doing anything to you.'

'Are you angry with me about last night, is that it?'

'Honestly I'm not angry. I'd love to see you, but it's just not possible tonight.'

'All right, little girl. How about later?'

'I'm not sure, I don't know—'

'I'll phone you at eleven. If you're not tired I'll pop round for an hour before going to the club. How's that?'

'Terrific.' I breathed a sigh of relief to get him off the phone without a nasty scene.

I borrowed Maddy's crochet dress and Michael actually gave a whistle when he saw me. 'You *are* growing up,' he commented.

He took me to a little restaurant, very dark and cosy, then he lectured me solidly about how I was mixing with bad company, and if I didn't watch it I would get into trouble, and all these people I was always with smoked drugs and things. Well, I *knew* that.

'I feel responsible for you,' he said. 'You can't come straight out of school and turn into the town swinger. What did your parents say about the papers today?'

'Nothing,' I muttered, I was sulky and disappointed. I thought he had wanted to have dinner with me, but he just wanted to tell me what a silly little girl I was.

'Anyway, what about you and that awful model?' I finally said, unable to keep quiet any longer, 'What do *your* parents think of *you* living with her!'

'I'm not seventeen years old,' he said grimly. 'I'm only trying to help you, Alex, you're only a kid.'

*I hated* him!

I was home by ten-thirty, having bid a cold goodbye to Michael immediately we finished dinner: Tony phoned promptly at eleven.

I would show Michael. I invited Tony to spend the weekend in the country at Mummy's house. Michael had called Tony common and loud. Well, let's see what he thought about this! If this doesn't make him jealous I don't know what will!

# 28

## TONY

You drift through life from day to day and everything's cool. Life is good, things swing along nicely, plenty of birds, friends, food, enough bread to gamble a little, eat out every night, hand Sadie a fiver occasionally. Beautiful!

Of course I always wanted to do a bit better, get my own joint. But I knew I didn't have to push, it would all happen. I could just relax and enjoy life. It was such a blast to have names I'd only ever read about treat me like their long lost brother, and fantastic birds available.

Then along come Miss Alexandra Khaled, auburn shining hair, big brown eyes, knockout body, young, innocent, classy, sweet, shy, kind. And I fall—POW!! In love.

It means an immediate change in my life. I need plenty more bread, not for gambling, or eating out, or handing more to Sadie. But I need to make a home. I have to have something to offer her.

She looks at me with those big trusting eyes and I melt. I never in my life felt this way before. I feel I must look after her, protect her from the world.

When she said she couldn't see me tonight I was destroyed. My whole day had hinged around seeing her in the evening. I was angry and jealous and sick to my stomach. But she explained so nicely, so sweetly.

Oh boy, I never thought I'd get caught like this. I've known a lot of women and I thought as far as they were concerned I had it licked. Screw 'em and leave 'em wanting more. Never failed. But now I was caught in that well-known trap.

When she said she couldn't see me, it was a physical feeling of pain.

Of course, I have to marry her. This is it. Put her in a little flat, give her a few kids. I wonder if she can cook?

I spent a miserable evening with Sammy and his whiney-voiced scrubber from the night before. We ate at a steak house and I'll swear she was giving him a quick one under the table. She sucked her thumb between mouthfuls of food, and wiped her nose with the back of her hand. Charming!

Eventually she went to the loo and Sammy said, 'What's the matter with you—what are you dragging for?'

I shrugged, 'Nothing, I'm fine.' I wasn't about to tell *him* what the matter was.

'What do you think of my bird? Still at school, isn't she a little darlin'?'

'You won't be happy until you get caught, schmuck. She's under age.'

'Who's going to catch me, then? She says 'er parents never ask any questions. She can come and go when she wants.'

'Sammy,' I shook my head sadly, 'what do you want it for?'

'You're kidding, aren't you?'

She came back. She looked all of fifteen in her wisp of a dress and long stockinged legs.

Eleven o'clock came very slowly. I tried to stay cool and phoned Alex.

She was adorable. 'I'm in bed, Tony. I've been home ages.'

'I'll come round and read you a bedtime story.'

Oh God, I was coming out with lines *I* didn't even believe.

'I'm just going to sleep, but I'll tell you what, would you like to come to the country for the weekend?'

'When?' I asked stupidly.

'I thought tomorrow afternoon, and we could come back Sunday evening.'

'Yeah, that would be great.'

Screw the club, it would have to manage without me over the weekend. A whole three days with my Alex. Couldn't be better.

'Shall we take the train?' she said. 'Or do you want to drive? It's only an hour's journey.'

I didn't think Sammy would see fit to part with his E-type over the weekend so I said, 'We'll take the train.'

'There's a four o'clock from King's Cross. Mummy will meet us the other end.'

I had forgotten about dear old Mummy. That sort of put a

dampener on things. What if Mummy told Daddy and Daddy told Fontaine? Oh well, I'd soon be away from 'Hobo'.

'Yeah, that's perfect. I'll pick you up around three.'

'What happened to you?' Sammy asked. 'You look like you found gold.'

'Yeah,' I laughed, 'let's go to the club.'

It was going to be one of those nights, jamming up early, plenty of faces. Franco on his toes, Flowers playing Wilson Pickett. Hal, Franklin and Massey in already. Massey with a zoftic blonde, Franklin alone as usual, and Hal stoned, celebrating his last night of freedom before Rome and Mamie.

I socialised a bit. It was too soon to put out the word I would be opening on my own, but it was as well to spread my charm heavy. I must remember to pinch the members' list and get it copied.

'The Twang' came in with a film group, pouty lips, mane of tangled orange hair, she had got over her temper with me. She gave a hug and a kiss. Her tits were hanging out of a black velvet dress. She wasn't a bad kid, we had had quite a lot of fun. She was certainly well built.

'Guess what, Tonee baby?' she squeaked, 'I'm starring in *Mud* with Steve Scott. Isn't that fabulous?'

'Yeah, great.' I felt full of goodness towards the world.

'What did *she* have to say?' Franklin asked when I sat down.

'She says she's starring with Steve Scott in *Mud*.'

'Huh!' exclaimed Franklin. 'Candy Cook is the lead, she's probably got a bit part.' He still hadn't recovered from his encounter with 'The Twang'.

'Franklin,' I said seriously, 'what are we going to do about you?'

'What do you mean?'

'I mean getting you laid, that's what I mean. What are you saving it up for? Wow—if I was your age with your connections I'd be having a ball.'

'I just haven't met the right girl.'

'Shit, man, by this time *any* girl would be the right one. You can't jerk off all your life you know.'

Franklin lapsed into silence and I went and had a scotch with one of the 'Must' just back from a record-breaking concert in Paris.

There's something about a scotch and Coke I like. It's a good long drink with hidden punch. I must have had about six or seven when I went to take a piss and realised I was well and truly loaded. I usually just get a little buzz on when I'm working, but tonight—like POW! it had really hit me.

I was sweating hot, having been dancing with Molly Mandy, who's a wild dancer. She had wandered in on her own and sat at our table. I had this vague idea of fixing her up with Franklin, but God-almighty, she'd eat him alive! Maybe that's what the kid needed.

Out of the blue I found myself dancing with 'The Twang'.

'Ooh! Tonee, this is fun,' she said. 'You never used to dance with me when we were together.'

'Funky Street.' Flowers freaking out at his stand. 'The Twang' shaking her boobies at me. Man, I was gone. Flowers grinning broadly. 'Jumpin' Jack Flash.' Sweat pouring off me. Hal having a screaming match with Franco. Everyone laughing. Everyone having a ball. Sammy doing it with his schoolgirl. 'Tramp.' Why did Otis Redding have to get it in a lousy plane crash? Flowers in mourning for weeks, more so than for Martin Luther King. 'You're Lookin' Good.' 'The Twang' falling out of her dress, giggling, tossing orange hair around. Suddenly she changed into Molly Mandy and I said, 'Do me a favour and ball Franklin.'

The music was getting slow, slower. Who was I dancing with? Carla Cassini, beautiful Italian movie star. She smelt fantastic, but ruined the whole thing with hairy armpits. 'You ees beeg man, yes?' 'I Left My Heart in San Francisco.' Was that Massey with Suki? And the zoftic blonde dancing with Hal? Hal never danced but he was swinging tonight. Who wasn't!

'My producer—he 'ave to return Roma for one day only, so I come see you tonight. Good idea, yes?' She was an armful of woman. What about Alex? Would one more time be wrong? 'Who Can I Turn To?' She moulded her body into mine, rubbing a leg between my thighs. Christ, she caught me in the balls and it hurt. 'We must be careful,' she muttered, 'I am followed—'ee always has me followed.' Can't take my eyes off you. She churned her body into mine, keeping perfect time to the music.

'I stay at 102 Marlofield, a leetle 'ouse. You come in one 'alf hour to the back window—I arrange everything.'

Shit, man! Franco and the Italian waiters were hovering at the edge of the dance floor trying to get a better look.

'I go now,' she said abruptly, and left me standing there.

It never rains but it pours. I sat down.

Molly Mandy was hard at work whispering in Franklin's ear. He looked a bit stunned. Man, the room was turning. 'The Twang' appeared. 'How about tonight for old time's sake?' She whispered in my ear, wriggling her tongue about in there at the same time.

Molly Mandy gave me a wink across the table. Massey and Suki came and sat down. A short fat guy who I didn't know came over to 'The Twang' and clamped a chubby hand on her shoulder. He had a cigar clamped between his teeth. 'You gonna stay with this jerk all night?'

'Oh, Chucky, sorry, I'll be right back.'

'You'd better,' he said.

'Who's that?' I asked.

'That's Chuck Van Marless Junior,' she said, 'the producer. I'd better get back.'

'So who's keeping you?'

She gave me a sad look. 'You're such a bastard, Tonee.'

Her voice got on my nerves. She wriggled her way back to Chucky junior, and the group she was with.

I love Alexandra.

What number Marlofield square did Carla say? After all I wasn't married—yet.

Franklin and Molly Mandy suddenly got up. 'We're going,' she announced with a big smile, flashing her gold fillings. Franklin studied the ground in embarrassment. At last, at last!

'What about my sister?' Suki said.

'Where *is* your frigging sister?' I asked.

'She's here—somewhere. She saw some friends when we came in, but she'll be over soon and she thinks Franklin is her date.'

'Listen, baby,' Massey said, 'I do not believe she's too anxious. You've been here an hour already, and where is she?'

Suki shrugged. 'Let's dance.'

They went off, happy to be together again.

I couldn't remember the goddamn number—a hundred and something, a hundred and two, that was it. I was going. After all a movie star is a movie star, and what Alex didn't know wasn't going to hurt her. It certainly doesn't mean I don't love her. Anyway it's a well-known fact that fellows need it more than birds. So what about Fontaine?

I grabbed a taxi, and remembering Carla's warning, had him drop me off in the square, where I wandered around looking for a hundred and two. It was impossible work finding the numbers, and pissing with rain, but I went from house to house peering at doors with my trusty cigarette lighter. Oh God, what one wouldn't do for a star!

I found it. I hoped she had some scotch and coke. I needed it. I pushed my way past clumps of trees to the back and started trying the windows. I was soaking.

Suddenly a light shone in my eyes and a loud voice said, 'I'd stay just where you are if I were you.' And then a big nasty copper loomed into view. 'What do you think you're doing then?' he enquired politely. One thing about our policemen, they've got lovely manners.

So there I stood wet through and just approaching a hangover in West London Central Police Station. Charming! The bloody copper had never heard of Carla Cassini, and nor had the couple who lived in one hundred and two Marlofield Square. Too late I realised it should have been Marlofield Street, but the sweet arm of the law didn't want to know about checking my story.

I imagined Carla waiting for me in a clinging black slip, the sort of thing she wore in most of her movies.

I was in a right mess now. What a scene! After long arguments they finally sent someone round to check my story at a hundred and two Marlofield Street, and Carla, the bitch, denied she'd even heard of me!! So then more arguments until I finally got them to phone 'Hobo', and Franco and Sammy came rushing over and identified me. Franco confirmed that Miss Carla Cassini had been in the club that night, and had been dancing with me. So they finally believed me and let me go.

Shit, man! Sammy was laughing so much that tears were rolling down his cheeks.

'I can just picture the scene,' he said, 'you trying to get in a window with an 'ard on, and the copper pouncing down on you!'

Oh very funny. Very funny indeed.

Franco was trying to look grave and concerned, wedged in the back of Sammy's E-type, but I knew as soon as we got back to the club the story was going to be all over.

'Now, I don't want this spread around,' I said grimly.

'Meester Blake!' Franco exclaimed in horror, 'I cut off my right arm eef I say anything.'

Lying sonofabitch!

# 29

## FONTAINE

I sat and planned my revenge. It was about time Benjamin was taught a lesson. God almighty, he was treating me like a wife!

I dressed, went out and bought the sable coat anyhow. Benjamin's credit was good, and they knew who I was. 'Send the bill to my husband's office,' I said, 'he always likes me to pick my own Christmas presents.'

That would teach dear old Benjamin to say no. Doesn't the old fool realise how lucky he is to have a wife like me? I am beautiful, elegant, chic, famous. What more could anyone want from a woman?

Tonight, when he expects me to entertain his beastly son I shall make mincemeat of them both. Benjamin can't expect to treat *me* this way and get away with it. First of all I intend to return to London tomorrow, with or without Benjamin. I will show him who calls the tune in *our* marriage. My God, if he thinks he can push me around the way he used to treat his dreary first wife, he can think again.

I put on a white lace Courrèges cat suit. Roger came by and fixed my hair in a devastating style, then Adamo made me a champagne cocktail, and I awaited my darling husband's return.

He puffed in promptly at six, followed closely by Ben junior, who peered at me through owl-like glasses.

'Hello, Benjamin, darling,' I purred coldly, ignoring the son, '*so* sweet of you to call me back.'

'Did you see young Ben?' Benjamin said pointedly.

'Yes, I saw young Ben,' I replied in a sing-song voice.

'Fontaine, pull yourself together. We'll talk about it later.'

'There's nothing to talk about. Oh, by the way, I bought the coat—it's in the bedroom, it's absolutely divine. Thank you, darling.'

His face sagged, but he was loath to argue in front of his precious son. He turned brightly to Ben junior. 'Well now, what restaurant would you like to go to?'

'Anywhere, sir,' Ben junior replied, studying the floor in embarrassment at being caught in the middle of an argument.

'What about you?' Benjamin turned to me, desperately trying to keep the proceedings bright.

'I don't think I'll come.' I savoured his look of annoyance, 'I have a headache.'

There was a short delicious silence, then Benjamin said, 'Make yourself comfortable, Ben, have a drink, look at the magazines. I think there's a new "Playboy".' He winked at his son as only a decrepit old man can. 'Fontaine, why don't you come in the bedroom and show me your coat while I shower?'

Oh, I see. He was going to forgive me for buying the coat if I came out to din-din like a good girl and was nice to dreary boring son.

I was right.

'Fontaine, don't be a bitch!'

' 'A bitch?'

'You know what I mean.'

'What?'

'The boy is sensitive, don't hurt him, make him at ease.'

'And how about *me*? I'm sensitive too, especially when some goddamn little secretary won't even put me through to you on the goddamn phone.'

'You must understand—'

'So must you. I don't expect to be treated like this.'

'You have the coat now, at least you can be civil.'

'Yes—I have the coat *only* because I ignored you and got it anyway.'

'Please, Fontaine, for the boy.'

'He's not a boy, Benjamin, don't baby him. He's probably bored stiff at having dinner with us anyway, and so am I—very bored by the whole thing.'

'I'll see you get the rest of the money you want tomorrow morning.'

'Oh, all right, but just remember to *never* treat me in such a way again.'

'Very well, Fontaine, but please let us have a nice amicable evening.'

I hate Benjamin. I hate a man you can tread all over.

His punishment wasn't over yet, he would see. As soon as he comes pawing me, expecting to go to bed with me, he will just have to wait. Just as he had to wait before we were married. Oh God, I had him mad for it then, and that's just the way it's going to be again. He'll have to beg for it. On his knees. Poor old bastard.

# 30

## TONY

Charming! Hauled down to the police station like a common criminal! Sadie would have a thousand fits if she knew. All over some bird that, if you want the truth, I didn't even fancy! Well, not much anyway. I mean if she hadn't've been who she was I certainly wouldn't have gone creeping down to Marlofield Square—Street—or wherever it was. Really I don't fancy anyone except Alex.

It is two o'clock in the afternoon, and I'm shaved and dressed (very casual—white sweater, black slacks, suede jacket). I am wondering what kind of jazz to take with me. A suit in case my darling wants to go out? Pyjamas? I don't even have any, on account of the fact that I always kip in the raw—lets the skin breathe, y'know.

In the end I bundled a couple more sweaters and my shaving gear in a bag. After all, a weekend in the country was bound to be slopping about.

I didn't feel too fantastic. Slight touch of your actual hangover. But I looked good, with some overnight tan I could have just got back from South of France.

Alex was waiting for me. Very pretty in a green trouser suit, with her hair tumbling around her lovely little face. She had a huge suitcase and, blushing, she said, 'I'm taking all my dirty washing home.'

Sweet!

'Do you want some coffee?' she asked.

'I've got a cab waiting.'

'Oh, O.K. Maddy won't be a sec.'

Maddy?!? Don't tell me she was coming with us. What a lumber!

She was. Maddy in a mauve trouser suit, with a big fat bottom, a John Lennon cap and plain face.

I had been looking forward to a nice quiet chat with my Alex, but it was not to be. On the train Maddy kept up a non-stop stream of unintelligent conversation, all about clothes and some schmuck called Jonathan and wasn't Christmas going to be absolutely 'super'. I gathered from the conversation that Alex was going to spend Christmas at Madelaine's home. Charming! I would have to talk her out of *that*.

'Mummy always goes to St Moritz for Christmas,' Alex remarked to me—*finally* including me in the conversation, 'it's so lovely there with the ski-ing and everything. This will be the first Christmas I haven't gone with her.'

'Only another week and I haven't bought *one* present yet,' Madelaine exclaimed. 'What do *you* want, Alex?'

Alex laughed. 'Nothing actually. Where are you spending Christmas, Tony?'

Where *was* I spending Christmas? The Elephant and Asshole I supposed. 'Er, I haven't decided yet.'

As a matter of fact Sadie and Sam don't keep Christmas—I mean, nothing special. Usually on Christmas Day I get up late and wander over to the Hilton with whatever bird I happen to be with, and eat their special Christmas lunch. It's very nice. Then I wander home, get into kip and watch the telly.

I fell asleep to the sound of the girls' chatter. I would get Alex alone later, I could wait.

'Wake up, we're here!'

I staggered off the train behind the girls, carrying Alex's enormous suitcase, Madelaine's ton-weight overnight bag, and my carryall. Tony the porter

The girls raced up the platform and I followed. Alex threw her arms around a fair-haired woman, standing beside a station wagon. She smiled at me when I came lumbering up with all the gear.

Alex said, 'Mummy, I should like to introduce you to Tony Blake.'

'Mummy' gave me a friendly smile. I could see where Alex got her beautiful brown eyes from. Her mother was an attractive woman, a lot better than any of the old birds Hal ever appeared with.

'So glad to meet you, Mr Blake. You'll have to excuse my

daughter leaving you to carry everything, she has absolutely no manners.'

We all laughed. I liked 'Mummy'.

We reached the house, I was shown around, then left alone in a mahogany lined guest-room with an adjoining marble bathroom. What a house! Stables, swimming pool—the lot. Servants darting around everywhere, three cars in the drive. I had imagined poor abandoned 'Mummy' living in a cottage with a daily help. Really, I was a bit choked. How could Alex have a billionaire father, a mother that lived like this, and *still* work as a crummy secretary? I couldn't understand it.

A butler came in with my bag. 'Shall I unpack for you, sir?' He looked disdainfully down his long thin nose.

Oh shit, man—if Sammy could see me now!

'No, that's all right,' I said airily, thinking of my two crumpled sweaters and a clean pair of pants with a hole in.

'Are you sure, sir?'

'Yeah, I'm sure,' I glared at him, hoping he would go away.

'Can I fetch you a drink, sir?'

Now that was more like it. 'Yes, I'll have a scotch and coke, plenty of ice.'

'Scotch *with* Coca-Cola, sir?'

'Yeah—*with* Coca-Cola.'

'Very good, sir.'

Skinny old bastard, didn't know what it was all about, stuck down in the country.

I opened my only piece of luggage and wished to hell I'd brought a suit. Alex and Madelaine had deposited me in this room saying gaily, 'We're going to change for dinner—see you downstairs at seven.' I had nothing to change into except another sweater, and I was saving that for tomorrow. I had an awful feeling that I'd brought the wrong gear. I hadn't even been alone with my baby Alex yet. Where the hell was her bedroom, anyway? I'd have to know that for later.

Long Thin Nose came back with a tiny slug of scotch in a glass, a full ice bucket and a bottle of coke.

I downed the scotch in one fell swoop. Then I changed sweaters and went off in search of Alex.

It was a huge bloody house with massive oak doors everywhere—all closed. I went downstairs and in front of a roaring fire I found 'Mummy' in a blue chiffon cocktail gown, with a red faced giant of an old chap in a dinner jacket.

'Ah, Mr Blake,' 'Mummy' said. I wished she would cut out the Mr Blake jazz. 'I'd like to introduce you to Doctor Sutton.'

I shook hands. Well, at least they were going out somewhere the way they were all dolled up.

'Mr Blake is a friend of Alexandra's from London.'

'Oh yes,' said Doctor Sutton. 'how do you do—yes, London, I shall be going there in three weeks time. Friend of Alexandra's. Charming girl, just like her mother, y'know—charming. Yes—very nice, very nice.'

'Would you care for a drink, Mr Blake?' asked 'Mummy'.

'Yeah—I mean yes, thank you, lovely, er I wish you'd call me Tony.'

'Certainly.' She smiled. She had a smile like Alex, only it was a little worn round the edges.

She summoned Long Thin Nose who smirked knowingly at me and said, 'Scotch *with* Coca-Cola, sir.'

'Yeah.'

'Now that's a funny drink.' Doctor Sutton wasn't one to miss out on a bit of conversation. 'Very funny, you drown the taste of the alcohol with the carbonated drink. You may just as well drink plain Coca-Cola.'

I wished the old goat would get going, and where was my Alex? As if on cue she came giggling in with Maddy. Both of them wearing quite dressy outfits. It suddenly dawned on me that maybe dressing for dinner meant dressing up for dinner.

Maddy confirmed my suspicions, 'Haven't you changed yet, Tony?' she asked, just as Old Long Nose was bringing me my drink.

'Hush, Madelaine,' 'Mummy' said, 'Mr Blake doesn't have to change.'

'Oh gosh, Tony,' Alex interrupted, 'I forgot to tell you we always dress for dinner. I thought you would know . . .' she trailed off lamely. 'Oh golly, I'm so silly, please forgive me, why on earth should you?'

Yeah. Why on earth should I know? After all I'm only a lousy ex-waiter. I felt like a right berk.

'Don't worry about it, Mr Blake. You look quite respectable as you are,' said 'Mummy'.

So I stood there with egg on my face while they all inspected my black and white striped (at least it was Simpsons) sweater and tight black trousers.

Madelaine stifled a giggle. What she needed was a good stiff kick up her backside.

'Dinner is served, M'Lady.' Old Long Thin Nose was back. I thought scenes like this only existed in the movies.

We all trooped into the dining-room, Alex holding my arm and whispering, 'Sorry!'

The dining-room table was loaded with enough silver to sink a ship. It's a good job I was once a waiter—otherwise I'd never have known which knives and forks and jazz to use.

Dinner was a gas, Doctor Sutton entertaining us with a story about a patient of his with a terminal disease; 'Mummy' telling us about how she was coming up to town for the January sales and what she was going to buy; and Alex and Madelaine occasionally giggling together.

I was well and truly fed up. After dinner, which dragged on, there was coffee in the study, then everyone started yawning and 'Mummy' said, 'we'd better all have an early night if we're to go riding in the morning.'

I tried to catch Alex's eye, but she was in a huddle with her girl-friend as usual.

'You *do* ride, don't you, Mr Blake?' asked 'Mummy'.

I'd kill her if she didn't stop calling me Mr Blake.

I felt like saying—'Yeah, baby, I ride, but not the way you have in mind!' Instead I said, 'No.'

'What a pity. But you can have a nice lie-in and we shall be back by lunchtime.'

Oh, very jolly.

Everyone said goodnight to everyone else, and the girls and I started upstairs while Mummy saw the Doctor out.

'Where's your room?' I hissed at Alex.

'Oh!' she looked flustered. 'Maddy's in with me.'

Charming! 'Then you come to my room.'

'Tony I *can't*, not here.'

I took her sweet little hand and squeezed it, 'I just want to talk to you, only talk, I promise.'

My body was talking already, I was as hard as a rock.

'All right, I'll try.'

I gave her a kiss on the cheek as Madelaine stood and stared.

'Make it soon.'

She nodded, 'If I can.' And then she was off with her girl-friend.

What a lousy situation. I mean what a drag this whole thing is. I looked at my watch. Only nine-thirty. I haven't been to bed at nine-thirty since I was ten!

I went to my room. No television, no radio, no telephone. Someone had turned the bed down and unpacked my bag. Well what the hell—I didn't care what some thin-nosed butler thought of me.

I lay on the bed and smoked a cigarette—then another one, then another.

This was ridiculous, nearly half an hour and no Alex.

I couldn't bear the thought that she wasn't going to come. My body was in a nervous sweat already. I would give her another five minutes—ten minutes—fifteen minutes. Goddamn it! Nearly an hour and where was she?

I went into the passage. No sign of life, just a dim light burning. Like an idiot I had no idea where her room was. I peered through the keyhole of the door next to mine, the room was in darkness. Then the next keyhole—it was a john—then the next—a cupboard. I was making great progress.

The passage curved round a corner, and there was a door with light showing under it. I bent down to peer through the keyhole and jerked back with astonishment. Naughty old 'Mummy'. She was spread out on the bed, yards of blue chiffon round her waist,

164

legs high in the air, and crouched above her was dear old Doctor Sutton. 'Mummy' was a right raver.

I couldn't help smiling. What a scene! Doctor Sutton still had most of his clothes on—couldn't be too comfortable!

Well, well, well. I dragged myself away from the keyhole—I was a doer not a watcher.

Now I felt horny. Where was Alex?

I went down the other end of the passage and started the keyhole routine again. Her room was in the same position as her mother's, but *she* wasn't. She was lying asleep in a divan bed with a small table separating her from Madelaine, also asleep.

I looked at her for a while. I felt like a thief. She was breathing softly with the covers pulled up to her neck and her hair spread out on the pillow. I had such a feeling of LOVE. Keeping a wary eye on Madelaine, who was giving out with a few snores, I gently pulled the covers off Alex. She was wearing a white frilly nightgown. She sighed and turned on her back.

I was eating her up with my eyes. My body was choking to hold her. I put my hand on her breast, so soft and still. Her eyelids fluttered and I quickly took my hand away.

She opened her eyes. 'Tony!'

'Sssh.' I didn't want the girl-friend awake. 'What happened to you?'

She looked a bit sheepish. 'I *meant* to come to talk to you but I fell asleep'.

Very flattering—I mean she really must have the hots for me.

'Well, come on,' I whispered.

'But it's so late, and what about Maddy?' she protested.

All the same she climbed out of bed and slipped on a pink quilted dressing-gown.

I took her hand. 'Maddy's fast asleep, and I'll have you back in bed in no time.' She didn't realise I meant my bed of course.

We crept off down the passage to my room, and she curled up in a chair and stared at me with those big brown eyes.

I paced about a bit and turned all the lights off except for a bedside lamp.

'What do you want to talk about?' she asked sweetly.

165

I stood behind her chair and stroked her hair. If I didn't have her soon I was going to explode.

'I'm sorry about dinner,' she said, 'I should have warned you we always dress. Mummy's a stickler for doing things properly.'

Yeah, baby! —

'Alex,' I said, my voice strangled. I started to undo the buttons of her dressing-gown.

She pushed my hands away. 'It's a shame you can't ride,' she said in a high little voice.

Oh but I can—I can.

My hands reached her beautiful breasts and I squeezed her nipples. She wriggled around in the chair, trying to get away.

'Stay still—relax,' I said. I was shaking, I wanted her so badly. I was a fine one to tell *her* to relax.

'What about Mummy?' she asked desperately.

I ignored *that*, and managed to slip her nightie over her head. Her hands flew to cover herself and she started to shiver.

'Come on, into bed.' Then I played the strong man, carried her over and plopped her on the middle of the bed. She still had on a pair of white panties and she lay quickly on her stomach, so all I could see was her velvet smooth back, rounded bottom through the panties, and long knockout legs.

I ripped my clothes off. If I wasn't quick I was going to blow the whole set-up. I lay on top of her. Oh Man, I could have made it all over those sexy legs! But I gathered a little control and pushed myself between the back of her thighs.

She tried to throw me off.

'Please, please, stop it, Tony, I don't want to—*please*.'

Birds were always saying no when they meant yes. But when she started to cry, loud sobs, I suddenly felt like the world's worst heel. This wasn't some bird I was on the make for. This was the wonderful girl I wanted to marry.

'Hey,' I got off and cuddled her softly. 'Quiet, darling, if you don't want to, we won't—no problem.'

She stopped crying, 'I'm sorry, Tony.' Then she got up and put her things on. I took her to the door and kissed her. She smiled at me. She looked like a little girl. 'Goodnight, Tony. Thank you.' Then she was gone.

Man, this is love! If I can give up what I just gave up I really have it bad.

And now I have a problem, and not even a 'Playboy' magazine in sight!

# 31

## ALEXANDRA

Maddy woke me in the morning by pummelling my back until I was forced to open my eyes. I yawned. 'What time is it?'

'It's seven, and where were *you* last night? I got up to go to the loo and you were gone. Did the devastating Tony drag you off to his room? I tried to stay awake, but you were ages.'

'I wasn't.'

'You were. Did he ravish your girlish body?'

'Maddy, shut up, you sound like some woman's magazine.'

'Did he screw you, then?'

'Maddy!'

I went off to the bathroom before she could bag it, and took a cold bath. Mummy say cold baths are better for you than hot ones.

I tried not to think about the previous evening with Tony.

Maddy was all huffy when I finished in the bathroom.

'You've become very secretive,' she remarked coldly.

We had a breakfast of scrambled eggs and bacon, then we set off riding. It was glorious fun. I had my own horse, Pinto.

I felt guilty about last night, guilty about upsetting Maddy, and guilty about everything in general.

We were riding through the woods and approaching a stream when suddenly Pinto reared up and I came tumbling off. 'Ouch!!'

Mummy and Maddy had already crossed the stream, but they stopped, and turned back.

I felt all right, nothing broken, but when I tried to stand my left leg gave way and I felt an awful pain.

'I think you've got a nasty sprain,' Mummy said.

'Oh, Alex!' Maddy lamented.

They piled me back on to Pinto who was now standing quietly, and back to the house we all went.

Mummy sent for Doctor Sutton, who came immediately. He is such a sweet old man. He brought me into the world and has looked after me ever since.

It was a sprain, and a nasty one.

'Off your feet for five or six days at least,' Doctor Sutton pronounced.

'Poor Alex,' Maddy wailed.

Mummy was very businesslike. 'Can't be helped. I think there's a two o'clock train to town that Mr Blake can take. What about you, Madelaine dear? Do you want to stay, or will you leave too?'

I groaned. I was beginning to feel sick. 'I think you had better go back, Maddy. I'm not going to be much fun to be around.'

'If you're sure, Alex. I'll stay if you like.'

'No.' I shook my head. Doctor Sutton had given me some pain killer and sleeping pills and I was feeling drowsy.

'Come along, Madelaine dear,' Mummy said, 'she'll feel better if she has some sleep.'

They went out of the room. My leg throbbed, my head ached and my eyes soon closed.

# 32

## TONY

Too bloody much! Sitting on another train next to best friend Madelaine, without so much as a last glimpse of my adorable little Alex.

'Rotten luck, isn't it?' Madelaine questioned for the sixth time. I think she gets some sort of perverted thrill seeing me so choked.

'Yeah,' I muttered, wishing she would shut up.

'What will you *do* tonight?'

'What I always do on a Saturday night, go to the club.'

'You're so lucky. I'm left in the lurch, my boyfriend's away and I hate staying in the flat alone.'

Tough!

We had five minutes of beautiful silence, then—

'I say, Tony, could I come to the club with you? I'd be ever so good, stay out of your way and everything.'

I frowned. Who needed her?

'Well no, Maddy, it would be a real drag for you, you'd get shoved around all over the joint, Saturday night's a mad-house.'

'*Please*, Tony, I don't mind. I'm sure Alex would want you to take me. In fact she did mention something about us sticking together.'

Sticking together? What was *that*?

Shit—why had my little darling gone and fallen off her god-damn horse?

'That's settled, then?'

Christ! Didn't she ever shut up? The poor guy that ever got lucky would probably have to gag her while he had it off.

'All right,' I said reluctantly. I didn't want her carrying tales to Alex about how I wouldn't take her to the club.

She prattled on about God knows what, I was bored by her. King's Cross at last!

'Can I share your taxi, Tony?'

Caught once more.

She talked all the way to Chelsea and left me with—'Can you pick me up about eight o'clock?'

Oh no, definitely no.

'Sorry, Mads, I've got to pop over and visit my mum and dad. If you want to come to the club I'll be there from about twelve.'

That should fix her. Her face dropped.

'What a shame. I thought we could have dinner first.'

'Sorry, darling, duty calls.'

'Oh, Alex will be disappointed when I tell her.'

Anyone would think it was Alex I was turning down!

'You know how it is. Maybe I'll see you later.'

I hopped back in the cab and muttered at the driver to get moving.

'See you later.' Madelaine shouted bravely.

She didn't intend to give up, but I doubted if she would come waltzing into the club alone at midnight.

I felt pretty blue. I'd been feeling like a king the night before on account of that whole scene with my darling, but now she was lying injured in bed and they hadn't even let me see her before I left. Dragtime. I had decided to talk to her about our plans, get everything settled over the rest of the weekend. I certainly wouldn't have minded staying at the house while she was in bed, but 'Mummy' had Madelaine and me out of there like a shot out of a gun.

My flat looked worse than ever. I could never expect Alex to move in here, even to start off with. Maybe if we got rid of Madelaine I could move in with Alex.

I was thinking of perhaps Caxton Hall for the wedding, do it quickly before anyone could object. I'd have to talk to her about it as soon as I saw her again, and when would that be? With randy old Doctor Sutton in charge, who knew?

Anyway—come Monday morning I am going to be out and looking for new club premises. As long as Alex is away I may as well get *something* settled.

# 33

## FONTAINE

Benjamin and I flew back to London in silence.

Our whole relationship has been based on silence ever since that ghastly evening out with Ben Cretin junior.

When we were coming in to land, Benjamin suddenly gripped my arm and said, white-faced and shaking, 'I want a divorce, Fontaine.'

Well of course I was astounded! 'You want *what*?'

He cleared his throat and I studied the network of tiny aged lines all over his face.

'I want a divorce,' he repeated.

I gazed out of the window completely at a loss. The old fool asking *me* for a divorce! How ironic. How humiliating. How dare he!

I smiled coolly. 'Sorry, old boy, but I don't think I care for that idea.' Inwardly I was in a burning rage.

'You have no choice,' he said sourly, 'I've had you watched.' He produced a thick wad of papers from his briefcase. 'I know *all* about you and Allen Grant and Tony Blake. I even have photographs.'

He handed me a glossy ten by eight of me and Tony on the bed in the New York apartment.

Oh my God, I looked awful, and Tony so hairy, like a great ape—ugh!

'Where did you get this?' I asked pleasantly.

'Adamo.'

'Oh!' That little bastard! I couldn't think properly. I had to see my lawyer immediately.

'There will be two cars meeting us at the airport.' Benjamin said, 'I have a suite at Claridges, and you may stay at the house until it's sold.'

My head was spinning. What had I done to this old man that he could treat me like this?

'Of course I will make you a reasonable allowance, though I don't have to, and we'll call the sable coat a farewell gift.' He stored his evidence back in his briefcase, and the wheels of the plane touched gently down.

For some utterly stupid reason my eyes filled with tears and I said, 'But I thought you loved me.'

He looked at me seriously, 'And I thought you loved me.' He unclicked his seat belt and stood up, 'Goodbye, Fontaine. Good luck.'

# 34

## TONY

I had a good kip. Didn't feel like seeing anybody, so went to a movie on my own and arrived down the club early. There was nobody in yet. I sat down and told Franco to have the chef fix me a steak and chips.

Flowers wandered in and sat down beside me. He looked moody and miserable.

'How's it going?' I asked.

He shrugged. 'Not good man!' He chewed on his fingernails.

'What's the problem?' I knew it was bound to be a touch, but I wanted to keep him sweet as I had plans for him and Tina in the new joint.

'I need a fast fifty for Tina, she's in trouble.'

Charming! A touch is a touch, but fifty?

He chewed on his fingernails some more while I did some quick thinking. I wanted them with me when I went, and what better way to guarantee that fact than by having him in my debt? Besides which, I liked Tina, she's a good, hard-working kid.

'O.K. I'll get it for you. Monday.'

Flowers beamed 'You're great, Tony. I knew we could count on you.' He rushed off to tell Tina the good news.

Fontaine will be definitely choked when I am gone. I don't give 'Hobo' ten days without me. The plan is to set the new place up, have it all ready to go, and then bye bye, Mrs Khaled.

Where is Mrs K. anyway? Still in New York, I hope, enjoying her strange scenes.

The money people started to arrive and were placed carefully out of the way. Flowers put on an early Antonio Carlos Jobim album. One of the 'Must' arrived alone and sat down with me. He was about the most intelligent of the group, but always high on acid. We discussed sounds and how the police were always raiding his joint, but he was too smart for them—he kept all his gear buried in the garden!

'Where's Lissy?' I asked. Lissy was his flaxen-haired sixteen-year-old-freaked-out wife.

'She's taking a health bath in Germany.'

'Oh.' I mean what else do you say to *that*?

Sammy bounced in alone. 'I've been workin' me bleedin' balls off!' He announced, 'I'll have a scotch and coke.'

I got up to greet some faces. A well known politician and his new wife. Who should they be with but mumsy old Vanessa and husband Leonard. She smiled nervously at me, huge tits escaping from purple tulle. Leonard shook my hand, good clean masculine stuff. I had a feeling he couldn't stand me. In this business you get a pretty reliable sixth sense about things like that.

Everybody started to arrive at once, and Franco got busy sorting them all out. There were certain places certain people would sit, and certain places they would not. Franco knew exactly, and he was great at arranging them all.

I stayed near the entrance, greeting, kissing, cuddling, flattering.

Vanessa came out to the Ladies room and whispered. 'Can I talk to you, Tony?'

'Yeah.' Why all the hush? We were well out of sight of hubby.

'Have you heard about Benjamin Khaled?'

'Heard what?'

'Apparently, and I know this from a very good source, my hairdresser actually.'

'Get on with it.' I was impatient.

'You must promise not to breathe a word of this to Fontaine. Do you promise?'

'Yeah, I promise.' She was impossible.

'Actually he's been seeing another woman, and not just any other woman—Delores! My dear, Fontaine will be beside herself with utter rage when she hears. She would never dream Benjamin could stray. Isn't it too, too frightful?'

Without tits I would never have looked at Vanessa in the first place, now, even with them, I couldn't fancy her. Gossip gives me a pain. Who cares? Good old Benjamin, getting one back on Fontaine. And with Delores yet! Sensational new model, on the cover of you name it she's on it. Yeah! Fontaine will be double choked!

I patted Vanessa on her fat bottom and winked. 'Don't believe it.'

'But it's true! Honestly Tony. Delores goes to the same hair-dresser as me and I heard that—'

'Still don't believe it.'

She pouted. 'Nanny takes the children out every day between three and five as before. Why don't you pop in to see me?'

I shrugged. That scene was definitely over. 'Yeah, maybe.'

She laughed nervously. 'Don't say maybe, say yes.'

I was saved by Sammy appearing. ''Ere, any loose stock around?'

Vanessa gave him a look of distaste and disappeared into the loo.

Sammy chuckled. 'You've always got a bird 'anging around you. What you got that I 'aven't?'

One of the good things about Sammy is that you never have to bother to answer him.

The evening roared on. I stayed sober, rejected a few girls and felt pleased with myself. I wasn't going to be unfaithful to my darling Alex. I didn't want to be, and I wasn't going to. There's true love for you.

Just before one, Madelaine appeared. 'I've had a simply dreadful time getting in,' she complained. 'I came at twelve and that ghastly foreign girl said you weren't here yet, and she wouldn't even let me in to wait. Then I came back and she *still* said you weren't here, so I waited 'til she wasn't looking and just came right on in. Really, I do think you should fire her.'

She looked lumpy in some sort of crochet dress, and a bit red faced. Tina had *strict* instructions *never* to let any unaccompanied bird in, especially if they asked for me.

I sat her down next to Sammy who looked her over with disinterest. I ordered her a Coca-Cola, wasn't getting *her* loaded. Then I did a fast vanish and sat down with a couple of songwriters who had the current hot show in town. Idle chat. Then up to greet old time movie star, five feet tall. He looked like a giant on the screen. He was with 'The Twang', fast becoming everybody's date.

'Tonee babee,' she squealed, 'you're going to be so proud of me, I'm signed for two new movies. First *Mud* and then a picture with my gentleman friend here.' She squeezed old time movie star's arm and giggled. Her left tit reached his mouth!

I wondered if she'd still be available for me if I wanted her, or did she only put out for a part in a movie now?

'That's wonderful,' I said, phoney bastard that I am.

'Yes, isn't it though? I'm so thrilled, it's all so wonderful! Have you got a good table for us?'

All of a sudden she was talking to me like a waiter!

'Franco will see to you.'

I went out front, where Tina said shyly. 'Thank you, Mr Blake.' The poor kid looked washed out.

'Why don't you go home? One of the boys can come out here.'

'Mr Blake, I'm fine—really.'

I felt like taking off early myself.

'Tony!!' A shriek from a deep throaty voice. 'You old sexy bastard. How *are* you darling? Still the greatest fuck in town, I bet!'

It was Margo Castile, famous sex change . . . lady. I mean *he* was originally a fishmonger or something, but after many operations *she* was a well-known personality around town. Rather exotic, lovely looking, but with this deep butch voice and language like a fishwife. She was with two men, a small beaming Italian and an English actor.

'Tony darling. When are you going to show *me* what you keep in those sexy tight pants?' She shrieked with laughter. She was always drunk.

'Yes, Tony,' the English actor lisped excitedly.' When are you going to show Margo?'

I smiled weakly. I wasn't ready for *this* group tonight. We all went inside.

'I say, let's have an organised fuck!' Margo shouted. 'All those that want to join in, hands up!'

'Shut up, you are awful,' giggled the actor.

I got them seated at a table and warned them to behave. Margo laughed and patted a pretty blonde girl sitting at the next table. 'You're sweet,' she drawled, 'perfectly sweet! Do you fuck?'

The girl gasped and turned away. Margo roared.

'Look, if you can't behave,' I said, 'I'll just have to throw you out.' I was always threatening her with that, but it never did any good.

'I promise to be a good girl,' she smiled at me 'Promise promise!'

She was a nut, but you couldn't help liking her. Back at my table, Sammy was chatting Madelaine.

''Ere, who is she?' He whispered.

I told him all I knew.

'Not much to look at, but I bet she's a lunatic in bed!'

He was welcome.

I suddenly decided the hell with it. I was going home. The place gave me a goddamn pain. I briefed Franco and quietly left.

Who needed it?

# 35

## FONTAINE

The old millionaire bastard can think again if he imagines he can treat *me* like this. Oh no, definitely not. I am not his ugly first wife, ready to be quietly discarded like a frightened white mouse.

Of course, the whole thing has come as such a surprise. Although I should have realised when he came to New York and wasn't ready to leap straight into bed with me that *some*thing was amiss.

There must be another woman. A scheming money grabbing *bitch*! I go hot and cold with sheer and utter anger. *How dare he*.

And as for that Adamo. I shall see he never works anywhere again. How revolting to think of him watching me in bed. Where on earth was he hiding? And Tony, Allen. Were they in on it?

I can't wait to phone my darling friend Vanessa. If there is gossip around, she will know of it.

As it was a Sunday I was forced to wait until at least ten to phone her, and then I got Leonard.

'She's still sleeping, Fontaine. We were at your club last night. When did you get back?'

'This morning. How was the club? Anyone interesting?' Leonard then started to tell me a boring story about how Margo Castile had done a striptease down to brief bikini panties.

'Fantastic bosom,' he added, 'all there, just like a real woman.'

'Injections, darling, you too could have one like that. Although what you're worrying about bosoms for with *your* wife's mammoth proportions I don't know.'

He laughed, slightly embarrassed. 'I'll get Vanessa to phone you when she wakes. I'm sure you two have a lot to catch up on.'

Did he know something?

I prowled around my house. My beautiful house that was up for sale. Oh, just wait until I get in touch with my solicitor tomorrow.

Vanessa didn't phone until twelve.

'Fontaine, sweetie, how are you? When did you arrive?'

'This morning.'

'You must be exhausted!'

'No, I feel wide awake actually. I thought I might come over and catch up on all the gossip. I'm sure there's lots of it.'

'I'm still in bed but I'd adore to see you. Come for lunch, Leonard's out golfing.'

'Divine.'

I was depending on Vanessa being able to tell me exactly what was going on.

I was right. She couldn't wait to tell me all about Benjamin and a ghastly scrubber model called Delores.

'Why on earth didn't you phone me in New York?' I demanded. My God, had I known I would have been in a much stronger position.

'I thought you knew,' replied my loyal friend, sloppy in a blue cashmere cardigan with a button missing. 'Apparently he's given her a huge emerald and diamond ring, a car, and several fur coats.'

'How nice.' My voice was acid.

'What are you going to do?' Vanessa gushed.

I shook my head slowly. 'Divorce the bastard, and take him for every penny he's got.'

# 36

## TONY

I have phoned my lovely Alexandra every day. But each time I get old hawk nose the butler or 'Mummy'. Both tell me Alex is fine, making wonderful progress, but can't come to the phone yet. Charming! Today is the last straw. Phoned as usual and was told Miss Khaled had left to spend Christmas with the Newcombes.

It's Christmas Eve, pissing with rain, and miserable. I have spent a lousy week searching for a new place. Haven't come up with anything. The club has been a drag, everyone away for Christmas. Even old Sammy hasn't been in.

I miss Alex like mad, in *every* way. It is getting difficult not to take some bird home and bang her purely for physical reasons. Fontaine is back, but I haven't heard from her. On top of everything else I have a lousy cold.

I spent hours trying to find the Newcombes in the phone book. Why hadn't I been nicer to Madelaine? Now she was with my Alex somewhere, and I couldn't even phone. Choked! Mind you, Alex should have phoned me or something. But then I remembered she didn't have my number or address. Oh well, get Christmas over with and then she'd be back, everything was going to be fine.

After Christmas Eve the club shut down for five nights, opening again on the night before New Year's Eve. I got flu and collapsed in bed during that time. Ate out of cans and spent a really wonderful Christmas in a cold sweat and fever.

Sadie came over once with a jar of chicken soup and a lecture about how this was all due to too much sex. Too much sex yet!! Ha!!

'You live like a pig,' she said. 'When are you going to settle down, get yourself a decent job. You should see your cousin Leon now, living in a big house at Finchley, a lovely wife, baby on the way. When are you going to find yourself a nice girl that you're not ashamed to bring home to your mother?'

I was too sick to tell her about me and Alex, she'd know soon enough. I gave her a hug and kiss and told her not to worry. 'I'll have a surprise for you soon,' I said.

Dear old Sadie, her one ambition in life was to see me married so she could have a few grandchildren to cluck over.

A doctor friend of mine came by, gave me a shot and told a few dirty stories. The next day, I felt better and got up. I had wasted away five days. Hey—it got me through the holiday season.

I shaved, dressed and phoned Alex. *Still* no reply at her Chelsea flat.

I phoned Ian Thaine and he was out. I wanted to get hold of the contract. I was sure to find a property this week.

I went to the club and looked through the reservations for New Year's Eve. The place was going to be a mad-house—booked solid.

When the hell was Alex coming back?

# 37

## ALEXANDRA

'Super to see you,' Maddy said, 'I have *so* much news.'

It was good to be out of bed and about again. My ankle felt fine, and I was looking forward to spending Christmas at Maddy's house.

'Is Michael here?' I asked anxiously.

'Coming down tonight, it's all over between him and that model girl, you'll be glad to know.'

'Oh,' My heart did a lurch. I couldn't *wait* to see him. 'What's it been like in London all alone? How's Jonathan?'

Maddy shrugged. 'All right. I say, Alex, I've met this awful man and I'm simply *mad* about him!'

'Who?'

'Well after I got back to London, Tony insisted I went to "Hobo" with him. I think I was next on his list. Then I met this friend of his, quite old, a raging cockney, but *so* funny and frightfully sexy. I just couldn't help myself. I did the most ghastly things with him!'

'Maddy! What about Jonathan? And what do you mean you were next on Tony's list?'

'I think he just goes to bed with as many girls as he can, and I was to be the next victim. That's what Sammy says anyway. I saw Jonathan one night, but he was so dull. Sammy makes hats and I went to his office one day and he gave me two. Alex, he's Jewish. My mother would have a fit!'

'Maddy, I can't believe it. Have you actually—well you know...'

'Not exactly—everything but, though. I think I shall after Christmas. I promised him I would. He's frightfully pleased I'm a virgin. Oh, and, Alex, I have the most juicy piece of news. Sammy said that Tony and your dearest stepmother are having a violent affair. What do you think of that?'

I felt sick. How could I ever have let him touch me? It was obscene. How awful. He had probably been laughing at me all along. Perhaps he had even told Fontaine about me. I shuddered.

'Maddy, you're kidding.'

'No, it quite true. Sammy told me all about it, said it's the only reason Tony is at "Hobo". Ghastly isn't it? I say, Alex, I thought we might pop down to the shops, get a few last-minute things.'

I shook my head numbly. 'You go, Mads, I've got a headache.'

# 38

## FONTAINE

'Mrs Khaled?'

'Yes.'

'My name is Ian Thaine.'

'Yes?'

'Er—you do know who I am?'

'No, Mr Thaine, I do not.'

'About the new club, our new club. Tony Blake *has* told you it's me that's putting up the money?'

'What new club?'

'The new club, the place that's going to take over from "Hobo".

181

I thought perhaps you and I should meet since we're going to be partners.'

'Mr Thaine, I don't have the slightest idea what you are talking about, but it sounds interesting, perhaps we *should* meet. Tell me, are you anything to do with "Thaine" shops?'

'I am Thaine shops.'

'How nice. Perhaps you would care to come for tea today, about four. Oh, and Mr Thaine, don't mention anything to Tony Blake about our conversation, let's just sort it out between ourselves first.'

# 39

## TONY

New Year's Eve is a drag. They should print little badges with that slogan on and have everyone who feels the same way as me wear one. A poor excuse for a giant booze up, wreck up and fuck up.

The club was festooned with balloons, paper balls, party hats, blowers, the lot.

I got there very early, choked because I had finally got an answer from Alex's Chelsea flat, and Madelaine had informed me that Alex was out and wouldn't be back until late. Out where? Madelaine Newcombe is an up-tight cow. I left the club's number and my home number and told her to have Alex phone me the minute she came in. I was going to get some things sorted out fast. In fact I didn't see any reason why we couldn't get married at once, nip into Caxton Hall and keep it a secret until the new club was all set. Great idea—maybe tomorrow—New Year's Day. It was the best way. Do it, then tell people. That way Fontaine couldn't try and stick her nose in.

Flowers appeared wearing yellow pants, black shirt, and embroidered sheepskin waistcoat.

'Very smart,' I said, thinking that some of my bread had ended up on his back.

He put on Sergio Mendes and went in the kitchen for food. Not a bad idea, there was at least another hour until people would start arriving. I hadn't phoned Sammy, Massey, or any of the boys. They were probably at Steve Scott's party. I wouldn't go near the little bastard, although his wife (Ha!) had phoned while I was sick and begged me to come.

I had a steak and a couple of scotches—had to get in some sort of festive mood. Then a sheepish Franklin arrived with Molly Mandy—dressed—though only just. She was beaming all over her face, and kept on throwing her arms round his neck and kissing him. He smiled politely. I guess he has finally blown his cherry!

Flowers launched into James Brown and the evening began.

On New Year's Eve it all starts much earlier and by eleven the place was pretty jammed. Franco and his boys were doing a great job serving chicken in the basket and champagne—standard fare for the special entrance tickets. Ian Thaine had a table booked for ten, even old Sammy had reserved. The thing was to make it before twelve, and by eleven-thirty a stream of faces appeared. 'The Twang', Suki with Massey, three of the 'Must', a couple of film stars, two Members of Parliament, and the whole group of models, photographers, actors, who made up the scene.

Then Fontaine, looking really fabulous in some kind of fantastic coat. I hoped Franco had somewhere for her to sit as I didn't remember her name being down as having booked. Trust her to try and screw up the table plans.

'Funky Broadway' was blasting out, and I laid a smile on my face and went to greet her.

She gave me an ice cold look and brushed past, followed closely by Ian Thaine, then Vanessa, Leonard, and a whole tacky group.

'Hi, Ian,' I put out my hand. He squeezed it limply. 'I've been trying to phone you, you're always out.'

Vanessa edged forward and I kissed her on the cheek. Her face was flushed and she looked uncomfortable.

Where the hell is Franco? Some schmucky waiter is sitting Fontaine down with Ian.

'Get me Franco quickly,' I hissed to another waiter.

Franco came running over, sweat streaming down his face.

'What's happening here?' I demanded. 'Get Mrs Khaled her own table.'

He rushed over to where they were all seated and spoke to Fontaine, then he rushed back to me and said, 'Is O.K., Mr Blake. Mrs Khaled is with Mr Thaine's party.'

'What?' I couldn't believe my ears. I stared over at the table and caught Fontaine's eye. She smiled coldly at me and then turned to Ian, beside himself with joy.

I had a funny feeling in the pit of my stomach that I had just blown a deal. Well, screw Ian Thaine and his millions. Who needed him anyway? I could find someone else, there must be lots of people who would be only too delighted to put up some loot for me. Yeah, but who?

Someone was throwing paper balls at me. It was the luscious Carla Cassini, squeezed into a black dress with lots of bosom popping out.

''Ello, Tonee darling,' she purred gaily, sitting safely with her 'Producer' and several other people ''appy New Year!!'

A whole group from Steve Scott's party came rolling in. I was getting loaded. What the hell. Then Sammy with Madelaine—what a daily double! Then Alexandra, my wonderful precious baby had come to see the New Year in with me after all.

I lifted her chin in my hand and smiled softly. 'Hello, my lovely.' She looked knockout in something pink and soft.

'Hello, Tony—you remember Michael Newcombe, don't you?'

Michael the schmuck. What the hell was *he* doing with her? 'Come on,' Maddy shrieked, 'let's sit down before midnight. I say, Tony, has Alex told you the super news, she and Michael are engaged! Can you imagine, we're going to be sisters-in-law!'

There comes a time in life when the bottom drops out. When everything just collapses and you don't care about anything. This was it for me. I stared at my Alex in disbelief, and she looked back at me with her big liquid brown eyes and I felt like I'd been kicked in the stomach by a thousand horses. I made it out to the kitchen and grabbed a bottle of scotch, drank from it until the fire burned through me.

I've never cried in my life. But the kitchen was so god-damned smoky and it gets underneath your eyelids.

Franco came in looking for me. 'Mr Blake, only five minutes to midnight.'

'Yeah, baby.' I was out of my skull. I weaved back inside and grabbed the nearest girl.

'Hey,' she protested as I dragged her up to the stand next to Flowers.

'O.K., everybody,' I yelled! 'Make the most of it. Five more glorious minutes—drink up.'

The girl pulled herself away from me. 'My boy-friend will be choked,' she said dashing off.

I got a waiter and told him to get Miss Cassini up here to announce the New Year. Smiling, escorted by two waiters, she was soon beside me, her 'Producer' beside her. Flowers was just finishing 'Land of 1000 dances' and the streamers were flying, balloons popping.

'Here, count down from ten.' I handed Carla the mike and she started to count—

'Nine, eight, seven.'

Why had Alex done this to me?

'Six, five, four.'

How *could* she do it?'

'Three, two, one—'appy New Year everyone!'

'Auld Lang Syne' blared out and everyone was kissing and laughing and shaking hands. I grabbed Carla and forced my mouth down hard on hers. She struggled, and I bit her tongue. Pay the bitch back for that night.

She pushed me away, and her 'Producer' gave her a stream of abuse in Italian.

I laughed and wandered into the crowd. Happy New Year. What was so bleedin' happy about it?

"'Ere, Tony,' Sammy was calling me over, 'come and 'ave a drink with us.'

'Oh yes, do,' Madelaine urged.

Sure. Sit and watch Alex and Michael gazing into each other's eyes.

'The Twang' appeared and I clung on to her, kissing her fleshy lips and pressing my leg between hers.

'What about you and me later?' I mumbled.

'Oohee, Tony, I can't. I'm with such an important director, and he says there may be a part for me in his next film.'

'Yeah, but I've got a part for you now.' I leered.

She giggled.

'Come on, come down to the office a minute, I've got something for you.'

She hesitated, then thought better of it. 'Another night, Tony, I really can't leave this very important director.'

Screw her then. The room was spinning. Screw everyone.

I could give one to Fontaine now, I could really wham it to her the way she likes.

I went over to her table. 'Happy New Year everyone.'

'Thank you, Tony,' Fontaine replied, twirling her finger in the champagne glass. 'Oh by the way, masses of luck with your new club. Ian has decided to become partners with me here, so count him out, but lots and lots of luck, I'm sure you'll do very well. Oh, and in the circumstances I think it's best that you don't work here any more. I've arranged for you to get two weeks' money, so you really needn't bother turning up after tonight.'

Her face weaved in front of me. Mean cold eyes, thin lips. She ignored me and turned to speak to Ian. They made a good pair. He didn't even dare look anywhere near me. I caught Vanessa peering at me, looking concerned, so I laughed. Didn't they all realise that the place would fold without me anyway?

The noise, the screaming, the bursting of balloons. People tangled up in streamers of coloured paper. I want my baby, Alex. Where is my darling girl?

I staggered out on to the balcony and shut away the gang bang. The cold air hit me like a punch and my eyes were running. I wished I hadn't drunk so much. I wanted to think clearly, sort things out.

I sat on the ground. It was spitting with rain.

Nice. I'd lost my girl, I'd lost my club. What was I going to do? I sat there for a bit and then I thought. So what? There's other girls and there will be other clubs. Life is *great* baby. So I went back inside and drank, danced, shouted, burst balloons, and threw streamers, and drank drank drank.

Then Hal appeared with his old dreamboat, Mamie.

'Hey, Tony, sweetheart, Mamie and I got married, say congratulations.'

I looked at Hal. The last of the great promoters was finally caught. Mamie was smiling and clinging to his arm fondly. She could have been his mother.

'We flew in from Rome to sign some papers, I'm taking over the studio you know.'

What studio? 'Great!' I tried to smile.

Mamie beamed. 'Tony dear, this is my dear friend, Delphine Cohen from Miami. This is her first trip to Europe and Hally and I are going to show her the sights.'

Delphine Cohen was a dyed blonde, somewhere in her late fifties. I nodded at her. She showed me a lot of teeth back. She was wearing a pale mink coat and lots of what looked like real diamonds.

We all sat down and I ordered champagne. Sammy came hopping over to see what was up. Mamie and Delphine went off to the Ladies room and Hal immediately grabbed a hold of me.

'Listen, Tony, don't be schmuck! I know it's not your scene but Delphine Cohen's old man practically *owned* Miami, and he dropped off with a heart attack six months ago, so she's hot as a pistol, raring to go. What are you going to do, hang around this joint all your life? Smarten up, fellow, look at me, I'm a big man now.'

I looked at Hal. He was so stoned his eyes held a permanent glaze.

Mamie and Delphine came back and we drank more champagne. Franco kept rushing over to me with minor dramas but I told him to stuff 'em. 'Hobo' wasn't my bag any more, let someone else run their ass off.

Delphine had plump arms with freckles on. I suppose she wasn't too bad for an older bird. Oh boy, more champagne. Much much more.

Mamie was saying, 'Tony, why don't you come to Rome with us for a few days. Hally's so busy now and we need a man to protect us on the streets. It's true what they say about the Italian men, poor Delphine's black and blue!'

Poor Delphine laughed and jangled a heavy diamond bracelet in time to the music. She was wearing a black dress cut wide and low to reveal a load of fat. I wondered if I could make it? I wondered if I *should* make it?

She was very suntanned, very lined, very over made-up, and very old-fashioned in her dress.

Hal gave me a wink. 'Yeah, Come to Rome, baby, we'll have a great time. What do you say, Delphine?'

'Sure,' she smiled at me, 'wonderful idea. Will you come?' Her eyes lingered on my face asking their own personal question.

I stood up abruptly. 'Yeah, maybe. I'll have to see. Excuse me, got to see what's going on, I'll be back in a minute.'

I rushed out to the desk.

'Happy New Year, Mr Blake,' said Tina.

A group of people were coming in, girls dressed up like Christmas trees, an agent and a well-known American actor. Automatically I went into the whole greeting bit. One of the girls was fantastic, long dark hair with pearls, a white-fringed outfit, staring green eyes. Someone introduced us.

She smiled at me and licked full pink lips.

I felt a familiar stirring, which I knew I should be keeping for Delphine Cohen.

The girl's name was Miranda. I asked her to dance. The agent and the actor had three other girls with them, so nobody minded. Flowers was freaking out on Clarence Carter. I gave him the signal and he switched to Jose Feliciano's 'Light my Fire'.

Miranda was tall and soft in my arms. I held on to her tightly. To hell with Delphine Cohen and all her loot, I wasn't getting caught in one of those sick scenes again.

So I'll be busted out. So what? Something will come along,

something that I won't have to sell myself for. And if it doesn't? Well, that's life. I can always wash dishes.

The girl in my arms isn't Alex, but she is certainly a beautiful girl. Creamy skin, and bright eyes.

'I wasn't expecting to meet anyone like you tonight,' I whispered, pulling her a little closer.

'Me neither,' she said, laughing softly. 'I only flew in from New York yesterday. I thought Englishmen had this reputation for being all uptight and stuffy.'

'What do you think now?'

She just pushed her body hard against mine.

We danced and danced. Hal and his group eventually left. 'Schmuck!' he came up and muttered to me. 'You're blowing a great set-up for another ding-a-ling!'

Fontaine swept out after three with her entourage. Ian Thaine smirking at her heel.

I didn't see my Alex go. I didn't want to, I just wanted to forget her.

Miranda and I left at six in the morning. She was trailing a load of balloons and we walked through the deserted streets to my pad.

I loved her face. It was serious and sexy. She had a boy's firm body with lovely small breasts, and I had to push her long dark hair away to kiss them.

'I just got disengaged when I left,' she said as I explored her with my hands. 'My fiancé could only make it in group scenes. Ugh! I hated that. My daddy said I should fly off somewhere and forget about him. He certainly knew what he was talking about. Oh, I love *that*!'

'My fiancé just got engaged to someone else.'

'How awful. Oh, oh, oh—do *that* again! You should come to New York to forget.'

'Yeah.' I climbed on top of her. She was a gorgeous girl. 'With what?'

She wriggled around. 'Hey, Tony, you're *fantastic*! just *too* much!! Listen. I know. You can come and work for my daddy, he's got all sorts of businesses. Oh—wow! Happy New Year!

Baby, baby, baby! Do that again. We've got this insane disco in New York called "Picketts". It would be just right for you and, ooh, Tony, that's so beautiful, so *wild*. I love it! I love it! Like yes! Wowee, Tony—you're *such* a stud!'

# L.A. Connections

# Power

## L.A. Connections 1

# Los Angeles
# 1997

IT WAS NEAR midnight when the gleaming blue Mercedes limousine pulled up outside the closed book store in Farmer's Market, on Fairfax. A uniformed chauffeur – dressed all in black, including leather gloves and impenetrable sunglasses – stepped out of the car and glanced around.

Nearby, a pretty girl sitting in her parked Camaro hurriedly said goodbye to her girlfriend, with whom she had been chatting on her cellphone, and left her car, locking it behind her.

"Hi," she said, approaching the weird-looking chauffeur. "I'm Kimberly. Are you here for Mr X?"

He nodded and opened the rear door for her. She climbed in. He closed the door and got in the front seat.

"Mr X requires you to put on a blindfold," he said

5

without turning around. "You will find it on the seat beside you."

*Okay*, Kimberly thought. *A kinky one. But that's nothing new.* Kimberly (real name Mary Ann Jones, formerly of Detroit) had been a Hollywood call-girl for eighteen months, and during that time she'd seen plenty. Wearing a blindfold in the back of a limousine was nothing compared to some of the things she'd been asked to do.

She put on the soft velvet blindfold and settled back, almost falling asleep as the limo sped to its destination.

Twenty minutes later the car slowed, and she heard the clanking sound of heavy gates opening.

"Can I take the blindfold off now?" she asked, leaning forward.

"Kindly wait," the chauffeur replied.

A few moments later the limo pulled to a stop. Kimberly adjusted her dress, a skimpy designer number she'd picked up at Barney's warehouse sale. Then she fluffed out her hair, blonde and curly.

The chauffeur opened the door. "Get out," he commanded.

She removed the blindfold without asking, and followed him to the entrance of a large mansion. He opened the door with a key and ushered her inside the dark entry hall.

"Wow!" Kimberly said, squinting at an enormous chandelier hanging above them. "Wouldn't want to be under *that* in an earthquake!"

"Here's your fee," the chauffeur said, handing her an envelope bulging with cash.

She took the envelope and stuffed it in her brown leather

shoulderbag – a Coach original she'd purchased in Century City that same day. "Where's Mr X?" she asked. "In the bedroom?"

"No," the chauffeur replied. "Outside."

"Whatever," she said, thrusting out her size 36C-cup breasts – purchased shortly after she'd first come to Hollywood, on the heels of winning a beauty contest back home.

"Whatever," the chauffeur mimicked, taking her arm and leading her through an ornate living room to French windows that took them out to a black-bottomed swimming pool.

The man had a firm grip on her arm – too firm for her liking. *And how dare he mimic her?* she thought. Where the hell was Mr X? She was ready to get this over and done with so she could get home to her live-in boyfriend – a sometime male model/porn star with muscles of steel.

"Mr X would like to know if you can swim?" the chauffeur said, stopping beside the pool.

"Nope," she replied, wondering why he didn't put on some lights – the place was downright gloomy. "Although I'm thinking of taking lessons."

"You'd better start now," the chauffeur said. And before she was aware of what was happening he had shoved her violently into the deep end of the pool.

She sank to the bottom, rising to the surface seconds later spluttering and choking, her arms flailing wildly in the air. "Help!" she screamed, gasping for air. "I told you – I . . . can't . . . swim."

The chauffeur stood by the edge of the pool, his member out, right hand working hard.

"Help me!" Kimberly yelled, struggling desperately before vanishing under the water for the second time.

The man climaxed over the girl's head as she surfaced again.

"You're *crazy!*" she screamed, before going down for the third time.

And after that, everything went black.

# One Year Later

L.A.
Connections
1

# CHAPTER ONE

MADISON CASTELLI did not particularly enjoy covering Hollywood stories. The lifestyle of the rich and decadent was not her thing, which is exactly why her editor, Victor Simons, had insisted she was the right person for the assignment. "You're not into all that Hollywood bullshit," he'd said. "You don't want anything from the so-called power élite, which makes you the perfect journalist to get me the real inside story on Mr Super-Power, Freddie Leon. Besides, you're beautiful, so he'll pay attention."

*Ha!* Madison thought ruefully as she boarded an American Airlines flight to L.A. *I'm so beautiful that three months ago David went out for a pack of cigarettes and never came back.*

What her live-in lover of two years *did* do was leave her a cowardly note all about how he couldn't deal with

11

commitment and would never be able to make her happy. Five weeks later she'd found out he'd married his childhood sweetheart – a vapid blonde with huge boobs and a serious overbite.

So much for avoiding commitment.

Madison was twenty-nine years old and extremely attractive, although she played her good looks down by wearing functional clothes and barely any makeup. But try as she might, nothing could disguise her almond-shaped eyes, sharply defined cheekbones, seductive lips, smooth olive skin, and black unruly hair, which she usually wore pulled back in a severe ponytail. Not to mention her lithe, five-foot-eight-inch body, with full breasts, narrow waist and long legs.

Madison did not consider herself beautiful. Her idea of good looks was her mother, Stella – a statuesque blonde whose dreamy eyes and quivering lips reminded most people of Marilyn Monroe.

Looks-wise, Madison took after her father, Michael, the best-looking fifty-eight-year-old in Connecticut. She'd also inherited his steely determination and undeniable charm – two admirable qualities that had not hindered her rise to success as a well-respected writer of revealing profiles of the rich, notorious and powerful.

Madison loved what she did – going for the right angle, discovering the hidden secrets of people in the public eye. Politicians and super-rich business tycoons were her favourites. Movie stars, sports personalities and Hollywood moguls were low on her list. She didn't regard herself as a killer, although she did write with searing honesty, sometimes upsetting her subjects, who were usually sheltered in an all-enveloping cocoon of protective PR.

Too bad if they didn't like it; she was merely telling the truth.

Settling into her first-class window-seat, she glanced around the cabin, spotting Bo Deacon, a well-known TV host with an equally well-known drug habit. Bo did not look good; puffy-faced and slack-jawed, it was amazing how he still managed to come to life when the cameras rolled on his popular late-night talk-show.

Madison hoped that the seat next to her would remain vacant, but it was not to be. At the last moment a breathy, busty blonde in a black leather micro dress was escorted aboard by two star-struck airline reps, who practically carried her to her seat. Madison recognized the girl as Salli T. Turner, the current darling of the tabloids. Salli was the star of *Teach!*, a half-hour weekly TV sitcom in which she played a comely swimming teacher who visited a different glamorous mansion every week, causing havoc and saving lives – all the while dressed in a minuscule one-piece black rubber swimsuit, which served only to enhance her pneumatic breasts, twenty-inch waist and endless legs.

"Wow!" Salli exclaimed, collapsing into her seat and fluffing out her mane of blonde curls. "Just made it!"

"Are you okay, Miss Turner?" asked anxious airline rep number one.

"What can I get you?" asked over-eager airline rep number two.

Both men were bug-eyed, peering down Salli's ample cleavage as if they'd never seen anything like it before. *And they probably haven't*, Madison thought.

"Everything's hunky-dory, guys," Salli said, favouring them with a toothy grin. "My husband's meeting me in L.A. If I'd missed the flight he would've been blue-assed pissed!"

"I can believe *that*," said airline rep number one, eyes still bugging.

"Me, too!" agreed the other man.

Madison buried her head in *Newsweek* – the last thing she needed was a conversation with this airhead. She vaguely heard the flight attendant asking the men to leave so they could prepare for take-off; then shortly after that, the big plane began taxiing down the runway.

Without warning, Salli suddenly clutched Madison's arm, causing her to almost drop her magazine.

"I *hate* flying," Salli squeaked, big blue eyes blinking rapidly. "I mean, it's not exactly *flying* I hate, more like *crashing*."

Carefully Madison prised the girl's fingers off her arm. "Close your eyes, take a deep breath and slowly count to a hundred," she advised. "I'll let you know when we're airborne."

"Gee, thanks," Salli said gratefully. "Didn't think of doing that."

Madison frowned. Clearly this was going to be a long flight. Why couldn't she be stuck next to someone more *interesting*?

She folded her magazine and gazed out of the window as the plane took off. Unlike Salli, she loved flying. The sudden rush of speed, that exhilarating feeling of excitement when the wheels left the ground, the initial ascent – it always gave her a thrill, however many times she'd done it.

Salli sat silently beside her, eyes squeezed tightly shut, pouty lips slowly mouthing numbers.

By the time she opened her eyes they were in the air. "Radical shit!" Salli exclaimed, turning to Madison. "You're *am*azing!"

"Nothing to it," Madison murmured.

"No, *really*," Salli insisted. "Your advice actually *worked!*"

"I'm glad," Madison said, wishing Miss Rubber Suit (she'd seen the show once – it was titillating trash) would keep her eyes closed for the entire trip.

Rescue arrived in the form of Bo Deacon, who came ambling over holding a glass of Scotch. "Salli, my darling!" he exclaimed. "You look absolutely edible."

"Oh, hi, Bo," Salli said guilelessly. "Are you on this plane?"

*Smart question*, Madison thought wryly. *It's so nice to be travelling with intellectuals.*

"Yeah, honey, I'm sitting over there," he said, gesturing across the aisle. "Got some old bag next to me. Whyn't we try getting her to trade places?"

Salli fluttered her long fake eyelashes. "How are your ratings going?" she asked, as if that would be the deciding factor on whether she changed seats or not.

"Hardly as hot as yours, babe," he leered. "Whyn't I go back and ask the old bag to move?"

"I'm kinda comfortable where I am," Salli demurred.

"Don't be silly," Bo said. "We *should* sit together, that

way we can talk about your next appearance on my show. Last time you were on we got better ratings than Howard."

Salli giggled, pleased with the compliment. "I did Howard's E cable show in New York," she said, small pink tongue licking her jammy lips. "He's *sooo* rude, but cute with it."

"You're the first broad I've heard call Howard Stern cute," Bo said, shaking his head.

"Well, he is," Salli said. "He's kind of big and gangly, and he's always talking about his little dick. *My* guess is he's really got a whopper!"

Madison realized she was actually sitting next to a real live cliché – the definitive Hollywood blonde. If she recounted this exchange to any of her New York friends, they wouldn't believe her.

"You know what?" Madison said, leaning forward, speaking directly to Bo. "If it'll help out, I can change places with you."

Bo noticed her for the first time. "Hey, little lady, that's very sweet of you," he said, putting on his "I'm a big star, but I can actually be nice to real people" voice.

*Little lady? Was he kidding?*

"On one condition," Salli interrupted.

"What's that, honey?" Bo said.

"I've *got* to sit next to this woman when we land. She's the greatest. She got me through take-off. She's like some kind of, you know, magical medicine man."

Bo raised an eyebrow. "Really?" he said, taking another look at Madison. "You one of those broads with special powers, honey? Maybe *you* should come on my show."

16

"Thanks for the offer, Mr Deacon," Madison answered coolly. "I have a hunch you'd be better off sticking with Max the chimp."

Bo winked. "So you watch the show, huh?"

*When I can't sleep,* she wanted to say. *When I've seen every old movie, and Letterman and Leno are in repeats, and I'm absolutely desperate.* "Sometimes," she said, with a pleasant smile, gathering her things before getting up and moving across the aisle to Bo's vacant seat.

The woman he'd referred to as an old bag was an attractive businesswoman in her forties diligently working on her laptop.

"Hi," Madison said. "I'm switching places with Mr Deacon. Do you mind?"

The woman raised her eyes. "The pleasure is all mine," she said. "I actually thought I'd have to *talk* to him."

They both laughed.

Madison settled into her new seat. This was definitely more her kind of travelling partner.

L.A.
Connections
1

# CHAPTER TWO

"I DON'T GIVE A FUCK," Freddie Leon said, staring coldly at the short, bearded man, who sat across the other side of Freddie's enormous steel and glass desk, uncomfortable in a Biedermeier chair.

"I'm telling you, Freddie," the man said, somewhat agitated. "The bitch won't do it."

"Listen," Freddie repeated. "If *I* say she'll do it, it'll happen."

"Then *you'd* better speak to her."

"I intend to."

"And soon."

Freddie's demeanour was as cold as an Eskimo's dick. "Don't push it, Sam," he said. He did not appreciate anyone advising him. He had not become the most powerful super-agent in Hollywood by listening to other people, especially

19

a man such as Sam Lowski, a half-assed personal manager whose only real claim to fame was his one big client, Lucinda Bennett – major diva, major pain in the ass, major talent.

Freddie Leon was a poker-faced man of forty-six. He had cordial features, ordinary brown hair, matching eyes and a quick, bland smile that rarely reached his eyes. Head and part-owner of the powerful IAA – International Artists Agents – he was nicknamed the Snake because he could slither skilfully in and out of any deal. Nobody ever dared call him the Snake to his face. His wife, Diana, had done so once. It was the only time he'd raised his hand to her.

Sam got up to leave. Freddie didn't stop him – he had nothing else to say.

As soon as Sam was out of the door, Freddie waited a beat and picked up the phone, speed-dialling Lucinda Bennett's private number. She answered, sounding sleepy.

"How's my favourite client?" Freddie asked, putting all the charm he could muster into his cold, flat voice.

"Asleep," Lucinda replied grumpily.

"Alone?" Freddie questioned.

An arch laugh. "None of your business."

Freddie cleared his throat. "What's all this I hear about you being a naughty girl?"

"Don't talk down to me, dear," Lucinda said languidly. "I'm too old and too rich to take that kind of crapola."

"I'm not talking down to you," Freddie replied. "I'm merely reminding you that good behaviour always wins in the end."

"I guess Sam crawled in to see you," Lucinda said, the

lack of respect she felt for her personal manager colouring her tone.

"Exactly," Freddie replied. "He tells me you're planning on backing out of the Kevin Page movie."

"He's absolutely right."

Freddie checked his irritation. Remaining cool was a requisite of his profession. "Why would you want to do a thing like that when the deal is already in place, and you're getting twelve million dollars?" he asked.

"Because Kevin Page is too young for me," Lucinda responded crisply. "I hardly want to look like an old hag on screen."

"I told you three weeks ago, Lucinda, it's in your contract – they'll hire the cinematographer of your choice. You can look eighteen if you want to."

"I'm almost forty, Freddie," she snapped. "I have no desire to look eighteen."

He knew for a fact she was at least forty-five. "Okay," he said calmly. "Twenty-eight, thirty-eight – whatever age pleases you."

"Don't try to placate me. Kevin Page is your client. He's made two hit movies, and now you think you can cement his career by teaming him with me."

"Not true. This deal is about you. It's essential that you keep reaching that younger audience. Demographics count." He paused before continuing. "You're an enormous star, Lucinda, there's nobody bigger. But you've also got to realize that there're plenty of young people who've never heard of you."

"Screw you, Freddie," she responded furiously. "I can do what I want."

"No," Freddie said, his voice hardening. "You can't. If you're as smart as I think you are, you'll do what *I* say."

"And if I refuse?"

"Then I'll no longer be your agent."

"Freddie, dear, sometimes I think you don't get it," Lucinda said, her icy diva voice piercing his ear. "Agents should be kissing my left toe to represent me."

"If that's what you want, Lucinda," he said, his tone perfectly cool.

"Maybe it is," she said, challenging him.

"Let me know," he said. And then he played his ace card. "Oh, by the way – remember that time way, way back, when you asked me to get hold of some early photographs your first husband took of you, and I was able to do so?"

"Yes."

"Strange thing," he said slowly. "I was going through my safe the other day, and it seems I still have a set of negatives."

Her voice rose, hot with disbelief. "Are you *blackmailing* me, Freddie?"

"No," he said evenly. "Merely trying to get you to sign a contract which has been on your desk for over a week. A contract that'll pay you twelve million dollars, star you with the hottest young actor in the country, *and* keep your career at the top, exactly where it should be." He paused, allowing her to mull over what he'd said. "Think about it, Lucinda, and let me know before the end of the day." Before she could reply, he replaced the receiver.

# POWER

Actresses! They'd had to suck so much dick on the way up that once they made it, all they wanted to do was cause trouble.

But nobody caused trouble for Freddie Leon.

He had the power, and he was not shy about using it.

# CHAPTER THREE

NATALIE DE BARGE consulted her Bulgari Swatch watch, a recent present to herself, and swore softly under her breath. How come time passed so quickly? She was running late again, and it made her crazy. She had so much to do before meeting her best friend and old college roommate, Madison, at the airport. *And*, on top of everything else, after driving to LAX, she then had to get back to the studio in time for her spot on the six o'clock news, where she was the showbiz news person on a local TV station. And although she enjoyed what she did, she certainly aspired to do more than cover trivial gossip and even more trivial showbiz events.

Natalie was an extremely vivacious twenty-nine-year-old black woman, with glowing skin, wide brown eyes and a curvaceous body. The bane of her life was the fact that she was only five feet, two inches tall. It pissed her off, because she would have loved to have been born long and lean like Madison, whom she was genuinely excited about seeing. They spoke at least twice a week, but it wasn't as good as living in the same city. Recently Natalie had split with her out-of-work artist boyfriend, Denzl. Quite convenient, since Madison was no longer with David. Ah yes, Natalie thought, they would certainly have plenty to discuss.

Natalie had already convinced herself that she hardly missed Denzl at all, although he *had* possessed a truly beautiful body. The sad truth was that sometimes a beautiful body was not enough. Denzl had leeched off her for over a year, and when she'd stopped paying the bills, he'd disappeared in the middle of the night with her expensive stereo equipment and entire CD collection of soul classics. She missed Marvin Gaye and Al Green more than she missed him.

"Hey, you," said Jimmy Sica, the night-time news anchor recently hired out of Denver. "What's with the hairstyle?"

Natalie turned, checking Jimmy out. He was six feet tall and extraordinarily handsome, which didn't impress her at all because she wasn't into perfect good looks – she preferred her men more on the edgy side. "I cut it," she said, casually touching her short, sleek do. "You like?"

"Makes you look about twelve."

She grinned. "Gee, thanks! I *think* that's a compliment in this town."

"Long hair, short hair – you always look great," Jimmy said, smiling. He had a gorgeous smile – and a gorgeous fair-haired wife, whose picture he kept prominently displayed on his desk.

"Why, thank you, Jimmy," she said, putting on an exaggerated Southern accent. "I never thought you noticed."

Jimmy flashed his best anchorman smile, revealing perfect teeth and a strong jawline. "All the guys around here notice you."

*Was Jimmy Sica coming on to her? No way.*

"I'm meeting my girlfriend later," Natalie said, quickly changing the subject. "She's flying in from New York to research a story on Freddie Leon."

Jimmy was suitably impressed. "The agent?"

"Is there another Freddie Leon?"

"Sounds like an interesting gig."

"Madison's an interesting woman."

Jimmy zeroed in for a long lingering look. "If she's *your* friend, I'm sure she is."

"Uh . . . maybe I'll bring her to the studio one day, give her the grand tour."

"I've got a better idea. My wife and I are having a small dinner on Saturday at the house – why don't you bring your friend over? My brother's in town, and one of my old college buddies. We can make it a party."

"What kind of party did you have in mind, Jimmy?" she asked coyly.

"Not *that* kind of party, honey," he said with a quick laugh. "Sorry to disappoint you, but I'm the straightest guy in town."

"I *know*," she said, flirting mildly despite the fact that he wasn't her type. "That's what I like about you."

He raised an expressive eyebrow. "Really?"

"Yes, really."

They exchanged smiles. *Hmm*, she thought, *he's definitely coming on to me.* Which made her slightly uncomfortable because he was married. Besides, he was way too tall for her.

"I'll run it by Madison and let you know," she said.

"Great," he said.

*Yeah. Great.* Maybe his brother would turn out to be the big love of her life – the prince she was forever searching for. Black, white, multi-coloured – the right guy had to be out there *somewhere*.

*Sure. And John F. Kennedy Jr is gay.*

"I'm outta here," she said, giving him a little wave. "See you later."

Jimmy Sica smiled his brilliant smile. "You can bet I'll be looking forward to it."

L.A.
Connections
1

# CHAPTER FOUR

THE PHONE RANG in Kristin Carr's pale peach apartment. It was past noon and she was asleep. In a vague fog she heard the loud ringing and waited for Chiew to pick up. To her annoyance, her lazy maid didn't do so.

Hazily Kristin realized it must be her private line. *Shit!* She didn't feel great. Too much Dom Perignon and coke the previous night, and a couple of Halcion to help her sleep. *Shit!*

Her long white arm snaked out from under pale peach satin sheets, groping for the receiver. "Yes?" she murmured, husky-voiced.

"Mr X would like to see you," said a female voice.

"Oh, God, Darlene. Not again! I told you after the last time, I'm not interested."

"Would four thousand cash change your mind?"

"Why me?" she groaned.

"Because you're the best."

Kristin thought about her two previous encounters with Mr X. The first time she'd met him in an underground parking lot in Century City as instructed. He was driving a dark pick-up truck with no visible plates and was dressed entirely in black, including opaque sunglasses and a pulled-down baseball cap. Without leaving the truck he'd requested that she strip naked in the parking structure – which fortunately was deserted – and while she circled bare-assed around his truck, he'd jacked off. When he was finished he'd silently handed her an envelope through the window containing two thousand dollars, then hurriedly driven off.

The second time she'd met him in the back row of a movie theatre in Westwood at noon. The darkened cinema was deserted, an Eddie Murphy movie played on the big screen, and Mr X was once more in deep disguise. He'd sat next to her, told her to remove her panties and hand them to him, then he'd satisfied himself on the panties and handed them back to her with an envelope containing cash. When she got out of the theatre he was long gone.

It was the easiest money she'd ever made and also the weirdest. Mr X gave her a bad feeling.

"He's a freak," she said.

"Force yourself," Darlene said.

"All right," she said grumpily, tempted by the exorbitant amount of money, although her instinct warned her to say no.

"It won't be so bad."

"How do *you* know?"

"It's not as if he beats you up or anything. In fact, you told me that last time he didn't so much as touch you."

"I wish he had," Kristin said heatedly. "Then at least I'd know he was *human*."

"His money says he's human. That should suffice."

"Okay, okay," Kristin said with a deep sigh. "What dump do I have to meet him at this time?"

"Hollywood Boulevard. A motel past La Brea. I'll fax you the exact address. He wants you there at seven. And wear white – including shoes, hose and sunglasses."

"Does that mean I get a clothes allowance too?" Kristin drawled sarcastically.

"Four thousand's not bad," Darlene pointed out. "That's a thousand up on last time."

"Big fucking deal."

"Have fun."

*Darlene's a great madam*, Kristin thought bitterly. *All she cares about is the almighty buck. Screw safety.*

She slid out of bed and into the shower. Kristin was the original golden girl – everything natural. A sweep of long blonde hair; all-American features; a curvaceous body with large breasts; and a tangle of fluffy gold pubic hair that turned grown men into horny little boys.

She looked like an angel. But she had a heart of stone and a calculator for a brain.

Kristin had a plan. The moment she had accumulated half a million dollars cash in her safe-deposit box, she was out of the business. Every little four thousand dollars helped.

But still . . . Mr X again, the second time in a week. She shuddered at the thought.

Reaching for a soft pink bathrobe, she wrapped it around her glorious body.

Oh, well, another day. Another step towards her goal. Eventually she'd be free.

L.A.
Connections
1

# CHAPTER FIVE

"WHAT A JERK!" Salli T. Turner exclaimed, her heavily glossed shell-pink lips turning down at the corners, signalling her disapproval.

"Excuse me?" said Madison. She had just settled back into her original seat and was busy thinking about her interview with Freddie Leon – an interview that, if all went smoothly, was due to take place very soon. Victor had promised to set it up through his connection with a mutual friend, even though Freddie Leon was famous for never speaking to the press. In the meantime, Madison planned on talking to his friends, acquaintances, clients and enemies. In fact, anyone who had anything to say about the man.

Salli leaned closer, allowing Madison a frightening close-up of her mascara-caked false lashes. *She's too pretty for that much makeup*, Madison thought. *Why doesn't someone tell her?*

"Bo," Salli said in a half-whisper. "He's a real horny asshole."

"I, uh . . . don't know him," Madison said, wondering why Salli had decided to confide in her.

"You don't have to," Salli snorted derisively. "He's a man, isn't he? And a famous one at that." She wrinkled her snub nose. "All these famous guys think they can get anyone. Do you *know* what he asked me to do?"

"What?" Madison asked, her natural curiosity aroused.

"Invited me into the john so we could make out," Salli whispered. "Only he didn't put it that politely."

"Are you serious?"

"Girl Scout's honour," Salli said. "Ha! Like I'd do it with *him* again. I mean, just 'cause I've got big boobs, blonde hair and the whole bimbo bit, men think I'm like *hanging* around, *waiting* for 'em."

"It must be a problem," Madison murmured sympathetically, wondering what Salli meant by "again".

"I can handle it," Salli said, summoning up attitude. "In fact, I get off on the attention." She shrugged, tugging at her short leather skirt. "Hey – I know I have the equipment, but it's not like I'm *dumb* or anything."

"I'm sure you're not," Madison said gently.

"No, I mean *really*," Salli said, becoming quite heated. "I've used what I've got to get where I am today 'cause it's the only way I could get noticed. Clint Eastwood used what *he* had to become a star. We're just different, that's all."

Madison didn't think it was prudent to point out that Clint Eastwood had been in the business for over thirty years, and had produced and directed many movies. Plus he had his own production company and an impeccable professional reputation. But who knew? Maybe thirty years down the line Salli would have the same – stranger things had happened.

"Here's the truth," Salli said, leaning even closer, so that Madison could smell her peppermint-tinged breath. "My boobs are silicone, 'cause I *know* big boobs turn guys on. I've had all the fat sucked out of my thighs, and some of it pumped back into my lips. I bleach my hair and wear sexy clothes. I'm the proof that it all works. It got me a TV series and a *sensational* husband. *Wait* till you meet Bobby, he'll be at the airport."

"I'd like to," Madison said.

"He's a stud!" Salli boasted. "He'd *kill* Bo Deacon if he heard how disrespectful he was to me."

"Then I suggest you don't tell him."

Salli widened her eyes. "I'm not *stupid*."

"Did you know Bo before?" Madison asked.

"A long time ago . . . before I made it," Salli said. "Then after I got famous, I was on his show a few times and we like *flirted* on camera. Nothing unusual about *that*, I flirt with them all – Letterman, Leno, Howard. *Everyone* does – Pamela Anderson, Heather Locklear, even Julia Roberts. That's the deal. It's expected." She picked up her drink. "Now I'm *married*, so he shouldn't be coming on to me. It's not nice."

"You're right," Madison agreed.

"Anyway," Salli continued, "I'm sure you're bored with hearing all about me. What do *you* do?"

"You'll hate this," Madison said wryly, thinking that maybe she should have mentioned it before.

"What?"

"I'm a journalist."

Salli burst into peals of girlish laughter. "Oh, no! A snoop! And here I am spilling the goods. Now I suppose I'll be all over the cover of the *Star* or the *Enquirer*. True confessions of a sex queen. I'm *such* a ditz!"

"Not *that* kind of journalist," Madison said quickly. "I write for *Manhattan Style*."

"Wow!" Salli responded, her big blue eyes full of surprise. "That's classy stuff. They'd never write about someone like little old *me*." A short hopeful pause. "Would they?"

"Why not? You'd be an interesting interview."

"You think?" Salli said eagerly.

"If you're willing to get into the whole Hollywood sex machine deal. If you were *really* truthful, we could probably have an intriguing piece. I'm sure you've got lots of tales to tell."

"You should *hear* some of my stories," Salli said, rolling her eyes. "I could lay stuff on you that'd make your tonsils hurt! Guys in this town – ha! There's *nothing* I don't know."

"Maybe I should talk to my editor."

"Wow!" Salli said, wriggling in her seat. "Can I be on the cover?"

"We have twelve covers a year," Madison explained.

"Only four of those are show-business-related. That's a tough prize to win."

"Every magazine wants me on the cover," Salli said guilelessly. "Truth is, I sell magazines."

"I'm sure. But my editor walks his own path."

"Remember those pictures of Demi Moore on the front of *Vanity Fair* – all naked and pregnant?" Salli said brightly. "I heard it *zoomed* their circulation. How about *me* naked? Would your editor go for that?"

Madison shook her head. "More *Playboy* than us."

Salli giggled. "I *know*. Only joking. I've been on *Playboy*'s cover three times. They adore me." She giggled again. "Or rather they adore my big boobs!"

"I can imagine you're very popular."

"Why are you coming to L.A.?" Salli asked.

"I'm interviewing Freddie Leon, the agent. You don't happen to know him, do you?"

"Wow! Freddie Leon," Salli sighed. "He's the man."

"I take it he's high on your list of important people?"

"Freddie Leon is only the most powerful agent in Hollywood," Salli said reverently, nodding as she said it, her blonde curls bouncing. "My ambition is that one day he'll represent *me*."

"Have you ever met him?" Madison asked curiously.

Salli hesitated before answering. "Well," she said tentatively, "once . . . a while ago."

"Yes?" Madison encouraged, sensing a story. "What happened?"

"I wasn't his type," Salli said flatly, as if the memory didn't please her.

Madison sensed a story. "Sexually? Or as a potential client?" she asked.

Salli wriggled in her seat. "One day I kinda tracked him in the underground parking of his office. He gave me the big brush." She frowned. "Maybe he's not into sex, 'cause believe me – I do *not* get turn-downs – I mean like *never*!"

"You went there to have sex with him?" Madison asked, surprised at Salli's openness.

"No!" Salli answered indignantly. "I went there to get his attention. I wasn't married then, my career was going nowhere, so I was taking a shot."

Madison decided that Salli's honesty was quite refreshing. There was a certain girlish naïvety hidden beneath the bleached blonde hair and outrageous boobs.

"Are we nearly there?" Salli enquired, beginning to get nervous.

"Yes," Madison said. "Time to prepare yourself. Remember what I told you – close your eyes, take a long, deep breath and slowly count to a hundred. I'll let you know when we're on the ground."

"You're the best!" Salli exclaimed. "Truth is, I don't have any girlfriends, they're all jealous." She gave a wan little smile. "Dunno why – they could have what I have for a price. Well, not *everything*," she added thoughtfully. "They certainly couldn't have Bobby – he's totally yummy and all mine!"

"How long have you been married?"

"Exactly six months, two weeks, three days and, if I had a watch, I'd probably say thirty-three seconds." She laughed, slightly embarrassed. "I don't sound *too* much in love, do I?"

"What does Bobby do?"

"He's like a major danger adventure guy. Rides motorcycles and cars, stuff like that. Jumps over, like, forty-two buses. All the things someone called Evel Knievel did years and years ago, in my grandma's day."

"Oh, yes, I've read about him. Bobby Skorch. The man who takes his life in his hands every day."

"That's my Bobby," Salli said proudly. "Are *you* married?"

Madison shook her head. "Too scary for me," she said, thinking briefly of David, who'd never asked. For two years they'd been inseparable; now they were total strangers.

"I was married before Bobby," Salli announced. "To a psycho freakazoid *asshole* actor."

Madison laughed. "Tell me how you *really* feel."

Salli frowned again, thinking about her ex. "He sued *me* for alimony. Can you believe it? He *still* thinks that one day I'll take him back. Moron *city*!"

"How long were you married to him?"

"Long enough for the bastard to break my arm a couple of times. Not to mention black eyes and bruises and all of that."

"Sounds like a charmer."

"*He* thought he was."

Salli didn't speak again until the plane landed. Then she opened her eyes and unbuckled her seatbelt. "That was a cinch!" she exclaimed. "Want a job as my flying coach?"

Madison smiled. "Think I'll pass," she said, standing up and stretching.

"If you don't have anybody meeting you, we can give you a ride in our limo," Salli offered. "Bobby's into the extra-extra stretch with the Jacuzzi in the back. It's *sooo* Hollywood, but since we're both from little towns, we get off on it!"

"That's okay," Madison said, still smiling. "My friend's picking me up."

"You've *got* to come visit me," Salli said, scribbling her number on a menu and handing it over. "You're *sooo* cool – and great-looking too, in a kind of like, *normal* way."

Madison laughed. "*Thanks*, I think!"

"I mean it," Salli said enthusiastically. "Our house in the Palisades is *amazing*."

"I'm sure."

"Oh, God!" Salli groaned, with an exaggerated shudder. "Here comes the letch."

And Bo Deacon was upon them, all washed and brushed – and drenched in a heavy cologne. He attempted to take Salli's arm, but she was too quick for him, niftily backing into a burly businessman who couldn't be more delighted that he actually got to touch the delectable Salli T. Turner.

An airline rep pushed past, eager to reach his two stars. Madison heard Bo say to Salli in a nasty whisper, "What's the matter, bitch? Trying to forget the people who got you where you are today?"

Madison shook her head and exited the plane, walking briskly through the airport to the luggage carousel.

"Girlfriend!" Natalie yelled, appearing out of nowhere. "You're here!"

Madison was delighted to see her. "*Finally*," she said with a big grin. "It was a long flight."

They exchanged warm hugs.

"The traffic was a monster," Natalie said. "I only just made it."

"You saved me a limo ride."

"How's that?"

Madison indicated Salli T. Turner and Bobby Skorch locked in a steamy embrace by the exit. "I could've hitched a ride with them."

"No way," Natalie said disbelievingly. "The delectable Salli T. Queen of the wet-dream brigade."

"I certainly could've. Salli's my new best friend."

Natalie laughed. "Does that mean you've traded my fine black ass for a bountiful blonde?"

"Yeah, right," Madison said dryly. "Can't you imagine me and Salli T. palling out? We've got so much in common."

"Hmm . . ." Natalie said, staring over. "The husband's pretty damn cute."

Madison glanced at Salli and Bobby, who were still making out, in spite of – or maybe because of – several hovering paparazzi. "All I can see is black leather, long hair, and tattoos."

Natalie gave a dirty laugh. "Sometimes I like 'em rough and colourful."

*Oh, God*, Madison thought. *Shades of college. We've only been together two minutes and we're already discussing men.*

"Here comes my suitcase," she said, lugging it off the moving carousel. "Let's go."

"Before you succumb to the limo ride?" Natalie teased.

"Don't be ridiculous!" Madison replied, laughing.

Within minutes they were in Natalie's car, heading for the Hollywood Hills, where Natalie shared a small house with her brother Cole, a personal trainer.

Madison gazed out of the window. Sunshine, palm trees, fast-food restaurants and gas stations. Ah, L.A., what a place!

In spite of her misgivings about Hollywood and its inhabitants, she was excited about her assignment. Freddie Leon was a high-profile power broker who'd managed to keep an exceptionally low profile in his private life. One wife. Two children. No scandal. And yet here was a man who controlled the most important talent in Hollywood. A man who had everyone's attention.

She was determined to find out everything – unearth the real man beneath the impenetrable image.

It was a challenge.

Madison always *had* relished a challenge.

# CHAPTER SIX

"I'M LEAVING NOW," Freddie Leon informed his executive assistant, Ria Santiago.

Ria glanced up from her desk as Freddie passed by. She was an attractive Hispanic woman in her mid-forties who'd worked for Freddie for just over ten years. She knew him as well as anyone – which didn't mean a lot, because Freddie was an intensely private person who was all business.

"Shall I phone Mrs Leon and tell her you're on your way?" Ria enquired, tapping a sharp pencil on her desktop.

"No," Freddie said. "I have to make a stop. I'll call her myself from the car."

"Very well," Ria replied, knowing better than to ask where he was going.

Freddie stepped into the private elevator he shared with his partner in IAA, Max Steele, and pressed the button for underground parking. When he stepped off the elevator, his maroon Rolls was waiting, waxed and gleaming, which pleased him because he was very particular about his cars – the slightest scrape or blemish drove him insane.

Willie, the parking valet, jumped to attention. "Weather man says it might rain, Mr Leon," Willie said cheerfully, careful to breathe in the other direction lest the Scotch he'd just swigged straight from the bottle hit Freddie in the face.

"The weather man is wrong, Willie. I can smell rain when it's on the way."

"Yessir, Mr Leon," Willie said respectfully, backing away even further. He knew how to kiss ass better than anyone; it got him a five-hundred-buck cash tip every Christmas.

Freddie got in his car and drove carefully from the IAA building – an architectural delight – his mind running over the events of the day, making sure he remembered every detail. The less committed to paper the better – that was Freddie's philosophy. It had worked well for him over the years.

He hoped Lucinda Bennett was not about to cause trouble. He'd negotiated a major contract for her, more money than she'd ever received before, and with Kevin Page as her co-star, their movie together was bound to be a hit. Now Lucinda was attempting to give him a hard time, which wouldn't work. His little remark about the negatives in his safe had definitely got her thinking.

What kind of Hollywood was it today when he had to talk an actress, whose career would be over in less than five years, into accepting twelve million dollars?

Talent. They were a breed unto themselves. Egotistical, ungrateful and predictable. Which is why Freddie was able to convince them he was always right. Deep down they were children who needed tough love and guidance. Freddie gave them exactly what they wanted. Max was his complete opposite. Max was Mr Smoothie. Divorced and always on the look-out for fresh new talent, Max cultivated the playboy image – a racy Maserati, a wardrobe of Brioni suits, a lavish home, and countless beautiful women. The difference between them worked. Freddie handled the major superstars, Max looked after the slightly lower-level luminaries.

Freddie smiled to himself, a smile that did not reach his lips. Max thought he was the smartest guy in town; in truth he was a joke, Freddie's own private source of amusement, for nobody fooled Freddie Leon. And Freddie knew for a fact that for the last three months Max had been involved in secret negotiations to land a high-powered studio job. And if he snagged it he'd leave IAA and Freddie without a backward glance, selling his interest in IAA to the highest bidder.

Freddie had his own future to watch out for. Max Steele was a traitor. And Freddie knew how to deal with traitors better than anyone.

*

Oblivious to Freddie Leon's knowledge of his negotiations, Max Steele wound up a long lunch at the Grill. His luncheon companion was a breathtakingly beautiful Swedish model who bore more than a passing resemblance to a young Grace Kelly.

Inga Cruelle wanted to make the difficult transition from supermodel to movie star.

Max Steele wanted to get into her Victoria's Secret lacy thong and fuck the life out of her.

They both had their agendas.

"So you see," Inga said, as they lingered over de-caff cappuccinos, her long delicate fingers toying with the rim of her coffee cup, "I do not wish to do what Cindy did. A starring role will be too difficult for my first attempt."

The ego of these girls was astounding, Max thought. However beautiful she was, what made Inga Cruelle imagine she could cut it on the big screen when there were hundreds of actresses out there – girls who really knew their craft – who couldn't even get in for an audition?

"Very wise," he said. Max was not movie-star handsome, but at forty-two he had an abundance of boyish charm, a full head of curly brown hair, an in-shape body and plenty of style. Plus his reputation as a cocksman was legendary.

"Elle seems to be doing it the right way," Inga mused, her long tapered fingers now twirling her coffee spoon. "She was quite good in the Streisand movie."

This was their second lunch together, and Max had played his role perfectly. They were the agent and the potential client. Nothing more. By this time Inga – who was used to reducing most men to slobbering idiots – must be wondering why he hadn't made any kind of move.

"Elle's a smart girl," he said briskly. "She works hard."

"*I'll* work hard," Inga said, her exquisite un-madeup face painfully earnest. "I'll even take acting classes if you think it's necessary."

*No, sweetheart. Why would you want to do that? You're a successful model. Don't put yourself out.*

"Right," he said. "Good idea."

"You are so understanding, Max, so helpful," Inga said, placing a delicate hand on his arm.

*Good. She was making the first move.*

"Listen," he said as sincerely as he could manage, "I want to help you, Inga, so I'm sending you to see a director friend of mine. Maybe, if he likes you, I can persuade him to shoot a test."

"A screen test?"

"Yeah, get a feeling of how you are in front of the camera."

Inga laughed, as if it was the most ridiculous thing she'd ever heard. "You've seen my photographs, Max," she said immodestly. "You *know* the camera loves and adores me."

"Still photographs are different. The movie camera has a mind of its own," Max said, marvelling at her conceit. "*You* brought up Cindy. Yeah, sure she's a knock-out, and she *looked* fantastic in her movie. But the big problem was her emotions simply didn't translate. She came across as a blank canvas."

"That is *exactly* why I do not wish to *star* in my first film," Inga said, as if producers were lining up to hire her.

"I could also set something up on a social level," Max said casually, baiting the trap. "Maybe a dinner at the Leons'."

"Your partner?"

"Freddie's dinners are legendary."

"Very well," Inga said. "Should I bring my fiancé?"

What was with this fiancé crap? It was the first *he'd* heard of it.

"I didn't know you were engaged," he said, slightly irritated.

"My fiancé lives in Sweden," Inga said, her precise accent a definite detriment to a film career. "He is arriving tomorrow to spend two days with me at the Bel Air Hotel, then he will fly home."

"Really?" Max said, even more irritated. "What does he do?"

"He's a very successful businessman," Inga replied. "We have known each other since school."

Max was not interested in the details. "When are you returning to New York?" he asked, wondering if she gave great head.

"Perhaps next week," Inga said. "My agency is impatient. However, I told them how important it is that I stay here until I have made a decision about my movie commitments."

"Sounds good to me," Max said, deciding that she probably didn't. Beautiful girls were not as into it as their plainer sisters. "Only I should warn you," he added, "no fiancés at business meetings. Leave him at the hotel."

"This will not be a problem," Inga said coolly.

Max snapped his fingers for the check, which the waiter immediately brought to the table.

*So, she has a fiancé*, he thought. *Am I wasting my time or what? No, she also has that hungry look. The look all these girls have when they want to be movie stars.*

"Time to get back to work," he said, signing the check and standing up.

# POWER

Inga slid out of the booth. She had on white slacks and a pale pink angora sweater, which gently covered the swell of her small, perfect breasts. He knew they were perfect and not silicone-enhanced because he'd seen the nude spread she'd done for famed photographer Helmut Newton in *Vogue*. Eight pages of Inga. Black stockings, matching garter-belt, stiletto heels, and a Great Dane sitting passively at her feet. Very classy. Very naked. Not at all crude.

Max decided the time had come to nail this delectable Swedish morsel. He wanted to go down on her – his speciality – in the worst way.

And soon.

Fiancé or no fiancé, he had no doubt she was a sure thing.

## CHAPTER SEVEN

L.A. Connections 1

# CHAPTER SEVEN

KRISTIN DID NOT possess white hose, which meant a trip to Neiman Marcus. Not such a hardship, as she enjoyed strolling around the luxurious store buying clothes she didn't need and perusing the tempting makeup counters. Shopping was therapeutic, it took her mind off everything, suspending her in a land of soft, sensual lingerie, Judith Leiber purses and Manolo Blahnik shoes.

Recently they'd installed a huge curved martini bar in the men's department. Kristin felt comfortable sitting at it, sipping a vodka martini, daydreaming that she was a perfect Hollywood wife with two darling little children and an important executive big-deal husband. A *faithful* big-deal husband – because all the ones she came across were lying whoremongers who cheated on their wives without giving their infidelities a second thought. And Kristin should know, she'd had most of them in the three years she'd been a call-girl in Hollywood.

Kristin and her younger sister, Cherie, had arrived in L.A. four years ago, with aspirations to become movie stars. Kristin had been nineteen, Cherie eighteen, and like hundreds and thousands of teenage hopefuls before them, they'd saved their money, left the small town they'd lived in all their young lives, and made the trek west in a beat-up Volkswagen.

Cherie was the true beauty of the family, or so everyone always said. Kristin was merely the sister who paled in comparison. But the two of them were the closest of friends, and did everything together.

As soon as they arrived in L.A. they rented a cheap apartment and both got jobs waitressing in a busy Italian restaurant on Melrose. Cherie lasted exactly one week before being discovered by one of the customers – Howie Powers – the bad-boy son of a rich business executive.

From the start Kristin knew that Howie was not good news. She found out that he was heavily into drugs, booze and gambling. She also discovered he was into taking his father's money and blowing it on fast cars and as many women as he could handle. That is, until he spotted Cherie and fell in love.

Howie pursued Cherie relentlessly, taking her to the best restaurants and clubs, showering her with expensive presents, treating her like a queen. It wasn't long before he persuaded her to give up her job and move in with him. Kristin warned her not to, but Cherie wouldn't listen. "He wants to marry me," she said, all starry-eyed and in love. "We're doing it after I meet his parents."

"And when will that be?" Kristin asked.

"Soon," Cherie replied. "He's taking me to Palm Springs to see them."

Kristin didn't believe it for a moment. Howie wasn't the marrying kind. He'd string Cherie along with promises until he grew tired of her, and then he'd dump her. Kristin knew the type – she'd experienced the rich-boy syndrome in high school when she'd given up her virginity to the captain of the football team and he'd boasted to everyone about his conquest. When she'd complained, he'd refused to speak to her again. A sobering lesson about men.

Kristin saw Howie as the sleazy playboy he was – especially when one day he came on to *her* while Cherie was out shopping. She loathed him, but at the same time she was forced to put up with him because of her sister. Until the night she discovered that Howie had gotten Cherie hooked on cocaine. Then she went crazy, fighting with both of them. Cherie told her to back off and mind her own business. So she did.

And two weeks later she'd gotten a midnight call informing her that on their way to Palm Springs to meet his parents, Howie had fallen asleep at the wheel of his Porsche, crossed the dividing line of the highway and smashed head-on into another car. The driver of the other car was killed, Howie was only slightly injured, and Cherie was in a coma.

Now it was four years later, and Cherie lay in a nursing home – a virtual vegetable – while Kristin was one of the most successful call-girls in town. She'd had no choice, somebody had to pay the hospital bills, and that somebody certainly wasn't Howie Powers – who'd instantly vanished out of their lives.

"Excuse me, do you mind if I sit here?"

Kristin glanced up. A man had settled on the stool next to her in spite of the fact that there were many empty places. He was handsome in a rumpled way – not at all Beverly Hills or Bel Air. He had on a white T-shirt, brown leather flying jacket, khaki pants and well-worn sneakers.

"Not at all," she replied carefully, wondering if he'd ever been a customer. Highly unlikely; he didn't look like a man who had to pay for it.

"I'm not coming out with a line," he said in a deep husky voice. "But can I ask you a big favour?"

*No favours, honey. Cash up front. I have bills to pay.*

"What?" she said shortly.

"This'll *sound* like a line," he said, grinning. "Only, believe me, it's not. You see, I gotta go to my father's wedding, and I haven't worn a tie in years, not to mention the fact that when it comes to clothes I have no taste. So . . ." He thrust two ties in front of her. "Whaddya think?"

"What do *I* think?" she said slowly.

"Yes. I need an opinion other than my own. And you look like a woman with an eye for the best."

"Why don't you ask a salesperson?" she suggested.

"'Cause they don't have your class and style," he said, his grin widening. "*You* will make me into the son my dad always wanted."

It was so long since she'd experienced a genuine pick-up that she couldn't help smiling. "You're not from L.A., are you?" she said.

"Nope," he replied. "Arizona. Drove here yesterday. The wedding's on Sunday. What's your pick?"

She stared at the two ties, both boringly conservative. "Come with me," she said, standing up. "I'm sure we can do better." And with that she led him toward the tie department.

An hour later, with a purple Armani tie in his shopping bag, they were still talking. She'd found out his name was Jake and he was a professional photographer – much to his banker father's disgust. He was thirty, unmarried and had moved to L.A. to pursue a new job with a magazine.

"The money's great," he said. "And it'll be a challenge photographing real humans instead of animals and landscapes."

"Real humans? *Here?*" Kristin drawled, sipping her third martini. "You *do* know you're in L.A."

"Don't sound so jaded," he said, "it doesn't go with your looks."

*What the hell are you doing?* she asked herself crossly. *Sitting here flirting with a total stranger. And actually liking it.*

"I have to go," she said abruptly, standing up.

"Why?" he asked, standing too. "Is there a husband I should know about?"

*No, honey. There's a career you wouldn't want to know about. I'm for sale. Lock, stock and fine ass.*

"A . . . fiancé," she lied, pushing the door firmly shut. "And he's *very* jealous."

"Don't blame him," Jake said, giving her a long lingering look.

She felt a jolt of unexpected excitement and wondered what it would be like to sleep with a man who wasn't a paying client.

*Don't even think about it. You're a whore – making money. And that's all you're interested in.*

"Uh . . . good luck with the wedding," she said.

"It's his fourth," Jake said. "He's sixty-two. The bride's twenty."

"I'm sure your tie'll look great."

"Why wouldn't it? You chose it."

They exchanged another long look, before she forced herself to move off towards the escalator.

Just as she was stepping on, he came after her. "I'm staying at the Sunset Marquis," he said. "I wish you'd call me. I'd really love to take your picture sometime."

She nodded. *No chance of that.*

"Goodbye, Jake," she said.

It wouldn't do to be late for Mr X.

L.A. Connections 1

# CHAPTER EIGHT

MADISON WAS ON the phone. "So?" she said, holding the receiver away from her ear because Victor always spoke in an overly loud booming voice, one capable of shattering eardrums "When am I getting my interview with Freddie Leon?"

"You just arrived, didn't you?"

"Stepped off the plane an hour ago."

"What's *wrong* with you?" Victor said loudly. "Can't you settle down for a couple of days and relax like everyone else?"

"I'm not in a relaxing frame of mind, Victor. I'm here to work."

"All work and no play . . ."

"Don't give me that cliché bullshit," she said crisply. "Besides, you should be thrilled I'm a total workaholic." A

57

short pause to let him think about *that* for a moment. "Now," she continued crisply, "when do I get to meet him?"

Victor sighed. "You're an impossible woman."

"Never said I wasn't."

"My contact's out of town until tomorrow."

"*Wonderful* timing."

"Nobody's perfect. Only you."

"Glad you realize it."

"Okay, okay, tomorrow I'll get it set. That's a promise."

"Good." She hesitated a moment before continuing. "Uh . . . by the way, Victor, this is a kind of off-the-wall suggestion . . ."

"Let me hear it."

"Well, on the plane I was sitting next to Salli T. Turner."

"Lucky you!" Victor boomed.

"I wasn't sure you'd know who I was talking about."

"My eleven-year-old son and I watch *Teach!* every Tuesday night. Kind of a male-bonding thing."

"How sweet."

"There's nothing *sweet* about Salli T. Turner," Victor chuckled, sounding uncharacteristically lecherous. "As my son would say – 'she's the shit!'"

"Victor!"

"Sorry," he boomed. "Did I just get carried away?"

"You certainly did," Madison said, laughing. "Totally unlike you."

"What is it you wanted to tell me about her?"

"Actually, I was thinking she might make a good interview."

"*You'd* be prepared to interview Salli T. Turner?" Victor asked, barely able to conceal his surprise.

"Why not? She's refreshingly honest, and I'm sure she'd be prepared to reveal *plenty* about what goes on in Hollywood if you're a young, gorgeous babe with . . . uh . . . quite remarkable assets. It would definitely be a feminist piece with a twist. What do you think?"

"I think if *you* like the idea, we should give it a shot."

"Good. I can fit it in while I'm sitting around waiting for Mr Leon."

"For Chrissake, Madison, stop complaining. I'll get back to you a.s.a.p."

"Do that," she said, replacing the receiver with a grin.

"What's up?" Natalie asked, handing her a glass of cold apple juice.

"Victor's got a yen for Salli T. Can you imagine? Victor *never* looks at any woman other than Evelyn."

"And Evelyn is . . . ?"

"His wife, of course. Rules him with an iron fist and a handy riding crop."

Natalie giggled. "You mean he likes to get his powerful little butt whacked?"

"Not so little," Madison answered, smiling back. "Victor's like a big cuddly bear. *Definitely* not an L.A. bod."

Natalie glanced at her watch. "Damn!" she said, grabbing her jacket. "I gotta get to the studio. Anything you need?"

"Don't worry about me," Madison said calmly. "I'm the perfect house guest. Put me next to a phone and I'm content."

"Cole'll be home soon."

"I haven't seen him in years."

"Then you're in for a shock," Natalie said crisply. "You probably remember him as a skinny, strung-out hyper teen monster. Right?"

"Right," Madison agreed, remembering how Natalie always used to despair because her younger brother was heavily into rap, gangs and getting high.

"Now he's Mr Focused. In fact, he's one of the most in-demand fitness trainers in L.A. Oh yeah," Natalie added, as she reached the door, "*and* he came out of the closet. See you later."

*Cole* was in the closet? Funky little Cole with his punk attitude and macho swagger? Madison shook her head. Who would've guessed? Certainly not she.

Reaching for the phone, she tried the number Salli had given her. No reply, so with nothing else to do she went into the tiny guest room and unpacked her one suitcase. She could have stayed at a hotel – Victor was quite generous with expenses – but Natalie would have been disappointed. Besides, she *wanted* to stay with her best friend, it was probably the only time they'd get to spend together all year. And they certainly had plenty to catch up on. Madison couldn't wait to get down to some good old girl-talk.

At six she clicked on the TV to catch Natalie's entertainment spot on the news. The male news anchor was impossibly handsome, with a dazzling smile. His co-anchor was a young blonde Diane Sawyer clone. The weather man was Hispanic. And then on came Natalie with her show-business news, sparkling with her own particular brand of personality and charm.

"I *hate* doing all that gossip crap," Natalie had confided in the car on their way from the airport. "But at least it gets my face on TV and it's good experience."

Just as Natalie was finishing her spot, Cole walked in. Or at least Madison assumed it was Cole, although this tall, muscled Denzel Washington lookalike in workout shorts and a Lakers tank bore no resemblance to the lanky teen rebel she'd last seen when she and Natalie had graduated college seven years ago.

"Cole?" she questioned.

"Madison?" he answered.

And they grinned at each other, exchanging "You look great!" and "It's been so long!"

*What a waste*, Madison thought, checking him out. Why were all the truly gorgeous ones gay?

"Got everything you need?" Cole asked, swigging from a plastic bottle of Evian.

"I told your sister – give me a phone and I'm happy."

"You here on business?"

"I write for *Manhattan Style*. Profiles on Power."

"Who're you nailing?"

"Freddie Leon, the agent."

"Cool guy."

"You know him?"

"Gave the dude a private session once when his regular guy was sick. Man, he was into it big time."

"A jock, huh?"

"Competitive, that's the vibe I got." Another swig of Evian. "Y'know, I train his partner, Max Steele."

"You do!" Madison exclaimed, sensing a major break. "Cole! I think I love you!"

"Huh?"

"Max Steele's number one on the list of people I need to talk to. When can you set it up?"

"Hey," Cole said, laughing. "Hold on – I said I train him, I do *not* arrange his schedule."

"All I need is a fast half-hour," Madison said, eyes gleaming.

"Max is a busy dude, always runnin' somewhere."

"Of course, I *could* set it up through the magazine," Madison mused. "But if *you* arrange it for me, it'll be so much quicker."

"We run the UCLA track every morning at seven a.m. Whyn't you jog on by an' I'll intro you."

"That's a great idea! I'll be there."

"Yeah . . . an' wear somethin' hot, he's into the femmes."

Now it was Madison's turn to laugh. "I want to *talk* to him, not fuck him!"

Cole grinned. "Hey – you never know . . . he's a real player."

Madison mock-frowned. "Behave yourself. I knew you when you were nothing more than a horny delinquent!"

Cole's grin widened. "Yeah, well, nothing much has changed. 'Cept now I'm horny in the opposite direction."

"So Natalie told me."

He grabbed an apple from the counter. "She kinda gets

a buzz from it – y'know, her brother, the fruit. When the two of us go out we take bets on which guys are straight an' which ones dance with Dorothy. I fake her out every time, 'cause my instincts *rule*!"

After Cole went off to shower, Madison tried Salli again. This time Salli answered her phone, all breathy-voiced. "Hi," she said. "This is Salli T."

"Remember me?" Madison said. "Your flying coach."

"*Course* I do," Salli said, sounding pleased. "Wow! You're actually calling me. Didn't think you would."

"I spoke to my editor. He loves the idea of an interview."

"That was quick."

"Very. Can I come by sometime after twelve tomorrow?"

"Well . . ." Salli said hesitantly. "I really *should* tell my publicist. He'll be mad at me if I arrange something on my own."

"Publicists have a habit of screwing everything up," Madison said crisply, trying to discourage her because dealing with publicists was a total pain in the ass. "Do it if you want, but I should warn you, by the time he gets into it, I'll probably be long gone."

"You're right," Salli agreed. "And I *do* want to be in *Manhattan Style*. It will be like a kind of new image thing for me, right?"

"We'll have fun," Madison promised.

"Okay," Salli said, like a little kid planning something naughty. "I'll give you my address and you can come to lunch tomorrow."

"Looking forward to it."

And she was. There was something very appealing about

Salli T. Turner. In spite of the obvious sex-bomb presen
tation – big boobs and clouds of bleached hair – she had a
certain sweetness and vulnerability. A kind of early Marilyn
Monroe quality.

Madison used her laptop to e-mail New York, requesting
a clippings file on Salli. Then she checked out her copious
notes on Freddie Leon, and finally relaxed, adding a slug of
vodka to her boringly healthy apple juice as she kicked back
in front of the TV and waited for Natalie to get home.

L.A. was turning out to be better than she'd thought.

# CHAPTER NINE

ON IMPULSE Freddie Leon decided to stop by Lucinda Bennett's Bel Air mansion. He was tired of waiting for the signed contracts, tired of being prisoner to her capricious will. He didn't usually make house calls, but since Lucinda was being so difficult, he felt a little hand-holding might be in order. *Hold a child's hand and you can lead them wherever you want* – his father had told him that when he was thirteen, and he'd never forgotten. Yes, it was time to put an end to all this nonsense, as only he could.

Nellie, Lucinda's faithful Bahamian housekeeper, answered the door. "Why, Mr Leon, what *you* doin' here?" Nellie asked, throwing up her massive arms as if to ward him off. "Madam – she no expectin' you."

"Correct, she's not," Freddie agreed, handing her the three dozen red roses he had prudently purchased at Flower

Fashions on the way. "Put these in a vase, Nellie, and give them to her. Tell her I'll be waiting in the living room."

"She be in the middle of a foot massage," Nellie confided.

"I'm sure you can disturb her," Freddie replied, striding into the tastefully decorated living room, overlooking a cool blue infinity pool. Lucinda owned several houses; this one in Bel Air was his favourite. He stood by the window staring out, aware that he might have a long wait. Knowing Lucinda, she'd have to get herself together, check her makeup, hair, clothes. Lucinda was one of the old-fashioned breed of stars, unlike the young actresses today who slumped into his office looking like they'd just stepped out of somebody's bed. Angela Musconni was the hottest young star around, and when Max Steele had encountered her leaving Freddie's office last week, he'd grabbed his partner by the arm and whispered in his ear, "You *gotta* be kidding? I wouldn't fuck her with somebody else's dick." Trust Max to say exactly what everyone else was thinking. Angela looked like a heroin addict on the run, but she was an excellent actress.

After twenty-five minutes Lucinda made her entrance. She was a tall woman with dramatic features and smooth, pale red hair worn in a becoming bob. She was not traditionally beautiful, more striking with her aquiline nose and piercing eyes, but her talent was ferocious and her fans equally so. Lucinda had been a star for almost twenty years.

"And to what do I owe this honour?" Lucinda asked, sweeping into the room, resplendent in a pale beige cashmere pantsuit and extremely high heels.

"I'm playing errand-boy today," Freddie said, kissing her on both cheeks.

Her finely pencilled eyebrows shot up. "Freddie Leon – errand-boy? I can hardly believe it."

"Believe it, sweetheart. I'm well aware of how insecure you get, so I'm here to personally pick up your signed contract."

Lucinda's finely rouged scarlet lips pursed dramatically. "Really?"

"Lucinda, dear, you should know better than anyone, there is *no way* I would push you into anything that wasn't right for you."

Lucinda collapsed into an overstuffed chair, kicking off her shoes like a petulant ten-year-old. "It's not that I'm being difficult, Freddie," she said. "It's simply that I don't want to look . . . foolish."

"How could *you* possibly look foolish?" Freddie asked forcefully.

"Well, Dmitri said—"

"Who's Dmitri?" he interrupted.

"Someone I've been seeing," she said, becoming uncharacteristically coy.

Oh, God, now he got it. She had a new man in her life, and like the legions before him, he was putting in his ten cents. "Have I met Dmitri?" he asked.

"No," Lucinda replied, still verging on the coy side. "But you will."

"I'm sure," Freddie said. "Is he around today?"

"He's out by the pool," Lucinda said. "Let's not disturb him, he might be sleeping."

*God, no!* Freddie thought. *Let's not disturb him if he's working on a tan. Jesus! Where do these women find these men?*

"Have I told you that you look incredibly beautiful today?" Freddie said, changing his strategy.

"No," Lucinda said, slightly flustered. "As a matter of fact you haven't."

"Well, you do. You're my most important client and that's why I'm here." He began pacing. "Sign the contract, Lucinda. Otherwise, this deal is about to fall through, and I wouldn't want that happening to you."

She hesitated. He could sense that she was almost his – not quite.

"But Dmitri said that if I was to star opposite Kevin Page, it might make me appear . . . older," she said, waiting for him to convince her that this was not so.

"You – older?" Freddie shook his head. "Every young guy in America will be *wishing* he was in Kevin Page's shoes."

"Yes?"

"Come along, Lucinda, let's go into your office, sign the contract and then I can get on with my day."

"If you're *really* sure . . ."

"Have I ever guided you wrong?"

Fifteen minutes later he was back in his car with the signed contracts on the seat beside him. Sometimes a little personal attention was all that was needed. And for a twelve-million-dollar deal, Freddie didn't mind putting out.

*

The two men playing racquet ball were going at it with a "take no prisoners" attitude. Both men were very fit; even so the vigorous workout was making them sweat profusely.

# POWER

Max Steele slammed the final shot, clinching the game. "Fifty bucks!" he yelled triumphantly. "And I want cash."

Howie Powers slumped against the wall. He was a sandy-haired man in his thirties, with crooked features, a stocky build and a permanent tan. "Shit, Max!" he complained, irritated at being beaten. "You gotta win at everything?"

"And what's wrong with that?" Max said cheerfully. "No point in playing if you don't plan on winning."

Howie stood up straight. "I might go to Vegas for the day tomorrow. Wanna come?" he offered. "We can hop a ride on my dad's plane, he's goin' on business."

"Don't you ever work?" Max said, grabbing a towel as they made their way to the locker room.

"Work? What's that?" Howie said, smirking.

Max shook his head. "Beats me why I hang with a bum like you," he grumbled. "You're useless."

"Why would I *wanna* work?" Howie questioned, genuinely puzzled. "I got plenty of bucks."

"Yeah, handouts from your old man."

"You're forgetting my trust fund," Howie said, with another satisfied smirk. "Who needs handouts? I only take 'em 'cause my old man insists."

"Aren't you ever bored?" Max asked, thinking how much he would hate having nothing substantial to do.

"Bored?" Howie said with a manic laugh. "You gotta be shittin' me. There's not enough time in the day to cover all the things I do."

Max nodded knowingly. "Yeah, like uh . . . go to the track, hang with the guys, play poker, smoke some primo grass, pick up girls, gamble, do a little coke, go out and get drunk . . ."

"Sounds like a life to me," Howie said, the smirk creeping back on to his face.

"*I'm* into work," Max said forcefully. "I get off on the power."

"You, you're an over-achiever," Howie said. "Me, I'm into getting my rocks off while I can still get it up!"

Max thought to himself that if *he'd* been born with a silver spoon up his ass, he'd probably enjoy the good life, too. But he'd had to work for everything he'd achieved – starting off in the mail room at William Morris, where he'd hooked up with Freddie. A fortunate meeting, for the two of them had risen together, until they'd made their break ten years ago and started their own agency. Now they were one of the top three agencies in town. In fact, right at this moment IAA represented the biggest stars, the hottest screenwriters *and* the best directors and producers in Hollywood.

And yet, in spite of their well-earned success, for quite a while now Max had been thinking of making a change. Being an agent was one thing, but running a studio would give him a lot more of the power he craved. Hey, if guys like Jon Peters could do it, he was in, like a sailor in a room full of hookers.

The only problem was telling Freddie, who had no idea he was thinking of defecting, and would throw a total shit-fit when he told him of his plans. But that was nothing Max couldn't handle.

Not a word until the deal was done. Only then would he think of the perfect way out.

L.A. Connections 1

# CHAPTER TEN

NATALIE RUSHED IN from the studio all smiles. "Did you catch me on TV?" she asked enthusiastically. "How about the bit I did on Salli T. and Bo Deacon?"

"Must have missed that," Madison said. "What did you say?"

"Oh, something like, 'Guess who flew into L.A. together,' you know – provocative inside gossip. The audience loves it."

"They *weren't* together," Madison pointed out.

"Who cares?" Natalie said airily. "They're both publicity hounds. They'll get off on hearing their names mentioned."

"If you say so," Madison murmured, not so sure that Salli would be thrilled.

"I *know* so," Natalie said confidently. "You should read some of the letters I get – all they want is the dirt."

71

"That's sad."

"No. That's just how it is."

"If you say so," Madison murmured.

"C'mon," Natalie said, full of energy. "Move your butt, I'm buying you dinner and hearing all about what happened with you and David."

"It's a short story," Madison said crisply.

"Good. You tell me yours, I'll tell you mine. Did you get to see Cole?"

"I certainly did," Madison said, grabbing her purse. "He came home, jumped in the shower, took off again and told me to tell you he won't be home tonight."

Natalie rolled her eyes disapprovingly. "He met some big showbiz executive – the type who picks a boy of the month. Trouble is, Cole won't hear anything against him."

"You're not his mother so quit trying to run his life, *especially* his love life."

"Ain't *that* the truth." Natalie sighed, as they headed for the door. "But hey – I'm *way* more street smart than he is, he *should* listen."

"He told me he trains Freddie Leon's partner, Max Steele," Madison said.

"Didn't I mention it?"

"No, you didn't. But Cole told me if I'm on the jogging track at UCLA at seven in the morning, he'll introduce me."

"Seven!" Natalie wailed, opening up her car door. "Honey, don't count on *me* to fix you coffee."

They went to Dan Tana's for dinner and sat in a cosy booth.

"Did I tell you I'm doing a piece for the magazine on

Salli T.?" Madison said, ordering a vodka martini because she felt like it, and knew it would guarantee a good night's sleep.

"Yes. Didn't old Victor get all excited when you mentioned her name?" Natalie said, requesting a beer.

Madison nodded. "I plan on getting her to talk about the men who run Hollywood. They all seem to have this thing about hookers and strippers with hearts of gold – y'know, Julia what's-her-name in *Pretty Woman* – the one with the big hair. And Demi Moore in *Striptease*. I'd like to get Salli's take on it."

"Good, you can give me all the leftovers," Natalie said, studying a menu. "I'll use them on my show."

"You're really into your show, huh?"

"Hmm," Natalie said, making a face. "Sometimes I am, sometimes I'm not. It's so predictable. All these people out there plugging books, movies and their goddamn exercise tapes – and *I* have to pretend I'm interested."

"What do you *want* to do?"

"Be a network news anchor, of course."

"Sounds like a plan."

"Yeah?" Natalie said ruefully. "How many black news anchors do *you* see?"

"Here's *my* philosophy," Madison said. "If you want something bad enough, you gotta go for it."

"Let's order," Natalie said. "*My* philosophy is – food solves a shitload of problems!"

A few sips of her martini and Madison began talking. "I think I genuinely loved David," she said wistfully. "But the truth is he got scared."

"Typical!" Natalie interrupted.

"Some men say they're okay with strong women, only when they find themselves with one, they can't handle the pressure," Madison continued. Natalie nodded her agreement. "We never talked about marriage," Madison added. "We were happy just being together. Until one day he went out for cigarettes and failed to come back." She paused, remembering, shaking her head because the memories were still painful. "The thing that hurt the most was that after he left, he ran off and married his high-school sweetheart. *That* was the *real* pisser."

"Girl, I know exactly what you mean," Natalie said. "Denzl and I had this great thing going until I woke up one morning and the slippery sonofabitch wasn't there. Nor was my CD collection, which, as you can imagine, *totally* freaked me. Losing him was one thing, but losing Marvin Gaye?"

They stared at each other and suddenly burst out laughing. "Who'd believe *this*?" Natalie exclaimed. "Two smart, hot-looking women like us, and we just got ourselves dumped!"

"At least we can laugh about it now."

"Maybe *you* can."

"Think about it," Madison said. "*You* weren't supposed to be with Denzl. And *I* wasn't supposed to be with David. Somebody bigger and better will come along."

"Hmm . . . bigger," Natalie said with a dirty laugh. "I like it!" Then she added quickly, "*Not* that I'm interested in getting involved again."

"Me neither," Madison agreed. "All this double-standard

crap about how only guys can go out and have sex whenever they want, and it doesn't mean a thing. Women can too. Why should *we* have to be in a relationship?"

"Right on!" Natalie agreed. "Give me a great-looking guy with a great body. We'll have great sex, and don't call me, I'll call you."

"Yes!" Madison said. "As long as they use a condom. Things sure have changed since we were in college."

"Oh, by the way," Natalie said, "the anchorman on my show asked us over to his house for dinner tomorrow night. I said we'd go. Okay with you?"

"You're not fixing me up, I hope," Madison said suspiciously.

"He's married."

"In that case, okay. I am *not* into fix-ups."

A waiter hovered by their table. "The gentleman at the bar would like to buy you two ladies a bottle of champagne," he said.

They both looked over to the bar. An ageing playboy with an ill-fitting black toupee perched on top of his head waved merrily.

"Tell the gentleman thanks, but no thanks," Madison said.

"Yeah, suggest he save his money for his old age," Natalie added. The waiter moved away. "That's the oldest pick-up line in the world," Natalie said, grimacing. "Surely the poor old dude could come up with something more original?"

"Pick-up lines are universal," Madison said wisely. "They go on for ever."

"How much you wanna bet he'll come over spouting another corny line?"

Madison shook her head. "No balls," she said.

"Is that a rug he's wearing, or am I seeing things?" Natalie said, stifling a crazed giggle.

"Do *not* make eye contact," Madison warned, suppressing her own laughter. "Otherwise, he *will* come over, and then we'll be forced to insult him."

Two minutes later the man was standing by their table. He was seventy-two and still considered himself a player. "Surely it's not true that two beautiful young women like you do not drink champagne?" he demanded.

"Hello," Natalie said, putting on a sugary, sexy voice. "I'm a stripper at the Body Shop on Sunset. Be there at ten tonight. Fifty bucks and I'll perform a special lap dance just for *you!*" The man took a step back. "See you later," Natalie said, barely able to contain her laughter. The would-be player hurriedly returned to the bar. "Guess he doesn't watch TV," Natalie dead-panned.

"I like your line," Madison mused. "Maybe *I* should use it sometime."

"Ha!" Natalie said. "Who'd believe *you* were a stripper? But me, black and pretty – why the hell not?"

"Oh, God! Don't start getting into racial stereotypes. You drove me insane with that crap in college."

"I'm simply saying it the way it is," Natalie said stubbornly. "*You're* a beautiful *white* woman. *I'm* a good-looking *black* woman. Guys *respect* you. They look at me and think – she's black, therefore she's easy."

"You're full of it."

"I live in this world," Natalie said, her voice rising. "I *know* I'm talking truth."

"What do you imagine *I* do – reside in a fairy-tale tower?"

"*You're* not black. *You* don't get it."

"I can't believe we're having this conversation again."

"Anyway," Natalie said, "I'm *glad* you're no longer with David, 'cause if he could run out on you, then he wasn't worth shit."

"The same goes for Denzl."

"What we *should* do is concentrate on our careers and become media moguls. You can *own* your magazine, and *I'll* be the first black Barbara Walters. How's that for a deal?"

"You got it going, girl."

"I love it when you try to talk black," Natalie said, giggling.

"What do you mean?"

"You're too uptight to get into jive talk."

"*Me*. Uptight?"

"You gotta loosen up – get yourself some attitude."

"What *kind* of attitude?"

"Like this, girl," Natalie said, high-fiving her. "Like this."

And they both broke into fits of raucous laughter.

L.A.
Connections
1

# CHAPTER ELEVEN

KRISTIN WAS putting the finishing touches to her appearance when the phone rang. She reached for it, and murmured, "Hello?"

"A change of plan," Darlene said, all business. "Tomorrow, not tonight."

"You mean Mr X is cancelling?"

"Not exactly cancelling, merely rescheduling."

"Oh," Kristin said, relieved and yet disappointed because she had wanted the money.

"Tomorrow. Same time, same place," Darlene said. "Which won't interfere with your lunch. You'll have plenty of time to rest up between appointments."

"Thanks so much," Kristin drawled sarcastically.

"I know you don't like seeing Mr X," Darlene continued,

"but what's not to like? He doesn't touch you, and he pays more than any other client."

"That's what's so weird," Kristin said. "I'm telling you, Darlene – there's something strange about him."

"Oh, *please*," Darlene said, dismissing her fears as if they didn't matter. "Guys with fetishes, what's so unusual?"

Kristin put down the phone feeling depressed. She'd wanted to get it over with and done with. She'd psyched herself up for another kinky encounter, now she faced a long evening ahead with nothing planned.

For a moment her mind wandered over the events of the day, and she thought about Jake, the photographer with the tie problem. He had no idea who she was or what she did. "I'd really love to take your picture sometime," he'd said. So why not? It certainly wasn't going to lead to anything. Why couldn't she do something *she* might enjoy for a change?

On impulse she picked up the phone and obtained the number of the Sunset Marquis.

When the hotel operator answered, she realized she had no idea what his surname was. "Uh . . . do you have a Jake staying there?" she said. "He's a photographer. I seem to have forgotten his last name."

"Let me check that out for you," said the operator obligingly, and a few moments later she was put through to his room.

He answered immediately. "Bunny?" he said.

"Not Bunny," she replied, wondering who Bunny was.

"Hey – *Kristin*," he said, sounding pleased to hear from her. "What a *nice* surprise. Why are you calling?"

Why *was* she calling? "Uh . . . I lied," she said.

"You did?"

"I . . . I don't have a fiancé. What I *do* have is a very jealous husband."

"And you couldn't wait to tell me."

"We're separated."

"That's encouraging."

A long pause, during which neither of them spoke. Kristin finally broke the silence, surprising herself. "Are you free for dinner tonight?"

"Me?" he said, obviously stalling for time.

"No. Mel Gibson," she said shortly, sorry she'd asked.

"Uh . . . are you saying that you *can* have dinner with me?"

"That's exactly what I'm saying."

"What time would you like me to pick you up?"

"I'll meet you," she said quickly, not wanting him to know where she lived.

"Okay," he said slowly. "And where will that be?"

Her mind wouldn't function. She didn't want to meet him where there might be people who knew her. "I'll . . . I'll come to your hotel," she said. Wrong! Now he would think she was easy. Ha! If he only knew *how* easy. Expensive, but easy all the same.

"If that's what makes you happy," he said. "What time shall I expect you?"

It was so long since she'd gone on a legitimate date that she had no idea what to suggest. "How about seven thirty?" she said, thinking that would give her plenty of time to change out of her pristine white outfit and get into something more suitable.

"You got it," he said.

"You're sure you can do this?" she asked, half hoping he'd tell her he was busy.

"Would I say yes if I couldn't?"

"No . . ."

"What's your number in case I need to reach you?"

"I'm not at home," she lied, quickly putting down the phone so she wouldn't have to answer his question. Then she was mad at herself. *What are you doing?* she thought. *Why are you going out on a stupid date with a stupid guy that you don't even know?*

*Because I'm entitled to have some fun sometime, aren't I? I'm entitled to behave like a real human being.*

*No, you're not. You chose to be a whore. Stick to what you know.*

She turned up at his hotel on time – punctuality was a prerequisite of the perfect call-girl. He was waiting in the lobby, still looking somewhat rumpled in his brown leather jacket and longish hair. She'd changed outfits ten times, finally settling on a simple black dress and a couple of pieces of good jewellery given to her by an Arab arms dealer. As soon as she saw him she realized she was too dressed up.

"Hey," he said, walking toward her. "This is a really nice surprise."

"It is?" she answered.

"You bet," he said, smiling. She smiled back. "Where do you want to go?" he asked.

"Uh . . . wherever *you* want to go."

"I'm the new boy in town."

She considered the possibilities. Clients took her to all

the expensive clubs and restaurants. A few of the maître d's knew her and what she did. "How about . . . Hamburger Hamlet?" she said, thinking fast.

"You look too pretty to hang out at a hamburger joint."

"Don't be silly," she said. "I love hamburgers."

"If that's what you'd like."

*I like you*, a little voice screamed in her head. *I like you because you're normal, because you're not going to pay me. Because you don't know what I do, or anything about me. I like you because you like me just for who I am.*

"My car or yours?" he said, walking her outside the hotel. "Yours is probably better because all I've got is a beat-up old truck, which, I can assure you, has definitely seen better days."

"Let's take yours," she said, thinking that tonight she wanted to feel like an ordinary girl out on an ordinary date. Nothing wrong with that.

"So," he said, helping her into his truck. "What made you change your mind?"

"About what?"

"About going out with me?"

"You never asked."

"'Cause when you got on that escalator today, I knew you had no intention of ever seeing me again."

"Why do you say that?"

"I can read people."

"See how wrong you were."

"I'm glad."

They went to the Hamburger Hamlet on Doheny and sat in a booth, side by side. Kristin ordered a double cheeseburger and an extra-thick chocolate milkshake. She felt like she was back in high school.

Jake had plenty to say. He talked about photography and the people he'd met and worked with. He told her about the six months he'd lived in New York and how he'd hated it. She learned that although he was an award-winning photographer with several prestigious exhibitions behind him, he did not take himself too seriously. He made her laugh about his ageing father and his father's future bride. She loved listening to him. He was interesting, funny, self-deprecating and undeniably attractive.

"I haven't done this in years," she said, enjoying every decadent minute as she sipped the thick chocolate shake through a straw.

"Done what?"

"Pigged out."

"How come?"

She hesitated for a moment. "My, uh, husband doesn't frequent places like this."

"Let me take a guess," Jake said, peering at her intently. "Your husband is very rich and much older than you – correct?"

She nodded. *Yes, Jake. They're all older than me, and they're all rich and lecherous and disgustingly kinky.* "That's right," she murmured.

"You're too beautiful to stay in an unhappy marriage," he said, his brown eyes genuinely concerned. "You're in a trap, you should get out while you can."

"I know," she said, thinking that marriage was a metaphor for the life she really led.

"Do you have a good lawyer?"

"The best," she answered, summoning up a mental picture of suave Linden Masters, the man who represented all of Darlene's girls.

"Then you should tell him you want out."

"I . . . I plan to," she said, studying his lips, wondering what it would be like to kiss him – a real kiss, not a paid-for performance.

He caught her looking and began asking more questions. She immediately became evasive, not wishing to tell him anything. After a while he realized he was being stonewalled and backed off, calling for the check.

"Come on," he said, getting up. "I'd better take you back to your car. It's been a tough day, and it's rapidly catching up with me."

A tough day? Choosing ties? What was *his* problem?

"Fine," she murmured, pretending to be totally unconcerned. "I'm tired, too."

This was unbelievable. He was in line to get something for free that she usually charged exorbitantly for, and he was *tired*! Or maybe he was meeting Bunny – whoever *she* might be.

Whatever. She didn't care.

Next time she'd think twice before trying to experience life like a normal person.

she was sure he had of the actresses and models he could

*L.A. Connections*
*1*

# CHAPTER TWELVE

THE RUNNING TRACK at UCLA was not crowded. Madison was surprised; she'd expected it to be packed. But then, of course, it was quite early. She'd gotten there just before seven and began jogging in place because it was chilly. She looked around to see if she could spot Cole and his client. No sight of them yet.

Cole had suggested that she wear something hot, but she was not into luring Max with her supposed sex appeal – she was sure he had all the actresses and models he could handle. So she'd put on a warm tracksuit, stuffing her long black hair under a red baseball cap.

She was busy doing leg stretches when Cole and Max finally came into view. Cole was certainly an impressive-looking hunk of male flesh. Max Steele paled in comparison, although he was still attractive in a flashy, up-front Hollywood-mogul way.

"Hey, Madison!" Cole said, waving at her. "What're *you* doin' here?"

"What does it look like I'm doing?" she replied, trying not to shiver. "Jogging, of course. You think us New Yorkers never get out on the track?"

"Didn't realize you were into it," Cole said, playing his part well.

"Oh, yes," she lied. Truth was she wasn't into physical activities at all, and had to force herself to go to the gym twice a week.

Max was busy checking her out. "Hello," he said, extending his hand. "Max Steele."

"*You're* Max Steele?" Madison said, feigning surprise. "This is such a coincidence."

"How's that?"

"Max Steele of the International Artists Agency?"

"Unless there's another Max Steele lurking around that I don't know about."

"I'm Madison Castelli. I write for *Manhattan Style*. I'm in L.A. to do a piece on your agency."

"Then how come I don't know about you?" Max said, still checking her out and liking what he saw.

"Because I'm supposed to be meeting with Freddie Leon tomorrow. I was told that *he* was the man to talk to."

"Oh, you were told that, were you?" Max said, obviously irritated. "Were you also told that Freddie and I happen to be partners?"

"I understand Freddie Leon runs the agency, but of course I've heard of you."

"That's nice," Max said sarcastically. "Truth is, you'll be hearing a lot more about me."

"I will?"

"Bet your pretty ass." She frowned. He didn't appear to notice. "Want to jog with us?" he asked.

"I'd love to." Second lie of the day.

They started out slowly – Cole moving to the front – while Madison stayed behind next to Max. "How did you get started in the agency business?" she asked.

He began to talk, telling her all about the mail room at William Morris, and how he and Freddie had made a daring escape and started IAA together.

Within minutes she was out of breath. "You know what?" she gasped. "I haven't done this in a while. Can we go somewhere for breakfast when you're through?"

"I haven't even seen your credentials," Max said, squinting at her. "Maybe I shouldn't be talking to you."

"My credentials?" she said, pretending to be offended. "I write the Profile on Power piece every month. Call my editor if you want. Victor Simons. I'm sure he'll be happy to fill you in."

"I don't have to," Max said. "On account of the fact I've decided to trust you. But I *would* like to see some pieces you've written."

"I'll have New York e-mail you my interviews with Magic Johnson, John Kennedy, Jr., Henry Kissinger. Oh yes, and there's an interesting piece I did with Castro when I visited Cuba."

"Okay, okay, I'm impressed," Max said, laughing. "You're too attractive to be that serious."

"And you're too smart to come out with tired old lines."

"Did you ever consider a modelling career?"

"Did *you*?"

He laughed again and turned to Cole. "How do you know this lady?"

"She went to college with my sister."

"What do you say," Madison interrupted. "Can we meet for breakfast when you're through jogging?"

Max nodded, sliding a small cellphone from his jogging pants pocket. "Anna," he said into the phone, "cancel my nine o'clock breakfast, and book me a table for two at the Peninsula."

Madison grinned. "I guess that's a yes."

*

Breakfast with Max went well. He regaled her with stories of all the people he'd discovered whom he claimed he'd then made into enormous stars. Madison listened intently. It was difficult eliciting information about Freddie Leon because all Max really wanted to do was talk about himself and his achievements. She did manage to get some choice quotes; Max was hardly modest.

She knew she was not being up-front with him regarding the interview, but she sensed that if he knew the piece was about Freddie Leon, he'd clam up. It was quite clear that Max's only interest was himself.

On their way out he offered to supply her with photo-

graphs and also suggested that later in the week she should
come up to his office and they'd continue their conversation.

"There's something else," he said, as they stood outside
the hotel waiting for valet parking to bring their cars.

"What's that?" she asked.

"I shouldn't be telling you this," he said. "It's strictly
confidential, and completely off the record."

"I'm intrigued."

"In the next few weeks I'll be making an announcement
that'll blow everyone away."

"How interesting. If I promise not to write it until you
give me a green light, can you tell me what it is?"

Max shuffled his feet – quite large in fashionable silver
and grey Nikes – then he looked around as though someone
might be listening over his shoulder. "I . . . I can't say
anything right now."

"Well . . . you know where to reach me. And yes – I'd
love to come by your office sometime."

"When are you seeing Freddie?"

"It's being set up right now."

"You want me to put in a word for you?"

"That would be nice."

"Only remember – you need a star for this piece, and
baby, you're *lookin'* at him."

"Right," she murmured, not appreciating the "baby"
one little bit.

"Good." And he got into his shiny red Maserati and
drove off.

L.A. Connections
1

# CHAPTER THIRTEEN

"DUNNO WHAT YOU DID, but I gotta say it – you're the freakin' best!"

"Thanks, Sam," Freddie replied, cursing his luck for running into the small-time personal manager in the parking area of his building. The very sight of the short, bearded man aggravated him. "Who are you here to see?"

"You, of course," replied Sam, tugging on his greying beard as he followed Freddie to his private elevator.

"I wasn't aware that we had an appointment," Freddie said, knowing full well they didn't.

"We don't," Sam said. "Took a chance you'd be free for a minute or two."

"I have a very busy morning, Sam," Freddie said, stepping into his elevator. "You'd best make an appointment with my assistant."

"Who needs appointments?" Sam said, trailing him into the elevator. "I can say what I have to on the way up."

*No escape*, Freddie thought sourly. "What's on your mind, Sam?"

"It's like this," Sam announced, quite full of himself. "I'm here t'do you a favour, but if you don't have time to hear what I havta say . . ."

Freddie swallowed his annoyance. "Go ahead," he said shortly.

"I'm givin' you the low-down," Sam said, speaking out of the side of his mouth like a character in a Damon Runyon movie. "Max Steele's plannin' on takin' a powder an' sellin' his share of IAA to the highest bidder. This I got from someone real close to the source."

Freddie had learned in life to always listen, never volunteer information. So instead of saying, "I already know," he was quiet for a moment. Then he said, "Tell me what you have."

"Well," Sam said, puffed up with his own importance, "your partner's been havin' closed-door meetings with Billy Cornelius regarding Orpheus Studios. An' from what my *very reliable* source tells me, Billy's plannin' on bringin' in your Maxie boy as head of production, with an eye to him taking over the whole shebang when Billy dumps Ariel Shore."

"Interesting," Freddie said, his poker-face giving nothing away.

"Word on the street is that these negotiations are CIA secret," Sam said, digging at his teeth with a dirty fingernail.

him, she was a killer in business with a charming manner and plenty of style.

Billy Cornelius was another matter. Billy, a skinny, red-faced, seventy-two-year-old billionaire, didn't just own Orpheus, he owned a whole slew of entertainment companies and business corporations. A media king – he was also a sonofabitch who'd stab you in the back soon as look at you.

Over the last year Max Steele had formed an alliance with Billy. An unlikely duo, but Freddie had never complained, because having Billy Cornelius on the side of IAA was a definite plus.

Ria buzzed him. "Your wife's on the line."

He picked up the phone. "Yes," he said into the receiver.

"I was wondering," Diana said tentatively, "would you like me to fax you the seating plan for tonight?"

Damn! He'd forgotten. They were having another one of Diana's boring little dinner parties. "Who's coming?" he said shortly.

"The people you approved last week," Diana answered, sounding uptight. "Remember? We went over the list together."

"Fax me the list and seating. I'll check it."

"I could do a good job if you'd let me," Diana ventured.

"No, Diana, leave it to me," he replied.

"Fine." And she put the phone down hard.

Freddie sat behind his desk quietly for a moment, wondering why he was always so mean to his wife. He knew he treated her in a cold, uncaring fashion, and yet he couldn't help himself. It was as if he resented the fact they were

"So I gotta say to myself I'd better alert Freddie – just in case he don't know."

Freddie gave Sam a long, cold look. "Do you think anything happens in this town that I'm *not* aware of? Do you honestly think that?"

Sam backed down. "Just makin' sure," he said, fidgeting nervously, because being in Freddie Leon's presence was enough to give anyone a case of the hives.

"I appreciate the information," Freddie said evenly.

"An' I 'preciate you gettin' that bitch to sign her contract," Sam grumbled. "What a cooze!"

Freddie froze him with a look. "Don't *ever* call Luci names," he said, as the elevator stopped at his private f "She's your client, and you should show her nothir respect. She's made you a lot of money over the year be wise to remember that."

"I . . . I kiss her goddamn ass," the little ma turning red in the face.

Freddie gave him another long, cold loo Ria's desk, entered his private office and sla Sam Lowski was the dregs; if he hadr Lucinda early in her career, he'd be now without her as a client, he was less than abhorred having to deal with scum. P right on the money – confirming wh

Ariel Shore was the studio hea friend of Freddie's. He'd obser and enjoyed her success, bec and knew how to play the ga married. Poor Diana. In public she was the perfect wife – never let him down, was always by his side, well dressed, cultured. At home she was available in the bedroom whenever he was in the mood – which wasn't often, because he'd lost interest in sex with his wife. They'd been married for over ten years, and there was no more of that sexual passion he'd felt in the first throes of their relationship. Also, she was the mother of his children; therefore, he could no longer regard her as a sexual object. Besides, sex drained a man's energy, and he needed every ounce of energy for his work. Thank God she had her charity functions and the children to keep her busy.

He considered the fact that news of Max Steele's upcoming defection was out on the street. If Sam Lowski knew, everybody must. Freddie decided the time had come to do something about it. Yes, he would deal with Max as only he knew how.

Ria knocked and entered his office carrying two faxes from Diana, which she handed to him. The guest list and the seating placement. He studied the guest list first. Max Steele was on it; he was bringing Inga Cruelle. Vaguely, Freddie remembered Max telling him about the gorgeous supermodel. "Most fuckable piece of ass you've ever seen," had been Max's description. "We gotta put her in something."

*Yes, we must,* Freddie thought. *We'll put her in the middle of a face-to-face confrontation between you and me, Max. Because if you think you're going to walk without telling me, you have another think coming.*

Freddie continued to study the list. Lucinda and her new

boyfriend, Dmitri. That should be interesting. Kevin Page and his current girlfriend, Angela Musconni – nothing like new young talent to give an evening heat. The other guests were a billionaire businessman and his wife, a New York financier and his L.A. mistress, and the head of one of the TV networks. Not a bad mix.

Freddie put down the list. An invitation to the Leons' was a much sought-after prize – he had to give Diana points for creating evenings that everyone fought to be invited to.

He buzzed Ria. "Get me Ariel Shore," he said abruptly. "And if she's not at the studio – find her. I need to speak to her immediately."

# CHAPTER FOURTEEN

KRISTIN HAD a regular, once-a-month client who liked to lunch with her before watching her perform with a girl of his choice. Over lunch he made her regale him with tales about her previous month's customers, and he in turn fed her unbelievable dish about Hollywood stars. Not that she was interested – she couldn't care less about who was doing what to whom. As a professional she kept her mouth shut and did her job to the best of her ability. Ratting on a john was a no-no.

So instead of revealing the truth, she made up tales of outrageous sexual goings-on, while her client listened with gleaming eyes and a satisfied smile.

Usually after her session with this particular client, she visited her sister in the nursing home just outside Palm Springs where – as long as Kristin could afford to pay the bills – Cherie resided permanently. Today she couldn't go because Mr X had rescheduled. Damn Mr X! Everything about him made her skin crawl. His disguise, his kinky demands. He was sinister, maybe even dangerous.

She dressed for lunch in a simple, pale beige Armani suit. Underneath the jacket she wore a plunging cream blouse and no bra so that the darkness of her nipples showed through the flimsy fabric. Her client enjoyed having other men in the restaurant look and lust. Little did he know that several of them were also clients of hers who knew exactly who she was and what she did.

He liked to lunch at Morton's, where he had a regular table. Kristin arrived first and sat down, wondering, as she always did, what this particular guy's trip was. He was powerful, not unattractive, with a manic if somewhat over-the-top personality. He could probably take his pick of most of the young actresses and models in Hollywood, and yet he chose to lunch with her once a month, and then pay for sex. Not so strange, really. If she was a date he'd be forced to make small-talk, send flowers, buy gifts, build up to the final moment. With her it was a sure thing, he'd pay her and she'd go home. No strings. A simple business deal.

Plus she had no objections to performing with another girl. Why would she? It was her profession. She knew that a lot of the women who did what she did were lesbians, so turned off by men and the way they treated women that they'd switched leagues. Although Kristin knew how to make all the right moves, she had no inclination in that direction.

She watched her client as he made his entrance, smiling

and joking with several people as he passed by their tables. He was a nice enough guy, she didn't mind their monthly meetings. It was seeing Mr X later that was freaking her out.

"Hi, Max," she said, as he sat down at the table.

"Hi, doll," Max Steele replied, summoning the waiter and ordering an iced tea. His mind was dodging this way and that. There was so much going on, and yet all he could think about was his date that night with Inga Cruelle. She was giving him a hard time and he liked it. Max considered the chase everything. Once he scored, he was out of there. Which is why he'd never married, and why he enjoyed meeting Kristin once a month. No demands, sensational sex, and the two-girls-together fantasy he'd dreamt about since first drooling over the centrefolds in *Playboy* at thirteen.

"How have you been, Max?" Kristin asked politely.

"Pretty damn good," he replied. "I'm in shape, business is zooming, it's all happenin', babe."

"Still single?" Kristin enquired, not really interested, but she knew he liked her to appear as if she cared.

He roared with laughter. "You know *me*, baby – one woman could never do it for me." He took a couple of healthy swigs of iced tea and leaned eagerly toward her. "So c'mon, honeysuckle, gimme the goods – what's been going on in hooker land?"

"Well," she said, toying with the glass of wine she'd prudently ordered, although she didn't usually drink on appointments. "There was this politician who came into town from Washington, someone *very* high up in the Senate."

Max leaned even closer; this was the kind of stuff he got

a buzz from. If only he could get names out of her, but she was adamant about never revealing her clients' identities. In a way it was a good thing because it meant she'd never talk about him. "You wanna give me his name?" he asked, hopeful as ever.

An enigmatic smile. "You know I can't do that."

He ran a hand through his curly brown hair. "You're somethin' else, babe. How come you chose to be a hooker, not an actress or model?"

"You ask me that every time, Max."

"What's the answer?"

"I can *choose* who I sleep with." *Not true*, she thought. *If you can choose, why are you meeting Mr X, when you know he's a sick pervert?* "Models and actresses – they have to cater to people, they're worried about their next magazine cover, their next movie. Me – I never have to worry about the next client, they're lining up."

"You gonna name the politician?" Max asked eagerly, hungry for information.

Kristin shook her head. "You know I'm not."

"Okay, okay," Max said, giving up. "But you can at least tell me what he got up to – or down to – depending on his trip."

"Well . . ." Kristin began, making up a fabulously erotic story that made Max's eyes bug.

Their ritual was always the same. An hour-long lunch, during which she fed him sexy stories which she swore were true, and some of which were. Then she'd follow his car to the Century Plaza Hotel, where he'd rented a penthouse suite ahead of time. Another girl would be waiting, and after snorting a little coke, the three of them would go into the bedroom. Max would sit in a chair, watching and barking orders, while they did everything he requested. Sometimes he joined in. Sometimes he didn't. Then he would hand out cash and everybody would go home.

She'd repeated this scenario with Max Steele for almost a year now, and the order of events never varied.

Idly she wondered how he'd react if she told him the only reason she was doing this was to support her sister who lay in a coma in a nursing home. Would he offer money and help her to get out of the business? Or would he merely put an end to their monthly meetings because she made him feel guilty? It was difficult to know.

Max glanced at his gold Rolex. He'd almost cancelled Kristin today, thinking he should save himself for the evening's activities. But then it had occurred to him that it might be better to indulge in some afternoon sex. That way he wouldn't be too anxious with Inga. He'd be in control, so if he *did* manage to get into her sexy little thong, he could give her the great lover treatment he was famous for. Sex with Kristin would keep his appetite at bay. She was very good at what she did.

He studied her face as she sipped her wine. She was quite a knock-out, in a totally different way from Inga. Blonde, fresh and pretty, the girl-next-door look with a body to die for.

Max had only been in love once, and that was with a girl in high school who'd treated him badly, humiliating him in front of his friends. He'd never forgotten her, never forgiven her either.

It was nice to be with a woman whom he controlled for an hour or so.

It was satisfying to be able to call every shot.

# CHAPTER FIFTEEN

"Hi." SALLI T. answered the door of her huge Pacific Palisades mansion herself. She was barefoot, wearing a skimpy little sundress that barely covered the top of her thighs. What was most evident were her long skinny brown legs, huge silicone boobs, white-blonde hair and an abundance of makeup. "It's *so* good to see you," she said, full of enthusiasm. "Come on in."

Madison entered the vast mansion, where she was immediately set upon by two small, fluffy white dogs who jumped all over her ankles, sniffing and barking.

"These are Muff and Snuff," Salli T. said, making no attempt to call them off. "Aren't they adorable? Bobby bought them for me on our wedding day. We took them on our honeymoon, and they crapped all over the hotel bedroom. Boy – was he *furious*! But you know what? Now he

105

loves them as much as I do." She scooped up one of the barking dogs and nuzzled its furry little face into hers. "I'm so *happy* when I'm around animals. Do you have a pet?"

Madison shook her head. "It's not that easy when you live in a New York apartment."

"Tell you what," Salli T. said brightly. "If these two ever have puppies, I'll send you one. I read this thing once where it said you live ten years longer if you own a dog."

"Ten years longer than what?"

Salli T. squealed with laughter. "You're so *funnee*!"

Madison looked around. The front hall was all soft pile carpets and soaring mirrored walls. Directly facing her was a giant portrait of Salli T., bare-assed, lying face down on a white sheepskin rug.

"That was from my first *Playboy* shoot," Salli said proudly. "I know it's kind of a trip to hang it in the front hall, but it sure gets a lot of attention!" She giggled. "Bobby *loves* it. He brings all his friends by – just to take a peek."

"I bet he does," Madison murmured.

An Asian man in tight orange pants and a white tank top appeared in the hall. "This is Froo," Salli said, waving in his direction. "Anything you want, all you gotta do is ask. He's fixing us lunch. And after, if you want a massage, he does that, too."

"No, thank you," Madison said quickly.

"You *sure*?" Salli said, leading her through the living room, outside to an Olympic-size, brilliant blue pool. "If you let him near your feet, it's totally orgasmic!"

Madison took in the view of the ocean, which shimmered like a glorious picture postcard.

"We can swim after lunch," Salli said. "It's *real* good for the boobs – keeps 'em up, if you know what I mean!"

"Didn't occur to me to bring my swimsuit," Madison said.

"That's okay, I'll lend you something."

The thought of her slim figure in one of Salli T.'s outrageous black rubber swimsuits brought a smile to Madison's lips.

"We're eating beside the pool," Salli said. "*Sooo* Hollywood. But, y'know, this is what I dreamed about when I was a little girl. I *wished* I'd get to live in a place like this. And my wish came true. Sometimes I have to pinch myself – isn't that crazy?"

"You know," Madison said, sensing that this was going to be a terrific piece. "That's exactly what I'd like to talk about. Your dreams, how you got here, the way the people you met on the way up treated you, the men in Hollywood, all of that stuff."

"Wow!" Salli giggled. "Usually people just wanna know how big my boobs are."

"Well, today," Madison said, "will certainly be different."

# CHAPTER SIXTEEN

JUST AS Kristin had finished dressing all in white for her meeting with Mr X, her phone rang. To answer or not to answer – that was the question. It might be Mr X cancelling again, or perhaps the nursing home with news of Cherie. She couldn't allow herself the luxury of *not* answering her phone, so she quickly picked up.

"Is this the hamburger queen?" said a male voice.

"Huh?"

"It's me, Jake. Am I catching you at a bad time?"

On impulse she'd given him her number, but she'd never thought he'd call. In spite of herself she felt a tiny buzz of excitement. "Well . . ." she said hesitantly.

He sighed. "Guess I am."

"No, no . . ." she said quickly. "I can talk."

"I realize this is kind of late notice," Jake said, "but I'm on my way to my brother's house for a home-cooked meal. Can you come?"

*No, Jake, I will be otherwise engaged with a disgusting perverted freak.*

"I'd love to, only—"

"I know, I know," he said ruefully. "You've probably got guys lined up around the block."

What did he mean by *that*?

"Actually, I have a business appointment," she said stiffly.

"I was thinking," he said, "what with me doing all the talking last night, I never got around to asking what *you* do."

*I'm a call-girl, sweetheart. Extremely expensive. Very talented. So if you know what's good for you – stay away.*

"I . . . uh . . . I'm a makeup artist," she lied. "I go to people's homes and give them a professional makeup."

"No kidding?"

"Yes. It's what I do."

"Hey," he said cheerfully, "in that case maybe I can hire you."

"Excuse me?" she said, frowning.

"Photographer. Makeup artist. We should work together."

One part of her wanted to keep talking, but sanity warned her to steer clear of all personal relationships. Getting involved could only lead to big trouble.

*Then why did you give him your phone number?*

*How the hell should I know?*

"Uh . . . I have to go," she said, aware that she sounded flustered. "I'm running late for my appointment."

"How about I give you my brother's address, and maybe you can drop by later when you're through?" A meaningful pause. "I'd very much like to see you again, Kristin."

*And I'd like to see you, too, Jake.*

"Okay," she said, reaching for a piece of paper and a pen.

She had no intention of going – but just in case she changed her mind . . .

*

On their way to Jimmy Sica's house in the Valley, Madison recounted her afternoon with Salli T. "I never thought I'd say this," she said. "But Salli's adorable. If I was a guy, I'd probably fall in love with her – silicone boobs and all."

"Oh, come *on*," Natalie said disbelievingly, racing her car along the freeway. "Salli T. Turner is the definitive Hollywood cliché. All giant tits and candy-floss hair."

"She *plays* that role," Madison explained. "Which is why she's so successful. But I'm here to tell you that underneath all the dumb gloss and glitter lurks a very nice little kid who's enjoying every moment. Trust me – this woman had it tough getting to the top."

"Sure," Natalie said with a toss of her head. "*I* can tell you about tough."

"Don't be such a mean bitch."

"I'm *not* a bitch," Natalie objected indignantly. "I'm merely voicing the way *everyone* thinks about her."

"No, you're being judgemental. If you got to know her, I promise you – you'd really like her."

"Okay, okay, if you say so," Natalie said, barely missing a huge truck as she skimmed past. "And how about the cute husband? Did you get to meet him?"

"He's in Vegas," Madison said, making sure her seat-belt was firmly buckled because Natalie's driving was a trip indeed. "He called ten times, and they had these lovey-dovey conversations. It was quite sweet. They certainly seem to be in love."

Natalie pulled a face. "Think I'm gonna throw up!"

"Will you stop being such a cynic."

"Thing *I'm* surprised at is you," Natalie chided, as she zoomed her car alongside a Ferrari. "I'd take a bet with you that their marriage will not make it to the end of the year."

"No, Natalie," Madison said, shaking her head. "You're wrong. What they have between them is genuine. Y'see, they both come from small towns, both arrived in L.A. determined to make it big. Now they've got everyone falling all over them to do anything they want, and they're loving it. I'm telling you, I like her a lot, and so would you if you got to know her."

Natalie was still unconvinced. "*Puleease*," she said.

"She told me some great stories," Madison offered.

This got Natalie's attention. "Hmm . . ." she said, eyes gleaming. "Tell me every detail."

"No. You'll have to read about them in the magazine like everyone else."

"Oh, come *on*," Natalie complained, almost rear-ending

a white Toyota. "You wouldn't do that to me – your best friend."

Madison placed her hands on the dashboard. "Oh yes I would."

"Here's the deal," Natalie said, blithely changing lanes. "*You* give me all the juicy bits before the magazine hits the stands, and *I'll* do a whole programme on it – y'know, give the mag a big plug so people'll be racing out to buy it."

"I hate to tell you this," Madison said, "but they race out anyway."

"Why can't you be like everyone else and get behind plugging something?" Natalie grumbled as she exited the freeway, cutting off a man in a sports car who gave her the finger.

"In my next life," Madison joked.

"You're no fun."

"Never said I was."

A few minutes later Natalie pulled her car to a shuddering stop in front of a modest country-style house on a quiet side-street. "Okay, so I'd better fill you in on Jimmy Sica."

"What about him?" Madison asked, releasing her seatbelt, relieved they'd arrived in one piece.

"He's incredibly handsome, with a lovely wife – picture displayed prominently on his desk." A succinct pause. "And . . . I think he's coming on to me."

Madison raised an eyebrow. "What do you mean, you *think* he's coming on to you? Either he is or he isn't."

"Well," Natalie said unsurely. "I *guess* he is, but somehow I can't believe it 'cause he's married to such a gorgeous woman."

"Oh, like you're *not* gorgeous. Is that your new trip – putting yourself down?"

"I'm not his type."

"Maybe it's not a *type* he's looking for. Maybe a fast blow-job would do it for him."

"Get your mind out of the gutter, girl!"

Laughing, they both got out of the car.

"You know, you're awfully naïve, Nat," Madison said, as they walked towards the house. "Married men are all the same, none of them would say no to a little action on the side."

"*Now* who's sounding cynical."

"It's the truth," Madison said defensively.

"Yeah, yeah, you and your truths."

"Listen, do what you want, but I'm here to tell you that I have absolutely no respect for married men who cheat."

"Get a life, girl. That's major unrealistic."

"I suppose so, especially when we have a president who does it all the time." She shook her head. "What in hell happened to moral values?"

Natalie shrugged as they reached the front door. "Moral values – what's that?"

"Wasn't it something we used to believe in when we were in college?" Madison said dryly. "Remember?"

"That was before all these tell-all books came out revealing every little detail."

Madison frowned. "I find it totally disheartening that every president from Kennedy on was running around the Oval Office with his dick in his hand and WD40 on his zipper!"

# POWER

Natalie giggled and pressed the doorbell. "A power hard-on! Tell me – please – where can I find one?"

Madison said sardonically, "Like I said – try the White House."

# CHAPTER SEVENTEEN

KRISTIN WAS EXCITED, and it wasn't at the thought of seeing Mr X again. As she sat behind the wheel of her car, driving towards her destination, she couldn't keep her mind off Jake. It was ridiculous really, because she was too smart to let anyone come between her and her goal of scoring enough money to get out of the call-girl business. And if she allowed herself to get involved, that's exactly what would happen.

*Forget about him*, her cold, calculating side warned her. *He's only another john who doesn't think he has to pay.*

And yet . . . he had a warmth and a laid-back sincerity, friendly eyes and a smile that melted her heart.

For the first time since she'd started in the business she actually felt a deep sexual longing. She *wanted* to sleep with him, she yearned to have long, leisurely unpaid-for sex, wake up in the morning to find herself safely enclosed in his strong arms.

*Get real.*

*Why should I?*

She pulled up at a stop light and began drumming her fingers nervously on the steering wheel. Enough thoughts about Jake; she'd better get ready to deal with Mr X and his bound-to-be-kinky demands.

She'd dressed all in white, as instructed, including a short dress and white-framed Christian Dior sunglasses. Darlene had faxed her the address of the motel where she was to meet him, and instructions to sit in her parked car outside cabin six until further notice.

A car pulled up next to her, and the male driver leered suggestively through the window. She pretended not to notice and drove quickly off.

The motel – way down Hollywood Boulevard – was a seedy, run-down dump. Automatically she checked that her car door was locked as she pulled into the dilapidated courtyard and drove up to cabin six.

A drunk ambled out of the shadows carrying a half-empty bottle of cheap booze. He winked at her, burping loudly as he lurched past her car.

Ten minutes passed. She tried to stay calm, thinking only of the four thousand dollars and how it would pay her sister's hospital bills for a while.

IF ONLY I DIDN'T HAVE TO DO THIS!

*Ah, but you do.*

A gloved hand knocked on her window. A man in a chauffeur's uniform all in black – his peaked cap pulled low over his forehead – opaque wraparound shades completely covering his eyes.

Was it Mr X?

She couldn't tell.

"Leave your car here and come with me," he said in a muffled voice.

She took a deep breath and got out of her car, locking it behind her.

"Over here," the chauffeur muttered, leading her towards a dark-coloured limo parked curbside.

He opened the rear door and she obediently climbed inside. He moved to the front of the car and slid behind the wheel.

"Where are we going?" she asked, a certain numbness taking over her mind.

"Mr X requires you to put on a blindfold," the chauffeur said, without turning round. "You will find it on the seat beside you."

She groped on the plush leather seat, found the blindfold and placed it over her eyes.

Four thousand dollars. Cash.

It didn't matter. This was the last time she was doing business with Mr X.

# CHAPTER EIGHTEEN

DIANA LEON greeted her husband at the front door of their Bel Air mansion. "You're late," she said crossly.

"Didn't realize I was on a time clock," Freddie said, entering the house, which was now full of caterers preparing for their dinner party.

"How can you do this to me?" Diana said, glaring at him.

"Do what?" he said, distracted and out of breath.

"Invite an extra two guests."

"You can fit 'em in," he said, hurriedly heading for the stairs.

"No, I can't," Diana said, angrily following him. "Our dining table accommodates sixteen people, now you've added two more."

"So we'll squeeze a little. No big deal."

"Why didn't you put them on our original list?"

"Diana," he said irritably, "do I tell you how to run the house?"

"No."

"Then don't tell me how to run my business," he snapped. "It's extremely important that Ariel is here tonight."

"*And* her husband, whom you can't stand," Diana pointed out, her voice tart.

"Sometimes you have to put up with the guy behind the woman, or *under* the woman, as the case may be."

"Ariel was here last month," Diana said, folding her arms.

"So now we're having her again."

Diana followed him into the bedroom. "Why did you leave it until the last minute?"

"Oh, for God's sake," he snapped, entering his private bathroom. "I have to take a shower. Leave me alone." And with that he slammed the door in her face.

Once rid of Diana, he stood in front of his marble vanity staring blankly into his shaving mirror. Moments passed before he cleared his mind and began thinking coherently. He still couldn't believe that Max would be stupid enough to attempt to sell out his half of IAA without consulting him first. Surely he had some idea of what it would be like to have Freddie Leon as an enemy?

No, Max Steele probably didn't, because Max thought with his dick most of the time which was useful when dealing with female clients, but as any fool knew, the brain has more staying power than the dick any day. The brain is *always* hard.

*

"Hello, ladies," Jimmy Sica said, throwing open the front door of his house and ushering them inside.

"Hi," Madison replied, as they entered the comfortable house. Natalie was right, Jimmy Sica was incredibly handsome in an *I'm-a-TV-anchorman-with-a-sensational-smile* way.

"Nice to *meet* you," Jimmy said, squeezing her hand a tad too tightly as a chocolate-box-pretty woman appeared behind him. "And this is my wife, Bunny," he added, putting his arm around Bunny's narrow waist.

"Bunny?" Madison questioned.

"I *know*," Bunny said, with a wide smile that matched her husband's. "It's *such* a silly name, everyone says so. I was nicknamed Bunny as a little girl, and it kind of stuck. I collected bunny rabbits, still do, only Jimmy makes me hide them in a closet."

"Now, now," Jimmy said, patting his wife on the ass. "Mustn't go giving away all our secrets. Madison's likely to write about them. She's a big-time writer from New York."

"I *know*," Bunny said, wriggling away from him. "You already told me, Jimmy pie." She dazzled Madison with a big smile, revealing perfect white Chiclet teeth. "Welcome to our home, Madison. We're *so* excited to meet you. I hope we can all become good friends."

*Oh God*, Madison thought. *Why did I agree to do this?*

123

*I'm perfectly happy alone. I could be writing my piece on Salli. I don't need to be with people. Especially these people.*

Natalie had gone straight to the bar, plopping herself down on a velvet-covered bar stool.

Jimmy ran over, deftly placing himself behind it. "What'll you have?" he asked.

"Isn't it Margarita time?" Natalie replied, flirting in spite of herself. "Can you make one?"

"Can *I* make one?" Jimmy said, as if it was the most ridiculous thing he'd ever heard. "*I* can make anything I put my mind to." He gave her a look that underlined his *double-entendre*.

Natalie quickly glanced around to see if Madison noticed, but Bunny was busy showing her a painting they'd recently bought of two rabbits being chased by a ferocious-looking fox. "The thing I like about this painting," Bunny explained to Madison in a serious voice, "is that the wicked old fox hasn't caught them yet. Isn't that something?"

"Uh-huh," Madison agreed, stifling a yawn.

A toilet flushed somewhere in the distance, then an exceptionally big, black man ambled into the room.

"Say hello to my college buddy, Luther," Jimmy said, steering him in the direction of Natalie. Luther towered over her. "Luther used to play for the Chicago Bears," Jimmy offered. "That is, until he got his shoulder busted."

"Wow!" Natalie said, thinking that this was one big handsome hunk of a guy. "I guess you're okay now, huh?"

"Still alive, sister," Luther said, with a huge grin. "Got me a nice little electrical business. Better than gettin' the crap kicked outta me every weekend – 'scuse my language. Oh, yeah, Jimmy tells me you're on TV with him."

"No," Natalie said. "Jimmy's on TV with me." And she smiled sweetly, realizing that if they ever had sex, she'd probably be crushed to death.

\*

"Kevin, dear," Lucinda gushed, balancing a martini in one hand and a caviar-loaded toast point in the other. "I'm *thrilled* we're doing a project together. I've seen every one of your movies – three in eighteen months. Poor over-worked boy, you must be *exhausted*."

Kevin straightened up from a terminal slouch. "Thanks," he muttered, considering that a word with his agent might not be a bad thing. Now that he'd seen Lucinda Bennett in the flesh he realized she was too *old* for the part, she'd make him look ridiculous.

"Hey, Freddie," he said, veering in the super-agent's direction. "We gotta talk."

"Later," Freddie said, dismissing him with a wave of his hand. Ariel was at the door, and he needed to speak to her before Max put in an appearance.

\*

Meanwhile, Max was pacing around his penthouse apartment in a fury, having just hung up on Inga. "I will be late, Max," she'd said, in her precise Swedish accent. "Go to the dinner and I will try to join you."

*Try* to join him. Was she totally nuts? Tonight was her

big night, an opportunity to meet important people in the industry, and the silly Swedish blonde was blowing it. "Why?" he'd demanded. "What are you doing?"

"It's private," she'd answered curtly.

Bitch! Bitch! Bitch! Just who exactly did she think she was?

"You'd better make it, Inga," he'd said, endeavouring to remain calm. "If you want to be in movies, you'd better make it soon."

"We'll see," she'd said, infuriating him even more with her casual tone.

Now he would have to walk in alone. Shit! If Max Steele got stood up, it would be all over town by noon tomorrow. *Shit!*

L.A.
Connections
1

# CHAPTER NINETEEN

JIMMY SICA was running around playing the perfect host, fixing Margaritas, making small-talk, flashing his unbelievable smile. While Bunny was busy showing pictures of their kids to the next-door neighbours, who'd dropped by for a drink, an extremely amiable Chinese couple whose grasp of the English language was somewhat elusive.

Madison could see that Natalie was getting along fine with Luther. *I wish I was at home, writing,* she thought for the twentieth time. *What am I doing here? This is not my kind of evening. I have enough casual friends in New York – no need to make new ones. And kiddie talk is not for me.*

She decided that after dinner she'd ask Natalie if she could borrow her car and leave. Luther would probably be only too delighted to drive Natalie home.

"And *this* is a photo of Blackie," Bunny announced

proudly. "Blackie was my precious itsy-bitsy black poodle who passed away last year." Her lower lip quivered. "I'm *still* grieving."

"Another Margarita?" Jimmy suggested. "We're waiting for my brother, he's always late."

"Okay," Madison said, trailing him back to the bar.

"First trip to L.A.?" Jimmy asked, taking her empty glass.

"I've been here several times before."

"I guess you must do a lot of travelling," he said, turning on the blender.

Madison watched the frothy liquid as it spun around in its glass cage. "Natalie tells me you recently moved here from Denver," she remarked.

"Six months ago," he said, refilling her glass and handing it back to her. He paused, giving her a long lingering look. "You know, Madison, I'm sure you've been told this many times."

"What?"

He flashed his handsome-anchorman smile, favouring her with another intimate look. "You're a powerfully attractive woman. In fact, you remind me of my first real love."

*Oh, get a life, Jimmy Sica. What a tired old line. You'll be telling me your wife doesn't understand you next.*

"Thanks," she murmured, ever polite. "You're not so bad yourself."

That shut him up for a moment.

Bunny ran over. "Where's—" she began.

But before she could finish her sentence, Jimmy's brother walked in. "I'm here," he said with a crooked grin, thrusting a bunch of flowers at her. "Late as usual."

"Thank *goodness*!" Bunny exclaimed, giving him a big hug and a squeeze. "We'd almost given up on you."

"Hey," he said, still grinning, "*never* give up on me, you know I always make it in the end."

Madison turned around to check out the new arrival. He was a rumpled version of the perfect TV anchor, only much sexier, with laughing brown eyes and longish brown hair.

"Meet my deadbeat brother, the photographer," Jimmy said with a twist of genuine affection. "Jake, say hello to Madison. You two should have a lot in common – Madison's a big-deal journalist."

"Yeah?" Jake said, giving her a firm handshake. "Big-deal, huh?"

"Not so big," Madison replied lightly, deciding that maybe tonight wasn't going to be such a dead loss after all. Jake had the look. And perhaps a quick fling with no responsibility was exactly what she needed.

"Who do you work for?" he asked.

"*Manhattan Style*."

"Very nice."

"It pays the rent."

"I bet it does."

"And you?" she asked.

"Mostly freelance."

"Really?"

"It pays the rent."

They smiled at each other, and then Natalie bounded over, giving Madison a not-so-subtle wink.

Jimmy put his arm around his brother's shoulders and walked him across the room. "You see how good I am to

**129**

you," he said in a low voice. "Not one, but *two* beauties. Take your pick, although personally I'd go for the journalist – she's got that icy-hot thing going. Very sexy."

"Spoken like a true married man," Jake said, rolling his eyes.

"Don't tell me you're *not* interested?"

"I met somebody."

"Who?"

"Just a girl. Nice. Pretty. Perfect."

"Oh, *shit*," Jimmy said, bursting out laughing. "You're not in love for Chrissake?"

"No . . ." Jake said, hesitating for only a moment. "It's just that there's something special about her – something I can't put into words. Hey, you'll see for yourself. I asked her over later."

"Can't wait."

"And *please*, do *not* hit on her," Jake warned.

Now it was Jimmy's turn to grin. "Like you said, I'm a married man, bro."

"Yeah, *right*."

And together they returned to the bar.

# Obsession

## L.A. Connections 2

L.A.
Connections
2

# PROLOGUE

THE BLONDE fell with a sickening thud – the razor-sharp
hunting knife cutting through her carotid artery as easy as
slicing butter. Blood pumped from her like oil gushing from
an open well.

The blonde attempted to scream, her eyes open wide
with the fear and knowledge of what was to come next. But
when she opened her mouth, blood gurgled out, spilling
down her body and soaking her clothes.

Then her assassin struck again – the lethal knife viciously
stabbing her breasts.

Once.

Twice.

Three times.

She sighed. A horrible death rattle of a sigh.

And within seconds she was dead.

# CHAPTER ONE

L.A. Connections 2

# CHAPTER ONE

MADISON CASTELLI regarded Jake Sica with a certain amount of guarded amusement as he entertained Jimmy's dinner guests with a hilarious story about a recent photo safari he'd been on in Africa. Jake had a kind of deadpan delivery that really caught her attention, even though she had no intention of getting involved again after her last disastrous relationship – absolutely no way.

*I'm twenty-nine, a successful writer for* Manhattan Style *magazine and single*, she thought, continuing to check Jake out across the dinner table. *Then why am I even thinking about this guy? Especially as I only just met him. Plus he doesn't seem at all interested – so what's my problem?*

She glanced over at Natalie, who seemed to be making out okay with Luther.

"You're a hoot," Natalie said to Jake, shooting Madison a sideways why-don't-you-do-something-about-him? look.

Madison did not respond, she wasn't about to encourage Natalie's not-so-subtle matchmaking, even though she did find Jake extremely attractive.

"I love this!" exclaimed Bunny, clapping her hands together like an excited little girl. "We used to entertain all the time in Detroit. What fun we had!"

"We sure did," agreed Jimmy, dazzling everyone with his smile.

"How about we play charades later?" Bunny suggested, still full of girlish enthusiasm.

"How about *not*?" Jake responded with a wry grin.

"I'm with you," Madison agreed, thinking that she couldn't stand parlour games – probably because she didn't consider herself very good at them, and she always strived to excel.

"Me too," said Luther, pushing his chair away from the table and stretching. "Man, I do *not* get off on all that goofin' around. Makes me feel like some kind of big old fool."

Bunny pulled a face. "It's *my* party," she said petulantly. "I can do what I want."

"Honey!" Jimmy said, embarrassed. "Whyn't we take a vote? See what everyone wants to do."

"No!" Bunny said, pursing her pink lips, her pretty features contorting into a scowl. "Don't want to."

"Sweetheart—" Jimmy started to say.

"Stop nagging me all the time!" Bunny shrieked, cutting him off, her baby blue eyes flashing major danger signals.

"Oh good," Natalie murmured, attempting to lighten things up. "A nice juicy family fight."

Bunny suddenly jumped up from the table. "I hate you all!" she screeched, before running from the room.

There was a stunned silence.

Jimmy's smile wavered. "She's only kidding," he said, getting up and hurriedly scooting after her.

"Holy *shit*!" Natalie exclaimed as soon as Jimmy was out of earshot. "What was *that* all about?"

Both Luther and Jake appeared unaffected by Bunny's outburst.

"Nothing," Jake said, with an unconcerned grin. "That was simply Bunny being Bunny, no big deal."

"Yeah," Luther agreed, reaching for a bottle of red wine and refilling everyone's glass. "Nothin' changes. She was always a trip."

"Does she usually scream at her guests like that?" Madison asked, quite surprised by their calm reaction.

"Bunny only throws a fit to get Jimmy's attention," Jake explained. "It's her way."

"Good for her," Madison said crisply, pushing her chair away from the table. "Only *I* don't have to stay around to watch."

"No, no," Luther said, chuckling. "You're not gettin' it. This shit's bin goin' on since college. They'll be back in a minute all cosy an' down each other's throats. It's their thing."

"Well, it's not mine," Madison said, standing up. "Besides, I've got work to do." She stared pointedly at Natalie, waiting for her to get up, too.

Natalie didn't budge.

"I guess I'd better call a cab," Madison said irritably, swearing to herself that tomorrow she'd hire her own car – no more being trapped somewhere she didn't want to be.

"Oh," Natalie said innocently, as if it had only just occurred to her. "You're in my car, aren't you?"

"Yes, Natalie, I am," Madison said, wanting to strangle her.

Natalie was not about to give up on Luther. "Maybe *Jake*'s going your way," she suggested.

Now all eyes were on Jake. Madison was furious, especially as Jake was not exactly leaping up to offer her a lift.

"A cab'll be fine," she said stiffly.

"I'll call one," Jake said. "I *would* drive you, but . . . uh . . . I'm kind of expecting someone."

*Oh great*, Madison thought. *He's got a late date, and Natalie's begging him to drive me home. How embarrassing is this?*

"Who?" Luther asked, all interested.

"No one you know," Jake replied, picking up his glass and taking a gulp of wine.

Natalie finally rallied. "I suppose I should be going too," she said, batting her long eyelashes at Luther, waiting for him to stop her.

He got the message. "No, baby," he crooned, giving her a long, slow-burn look. "It's *way* too early for you to leave."

"Gotta get my beauty sleep," she said, doing the eyelash thing again.

"Honey," Luther said, right on cue, "you're so fine you don't *need* no beauty sleep."

*Oh God*, Madison thought, *do I really have to listen to this?*

And then the phone rang, and all hell broke loose.

# CHAPTER TWO

ARIEL SHORE was a statuesque brunette in her late forties with an abundance of charm and a deceptively bland manner. Beneath the wide and welcoming smile lurked an astute woman who knew the movie business inside out – a woman who could sweet-talk like nobody else and then – if she felt like it – blow a deal right out of the window without a second thought.

Ariel had started her illustrious career in advertising, moved on to marketing, produced a couple of low-budget films, until finally she'd caught the attention of Billy Cornelius, who'd championed her rise to head of his studio. Some said Ariel and Billy were lovers. Freddie Leon didn't believe it for a minute, Ariel was way too smart to sleep with her boss. Besides, Billy's feisty little wife, Ethel, watched him like a bird-dog – ever since he'd nearly left her for a curvaceous starlet with big silicone-enhanced lips and a talent for latching on to other women's husbands. Ethel had seen to it that the girl was run out of Hollywood – forcing her to seek employment (and other women's husbands) in Europe.

Like Freddie, Ariel was career driven – which is why the two of them got along so well. They usually managed to have lunch a couple of times a month where they exchanged information, a lunch they both enjoyed because they genuinely liked each other.

Freddie greeted her at the door of his house, hugging her close, whispering in her ear how glad he was she'd made it.

"This was very short notice, Freddie," she scolded.

"Only for you."

"I know, Ariel," he replied, poker-faced as usual. "I appreciate it."

"So you should. You owe me, Freddie. And I *always* collect."

"Like I doubted it," he answered, thinking that when he told her that Billy Cornelius was planning on replacing her with his erstwhile partner Max Steele it would be payment enough. "Come on in," he added, placing his arm around her broad Armani clad shoulders.

Ariel nodded and strode ahead of him. She was an assertive woman with complete confidence in her ability to charm and conquer.

As Freddie followed her into the living room, he wondered how confident she'd feel when she heard of Billy Cornelius' plans to replace her.

Diana stepped forward, greeting Ariel with a weak smile. Although Diana rarely voiced her opinion about any of her husband's business associates, he knew she couldn't stand Ariel – whom she considered brash and overbearing. He also knew that Diane suspected he might be attracted to the striking studio head, and had once accused him of just such a thing. He'd laughed off her suspicions: Ariel was too important for him to sully their relationship with sex.

"Hi, Ariel," Diana said with about as much enthusiasm as a dead rattlesnake.

Freddie narrowed his eyes, it infuriated him when Diana exhibited attitude.

"Honey!" Ariel exclaimed, ignoring Diana's coolness. "How *sweet* of you to include me." And before Diana could summon up a reply, Ariel was heading in the direction of hot, sexy young movie star Kevin Page.

"I thought you said she was bringing her husband," Diana hissed.

"She's obviously alone," Freddie replied, too preoccupied to bother with trivia.

"This ruins my table placement," Diana seethed, tight-lipped.

"Get over it," Freddie said, completely unconcerned.

Diana favoured him with a hate-filled look which he ignored.

Later, at the dinner table, all was back on track. Lucinda Bennett was holding court, telling lurid tales of her early days in Hollywood and how every man on two legs was after her. Kevin joined in with hilarious stories about a particularly stoned director he'd recently worked with. And Ariel added anecdotes of her own early experiences.

Freddie noted that Max was uncustomarily quiet. Either he was contemplating what he considered his rosy future, or he hadn't gotten over Inga Cruelle's obvious snub.

Earlier Freddie had cornered Ariel and informed her of the facts about Max and her job as he knew them. She was genuinely shocked. "I don't think Billy would make a move like that without telling me," she'd said. "Everything's going so well at the studio. We've had two enormous hits this year."

"*And* a couple of flops," Freddie had reminded her.

"The hits make up for the flops," Ariel had replied, not quite as pleasantly as usual.

"I'm merely telling you what I know," Freddie had said. "I'm planning on talking to Max tonight, and I want you involved. After all, you and I are on the same side."

Ariel had nodded, but Freddie knew she was angry, as well she should be.

He glanced around the table. Diana's other guests were doing fine. The billionaire businessman and his wife, and the New York financier and his L.A. mistress were completely enthralled to be in the company of stars. Good, Freddie thought, now both men would owe him favours – exactly the way he liked things to be.

Brock Martin, the head of one of the TV networks, was also enjoying himself. He had his eye on Kevin Page's date, the young actress Angela Musconni, she of the pouting lips and seductive eyes. Angie was only nineteen, but her knowing eyes signalled promises of wild sensual experience and Brock felt he was in with a chance.

"I don't do television," Angie kept on insisting, as Brock offered her a mini-series, weekly series, or if she preferred, a major development deal.

"Not even for me?" Brock finally said, perplexed by her lack of interest. He considered himself a stud, having started his career as an actor many years ago, and he simply couldn't understand why Angie wasn't reacting with more enthusiasm.

"Tell ya what," Angie said, her New York twang reverberating along the dinner table, "if I ever *do* decide t'do TV, it'll *only* be for you. How's that?"

Her pronouncement pacified him, he gave a satisfied smile. She flashed him the eyes, while under the table her child-size hand groped its way up Kevin's thigh, searching for his zipper, so she could pull it down and investigate the possibilities. Angie got off on living dangerously.

Kevin slapped her hand away, he was having a good time listening to Lucinda Bennett and didn't need distractions. Freddie had been trying to persuade him to star in a movie with Lucinda. He'd turned it down, said she was too old. Now he'd decided that maybe Lucinda wasn't too old after all, and he'd better take another look at the script and alert Freddie to his change of mind.

"So, Max," Freddie said quite loudly, "isn't there something you've been meaning to tell me?"

Ariel sat up very straight. A silence fell across the table.

Max jumped to attention. "What would that be?" he

asked, still wondering where the hell Inga Cruelle was. How dare the Swedish bitch stand him up.

"Come on, Max," Freddie said, playing with him. "You and I have never kept secrets."

"Yes, Max," Ariel said, joining in, her voice sounding ever so slightly strained. "There's a rumour going around."

"A rumour?" Max said warily. Where the fuck was *this* leading?

"That's right," Ariel said, honouring him with one of her charming smiles. "A rumour that you're after my job."

# CHAPTER THREE

DETECTIVE CHUCK TUCCI hitched up the waistband of his moss-green pants, which were uncomfortably loose on account of the fact that over the last six weeks he'd lost twelve pounds – thanks to Faye, his wife, who, much to his disgust had put him on a rigid diet. He hadn't wanted to lose weight. He was forty-nine, six feet tall and perfectly happy at two hundred and twenty pounds. However, Faye had insisted, nagging on about his heart and cholesterol level, and all other kinds of ominous ailments. He wouldn't have taken any notice of her, but when she said he felt too heavy lying on top of her when they made love, he'd decided he'd better acquiesce. Hence the diet. Hence the loose pants. Hence his bad mood.

The body of the murdered blonde lay before him in a spreading pool of thick, crimson blood.

Another dead body.

Another brutal murder.

Only this time things were different. This time the victim lying spread-eagled on the ground, half in and half out of the luxurious living room, was extremely famous.

Detective Tucci stared down at the once gorgeous woman, her half-naked body vulnerable and exposed, the clothes ripped from her body in a frenzy of violence. Somebody had hacked her to death, viciously stabbing her at least seventeen times, almost severing her right breast.

The white dress she'd been wearing was in blood-splattered shreds around her. No underwear in sight. Blonde pubic hair shaved into the shape of a heart. A small tattoo of a colourful bird just below her pierced navel. Fashionable metallic blue polish on her finger and toenails. She was a beauty.

As he took in the details he let out a deep and weary sigh. This was not his first violent murder; it was his twenty-sixth. However, this was his first famous one.

On his way into the well-appointed living room with its sweeping views from the huge glass windows, he'd passed a portrait of the victim. Young, blonde, pretty. Like a top-of-the-line Barbie doll, her youthful body captured in a giant nude painting hanging on the wall.

Now she was dead, gone, her sexy image for ever frozen in time.

The police photographer arrived and methodically began setting up his camera and harsh, glaring lights. He nodded at Detective Tucci and soon began his grizzly work, photographing the dead female body from every possible angle, while several cops wandered all over the house, sealing off areas.

Detective Tucci was particularly concerned with the security outside the house, for he was well aware that once the news hit the airwaves, the press and TV crews would descend, swarming around like packs of particularly ravenous vultures. Bad enough when the victim wasn't famous. This time it would be a circus – rivalling the Nicole Simpson/ Ron Goldman/OJ débâcle.

Salli T. Turner. Pneumatic princess of the small screen. Bountiful blonde with the amazing body and sweet, sweet smile. The girl in the black rubber swimsuit.

Adorable girl.

Dead girl.

He continued gazing down at her lifeless, mutilated body and sighed again. Sometimes he thought Faye was right – it was time to retire and get out of the violence business once and for all.

This was one of those times.

# CHAPTER FOUR

L.A. Connections 2

# CHAPTER FOUR

"I CAN'T BELIEVE IT!" Madison gasped, barely able to absorb the shocking news. "It's impossible. I was with her only a few hours ago. There has to be some mistake."

"No mistake," Jimmy said grimly, his handsome face alive with the scent of a sensational story.

"Our boss never makes a mistake," Natalie agreed, agitated because she hated violence and backed away from covering any stories that even touched on it. Now she was stuck, because she and Jimmy had been summoned to their TV station to get a handle on the case.

Madison shook her head, still trying to get her mind around the horrifying news. Salli T. Turner. So alive and vibrant and sweet. It seemed impossible that she was dead, gone, brutally murdered.

"I'm sorry," Natalie said quietly. "I know you liked her."

"I did," Madison said in a low voice. "How exactly did it happen?"

Jimmy shrugged. "All we know is she was stabbed to death in her house."

"Is it on the news?"

"It will be by the time we get there."

"How did your people find out?"

"Our news director has someone in the police department. We hear everything early." He turned to Natalie. "C'mon, kiddo, we'd better get going."

Reluctantly Natalie picked up her purse, and they all trooped into the front hall.

Bunny emerged from the bedroom and stood with her arms crossed glaring in sulky silence as everyone prepared to leave.

"You'd better take my car," Natalie said to Madison. "That's if you're okay to drive. I'll go with Jimmy and catch you at home later."

"No," Madison answered quickly. "I should go with you. I'm probably one of the last people to see Salli alive, the detectives will want to talk to me."

"She's right," Jimmy agreed, ignoring his wife's baleful glares.

"Hey," Luther joined in, "what can *I* do?"

"You can call me later," Natalie said ruefully. "I'll need some kind words. Right now I'm totally freaked."

"Me too!" Bunny burst out, lower lip quivering. "This stupid murder has completely spoiled my dinner party."

Madison exchanged glances with Natalie. Jake shook his head. Jimmy threw his wife a furious look, grabbed her arm, and marched her back into the bedroom. Everyone could hear his angry growl – "Do you *always* have to sound like the town idiot? Why can't you keep your mouth shut for once?"

The uncomfortable silence in the hall was broken by the sound of the doorbell.

"I'll get it," Jake said, throwing open the front door. And there stood Kristin Carr, a tentative, slightly nervous smile on her glowing girl-next-door face.

"Uh . . . hi," Jake said, genuinely pleased to see her. "Didn't think you'd make it."

Kristin glanced past him, taking in the group of people in the hall, immediately noticing two women – a very attractive, dark-haired one, and a pretty black woman who had a familiar face. *Oh God*, she thought, swallowing hard, *I hope they're not women I've partied with. I'll die if they are.* She couldn't stand Jake's surprise and eventual disappointment, for he had no idea what she did for a living. "I guess I'm late," she said, standing awkwardly in the doorway.

"Not at all," Jake replied, blocking her way into the house, thinking that he wanted to get her out of there so he could have her all to himself. "In fact, you're right on time for me to take you for a drink."

"But I thought—" she began, wondering why he didn't invite her into the house.

"Everything changed," he interrupted, speaking fast. "I'll explain later."

"Fine," she said, feeling as if she'd walked into an uncomfortable situation – exactly what she *didn't* need after

**153**

her gruelling session with Mr X. She sighed, closing her mind to the memory of stripping naked in the back of Mr X's limo and pretending to pleasure herself as per the chauffeur's instructions. Of course, the chauffeur *was* Mr X, no doubt about *that*.

"C'mon, let's go," Jake said.

"Wait up, bro," Luther interrupted, elbowing his way past Jake. "Don't we get to meet this fine lady?"

"Sure you do," Jake said easily, knowing that a fast exit would've been too simple.

Jimmy emerged from the bedroom. "We're outta here," he said brusquely. Then he, too, noticed Kristin, and stopped short. "He–*llo*," he said, turning on the well-known Sica charm.

Jake moved between them, well aware what a lecherous bastard Jimmy was. "My brother," he said. "Jimmy, say hi to Kristin."

Kristin took a step backwards, civilians made her edgy – especially this group.

Jimmy was now busy flashing his perfect anchor-man smile. "And where has he been hiding *you*?" he leered.

Kristin recognized the type. She also recognized him from the TV news, and that made her even more nervous. "Uh . . . away from you I guess," she mumbled, grabbing on to Jake's arm, wishing she was someplace else.

Madison observed the scene. It didn't take a genius to realize Jake was off the market. He definitely only had eyes for this fresh-faced blonde dressed all in white. "Are we leaving or not?" she asked Jimmy impatiently. The journalist in her had kicked in, and she was not interested in anything except finding out what had happened to Salli. She was *certainly* not interested in Jake Sica.

Jimmy took his eyes off Kristin and jumped to attention. "You got it, Madison," he said. "We're on our way."

"Good," she said. And along with Natalie, the three of them left the house.

L.A.
Connections
2

# CHAPTER FIVE

THIS WAS NOT at all how Max had planned it. He should have known his karma was bad when Inga failed to show. Now he had Ariel on his case with her big phoney smile and faintly Southern accent. Another bitch. Truth was, they were all bitches – the only honest woman he'd ever encountered was his once-a-month hooker, Kristin. At least he knew exactly where he stood with her. Money on the table up front and unbelievable sex.

He decided to play it dumb. Stonewall both Freddie and Ariel. Screw it, he didn't have to answer to anyone.

"What?" he said, quite rudely, so they'd both get the message they were pissing him off.

"I said," repeated Ariel, refusing to back down, "there's a rumour going around that you're campaigning for my job."

Shit! Someone had loose lips, Billy Cornelius had promised him total secrecy until they were ready to make their announcement. Bluff it out, that was the only way to deal with it.

"I'm flattered that you think I could handle your job," he said calmly. "Truth is, I can barely handle my own." Self-deprecating laugh. Quick glance at Freddie. The ball was now on their side of the court.

Diana, who was totally ignorant of what was happening, did not like the way the conversation was going. She sensed trouble and was not about to let it disrupt her dinner party. "What are you all talking about?" she asked impatiently.

Freddie threw her a look. She caught his displeasure and decided to shut up. Freddie was not pleasant when he was angry: he had a violent, out-of-control temper.

"Beats me," Max said with a casual shrug.

"You know, Max," Ariel said icily, "I always *knew* Freddie was the heart of IAA. You were merely the gofer with whom people dealt when they couldn't reach *him*." A meaningful pause. "How *sad* to always come second."

The guests at the dinner table fell silent. Even Lucinda was quiet, preferring to listen to the drama taking place rather than continue charming everyone with her fascinating stories of Hollywood past.

"Fuck you, Ariel," Max spat, regretting the words the moment they left his mouth. Cool was everything, and he'd just blown it.

"That's enough," Freddie interjected angrily. "This is neither the time nor the place to get into a discussion."

"*What* discussion?" Max blustered, red in the face. "I'm supposed to sit here while Ariel accuses me of all kinds of shit, and then insults me? Oh no, Freddie, it ain't gonna happen."

Freddie rose from the table, it was time to put Max firmly in his place. "Come into the library, Max," he said, his face impassive. "We'll talk in private."

"Got nothing to talk about," Max replied, hating the whiny tone he heard in his own voice.

Diana stood also. Damn Freddie. He'd planned the whole thing. He'd *wanted* to humiliate Max in front of everyone so that the Hollywood rumour mill would gossip about what an asshole Max Steele was, and how Freddie Leon had caught him with his pants down.

Well, she was not going to stand for it. Max deserved better. He'd always been a good friend to her, and in spite of his appalling taste in the women he dated, she genuinely liked him and she strongly suspected he liked her back. In fact, if she weren't married it was quite possible that she and Max might have got together.

The very thought brought a blush to her cheeks. Abruptly she left the dining room and marched into the kitchen, where the help and the caterers were all gathered around the small portable TV.

"What *is* going on?" she demanded, not at all pleased they were slacking off when they should be hard at work.

Ronnie, her regular barman, black and capable, a middle-aged veteran of the more upscale Hollywood parties, stood to attention. "Breaking news, Mrs L," he said excitedly. "Big murder in the Palisades."

Diana frowned. "I couldn't care less *who's* been murdered," she said tartly. "We have a dinner party in progress. Kindly get back to work immediately. And that's an order."

L.A.
Connections
2

# CHAPTER SIX

DETECTIVE TUCCI was still contemplating the body of the
murdered blonde when Officer Andy Flanagann sidled up
alongside him. Officer Flanagann had been the first person
on the scene – summoned by a neighbour complaining
about barking dogs and loud music. By the time Detective
Tucci had reached the murder scene, the dogs were locked
in the kitchen and the music turned off. Nothing else had
been touched.

Tucci had already decided that Andy Flanagann was too
young for the job, although he had a fresh-faced enthusiasm,
and at least he seemed competent.

"You'd better come with me, Detective," Officer Flanagann muttered, avoiding looking at Salli's mutilated body.

"What's up, now?" Detective Tucci asked, his stomach
rumbling.

"Another victim," Officer Flanagann said flatly. "Male. Shot in the face. Discovered the body outside the guest house."

"Jeez!" Tucci exploded, thinking, *There goes dinner*. A double homicide was always twice the work and twice the aggravation – especially when both murders were committed by different means. A stabbing and a shooting. Perfect.

"Sorry," Officer Flanagann mumbled, like it was his fault.

Detective Tucci hitched his pants up again and, armed with a heavy-duty flashlight, he followed the young officer across the flood-lit lush green lawn surrounding an azure blue swimming-pool. Salli T. Turner must have worked hard to afford such a palatial spread. Their path was dotted with giant palm trees, potted bougainvillea and fragrant peach and lemon trees. Some people really knew how to live. Pity she'd had to die before her time.

Tonight Faye was making turkey meatloaf with her secret salsa sauce – a special treat. Tucci imagined her taking the pan out of the oven and leaving it to cool while she called him into the kitchen to eat. Ah yes, he'd desert his precious Lakers on TV, and race to her side. Faye was a good cook, and at forty-two still a most attractive woman. Half Hispanic and fiery with it, she had jet-black hair and a pocket Venus body. They'd been married five years, his first wife had died of cancer. He loved Faye very much.

"It looks like one bullet," Office Flanagann offered. "Seems like the victim might have been on his way to the main house to investigate the noise."

Tucci nodded. Amateur detectives irritated him. It was *his* case, *he'd* solve it, he didn't need any help.

The male victim was sprawled on his side, half on the walkway and half on the grass leading from the guest house. He had no face, just an angry mud-patch of blood and bones.

It was not the first time Detective Tucci had seen someone who'd been shot in the face. It was never a pretty sight. His stomach churned, this time not from hunger, and he wished he was at home.

Carefully aiming his flashlight, he studied the dead body. Male. Slight and skinny. Clad in psychedelic shorts and a midriff-baring white tank. Pierced navel. Glossy black shoulder-length hair. Oriental hair.

Detective Tucci leaned closer, his flashlight skimming up and down the lifeless form.

"No weapon," Officer Flanagann said helpfully. "I checked all around."

"Did you go in the guest house?"

"The door was open. I inspected the premises. It does not appear to be a home invasion."

Tucci continued staring at the body. "Houseman," he said, thinking aloud. "Get the photographer down here. And make sure nothing's touched."

"Yes, Detective," Officer Flanagann said, jumping to attention. "I'll take care of everything."

L.A.
Connections
2

# CHAPTER SEVEN

KRISTIN SAT next to Jake in a booth at the bar in the Beverly Wilshire Hotel. He'd ordered a beer, and she was sipping Evian. Both of them were treading carefully.

"I'm really glad you came by," Jake said, trying hard not to stare, for she was truly gorgeous in a refreshingly whole-some way. "I was beginning to kind of wonder if you'd show."

"Did you think I would?" she asked, feeling like a real girl on a real date and liking the feeling a lot.

He shrugged. "Wasn't sure," he answered honestly.

She smoothed down the skirt of her white dress with the palms of her hands. "Can I ask you something?" she ventured, studying the way his eyes crinkled when he smiled.

"You can ask me anything you like."

She hesitated a moment. "Well . . ." she began, not even

embarrassed because she was determined to know, "I noticed two attractive women in the hall. Was one of them with you?"

*Why am I asking him this?* she thought. *I hardly know him. And yet . . .*

"Oh sure," he said, laughing. "Like I'd invite you over to join me and my family, and there I'd be with a date." His brown eyes were full of amusement. "C'mon, Kristin, what kind of a guy d'you think I am?"

"A nice guy," she answered softly.

He took a swig of beer. "Now you're making me sound boring."

"No, I'm not."

"Yes, you are."

They grinned at each other. He was delighted she'd wanted to know whether he was with Natalie or Madison: it showed that maybe she was interested.

"Your brother's on television, isn't he?" Kristin asked, carefully picking a slice of lime out of her drink and sucking it.

"Jimmy's a news anchor," Jake replied, eyes fixated on her full lips.

"I recognized him."

"He'd like that. His ego's bigger than his brain."

"Do you two hate each other?" she asked curiously.

"Naw. He can be a real jerk, but he's still my brother."

"And so the two of you are going to your father's wedding?"

"Wouldn't miss it. My dad's the character of all time." A beat, then, "Hey – why don't you come?"

She shook her head, natural blonde hair swirling around her pretty face. "I don't think so."

"Why not?" he asked, hoping he might persuade her to say yes. "We could have fun."

"I'm not used to having fun," she said quietly.

He looked at her quizzically. "What does *that* mean?"

"I work all the time," she said, tapping her clear polished nails on the table. "My sister was in a bad car accident, and . . . I look after her – pay the bills. She's been in a coma for over three years."

Impulsively he took her hand. "You poor kid."

"No," Kristin said fiercely. "*She's* the poor kid. *I'm* the one who's still able to walk around."

"Does that mean you have to support her?"

"I don't *have* to do anything," she said, her voice tightening as she withdrew her hand from his.

"What about your husband? Doesn't he help out?"

A moment of silence. "I . . . uh . . . wasn't quite truthful with you, Jake," she lied, remembering the fictitious rich husband she'd made up to protect herself. "I left my husband six months ago. He doesn't pay me a dime."

"Then you're single?"

"Separated."

He fixed her with a long penetrating gaze. "Glad to hear it."

"Why?"

"Now isn't that a silly question?" he said teasingly.

She lowered her eyes, his gaze was too intense for comfort.

"So . . . tell me, Kristin," he continued. "Are you involved with anyone?"

She was silent again. Was sleeping with a variety of men rich enough to pay for her exclusive services being "involved"?

No. That was business.

*And business and pleasure do not mix.*

A harsh reminder that she shouldn't be sitting here with a man she found undeniably attractive.

"Hey," Jake said, pushing gently, "do I get an answer?"

"I . . . I don't have time to be involved," she said. "Have to keep working to pay the bills."

"That's *not* a healthy attitude."

She shrugged, studying his lips, wondering what it would be like to kiss them. "I know," she said. "But what can I do?"

"Spend more time with me for a start," he said playfully. "I'm new in town. I need a tour guide, someone to show me what *not* to do."

"I *am* spending time with you."

He took her hand again and she experienced long-lost shivers of desire. "I've never met anyone quite like you, Kristin," he said, his brown eyes sincere and probing. "Are you feeling the same way I am?"

She nodded, unable to stop herself, even though she knew she was venturing on to dangerous ground.

"Then shouldn't we do something about it?" he suggested.

"Like what?" she murmured, knowing full well what he meant.

"My hotel or your place?" he said, deciding to go for it.

Her place was her sanctuary, she never took clients there.

Only Jake wasn't a client. He was a man she desperately wanted, and maybe if she slept with him she would get over her overwhelming desire for him, and then normal life could resume.

"My place," she whispered, still flushed with excitement.

He squeezed her hand. "I'll get the check."

L.A.
Connections
2

# CHAPTER EIGHT

BY THE TIME Jimmy and Natalie reached their TV station, news of the Salli T. Turner murder was spreading across L.A. like an out-of-control brush fire, which really pissed Jimmy off because he'd expected to be first on air with the news.

Madison followed them into the news room, still dazed by the shocking murder. She kept on thinking of her lunch with Salli – a woman so vibrant and alive. Now Salli was dead, and it didn't seem possible.

Garth, the news director, a tall man with angular features and sparse yellow hair plastered to his scalp, was not pleased either. "What the hell took you so long?" he screamed at Jimmy, ignoring both Natalie and Madison.

"I live in the goddamn Valley for Chrissake," Jimmy retorted bad-temperedly. "Pay me more money and I'll move closer."

"Never mind," Garth growled. "You're on a special news break. Get moving."

"Thanks," Jimmy said sarcastically, taking off for the makeup room.

"As for you, sweetie," Garth said, turning to Natalie, "prepare me a eulogy for the eleven o'clock news. Something that'll break everyone's heart *and* keep 'em watching." He licked his thin lips. "We'll use plenty of footage of Salli bouncing along the beach in her sexy black rubber suit. Nothing like T and A and a good murder to guarantee mega-ratings."

"I was thinking," Natalie blurted, "maybe Madison should do it, she was with Salli today."

Madison threw Natalie an amazed look. "*I'm* not appearing on TV," she objected. "What's gotten into you?"

Garth took notice of Madison for the first time. "Who're you?" he asked rudely.

"Someone with better manners than you," she shot back, not thrilled by his brusque attitude.

"Madison's my journalist friend from New York," Natalie quickly explained. "She flew out on the same plane as Salli. And today she was at Salli's house having lunch."

Garth's long, thin nose smelled an exclusive. "You were?" he asked, practically salivating.

"That's right," Madison replied curtly. "And I can assure you I have absolutely *no* intention of talking about it on TV."

"Why not?" Garth demanded.

Madison frowned. What was wrong with Natalie for trying to use her? And who was this total *idiot*? "Don't you people *care* that a beautiful young woman has been *murdered*?" she said furiously. "What is this to you? Nothing more than a ratings race?"

"Now, now," Garth said gently, realizing she could be useful. "Understandable you're upset. But the public has a right to know. As a journalist you should understand that."

"Sorry," Madison said shortly. "I don't think they have a *right* to anything."

Garth scratched his head. Nothing worse than a stubborn woman – especially a stubborn female journalist. "How much?" he asked wearily, as if money could solve any problem.

"How much for what?" she said, still frowning.

"Money. For you to get on air."

She gave him an icy glare. "You just don't get it, do you?"

"No, honey," he answered patronizingly. "It's *you* who don't get it. News is news, and if you *were* with her today, we're sitting on dynamite. So tell me what it's gonna take to get you in front of the camera?"

Madison couldn't believe what a moron this guy was. "Nothing *you* have to offer," she said, throwing him a dismissive look.

"Drop it, Garth," Natalie interrupted quickly, sensing that Madison was about to lose it. "It was a dumb idea. Sorry, Maddy."

"No, honey," Garth sneered. "For once you got it right."

"Hey," Madison said, directing her words to Natalie, "I'm out of here. You work for this asshole, *I* don't."

"Who're *you* calling names?" Garth said, a plum-red flush spreading up from his neck.

"Forget it," Madison said. "Let's just say it *wasn't* a pleasure."

"Maddy—" Natalie began. But it was too late – Madison was on her way out.

Angrily she made her way to the front desk and requested the young man at reception to order her a cab. Then she used her cellphone to reach Victor Simons in New York, where it was now one thirty in the morning.

"Listen to me, Victor," she said, her words tumbling over each other as she was overcome with a sudden rush of adrenaline.

"What?" Victor mumbled, half asleep and disoriented. "It better be important."

"It is," Madison said, finally realizing that she did have a hot story, and she'd better pursue it. "Salli T. Turner was murdered tonight. Stabbed to death."

"You sure?"

"*Very* sure."

"Weren't you having lunch with her today?" Victor asked, sounding a lot more alert.

"Yes. I was at her house earlier."

"Then it must've—"

"—happened after I left," Madison said, finishing the sentence for him.

"You should—"

"Don't worry, Victor, I'm on to it. In fact, I'm heading for the murder scene right now. Expect to hear from me later."

# CHAPTER NINE

MAX STEELE was not about to be lectured to by the likes of Freddie Leon – "the Snake", as everyone referred to him behind his back. Screw Freddie. Screw 'em all. Max was on an I-hate-everyone roll.

The plain truth was that Ariel was right, people regarded Freddie as the major partner in IAA, Max Steele always came second. Oh yes, he knew what they said – "If you can't get to Freddie, settle for good old Max."

Dammit! He'd had enough. He was glad he was splitting. Once he was ensconced as a studio head, he'd be a man to be reckoned with, not some little unimportant agent.

Freddie attempting to edge him into the library had pissed him off. He'd stormed out. He had nothing to say until he'd figured out exactly how he was going to say it.

Now he was in his red Maserati cruising along Sunset

with All Saints on his CD player, wondering what the hell he was going to do to calm down.

He shouldn't have pissed Ariel off – he knew that for sure. She was a cunt – but she was a cunt with connections. *No bad karma.* That was his new motto.

*I need a snort,* he thought, *a touch of the magic white powder to calm me down and make me feel smooth as velvet.*

Howie would have what he needed. But hadn't Howie mentioned he was going to Vegas with his old man?

Yeah. Maybe. One never knew with Howie, he was a number-one degenerate fuck-up, typical son of a rich man. Money no problem, there was always more where that came from. Never kept a job for longer than two weeks. Never met a beautiful woman he didn't want to sleep with. Never encountered a drug he wasn't willing to try. Max reckoned Howie had brain damage from all his excesses.

Still . . . you could relax with a guy like Howie, have some laughs. And sometimes Max needed laughs when business got too intense.

He pulled his Maserati up outside *Riptide* on Sunset and left it with an eager valet. Max was known around town as an excellent tipper.

*Riptide* was the latest place to hang – a restaurant club with good food, a crowded bar, and many beautiful and available women. Not that beautiful available women were hard to come by in Hollywood. Truth was, they were everywhere – would-be models and actresses who flocked into town hoping to become the next Pamela Anderson or Claudia Schiffer, and ended up posing for *Playboy* or getting walk-ons in some horny producer's movie. Then there were the women who'd made it – the television stars with their own series, and the supermodels with their lucrative cosmetic contracts. And above all of them were the mega-stars such as Sharon Stone, Michelle Pfeiffer and Julia Roberts – talented females who'd gotten to the top in spite of the odds.

Max liked to sample all levels. Howie usually settled for the would-be's, claiming they were more grateful.

Bianca, the shapely Brazilian maître d', greeted him warmly as well she should, he'd gotten her the job after a night of interesting sex on a friend's yacht in the Marina. Banking favours was Max's speciality.

"Hi, Max, joining Howie's table?" Bianca asked, gold hoop earrings jangling on exceptionally small earlobes.

"Thought he was in Vegas," Max replied, giving her a friendly pat on her black-satin-clad ass.

"He's here," Bianca said, leading him through the crowded restaurant. "You know," she said, over her shoulder, "I can't believe the news about Salli T. Turner. She was in here all the time with that shit-heel husband of hers. I wouldn't be surprised if *he* was the one who did it."

"Did what?" Max asked blankly, waving at various friends and acquaintances as he trailed Bianca through the room.

She stopped short. "Haven't you heard?"

"What?"

"Salli was stabbed to death," Bianca said, lowering her voice to a horrified whisper. "They're saying whoever did it cut off one of her breasts."

Max shuddered. "Jesus!"

"It's so horrible! Did you know her?"

Max nodded, remembering the time Salli T. had come

to the office with the intention of seeing Freddie. Naturally Freddie was completely disinterested, so Max had ended up feeling sorry for her, and taken her for a drink in the bar at the Peninsula where he'd given her career advice. In return she'd offered him a blow-job. He'd turned her down. Not his type. Too obvious with the fake boobs and cascades of platinum hair. But sweet with it, almost naïve in a way.

"When did this happen?" he asked.

"Earlier tonight," Bianca answered. "I'm getting myself a gun. If it can happen to her it can happen to anyone."

"Now don't go getting paranoid," Max said, not mentioning that he'd had a hidden compartment specially built into his Maserati to house a fully loaded Glock.

"Why not?" Bianca demanded, dark Brazilian eyes flashing. "It's the truth."

"Was it a break-in?"

"Nobody seems to know. It's all over the TV."

And then they were at the booth. And there sat Howie in a three-thousand-dollar Brioni suit, four-hundred-dollar Lorenzini shirt, and a hundred-and-fifty-dollar Armani tie. There was nothing cheap about Howie – especially when he was spending his old man's money.

On the table in front of him was a half-empty bottle of Cristal in a silver ice-bucket, with two glasses, and a large glass dish filled to the brim with the best Beluga caviar.

Lounging next to Howie on the comfortable leather banquette was Inga Cruelle, a blank expression on her perfect supermodel face.

"Jesus!" Max exploded.

This was not turning out to be his perfect day.

# CHAPTER TEN

ANGELA MUSCONNI was bored. She'd had enough of watching the goings-on at the grown-up table. She was nineteen years old, for Chrissake, too young to sit around with a bunch of boring old farts.

Kevin Page had talked her into coming with him. "C'mon, babe," he'd said persuasively, still impressed with his own sudden fame. "It's a movers-and-shakers deal – we gotta go."

"What do I care?" she'd answered with a couldn't-care-less shrug. She'd met enough so-called movers and shakers on her way up. They were no big surprise, star fucks, every one.

When she'd first come to Hollywood, nobody had wanted to know her. Oh yeah, a blow-job was acceptable to certain producers, who'd promised her everything and then forgotten her name. Apart from that she was treated like a nothing – a dumb little street-kid.

Now they all wanted to suck up to her, including Brock Martin, who really thought he was hot shit on a plate. Of course, Brock didn't remember two years ago when he'd tried to pick her up at Farmer's Market on a Saturday morning, and offered her money for a hand-job. Pervert! Out trolling for teenagers when he had a wife and two kids at home.

She'd been broke at the time and quite tempted, now she could reject him and enjoy watching him beg. It was amusing for five minutes, after that it was a yawn.

She didn't get it. What fun was there in sitting around a fancy dinner table with waiters serving all kinds of gourmet crap when she and Kevin could be making out, eating pizza or cruising the clubs?

And what was with Kev brown-nosing Lucinda Bennett's saggy ass? She was old enough to be his *grandmother*, for Chrissake.

Angie sighed, sometimes Kev was so out of it. Even though he was five years older than her, he was not nearly as street smart. If she was planning on staying with him, she'd have to teach him how to operate.

Restlessly she got up from the table. "Goin' to the john," she mumbled. Like anyone cared. Kev certainly couldn't give a rat's ass.

She wandered through the ornate living room, taking in the silver frames filled with signed photos of presidents and movie stars. Then she checked out the tastefully lit expensive art hanging on the walls. There was a Picasso here, a Monet there. *Bo—ring*.

The only place where any sounds were coming from was the kitchen, so she gravitated in that direction. Peeking around the door, she was amazed at the size of the industrial-looking room. Holy shit! The fucking kitchen was bigger than her New York apartment!

A bunch of people were busy, busy, busy. Ah, this must be the staff – her kind of people. She'd grown up in New York, where her mom worked as a maid and her dad drove a union truck. Recently she'd bought them a house in Paramus. They'd moved from Brooklyn and hated it. Too bad.

"Hi, guys," she said, wandering into the enormous space filled with industrial ovens, several dishwashing machines, thick wood-block cutting boards and two giant centre islands. "Can I bum a cigarette?"

Ronnie, the barman, who was stationed in front of the TV, dragged himself away. "Sure, Miss Musconni," he said, groping in his pants pocket for a pack of low-filter Camels. "Only don't smoke it around Mrs Leon, she don't allow smoking in the house."

"Really?" Angie said, with a wicked grin, plucking a cigarette from his crumpled pack. "I'd like to see her try to stop *me!*" She got off on the clout that came with movie-stardom – it gave her a constant high. "Hey," she said, edging nearer the TV. "What's going on?"

"Big murder in Pacific Palisades," Ronnie announced. "Up the street from Steven Spielberg's place. We're watching live coverage from outside the house."

"No shit?" Angie said, moving closer to the small screen. "Who got wasted?"

"Salli T. Turner," Ronnie answered, twisting his head to make sure Diana Leon wasn't creeping up on him. Mrs Leon was the most demanding of Hollywood wives, she had a nasty habit of appearing unexpectedly.

Angie's hand flew to cover her mouth. "God, no!" she gasped. "Not Salli!"

"Did you know her?"

"Yes," Angie whispered, her face ashen.

"That's too bad," Ronnie said.

"Who . . . did . . . it?"

"They don't know, Miss Musconni."

"I do," Angie said fiercely. "He always threatened he was going to kill her, now the bastard has."

"Who?" Ronnie asked, hoping for the inside scoop so he could sell the information to one of the tabloids.

But Angie was not talking, she was already on her way back into the dining room.

*

Diana threw Angela a furious look. Wasn't it bad enough that Freddie had tried to ruin her dinner party by fighting with Max? Now this so-called actress had burst back into the room, telling everyone about the murder.

Diana knew exactly what would happen next, they'd all be dying to go home and huddle in front of their televisions. Damn! Why couldn't Salli T. Turner have gotten herself murdered on another night?

Angie announced the news, then immediately dragged Kevin off, barely saying goodbye.

*Good riddance*, Diana thought sourly.

Soon all the remaining guests were talking about the OJ case – reliving the most notorious murder trial of the century. Everyone who lived in L.A. had an opinion. But the discussion didn't last long, because after Angie and Kevin's abrupt exit – just as Diana expected – they all wanted out. Brock Martin was first on his feet, anxious to run over to his TV station. Lucinda was next, television junkie that she was. And Ariel couldn't wait to split.

Freddie was not at all fazed by everyone making a fast exit, but Diana was seething, although she put on a good act of saying goodbye graciously.

As soon as the last person left, she turned on Freddie. "I don't ask much of you," she said, tight-lipped. "But one thing I *do* expect is that when we're entertaining, you behave like a gentleman. My dinner parties are important to me, and you ruined tonight."

"What *are* you talking about?" Freddie snapped, in no frame of mind to suffer one of Diana's moods.

"How dare you air your problems with Max in front of my guests," Diana said, her voice rising.

His eyebrows rose. "*Your* guests, Diana?"

She backed down. "Our guests," she conceded.

"I hope you're not telling me how to run my business," Freddie said, grim-faced.

"No . . . But Max is your *partner*, your *friend* . . ."

"Bullshit," Freddie said harshly. "I made him – and let

**183**

no one forget it. He thinks he's capable of running a studio. Ha! Any moron could run a studio better than him."

"It'll be in Army's column tomorrow," Diana fretted. "It doesn't make *you* look good."

"Diana," Freddie said coldly, "stay out of my business."

"Fine," she replied, turning her back on him and hurrying upstairs, wondering if any of the staff had overheard their argument. God! That's all she needed. Ronnie, the barman, running around the Bel Air and Beverly Hills circuit telling everyone that the Leons were in a big fight. Freddie was as high profile as any movie star. Mr Super-agent. Mr Power. He was as big as Mike Ovitz had once been, before the débâcle at Disney.

Once upstairs, Diana sat at her dressing-table and wondered what Max was doing now. She understood why he had to leave the agency: it was because Freddie had always kept him in the background – kind of like the court jester. But she knew the truth. Underneath Max's brash exterior lurked a caring, sensitive man. And one of these days she planned on finding out exactly how caring and sensitive he was.

The intercom buzzed. "I'm going for a drive," Freddie said, his tone cold and flat. "Don't wait up."

*Not to worry*, Diana thought. *I have better things to do with my time.*

L.A.
Connections
2

# CHAPTER ELEVEN

JAKE FOLLOWED Kristin into her apartment, looked around, and let out a long low whistle. "Some place," he said, admiring the expensive décor.

"Uh . . . thank you," she answered nervously. He was right, her apartment *was* nice. And so it should be: working with a decorator, she'd overspent, but the result was soothing and tasteful, exactly what she'd been looking for. She considered her apartment her haven, the one place she could be alone. Now she was bringing Jake – a virtual stranger – into her private domain.

*Am I insane?* she thought. *Why am I doing this?*

*Because you like him.*

*No, I don't like him. I'm merely lonely. I need the arms around me of a man who isn't paying. Is that a crime?*

*Yes, because you're setting yourself up to get hurt.*

"Would you like a drink?" she asked, still feeling ridiculously skittish.

"Wouldn't mind a beer." He laughed. "Bet that's something you *don't* have."

"It's not my drink of choice, but I can offer you vodka or wine."

"Not a heavy drinker, huh?"

"I never drink by myself."

"So you're a good girl," he said teasingly.

"Now you're making *me* sound boring," she countered.

"Wouldn't want *that*," he said, coming up behind her, putting his arms lightly around her waist.

She turned in his embrace and began to say something, but he stopped her with his lips, and they were as good as she'd known they'd be.

He kissed her for several long slow-motion minutes. She couldn't remember the last time she'd been kissed, because paid-for sex did not usually involve that kind of intimacy. The sensation was unbelievably heady and yet fraught with danger.

Finally she forced herself to push him away. "I need a drink," she whispered.

"So do I," he agreed. "We're both nervous."

"You're nervous, Jake?" she asked, surprised. "Of what?"

"*You* make me nervous. In fact," he added with a rueful grin, "you made me nervous the first time I spotted you in Neiman's."

"I did?"

"You certainly did. I mean, there I was, minding my

own business, searching for a tie. And there *you* were, sitting at the martini bar, looking to break my heart."

"I was not," she objected. "If I might remind you – it was *you* who picked *me* up."

"No. It was *you* who came and sat beside me."

"Liar! Liar!" she said, enjoying the game. "I was already there – *you* sat next to *me*."

"I did?"

"You did."

"Then I must be smarter than I thought."

She laughed softly. "You're so romantic."

"Was your husband romantic?"

"Please don't talk about him," she said, quickly moving over to a side table where she kept glasses, red and white wine and a bottle of vodka. It was not like she ever entertained – the set-up was purely decorative.

Once more, Jake came up behind her. "I'll play barman," he said, taking the bottle of vodka out of her hands.

"If you insist," she said, shivering slightly.

He poured them both a healthy shot. "Where's the ice?"

"In the kitchen."

She watched him as he went into the kitchen. He was very watchable, tall and lean with a long-legged stride that she found irresistibly sexy. She could hear the jangling of ice cubes as he removed them from the freezer. When he returned he handed her a glass. "Okay, this is the deal," he said. "I'm making a toast."

"To what?"

"To you – because you're beautiful, inside and out."

*Oh no, Jake, don't say such things. The truth is that I'm ugly and I never want you to find out.*

"I know this is all happening fast," he continued. "But I feel I've got to tell you."

"Tell me what?" she asked, holding her breath.

He took a long beat, then – "This'll sound like another line – only it's the truth. I . . . uh . . . I guess I've never felt this way before."

*Oh, God! Please don't get carried away, Jake. Take this for what it is, one night of love. One long, leisurely, unpaid-for night of love.*

"How about you?" he demanded, staring at her.

She stalled, pretending she didn't understand. "How about me what?"

"Jeez!" he said, perplexed. "I'm declaring all kinds of true feelings and you're stonewalling me. What's going on, Kris?"

Nobody called her Kris, it felt familiar and endearing. She shrugged. "I . . . I don't know," she murmured. "Something . . ."

"Yeah . . . something," he agreed. And then somehow or other he was kissing her again, his body pressing hard against hers, his lips insistent and intoxicating.

She felt herself dissolve inside. This was too good to pass up. One night. Didn't she deserve one night of happiness?

Jake's hands slid down her shoulders to her breasts and began fingering her nipples through the flimsy folds of her white dress – causing her to catch her breath. She'd faked sexual excitement for so long that the real thing was almost a surprise. She shivered with anticipation, it was as if she'd never been touched there before.

Slowly he started easing her dress off her shoulders. She leaned back, making it simple for him.

He released her breasts from the thin material and bent to kiss them, rolling his tongue around her nipples in a way that immediately started to drive her crazy. She sighed loudly, knowing for sure that she never wanted him to stop.

"You . . . are . . . so . . . beautiful," he murmured, his tongue continuing to drive her crazy. "So . . . fucking . . . beautiful."

*I'm a professional, Jake, I have to keep in good shape.*

"Thank you," she whispered, wondering if it would seem too bold if she went for his belt and removed his pants.

"I haven't been with a woman in over a year," he admitted. "Unless sex means something, it's not for me."

Words to stop anyone in their tracks. "I . . . uh . . . can understand that," she managed.

"The reason I'm telling you is so that you know you can trust me."

Trust him? What did he mean? And then she got it. He was informing her that he didn't have AIDS or any other catchable diseases.

Oh, God, now he was waiting for her to give him *her* sexual history.

*Well, Jake, it's like this. I'm a whore. But you can feel perfectly safe because if they touch me I always insist they use a condom. And I visit my gynaecologist twice a month. And . . .*

*oh shit, why am I fooling myself? This silly charade of falling in love has nowhere to go.*

*And yet . . .*

"I haven't slept with anyone since my husband," she murmured.

"Well then," he said, obviously pleased with her reply. "You and I are about to make this a night to remember."

L.A.
Connections
2

# CHAPTER TWELVE

MADISON HAD the cab take her to a car-rental office, and now she sat behind the wheel of a green Ford Galaxy driving toward Salli's house in Pacific Palisades. No more depending on other people to get around.

Her thoughts were full of Salli as she tried to dredge up every detail of their lunch together. She remembered walking into Salli's luxurious house – her sense of how unlike New York City living it was with its big, high-ceiling rooms leading out to lavish gardens, and an enormous swimming-pool. The sun was shining and music was playing in the background. It was the radio, because every so often a male disc jockey would announce his last three choices. She remembered the dogs, yappy little things racing all over the place.

"They're my babies," Salli had said, scooping them up

191

in her arms. And then later Salli had confided that she couldn't have kids – something to do with an abortion that had taken place when she was fifteen. "I was dirt poor," she'd said with a sad little laugh. "So I guess I got me the town butcher."

"Is that off the record, or can I use it?" Madison had asked, playing fair because she didn't want to take advantage of Salli's almost naïve openness.

"Go ahead, print the truth for once," Salli had answered boldly. "I'm sick of all the lies." And then she'd *really* started talking.

Good journalist that she was, Madison had made short-hand notes in her head as Salli rambled on, even though her mini-tape machine was recording every word, because nowadays the lawyers wouldn't allow the magazine to print an interview unless there was tape to back it up.

Sitting beside the pool, chewing on carrot sticks because she was on a constant diet, Salli began peeling back the layers of her life.

\*

*Small town girl Salli got pregnant, had an abortion, won a local beauty contest at the age of fifteen, fought with her widowed father, dropped out of school and took the bus to Hollywood with exactly one hundred and three dollars in her cracked white patent-leather purse. She had brown frizzy hair, slightly buck teeth and quite a bit of puppy fat. But she was still pretty enough to make heads turn.*

*She faked her ID and immediately got a job as a waitress in a strip joint out by LAX airport, where she was so impressed by most of the strippers' attributes that she decided she'd better do something about her own modest 34-B's. With that goal in mind she began saving her money.*

*While she was waiting, a cab-driver boyfriend took a nude Polaroid of her and sent it to* Playboy. *Eight weeks later they rejected her as too skinny. This infuriated Salli, who immediately became determined that one day she'd be on the cover.*

*New tits became more important than ever. She found herself an agent and started doing extra work. Naturally, the agent, an older man with grown kids, fell in lust with her. Of course, he had no clue she was barely sixteen. She held out going to bed with him until he came up with the money for her new boobs. It took a year because – being a nice family man – he was riddled with guilt. Eventually he left his wife, paid for her operation, and on the night they finally slept together – expired on top of her before consummating the act. It was a traumatic experience, one that Salli did not forget in a hurry.*

*After that she became an expert tease – never letting any man get too close, although they all tried. Instead she concentrated on making herself the best she could be.*

*The new boobs gave her a head start, they changed her life. Instead of waitressing she turned to exotic dancing and began making enough money to continue her transformation from small-town beauty queen to Hollywood starlet. First she dyed her brown hair a Marilyn Monroe platinum blonde. Then she had her teeth capped and managed to lose a staggering twenty-five pounds. With her new glamorous look – all big boobs, tiny waist and long legs – she soon found a new agent and began getting small roles on TV shows and in films. If she'd wanted to do porno she could've made a killing, but sensibly she opted not to go that route. Instead she specialized in playing dumb blondes with spectacular bodies. An easy task. What wasn't easy was fighting off all the men. They came on to her in droves – including married famous ones who all had the same excuse. "My wife isn't into sex, so suck my dick." Sometimes she did, sometimes she didn't. She had to like a guy before she did anything.*

*It was a long haul, but Salli finally made it back to* Playboy. *This time they were all over her, and not only did she get the cover, but four pages of photographs inside* and *the centrefold.*

*Fame at last. Her spread was so popular that a year later she did it again. And then her career really started to take off, culminating in her own TV series* Teach! *and yet another* Playboy *cover.*

Teach! *became the* Baywatch *of the nineties, and Salli became the heroine of horny teenage boys across the world.*

*Along the way she married an actor, Eddie Stoner, divorced him two years later. And was currently married to the infamous Bobby Skorch – a man who regularly risked his life for a living.*

\*

Once more Madison wondered what had happened after she'd left. Salli had seemed in such a good mood, upbeat and enthusiastic about her future. She'd told Madison she planned to stay on *Teach!* for one more year, and then take a shot at movie stardom.

Now it was all over. And there had to be a reason why.

Madison drove on determinedly towards Salli's house.

# CHAPTER THIRTEEN

"I DON'T BELIEVE THIS," Max said, enraged.

"Howdy, pal," Howie said, oblivious to his friend's anger. "Meet Inga."

Max glared furiously at the exquisite supermodel lounging casually on the leather banquette in a barely there black dress. "What the fuck are *you* doing here?" he exploded.

"You two know each other?" Howie asked, obviously surprised.

"Not only do we know each other," Max blustered. "But Inga was my date tonight, and Inga failed to show."

"Don't be so silly, Max," Inga said in her infuriatingly precise accent. "I was *not* your date. We had a business appointment I could not make. And kindly do not use foul language."

Max's famous smoothness slid away as his face contorted

with frustrated rage. This Swedish bitch was dissing *him*, Max Steele. No fucking way. And what the hell was she doing with a low-life like Howie, his supposed friend?

"Am I in the middle of something here?" Howie asked, all playboy innocence.

"Not at all," Inga answered coolly.

"Did we, or did we not, have an appointment?" Max demanded, dropping the word date.

"A vague arrangement, nothing definite," Inga said, dipping two fingers into her champagne glass, then delicately licking them in a highly suggestive way.

"Hey," Howie said, sliding out of the booth, "I'll be in the head if anyone needs me."

Max sat down on the leather banquette. "Inga," he said, regaining his composure, "you were supposed to meet me at Freddie Leon's house, remember? It was an important sit-down dinner, *and* it was place-carded. Your absence was embarrassing – not to mention rude. You can't get away with shit like that in this town and expect to work." He glared at her, waiting for a reaction. "Do you understand me?"

Inga regarded him for a long, silent moment. "Inga does what Inga wants," she said at last. "And I can assure you, Max, that when the right project comes along, they will be begging for Inga to appear."

Max was stunned. Just who did this broad think she was?

"Honey," he said, "keep on believing *that*, and you can watch your movie career *never* take flight." Abruptly he got up from the table. "I'm off the case – find yourself a new agent."

Howie was in the men's room snorting a line of coke from the dark green marble counter-top. The attendant was looking the other way on account of a fifty-dollar tip.

"You're lucky I'm not undercover Vice," Max said, stealing a healthy pinch of the white powder and rubbing it into his gums.

"They'd never get in the door," Howie said with a manic chuckle. "This place is protected."

"Protected my ass," Max snapped.

Howie slipped the small plastic straw into his pocket and wiped the tip of his nose, getting rid of any tell-tale white powder. "What's with you and the babe?" he said. "She really break a date with you?"

"Nobody breaks a date with Max Steele," Max said stiffly. "It was purely business and the stupid bitch blew it."

"*I've* got something I'd like her to blow," Howie chortled, grabbing his crotch in an exaggerated manner.

"Where'd you meet her?" Max asked, still fuming, but hiding it well.

"Cocktail party at Cartier's earlier. She was standing there looking hot, so I bought her a trinket."

"Trinket?" Max questioned.

Howie laughed sheepishly. "So it was a gold tank watch. Big deal. It got me a date, an' you gotta admit – she's the business. Makes Cindy look plain."

"Models *are* better-looking than actresses," Max admitted, feeling better as the coke began to take effect. "Although – you gotta remember – they're also stupider."

Howie gave a ribald laugh. "I wanna fuck her, not take a lesson in physics."

"I heard a rumour she's got the clap," Max said, his mean streak surfacing.

"No shit?" Howie said, too stoned to care.

By the time they returned to the booth, Inga was gone. "She must be in the john," Howie said.

With a deep sense of satisfaction Max knew better. She'd dumped on Howie just as she'd dumped on him.

Supermodels. Tall and tan and young and dumb. He'd know better than to ever chase after one of *them* again.

# CHAPTER FOURTEEN

"WHY DID we have to leave?" Kevin whined, as Angie recklessly raced his black Ferrari along Sunset. "I was havin' fun."

"If that's your idea of fun," Angie sneered. "Then you, like, need *major* detox."

"Fuck you!"

"Fuck you, too!" she retorted, screeching the powerful car to a halt at a stop light. "I'm not into all that phoney b.s. If you weren't a friggin' movie star, those people wouldn't talk to you."

"So?" Kevin said belligerently. "I *am* a friggin' movie star."

"You're not Leonardo DiCaprio."

"Wouldn't want t'be," Kevin said sulkily, thinking that it was about time he dumped Angie. She was too bossy by far, and now that he had two big box-office successes behind him, he could get any girl he wanted. Angie didn't know it, but she was busy bossing herself out of a gig. "Where we goin'?" he asked, noticing that she'd zoomed past the street where they'd set up house together.

"I need to score," she said, rubbing her forehead. "I'm, like, totally bummed."

*You need to clean up your act*, he thought. Angie was heavily into drugs and he wasn't. Been there. Done that. He had no desire to become the next Robert Downey Jr or Charlie Sheen. Those guys were old enough to know better.

"Fuck," he mumbled. "I can't go scorin' drugs with you. It's not good for my image."

"You never do anything for me," she complained. "Never."

"It's time you got out of that whole drug scene," he said, thinking about Lucinda Bennett and the movie they were going to make together.

"I don't need a freakin' lecture," Angie snapped. "I just lost a very close friend."

"I never heard you mention Salli."

"That's 'cause we had a big fight before you and I got together."

"Big fight about what?"

"We used to share an apartment." Angie sighed. "That is until she stole my boyfriend who wasn't even worth stealing. He was a sonofabitch. I bet it was him who killed her."

"What're you talking about *now*?"

"Eddie Stoner."

"Eddie Stoner," Kevin repeated. "The actor?"

"You know him?"

"Think I worked with him once."

"Did you or didn't you?"

"Who remembers?"

"Anyway – he was a rough bastard, so I figured if Salli wanted him so much, she could have him. I moved out, and a couple of weeks later she and Eddie got married in Vegas. What a *dumb* move. All he had going for him was a big dick and a sharp right hand. He used to beat the shit out of me, and as soon as they were married, he started on her. One night she phoned me, hysterical. I told her, 'Don't come cryin' to me – you wanted him, you got him.' And I didn't help her. Then she started to get famous and all of that shit. Eventually she dumped Eddie and got a divorce. It was a real drag. I know she had to call the cops on him a few times, and I know he threatened to kill her. That was his thing – he threatened to kill *me* when we were together. I'm surprised he didn't come creeping back when I made it, considering *I* made it bigger than her." She paused, then added thoughtfully, "Maybe I should tell the cops what I know."

"You can't go around accusing people," Kevin said, frowning. "You want us *both* dragged through the tabloids?"

"Okay, Kev," Angie said, her mind on other matters. "Let me score a gram or two an' I'll think it over."

"You gotta get out of the drug scene," Kevin repeated sternly.

"I can," she answered defiantly. "Anytime I want."

"Sure."

"Yeah, *sure.*"

"You're difficult, Angie, you never listen."

"I know, you've told me a million times. But what would you do without me, Kev? You'd be running around this town with your cock in your hand, and they'd all be taking you for the ride of the century. Right?"

"If you say so."

And he wondered exactly how he should go about dumping her.

L.A.
Connections
2

# CHAPTER FIFTEEN

DETECTIVE TUCCI called his wife, Faye, and told her that, just as he'd expected, the area around the house was turning into a media circus. There were TV trucks with their news crews, reporters, and crowds of people milling around outside on the street. Everyone was contained behind police lines, while helicopters hovered overhead, and in the house the phone did not stop ringing. Even though it was late at night, word had spread fast.

Detective Tucci swore softly under his breath. There would definitely be no dinner tonight, not unless it was take-out pizza, and he hated to do that to his stomach.

By midnight the police photographer had finished his grizzly task, and the medical examiner was now in charge. Later Salli's mutilated body was put on a stretcher and taken off in an ambulance headed for the morgue where an autopsy would take place and evidence would be gathered.

When the ambulance attendants loaded Salli's body aboard, the crowds went wild, screaming and yelling her name. Detective Tucci couldn't help wondering if the murderer was out there somewhere, watching . . . waiting . . . getting his kicks.

The facts as Detective Tucci knew them were as such: there was no sign of a break-in, which meant that Salli had obviously known her killer, and had probably let him into the house. She must have been comfortable with him – if indeed it was a male – because she'd taken him into the living room and out by the pool. In the sink behind the bar Detective Tucci had found two hastily washed glasses. He'd immediately put them into a plastic bag and sent them over to the lab to be checked.

So, he decided, whoever the killer was, he had entered through the front door, Salli had greeted the person, they'd had a drink together, walked out near the patio, and then for some unknown reason, he or she had worked themselves into a frenzy and stabbed her to death.

The houseman had probably been on his way to see what all the noise was about, because according to neighbours, loud music had been playing, and the dogs were barking non-stop. On his way, Froo, the Asian houseman, had encountered the killer, who'd shot him point-blank in the face – which indicated that Froo would have recognized the man – or woman.

For the last two hours Tucci had been trying to contact Salli's husband, Bobby Skorch. Apparently Bobby was in a car somewhere on his way back from a gig in Vegas. His cellphone was turned off, and he appeared to be unreachable.

Detective Tucci wondered if Bobby had murdered his wife. It wouldn't be the first time a husband was responsible. Maybe Bobby Skorch had driven back from his appearance early, fought with Salli, stabbed her to death, then got back in his car, driven away and would turn up later – the distraught husband. It was hardly an uncommon scenario. Crimes of passion were not unusual.

Detective Tucci sat at a table in the kitchen making numerous notes. He was known for his detailed accounts, and he enjoyed making sure that he didn't miss one single thing.

Somewhere in this puzzle there was an answer, and he fully intended to find out what it was.

# CHAPTER SIXTEEN

MADISON PARKED a couple of blocks from the house. There were TV camera crews and reporters everywhere, not to mention huge crowds of onlookers. The police had already roped off the area around the house and there was a strangely festive atmosphere – as if people were revelling in the action.

She left her car and hurried over to the nearest cop. "Who's the detective in charge of this case?" she asked, flashing her press pass.

"Can't give out any information at this time," the cop said, barely glancing at her.

"I understand that," she said evenly. "However, I know he'll want to talk to me, so please would you get a message to him. My name's Madison Castelli, I'm a journalist from New York, and I spent the day with Ms Turner in her house."

"Really?" the cop said disbelievingly.

"Yes, really," Madison replied.

"Can you prove that?"

"How am I supposed to prove it?"

"With all due respect, ma'am, there are a lot of people here trying to get into the house . . ."

"I'm sure there are, but if you tell the detective that I was with her today, I'm certain he'll want to see me."

"I told you, ma'am, I can't do that, there's too much going on."

"Look," Madison said, fast losing patience, "I work for *Manhattan Style*, my editor is Victor Simons." She handed him a card. "This is his number. If you give this to the detective in charge, he can check with my editor and verify my story. Other than that I don't know what I can do, but I *do* know that he'll want to see me."

"Not tonight, ma'am. Maybe he'll interview you tomorrow. Why don't you leave your name and number and go on home."

"Can I be sure he'll get it?" she said, swallowing her aggravation, because she knew it wouldn't do any good to lose her temper.

"Absolutely, ma'am."

"I have an audiotape of Salli at my house. On it she talks about everything that's going on in her life. I'm sure it will be helpful."

The cop took another look at her. Maybe she wasn't handing him a bullshit story, maybe she was legit. "Whyn't you wait here a minute," he said. "I'll go check."

"Thanks."

She watched as the cop made his way into the house. Where were Natalie and Jimmy? They should be here already. She could see quite a few on-the-scene reporters standing on the street doing remotes to their TV stations.

The cop returned after a few minutes. "Detective Tucci says he'll be in touch tomorrow."

"Are you telling me he doesn't want to see me now?"

"That's right, ma'am."

"Then I guess I'll write the story my way, and mention the detective on the case refused to see me. I'm sure the *L.A. Times* will be interested in a first-hand account."

"Whatever you say, ma'am."

"I'm merely telling you what I plan to do so you can pass it on to Detective Tucci."

"I'll let him know."

She returned to her rented car, drove to the nearest gas station, went into the phone booth, and looked up Tucci in the phone book. Then she started making calls. Third time lucky.

"Is Detective Tucci there?" she asked the woman who answered.

"I'm sorry, he's not."

"Am I speaking to his wife?"

"Yes. Can I help you?"

"It's most important that I get in contact with your husband. I have information pertaining to the case he's working on. I talked to an officer in charge of crowd control, and I'm not sure if he gave Detective Tucci my message. I work for *Manhattan Style* magazine."

"I know that magazine," Faye interrupted. "I read it every month."

"Glad to hear it. Then you might know me – Madison Castelli?"

"Certainly, Miss Castelli – I've read your work. I like it a lot."

"Call me Madison. And your name is?"

"Faye."

"Okay, Faye – well, um . . . tell your husband I had lunch with Salli today, I have an audiotape of our interview, and I'd like to see him personally as soon as possible."

"I'll do that," Faye said, impressed. "You can depend on me."

Madison gave Faye her phone number, then, secure in the fact that she'd done her duty, she got in her car and drove back to Natalie's.

Cole was sprawled on the couch in front of the TV staring at the screen. "You heard the news?" he said as she walked in.

"Yes."

"I used to train Salli, y' know."

"You did?"

"Yeah, a couple of years ago, when she was married to her first husband, Eddie. He was a maniac. She was a sweetie."

Madison sat on the edge of the couch. "Tell me about him."

"Salli used to confide in me," Cole said. "To everybody else she'd say she got a black eye or all bruised up walking into a door. One time he broke her arm and she had to go to the hospital. She called the cops on him a couple of times, but he'd always talk them round. She was lucky to get away from him."

"Are you saying you think he did it?"

"Wouldn't be surprised," Cole said, with a shrug. "He had a way hot temper. That dude was always pissed about something."

"Like what?"

"You know the deal. He was a small-time actor who worked plenty, but was never the star, which made him *real* sour. I stopped working out with her when Eddie began getting jealous."

"Of you?"

"Yeah."

"But you're gay."

Cole laughed mirthlessly. "Try telling Eddie. He didn't want her around *any* guy who looked good. He wanted control, that's all he was interested in. I'm kinda surprised she got away, it took a lot of strength."

"What was his name again?"

"Eddie Stoner."

Madison got up and went to her laptop, where she put in a request to New York for information.

*Eddie Stoner. Let's find out exactly who you are.*

# CHAPTER SEVENTEEN

"Oh ... my ... God," Kristin murmured, stretching luxuriously. "That was pretty ... damn ... good."

Jake pinned her arms above her head, holding her wrists tightly so she could barely move. "That wasn't pretty damn good," he said sternly. "That was sensational, *and* you know it."

"Of course I know it," she said, giggling softly. "You don't have to torture me to make me talk."

"And what makes you think I'm about to torture you?" he asked, mock-serious.

"I don't know, maybe you'll make love to me again."

"Would that be torture?"

"Oh yes. Beautiful, incredible, fantastic torture."

He laughed. "I guess I'm going to have to make you beg."

"Really?" she said, attempting to roll out from under him.

"Yup," he said decisively. "I'm gonna have to do it."

"Okay, how do I beg?" she said, realizing she'd never felt so relaxed and carefree and happy as she did at that very moment.

"You say, 'Please Jake.'"

"Please Jake," she repeated, unable to keep the laughter out of her voice.

"Now say, 'I beg you, Jake, to give me more.'"

"I'm not saying that."

"Don't argue. I'm trying to teach you."

"Dear Jake," she said, smiling. "That was so damn good that I'm *begging* you for more."

He bent his head to her left nipple, teasing it with his tongue. "Keep begging," he said. "I like it."

She felt his hardness against her naked thigh, and sighed with pleasure. "Isn't it time you begged me?" she suggested, after a few moments of utter bliss.

"Huh?"

"I want to hear *you* beg."

"You do?"

"Right now, soldier!"

"Hey!" A big smile spread across his face. "This is like we've been together for years."

She laughed softly. "Well, we haven't."

"Oh, *big* surprise," he said jokingly. "But we're going to be – right?"

*Why did he have to spoil everything*? "Jake," she said, searching for the right words, "I haven't been completely honest with you."

214

"Don't want to hear about it now. You can be completely honest with me over lunch tomorrow. But right now, let's just enjoy the moment."

She tried to roll away again. He turned her back towards him and began sucking on her lower lip. "I never realized," she gasped, "that kissing could be so erotic."

"Then you've got a lot of learning to do."

"Will you teach me, Jake?"

"You want me to?"

"Yes."

"Well, first you've got to gently caress the lips with your tongue very, very slowly. Like this."

"Oh, you're good," she said, shivering.

"So I've been told," he answered confidently.

"And who told you?"

"Huh?"

"Well, you informed me you hadn't been with a woman for over a year," she said curiously. "So who told you?"

A long pause before he spoke. "My wife," he said at last. "She died in a car crash a year ago."

"Oh, God, I'm sorry – I didn't know."

"Hey, listen, I'm over it. You know the old cliché – there's nothing like time to heal. Anyway, we were separated when it happened."

"Were you getting a divorce?"

"She was seeing another guy. In fact, she was on her way to visit him when a truck came out of a side-street and totalled her car. She had no chance."

"Are you telling me she left you for someone else?"

"Yup, that's exactly right. Which is why there hasn't been anyone since. Because how could I trust anyone after that? Megan was my high-school sweetheart, we were married straight out of school. I thought we had a pretty good marriage, and then . . ." He trailed off.

"Jake, I . . . I'm really sorry."

"When somebody lets you down it's difficult to trust again. But then I saw you sitting in Neiman's, and you had this great luminous quality, and I *knew* you were special. And now, days later, here we are. God works in mysterious ways, huh?"

She was suffused with guilt. Why did this have to happen? Why did she have to fall in love with a man to whom she could never tell the truth? And how was she going to extract herself from this situation? Because there was absolutely no way she could ever tell him.

"Hey," Jake said, "this wasn't supposed to turn into a confessional. This is you and me starting out, it's not about either of our pasts. But while we're on the subject, is there anything you want to tell me?"

*Plenty*, she thought, suffused with guilt. *But there's no way I'm going to.*

She put her arms around him to hide her shame, and hugged him very tight. She was definitely going to make this a night to remember, because after this one night of passion, she'd decided she would never see him again.

"So," Jake said, smiling, "what did I do to deserve such affection?"

"Everything," she murmured.

And then he was kissing her again. And before she knew

it they were making love for the second time. And it was so amazing, so different, so satisfying.

And just as she was heading towards another great climax, the phone rang, jangling her back to reality.

"Ignore it," Jake said, still inside her, pinning her beneath his body, the feel of him driving her crazy.

She wondered who it could be, but she didn't have to wonder long, because after three rings her answering machine picked up.

*Oh God*, she thought, panic-stricken, *I forgot to turn the damn machine off*.

Jake was also close to a climax, so there was no way she could escape to turn down the volume.

"Hi, Kristin, sweetie," said Darlene. "Boy, has Mr X got a hot nut for *you*. Talk about obsession. Can you believe he wants to book you again tonight, *and* he's willing to spring for another five thousand big ones for the privilege? Twice in one night. Honey, you've really got it going." A husky giggle. "What's your secret? A mink-lined snatch? Call me back a.s.a.p. The man is waiting."

L.A. Connections 2

# CHAPTER EIGHTEEN

MADISON AWOKE to Natalie pushing her shoulders. "What's up?" she mumbled.

"There's a Detective Tucci on the phone," Natalie said, already dressed and made up. "Isn't he the detective covering the Salli T. Turner case?"

"That's right," Madison answered, suppressing a yawn.

"Why's he calling *you*?" Natalie asked curiously.

"Because I phoned his house last night. I couldn't get into the location and I thought I should talk to him about the audiotape I have of Salli." Leaning over, she reached for the phone. "This is Madison Castelli."

"Miss Castelli," Detective Tucci said, his tone slow and measured, "I understand you have some information for me."

"Yes, I do. You see, I was with Salli yesterday. She gave

219

me an in-depth interview for my magazine. In fact, I have the tape if you'd be interested in hearing it."

"Most definitely."

"Shall I come to the station?"

"That's very accommodating of you, Miss Castelli, but I'll be at the Pacific Palisades house all day. Can you come there?"

"Certainly."

"I'll expect you as soon as possible."

Madison replaced the receiver. "There goes Freddie Leon for the day," she said wryly.

Natalie handed her a cup of much-needed coffee. "What do you mean?" she asked.

"If I'm going to meet the detective, how can I get in to see Freddie today? I was planning on dropping by the IAA office to visit Max Steele."

"You couldn't anyway," Natalie pointed out. "It's Sunday, they'd be closed."

"Oh, right."

"And regarding Max Steele," Natalie added, "there's a story about him in the *Times*. Seems he's leaving IAA to head up Orpheus Studios."

"You're kidding?"

"It's on the second page."

"Really?"

"Is this a surprise?"

"He told me he had some news, only I didn't realize it was going to be public knowledge so fast. I'd better call him."

"He's probably sleeping."

Madison reached for her robe and got out of bed. "What happened after I left last night?"

"Oh, Garth was his usual uncharming self," Natalie said. "I was at the station all night interviewing anybody who knew her. It's media-frenzy time, all anybody's talking about. And once they find out you were with her, *you'll* be a media sensation, too."

"Thanks a lot," Madison said. "If you hadn't told your news director—"

"What can *he* do?"

"Tell other people, to punish me for not appearing on his shitty show."

"It's not a shitty show," Natalie said defensively.

"Sorry, I didn't mean that."

"Yes, you did!"

"C'mon, Nat, let's not start the day off badly. Did they reach Salli's husband yet?"

"Yeah, there's coverage of him going into the house. He looks wrecked."

"What about the *ex*, Eddie Stoner? Have they questioned him?"

"They're looking. Nobody seems to know where he's at."

"Is he the prime suspect?"

"Can you imagine what the tabloids are going to do with this story?" Natalie exclaimed.

Madison nodded. "It'll turn into another OJ and Nicole circus."

"You got it," Natalie said. "Only this time they won't be able to play the race card. Thank God!"

"No, but you can bet they'll play the sex card," Madison said. "You know, sexy blonde, big boobs, all of that sexist crap – like Salli was asking for it."

"You think so?"

"I *know* so. She was beautiful, rich, sexy *and* a woman. Major strike against getting any kind of fair treatment." Madison sighed. "This whole thing makes me sick. Yesterday she was alive, today's she's dead. I simply can't believe it."

"Me neither," said Cole, entering the room. "How's everyone doin' today?"

"Not great," Madison replied, shaking her head.

"I heard on Channel Five that Salli's dad is flying in from North Dakota," Cole said. "And there'll be a private funeral tomorrow. I'd like to go."

"That's a tough one," Natalie said. "Salli had so many fans, they'll all want to be there."

"I'd still like to go," Cole said.

"So would I," Madison agreed. "How can we arrange it?"

"I'll see what I can find out," Natalie said. "Right now I've got to get back to the studio. Then Luther wants to take me to lunch, and girl, I am *not* passing *him* up."

As soon as Natalie left, Madison decided to call Max Steele. She had his home number, so she picked up the phone and got through immediately. "Hi, Max," she said. "This is Madison – remember? Breakfast yesterday?"

He sounded groggy. "What's doin'?"

"I read your news."

"News?"

222

"You told me you had an announcement, however, you didn't tell me it was going to appear today."

"What announcement?" Max said, kicking off his bedcovers, realizing he was suffering from a monster hangover.

"Is it true you're taking over Ariel Shore's job at Orpheus?"

"Shit!" he said, sitting up. "Where'd you hear that?"

"It's in the *Times*."

"Christ!" he said. And he knew what had happened. Freddie had opened the door before he was ready to leave, and shoved him out. Hard. Now Billy Cornelius would be mad as hell, and there was nothing he could do about it.

"Off the record," Madison said. "Would you mind giving me Freddie Leon's home number?"

"Why?" Max said suspiciously. "You wanna ask him about this?"

"No, this has nothing to do with you. I'm simply looking to find out everything I can about him. That *is* why I'm out here."

"If you want the dirt on Freddie, talk to his secretary – Ria Santiago. She knows things nobody else does."

"Would you happen to have *her* phone number?"

"Yeah, I'll give you both numbers." *Nothing like a little sweet revenge*, Max thought.

Madison hung up and glanced at her watch. It was too early to call anyone else: waking Max was one thing, but she figured she'd be nice and let the others sleep for an hour or so, although she was sure Freddie Leon was an early riser – he looked the type.

While she was waiting she called Victor in New York,

where it was three hours later. "I'm holding the press for your story," Victor said. "I need it like yesterday."

"I'm seeing the detective on the case this morning. As soon as I get back I'll write it up and fax it to you."

"Good," Victor said. "And maybe you can include the name of the killer."

"Yeah, sure, Victor," she drawled. "Why not? Simple."

"No need to be sarcastic, Maddy. I'll talk to you later."

"Yes, Victor, later."

# CHAPTER NINETEEN

ARIEL SHORE arrived at Billy Cornelius's house at eight in the morning and insisted upon seeing him. Ethel, his feisty wife, was still asleep. The butler, a prudent man, did not wake Ethel. Instead he ushered Ariel into the living room, where she waited impatiently for ten long minutes.

When Billy finally appeared, she thrust the *L.A. Times* in his face. "What's *this*?" she said through clenched teeth, towering over him.

Billy Cornelius stared bad-temperedly at the newspaper. "What're you talking about?" he snapped, his left eye twitching.

"This ridiculous story about Max Steele getting my job," Ariel said. "Read it."

Billy scanned the story with beady, red-rimmed eyes. "Bullpuddy, hogwash," he said.

"It better be," Ariel said sternly. "Because I'm sure you wouldn't relish Ethel finding out about us."

Billy curled his lip. "You wouldn't do that, Ariel."

"Think again, Billy, I certainly would."

"You promised."

"I *know* what I promised," she said, marching up and down. "And I know what *you* promised. You break yours, I can break mine. What is this crap with Max Steele anyway?"

"I was planning on telling you," Billy said. "I considered bringing him in as head of production. Nothing definite."

She arched a disgusted eyebrow. "Without informing me?"

"Max is a go-getter, he knows everyone."

Ariel planted herself in front of her so-called boss. "Listen to me, Billy, and listen carefully. *I* run the studio. You do not make decisions like that without my input. Max Steele will have nothing to do with Orpheus. *Nothing.* Is that perfectly clear? Because if it's not, I'm sure that Ethel will be able to make it *very* clear to you."

"You have nothing to worry about," Billy said, backing down in the face of Ariel's fury.

"And next time you sneak around behind my back," Ariel said, eyes glittering dangerously, "you'd better be more careful. I want a retraction, and I want to see it in Monday morning's paper. Do we understand each other, Billy?"

Billy Cornelius nodded. He might be one of the richest men in America, but when Ariel Shore screamed, he jumped.

L.A.
Connections
2

# CHAPTER TWENTY

WHEN DIANA awoke on Sunday morning she realized that Freddie had not returned home the night before. It wasn't the first time he'd stayed out all night.

Nevertheless she was livid. How dare he think he could simply walk out and not return.

And where exactly was he? Not that she was worried about other women – Freddie had never been a sexual being. Even at the beginning of their marriage they'd made love infrequently; then, several years ago, their lovemaking had stopped altogether.

No, it wasn't another woman. It was Freddie's way of hurting her. First he ruined her dinner party, then he stayed out all night. What a cold bastard he could be.

The children were away in Connecticut staying with her mother, so the house was quite peaceful. She got out of bed and marched downstairs to the kitchen, where the caterers had done a masterful job of cleaning up.

Throwing open the fridge she surveyed the leftovers, wrapped neatly in Saran Wrap. Cold hors d'oeuvres always appealed to her, so she took out an egg roll and wolfed it down without thinking. Then she stomped around the house, making sure everything was in place and that the catering staff hadn't stolen anything. Diana lived in fear that someone was going to rip her off. It could be because she had been brought up by extremely strict parents in Utah who suspected everyone of stealing. She'd never forgotten her stern upbringing.

The Sunday *L.A. Times* was neatly laid out on the kitchen table, alongside the *New York Times*. Usually Freddie got to them first, he was fastidious about his newspapers and did not like anyone else touching them before him. However, today Diana felt it was her duty to mess them up before he got home.

The heading of a story on page two caught her attention.

## ARIEL OUT, MAX IN
### MAX STEELE TO LEAVE IAA AND
### JOIN ORPHEUS

How could this possibly have gotten into the newspapers so fast? Somebody must have leaked it early, long before Freddie and Max's confrontation.

Diana read the story quickly, then rushed to the phone.

Max answered immediately. "Yes?" he snapped, sounding most unfriendly.

"Max, this is Diana. Can we meet?"

"Why?" he asked suspiciously.

"There's something I wish to discuss."

"Is it about Freddie?"

"He mustn't know we're meeting."

"Whatever you say, Diana."

"Nine thirty at the Four Seasons. The dining room."

"I'll be there," Max said.

"Good," Diana replied.

She'd known he wouldn't turn her down.

L.A.
Connections
2

# CHAPTER TWENTY-ONE

EDDIE STONER was awakened from a liquor-induced sleep at six a.m. on Sunday morning by two burly cops, who burst rudely into his apartment and informed him he was under arrest. He was between girlfriends at the time, so there was no one to buffer their entrance.

"What the fuck is *this* about?" Eddie mumbled, as they instructed him to get out of bed.

"Parking tickets," cop number one said. "You got thirty-four of 'em, all unpaid. You're under arrest, bud, so let's go."

"Parking tickets!" Eddie Stoner said, throwing off the sheet, knowing he was naked and not caring. Let the cops get an eyeful and see what they *didn't* have.

"Yeah, unpaid tickets," said cop number two, proceeding to read him his rights.

"Jesus Christ!" Eddie grumbled, reaching for his pants. "Don't you guys have anythin' better t'do?"

"Where'd you get that scratch on your chest?" cop number one asked.

"Didn't realize gettin' a parkin' ticket meant havin' to explain my physical state," Eddie replied, running a hand through his mane of dirty blond hair. "There's one on my ass, too. Wanna take a peek? My girlfriend's got long fingernails."

"Get dressed," cop number two said.

Eddie Stoner shrugged, threw on a T-shirt and some sneakers. "Fuck!" he said. "You're haulin' me in for parkin' tickets. Who the fuck'd believe *this*?"

# CHAPTER TWENTY-TWO

MADISON PLAYED the tape in her rented car on the way to Salli's house. It was truly heartbreaking to hear Salli explain her life in her own words – exactly as Madison remembered. She found it particularly interesting when Salli talked about Eddie Stoner. "Eddie was basically a good guy," Salli said in her breathy voice. "Just frustrated, 'cause, like, his mom drove him loco. Never left him alone for a moment, laid a big fat guilt trip on him 'cause his father ran out on them when Eddie was twelve. So, like, he always felt kind of responsible for her. An' she got off on that – telling him he was a bum and no good. Guess he wanted to prove her right. She hated me, thought I was a little tramp. Said so to my face. Well, I guess I gotta confess – Eddie did beat me up a few times. But it wasn't his fault, and later, he was always so nice and loving, begging my forgiveness. I had to escape, though. Otherwise he would've dragged me down with him."

Madison listened to her own voice on the tape. "If I remember correctly, Salli, you told me on the plane that Eddie was a psycho freakazoid asshole actor who sued *you* for alimony. You also told me that he thinks one day you'll take him back."

"Wow!" Salli's voice again. "*You*'ve got a good memory."

"So which is it? Was he a sweetheart? Or a wife-beater?"

"A little bit of both," Salli said. And then, wistfully, "But I must've loved him at one time."

Madison switched the tape off. She wished she'd asked more questions about Eddie Stoner.

Now it was too late.

\*

"Nice of you to come, Miss Castelli," Detective Tucci said, greeting her at the door. He was a tall, heavy-set man with brown hair and faded blue eyes. Not unattractive, he took Madison's arm and led her inside the house. Walking through the hall without Salli there to greet her felt strange. Automatically, she glanced up at the giant portrait. It was still there, a naked Salli, smiling down at everybody.

"Merely doing my duty," she replied. "When I leave here I'm writing a piece for my magazine, and I thought I should let you know what I have, in case it might be useful for your investigation."

"That's very thoughtful of you, Miss Castelli."

"On the tape, Salli talks about her ex-husband, Eddie

Stoner. When we flew into L.A. a couple of days ago, she was telling me he always expected they'd get back together. Do you think he could've—?"

"Mr Stoner's already in custody on parking-ticket violations," Detective Tucci said. "Of course, that's official information, not for publication. I can trust you, Miss Castelli, can't I?"

"Please call me Madison," she said, nodding. "I spoke to your wife, she was most charming on the phone."

"Faye's a good woman."

"Salli was a terrific girl," Madison said. "You've only seen the public image, but to know her was to realize that she had a certain sweetness that really came through. I'm so saddened by this horrible tragedy."

"The world seems to be," Detective Tucci said. "There's already several websites set up to discuss her murder."

"I can imagine."

"May I listen to the tape back in my office?" Detective Tucci said. "Then maybe I can ask you questions about it later."

"I made a copy for you."

"You're very organized."

"I'm a good journalist."

"My wife said that. She speaks very highly of your work. Faye's the one with the time to read magazines, I don't."

Madison laughed politely.

"Are you from here?" he asked.

"New York," she said. "I'm in L.A. preparing a story on Freddie Leon."

"I'm afraid I don't know who that is."

"Your wife would, I'm sure."

"Oh, yes, Faye – she knows all about show-business."

Madison smiled again. She liked this man, he was warm and seemed to care.

"Did you meet the houseman yesterday?" Detective Tucci asked.

"Froo. Yes, I did. I gather he's the other victim."

"We think he heard noises and came to investigate."

"Well, Detective, if there's anything I can do, please don't hesitate to call me."

"You say she had a certain sweetness?"

"That's right."

"I'd like to solve this one."

"Tell me, do you think it could be the ex-husband?"

Detective Tucci shook his head. "I never make random guesses. With DNA today we'll be able to find out in no time."

"Just like they did with Nicole Simpson, right?" Madison said, unable to resist the dig.

"That was a botched case."

"I'm sure you won't botch this one. I trust that you'll do Salli justice."

"It's my intention, Miss Castelli, it's certainly my intention."

L.A.
Connections
2

# CHAPTER TWENTY-THREE

MAX COULD NOT believe what was happening to him. One moment he was a partner in the most successful talent agency in Los Angeles, the next he was about to head up a studio, and now Billy Cornelius had just got off the phone, telling him that things had changed, and there was no way they could work together.

"What do you mean changed?" Max had blustered.

"You should never have leaked it," Billy had said. "Too late now. The deal's off."

Max was furious. Now he'd have to go crawling back to Freddie and say, "Let's forgive and forget." Only Freddie was not the forgiving kind. Everyone knew that.

Max couldn't help thinking about Inga Cruelle. He'd always had great success with women; how dare she treat him as if he was simply another guy on the make?

He glanced at his gold Rolex, it was almost time to meet Diana. Before he did, he had a plan.

He went to the phone and called Kristin. To his annoyance her answering machine picked up.

"Hey, baby," he said, "this is Max Steele. I've made a decision. I'm taking you out of the business, honey. Making you exclusive. You tell me what it'll cost to set you up, and I'll do it." He paused for a moment, quite pleased with himself. "I've been thinking about things. I want you to be with me. Y' see, I need somebody like you around, somebody to keep me focused. I can introduce you to people, change your life. Nobody'll know who you are, or what you used to be. This is gonna work out, Kristin." Another pause. "I have a meeting at eleven, so call me any time after twelve an' we'll work something out. Okay, honey?"

And when he hung up the phone he was convinced he had her. Beautiful Kristin beside him would change his luck.

*

Diana was about to leave the house when Freddie walked in. He was unshaven, his eyes kind of wild looking, and his clothes crumpled. Most out of character for a man as fastidious as Freddie Leon.

"My God!" Diana said, staring at her dishevelled husband. "You look as if you slept in your clothes. What hotel took you in looking like that?"

"Diana, leave me alone," Freddie said, pushing past her

238

on his way upstairs. As far as he was concerned, his wife was becoming more trouble than she was worth.

"Yes, Freddie, I will," she called after him. And set off to seal her future with Max Steele.

# Murder

L.A.
Connections
3

L.A.
Connections
3

# PROLOGUE

ON THE beach in Malibu, two teenagers ran down to the water wearing black rubber wet-suits, their surfboards tucked under their arms.

"Great waves, dude," said one.

"Sweet," agreed the second one.

And just as they were about to enter the water, they noticed a fan of long blonde hair and one delicate arm tangled in seaweed.

They glanced at each other. "Holy shit! What's that?"

"Looks like a body."

Together they dragged the lifeless form out of the water and laid it on the sand.

It was a female. Gorgeous, blonde, and very, very naked.

Another murder.

Another beautiful day in L.A.

# CHAPTER ONE

DETECTIVE CHUCK TUCCI was tired. He'd only had two hours of sleep and was now feeling the effects. He was also aware that very shortly he'd have to give some kind of press conference to satisfy the hordes of media still hovering outside the murdered star's home like hungry vultures waiting for something to be thrown into their gaping mouths. Tucci knew exactly what he'd like to throw – several hand grenades.

Early in the morning, Faye had packed him a care package – one corned beef, lettuce and tomato sandwich, his favourite, *and* a carton of her home-made coleslaw, which she knew he loved. He'd missed dinner the night before, and when he'd finally arrived home at some ungodly hour, Faye had been asleep. As soon as he'd made enough noise to wake her, she got up and, in spite of the fact that he was supposed to be on a diet, she'd hurried down to the kitchen and fixed him a delicious plate of scrambled eggs. Faye was a good woman. He often gave thanks for the day he'd met her: he'd been investigating a murder in Malibu, and she had been the social worker sent to collect the two children in the house. Three months later they were married.

Last night he'd wolfed down the plate of eggs and begged for more. "You can't eat anything else this late," Faye had scolded, wagging a disapproving finger at him. "It's bad for your stomach."

Bad for his *stomach*? Given half the chance, he would've devoured everything in sight, despite having spent the evening in the company of two bloodied bodies he'd had to inspect and watch being photographed. Finally, when forensics were finished, he'd observed the bodies being hauled off to be autopsied, and then he'd prowled around the house, making copious notes in his blue leather notebook. After that he'd interviewed the neighbours, and now, in the morning sunshine, all that was left were the chalk marks to show exactly where the unfortunate victims had fallen.

Tucci shook his head and tried not to think about food. His care package was sitting in the victims' kitchen where he'd left it, and there it would stay until he got desperate. He was now waiting to interview the infamous Bobby Skorch. A few hours ago, Bobby's lawyer, Marty Steiner, had arrived at the house and rushed straight up to the master bedroom, where he'd been huddled with his client for the last two hours. Marty was smoothness personified, with his slicked back silver hair, smug face and expensive jogging suit. A "dream-team" reject, he was a man obviously determined to hit the headlines. One look and Tucci had immediately tagged him "Hollywood lawyer", although he'd promised himself not to make such quick judgements. Faced with Marty Steiner, the temptation had proved irresistible.

He glanced at his watch, noting that the brown leather strap was worn and that he needed to buy a new one. Maybe next weekend he and Faye would go shopping. Faye loved wandering along the Third Street promenade, checking out the stores, and as long as they got to stop for a hamburger or a hot dog, he didn't object.

Now that his mind was back on food, his sandwich, packaged in Saran Wrap, was beckoning him. Finally he gave up and hurried into the kitchen.

Salli T. Turner's plump, middle-aged Filipino maid, Eppie, sat at the end of a long marble counter, crying into a glass of milk and a plate of cookies. Earlier he had questioned her; between sobs she'd told him she didn't know anything. According to Eppie, she arrived at the house every morning at eight a.m. and departed at three p.m. When she left yesterday, Missy Salli – as she called her employer – had been happily lunching out by the pool.

He'd asked her about Bobby Skorch. "They very much in love," Eppie had answered tearfully. "Always laughing."

Well, Bobby Skorch wasn't laughing now, Tucci thought grimly. And he wasn't talking either. Not that he had any obligation to do so – but if he didn't, it would cast a deep pall of suspicion over him.

Tucci's eyes swivelled to the end of the marble counter where he'd left his sandwich. It was gone. So was his carton of home-made coleslaw. "I . . . uh . . . had some food I left here," he said, trying to ignore his rumbling stomach.

"What?" Eppie said rudely, like she couldn't believe he was thinking of food at a time like this.

"A sandwich," he said, clearing his throat. "And a carton of coleslaw."

"Oh," Eppie answered vaguely, lowering her swollen and red-rimmed eyes. "Didn't know it was yours. I ate it."

"You *ate* it?" Tucci said incredulously.

"Sorry," Eppie said, stuffing another cookie into her mouth. "It was only an itty-bitty *snack*." And then, noticing that the detective was not pleased, she burst into sobs again, almost choking on her cookie.

"Goddamn it!" Tucci mumbled under his breath, just as his partner, Lee Eccles – summoned back from a fishing trip – arrived.

"Jeez!" Lee exclaimed. "There's a friggin' circus goin' on outside. What in hell happened here?"

L.A.
Connections
3

# CHAPTER TWO

MADISON SAT in front of her laptop at the kitchen table, diligently attempting to compose a story about Salli. It was not easy.

She stared blankly at the screen, pushing back her long dark hair and sighing deeply. In a way, it was probably best to get it all down on paper, yet in another way she was so upset by Salli's murder that she wasn't sure she could remain completely detached.

Drumming her fingers on the table, she wondered what to say about the girl everybody *thought* they knew, but didn't really know at all. Salli T. Turner, the sizzling platinum blonde who regularly appeared on *ET* and *Hard Copy*, and was often featured in the tabloids – photographed running into parties, emerging from clubs and discos, clad in revealing tight rubber dresses and exceptionally high heels, her bountiful cleavage well displayed. She always seemed to be waving and laughing, her mega-watt smile lighting up the night.

And yet, beneath the boobs and abundance of blonde hair had lurked a very simple girl, a very *nice* girl. And even though they'd only known each other a short time, Madison had liked her a lot, for Salli had possessed a naïvety and freshness which was surprisingly endearing.

Abruptly she closed her laptop. She didn't feel like writing; she felt like crying. This horrific murder was so senseless. *Why* had it taken place? What had Salli done to merit such a frenzy of violence?

Madison knew what she *should* do – forget about the murders and concentrate on Freddie Leon, since he was the main thrust of her trip to L.A., and she'd done virtually nothing about arranging an interview. Of course, the elusive Freddie Leon was notorious for not granting interviews, but Victor had assured her he could set it up.

*Yeah, Victor*, she thought sourly. *When?*

To take her mind off Salli, Madison decided to call Freddie Leon's long-time secretary, Ria Santiago. She had to stop thinking about Salli, it was all too dark and depressing, and she'd been depressed enough when she'd arrived in L.A. – what with David's walk-out and subsequent marriage. Damn David! Why couldn't he have been honest with her?

Men! She'd had it with them. If only she could find one like her father, Michael, the best-looking and nicest man she knew. He and her stunningly beautiful mother, Stella, had an idyllic marriage. They'd been together thirty years and hardly ever spent a night apart. Madison missed them since they'd given up their elegant New York apartment and moved to Connecticut. It was far too long since she'd spent a weekend with them. As soon as she was through in L.A., that's exactly where she planned on going.

Before she could punch out Ria Santiago's number, Cole came into the room. "Hey," he said, reaching for the coffee pot.

"Hey," Madison responded.

"Didja go see the detective?" he asked, pouring himself a mug of black coffee.

"I sure did."

"Anythin' new?"

"Nothing that I know of."

"It's shit," Cole mumbled, pulling out a chair and sitting down. "Salli didn't deserve to get taken out like that."

"I know," Madison said in sombre agreement.

Cole reached for the TV clicker and tuned into the *E* channel, where they were already showing a quickly put together retrospective. There was Salli in red. Salli in blue. Salli in skintight. Salli in her famous black rubber swimsuit. And then the male star of *Teach!* appeared, an actor past his prime, who still thought he was a major stud. "Everyone was in love with Salli," the actor said, Hollywood casual in well-fitting linen pants and a chest-baring silk shirt, his capped teeth catching the light. "Salli was a *very* special person."

Commercial break.

"Would you switch to Natalie's channel?" Madison asked.

Cole obliged. There was Natalie on the screen, vibrantly

pretty in a shocking pink jacket and short, white dress. "The Salli everyone knew and loved came from a little town outside Chicago," Natalie said. "And we have learned from family and friends that ever since Salli took her first steps, she wanted to be an actress."

Cut to baby pictures of Salli. A fat little cutie. And then on came a "friend of the family" – a stone-faced woman with badly dyed red hair and an eyelid twitch. "I knew Salli since she was two years old," croaked the woman, her voice a gin-soaked rasp. "An' to know her was to love her."

"Jesus!" Madison murmured. "They'll be crawling out from everywhere."

"Who?" Cole asked.

"People who met her once in their lives. It's *their* chance of glory."

"Guess you're right."

"It happens every time somebody famous dies."

"Yeah," Cole agreed.

"Where's her family? Her mother?"

Cole rubbed his faintly stubbled chin. "Didn't Salli tell you about her mom when you interviewed her?"

"She hedged – I didn't pursue."

Cole took a deep breath, his handsome features deadly serious. "Salli's mom was murdered when she was ten. It was her big secret."

Madison felt a cold chill creeping up her spine. "How do you know this?"

Cole was silent for a moment before replying. "There was a time Salli an' I were pretty close," he said, refusing to make eye contact. "She kinda viewed me as a challenge – y'know, the good-looking guy who wasn't into having sex with her. It drove her nutty. Salli liked to think she could get any man she zeroed in on. Sex was her big validation, her comfort zone."

Madison raised an eyebrow. "And did she get you?"

"We did it once," Cole admitted sheepishly. "For God's sake, *don't* tell Natalie."

"Of course not."

"It was before she got really famous."

"And that's when her then husband, Eddie, became jealous of you?"

"He suspected something was goin' on, even though he knew I was gay. So he made her stop using me as her trainer."

"I don't get it," Madison said, frowning. "If you're totally gay, how did she—"

"Hey," Cole said, throwing up his muscular arms, "I'm gay, not dead. And Salli knew exactly what to do to turn me on. She was an expert at sex. It was her game, and man, that girl always played to win."

Madison nodded understandingly. Nothing really surprised her. And Cole was right, Salli *had* gotten off on all the attention.

Cole stood up. "I'm goin' for a hike," he said. "Wanna come?"

She shook her head, everyone was so energetic in L.A. Didn't they know how to relax? "I'll pass," she said. "I'm hoping to interview Freddie Leon's secretary."

"*You*, girl, are missin' out," Cole said, heading for the door. "Nothin' like a good hike in the hills to set your head straight."

"Thanks for the offer," she said, reaching for the coffee pot and refilling her cup. "Maybe some other time."

As soon as he left, Madison called Ria Santiago, identified herself, and told the secretary she was writing a piece on Freddie Leon for *Manhattan Style*, and would like an opportunity to sit down and talk.

Ria's response was cold. "Does Mr Leon know about this?"

"I'm hoping to meet with him tomorrow."

Ria: "I doubt it. Mr Leon does not give interviews."

"I'm sure he'll make an exception."

"I'm sure he won't."

And then the bitch hung up.

# CHAPTER THREE

KRISTIN CARR sat in front of her dressing-table mirror, staring at her reflection. She knew that at twenty-three she was undeniably gorgeous, but she also knew that what was reflected was merely her outer image. Inside she was a whore, and she was certain that everyone knew it.

*Prostitute, hooker, call-girl, whore.* All names that described her profession. Not that it was a profession she'd deliberately chosen. No, it was something she'd taken up because it was the only thing she could do to make enough money to keep Cherie at the private nursing home.

*I sell my body for the almighty dollar*, Kristin thought sadly. *I allow men to use me any way they want. I'm meat. They devour me. And everyone is happy. Everyone except me.*

The sinister Mr X crossed her mind and she shuddered. His sick demands were beyond the merely kinky, but he paid well for the privilege of humiliating her. And that's why Darlene had phoned the night before, leaving her the message that Mr X wanted to see her again – even though she'd been with him earlier that same evening.

The problem was that Kristin had taken it upon herself to have a life – much as her inner voice had warned her not to. Instead of listening to her gut feeling, she'd gone ahead and fallen in lust with Jake. A bad move, because their relationship – such as it was – could go nowhere. Especially now, after he'd heard the message from Darlene – loud and clear.

Kristin had felt Jake shrivel up inside her before he'd rolled away.

She hadn't known what to say. In fact, neither of them said a word. After a moment or two, Jake had gotten off the bed and hurried into the bathroom.

*Punishment,* she'd thought. *Punishment for imagining I could have a life.*

She'd reached for her silk robe at the end of the bed, sat up and put it on. When Jake emerged, he was fully dressed and ready to leave.

"I forgot," he'd said, hardly able to look at her, "I'm expecting an important call."

Disappointment had flooded over her. Didn't he want to discuss it?

*So what?* she'd thought defensively. *Maybe this is best. What could he say? Excuse me, Kristin, why didn't you tell me you were a hooker?*

*Sorry, Jake, I forgot.*

"Uh, I'd like to explain," she'd ventured, hoping for at

least a chance to say something – even if it was only an apology.

"No, Kristin, really," he'd said, anxious to leave. "There's nothing you have to explain to me. The truth is, your lifestyle and mine, they uh . . . simply don't mesh."

*Was that it? Was the non-paying customer leaving?*

"I understand," she'd said stiffly, thinking that if he didn't want to get into it he wasn't worth having anyway. "I'll see you around."

"Yeah," he'd replied. "Guess so." Then he'd stopped at the door, turned and stared at her accusingly. "I wish you'd told me," he'd said.

"Why?" she'd said, filled with hurt.

"Because it isn't fair you didn't. I would've used a condom."

The final blow. How *dare* he say that to her as if she was a common street prostitute? "Fuck you," she'd yelled, suddenly furious. "Fuck *you!*" And she'd gotten up and chased after him, slamming the door on his retreating back. Then she'd gone to her dressing-table and sat there, staring . . . staring . . . staring at her reflection.

When Max Steele, her once-a-month client, phoned in the morning, she had not picked up. Instead she listened to his message on her answering machine. He wanted to make her exclusive, change her life.

*Okay, honey,* she thought. *I can do that. If you want to pay me the kind of money Mr X does, you can have me. Because nobody else wants me. I'm used goods. So, Max Steele, I am all yours.*

L.A. Connections 3

# CHAPTER FOUR

"YOU'RE LATE," Detective Tucci said to his partner, thoroughly grumpy because the maid had devoured his sandwich – not to mention an entire carton of Faye's home-made coleslaw.

"Hey, buddy, *you* try gettin' back from a fishin' trip in the middle of nowhere," Detective Lee Eccles complained, frowning. He was a tall, stoop-shouldered man with a weathered face and exceptionally large hands. "It ain't easy," he grumbled. "An' *then*, when I stopped by the station – my freakin' luck – I got sent out on another homicide. Or a suicide – who the fuck knows? Knock-out blonde babe washed up on the Malibu shore. Legs from here to Cuba. Forensics are runnin' a check on her now."

"You missed the big one here."

"My freakin' luck again. Fill me in. Tell me what we've got."

"Two dead bodies: one female, one male. The female stabbed multiple times. The male shot once in the face. The female's husband arrived home at three a.m. Gave him the news, he shut himself in the bedroom. His lawyer, Marty Steiner, arrived this morning – they've been locked in there together for a couple of hours."

"That piece a shit," Lee spat in disgust.

"You know him?"

"Some freakin' asshole," Lee said, picking at his teeth with a dirty fingernail. "Had dealin's with him before."

Lee Eccles and Detective Tucci had been partners for an uneasy six months. Tucci's previous partner had been a veteran detective, now retired. Lee was smart enough, but too abrasive for Tucci's taste. His favourite off-duty pastime was hanging out in bars and strip clubs, and he constantly talked about women in such graphic terms that he offended Tucci's sensibilities. His remarks were so sexist and derogatory that Tucci had once complained.

"Get yourself to a fuckin' monastery," Lee had responded with a mean scowl.

"What the hell does *that* mean?" Tucci had growled, and they'd almost gotten into a fist fight.

Since that time they had tolerated each other, but there was no real camaraderie.

"You don't look so good," Lee remarked.

"Didn't get any sleep," Tucci replied. "*And* I'm hungry."

"You're always freakin' hungry," Lee said, impatiently

cracking his knuckles. "If you stopped eatin' so damn much, you wouldn't have such a big gut."

"I'm dieting," Tucci admitted, stung by the criticism.

Lee guffawed. "Yeah, until the next doughnut comes along!"

Tucci didn't bother answering. His gut wasn't *that* bad – Faye said she loved cuddling up to him. "You're huggable," she often said. *Hmm* . . . he thought, it would be nice if she changed that to "fuckable". Not that they had any problems in *that* department.

"What's the deal?" Lee said impatiently. "We gonna wait 'til the husband decides to come out an' speak to us? Whyn't you go knock on the door an' tell him we need t'interview him *now*."

Lee was right for once, Tucci thought. He had definitely had enough of sitting in this house of death. Still, he had to do it by the book. "Bobby Skorch doesn't *have* to talk to us," he pointed out. "*You* know that."

"He'll talk. For your info, when I was over at the station I took a gander at the ex. The dumb jerk is sittin' in a cell sweatin' it. Apparently he called his lawyer, who ain't exactly breakin' a leg to post bail."

"Really?" Tucci said.

"Yeah, and you'd better get your fat butt outside an' make some bullshit announcement to the media," Lee added. "The natives are gettin' ornery, nearly pulled me to pieces on my way in. An' while you're out there, take a look at the ass on that little Chinese chick from Channel Four. Now *she's* a piece! I wouldn't mind reamin' it up *that* juicy rear." Tucci threw him a disapproving look and Lee chuckled heartily. "What's your problem? Can't get it up with anyone 'cept Faye?"

"Do me a favour," Tucci said, clenching his teeth and willing himself to remain calm. "Leave my wife out of this conversation."

"Oh, yeah, yeah, your wife," Lee said mockingly. "Faye's too fuckin' good to mention." A ribald laugh. "Face it, Tucci, she's got your balls in a lather an' your dick strapped to her left tit."

"That's enough," Tucci said, his face reddening. He knew that Faye and Lee had a history of sorts. She'd gone on a date with Lee once, long before she met him, and Lee had behaved badly. She wouldn't reveal the details, but suffice to say that whenever Lee's name came up she made a disgusted face.

"Yeah, yeah," Lee said, cracking his knuckles again. "So show me where you found the dead broad. Shit, I'm sorry I missed out on *this* babe. Wouldn't've minded an in the flesh close-up of *those* tits."

Tucci decided that was it. As soon as he could, he was making an appointment to see Captain Marsh and requesting a new partner.

L.A.
Connections
3

# CHAPTER FIVE

DIANA LEON pulled up outside the Four Seasons, left her car with a parking valet, and entered the hotel. She felt oddly apprehensive. It was the first time she would be with Max Steele on her own. And yet, why not? Max and Freddie had worked together for many years, and she'd always had a friendly relationship with her husband's partner – although deep down she knew it was more than that, and now it was time they both voiced something that was becoming painfully obvious.

*Yes, Max*, she hoped she had the courage to say. *I'm married to Freddie, but it's a marriage in name only. And since you're not attached to anybody right now, and you're departing IAA, I suggest that I leave Freddie and come with you.*

Diana was forty-three years old and this was the boldest

move she'd ever made. She had been married to Freddie for fifteen years. Now, finally, she was doing something on her own without getting Freddie's permission.

She giggled nervously to herself, feeling like a silly schoolgirl. If Max was in agreement, *could* she leave Freddie? *Would* she leave? The situation was in Max's hands; she would have to feel her way carefully.

"Mrs Leon," the maître d' greeted her warmly, "how nice to welcome you again to the Four Seasons. Mr Steele is waiting."

Oh, God! She was having breakfast with Max Steele, a notorious womanizer. What must people think?

As she approached the table, Max stood up to greet her. She experienced a fleeting moment of sheer panic. Max was so unlike Freddie, who was always in control. Max was an unpredictable wild card and he excited the hell out of her.

"Hi, Diana," Max said.

She noticed that his hair was slightly mussed in a most attractive way, and that his suntan, as usual, was glowing. He was dressed all in white from his pristine pants to his casual summer cashmere sweater.

"Hello, Max," she said, hoping that she'd picked the right outfit. The girls he dated were always outrageously under-dressed in flimsy little mini-dresses and barely there tank tops. This morning, after much thought, she had chosen a Calvin Klein blue blazer, worn over a pale blue silk shirt and beige linen slacks. Casual, elegant and understated – that was her look and she wore it well.

"I was kind of surprised to get your call," Max said.

"Well," she answered, choosing her words carefully as

she sat down, "I was surprised and upset about what happened last night."

Max nodded his agreement. "Yeah. That husband of yours," he said, picking up a coffee spoon and tapping it on the table, "couldn't say what he had to say in private. Had to do it in front of that fucking, I'm sorry, in front of Ariel. She's not my favourite person."

"Nor mine either," Diana said quickly. "In fact, if it was up to me, I wouldn't have her in my house. She's duplicitous. I'm sure she got to where she is by sleeping with Billy Cornelius."

Max laughed. "C'*mon*, Diana," he teased. "I've never heard you talk like that about people. You're always Miss Straight-laced."

"Is that what you think of me, Max?" she said, giving him a bold look.

Max was no fool, he caught the signals. Diana Leon was flirting with him. "Uh . . . never really thought about it," he said, wondering where this was leading. The waiter came over and hovered by their table, order pad in hand. "What'll you have, honey?" Max asked.

She liked the way he called her "honey". It was casual, yet extremely intimate. "Maybe some tea."

"No toast? Eggs? Waffles?"

"No, just tea. Earl Grey," she said, speaking directly to the waiter.

"The lady wants tea," Max said. "And bring me another orange juice, two eggs sunny side up, one slice of crisp bacon, three pieces of toast not too well done, and more coffee."

"Yes, Mr Steele," said the waiter.

"So," Max said, leaning back and surveying the room. "What can I do for you, Diana?"

*You can ravish me,* she longed to say. *You can take me to bed and do all the things to me that you do to your numerous girlfriends. And I will love you, care for you, and be the faithful woman for ever by your side.*

"I wanted to say, Max, that whatever happens, you have my full support."

"That's good to know," he said, his wandering eyes checking out a pretty brunette with long tanned legs on her way out of the dining room. "The truth is, Diana, I changed my mind."

"You changed your mind?" she repeated, not sure what he'd changed his mind about.

"Freddie and I have been through so much together; there's no way I can leave the firm. I simply can't do it to him."

The waiter returned and refilled Max's coffee cup. Diana waited until he had left before speaking. "I'm sure you're aware that in the *Times* today there's a story about you taking over at Orpheus Studios," she said.

"It's all bullshit," Max said sharply. "They write these stories before anything's signed. I spoke to Billy Cornelius this morning and told him the deal is off."

"You *did*?"

"Yes, honey. Y'know, on reflection, I reckon I was going through some kind of mid-life crisis thing. Freddie'll understand."

"But, Max, if you feel you can do better elsewhere, then

you *should* move," she said, a slight tinge of desperation creeping into her voice.

"Hey, hey," Max said, with a half-smile, "don't encourage me."

"I'm encouraging you to be yourself," Diana said, her expression earnest.

"Did Freddie send you?" he asked curiously.

"No, he didn't," she responded indignantly. "As a matter of fact, Freddie failed to come home last night. I have no idea where he was. He walked in when I was leaving this morning, looking dishevelled."

Max stared at her disbelievingly. "Freddie, dishevelled?"

"Yes, Freddie."

"Don't tell me he's got a broad . . . I mean, no disrespect to you, Diana."

"There's no one else, Max," she said confidently.

"If you say so . . ."

"The truth is," she said, leaning towards him, lowering her voice to a whisper, "Freddie doesn't like sex."

"Doesn't like sex, huh?" Max said, storing that little piece of information away for future use.

"I can speak to you in the strictest confidence, can't I?"

"Sure, baby," Max said agreeably. Hey, bonding with Freddie's wife was a kick. This way he could get the inside track on everything.

Diana wondered if she had said too much. No. Why *shouldn't* she confide in Max? He would never betray her. "Freddie's not a sexual being," she said. A long, meaningful pause. "But *I* am . . ."

Oh, Jesus. Was she coming on to him? Freddie's uptight

wife? No way. And yet . . . she had that predatory look, a look Max knew only too well. Women on the make . . . he'd had more of those than he cared to remember. Usually actresses. Hey, it wasn't *his* fault if he was irresistible to women.

"Diana," he said carefully, "I'm not sure you should be here with me."

Her slate-grey eyes stared boldly into his. "Why not?"

"Because . . . uh . . ." he began, thinking fast, it wouldn't do to insult her by telling her he wasn't interested, "because I . . . uh . . . well, I guess I'm very attracted to you," he lied.

Her face lit up. He had said the right thing. "You *are*?"

"Yes, Diana, honey. But, believe me, this is not the time for either of us to do anything about it."

"Why not?" she demanded, bedroom eyes materializing out of nowhere.

Oh, shit! She wasn't going to give up easy.

"Trust me. It's not."

Tentatively she reached across the table, placing her hand gently over his. "I've waited so long for this moment, Max. Something told me it was inevitable."

He slid his hand out from under hers, indicating the approaching waiter with his eyebrows. "Be cool, Diana," he said in a low voice. "The tabs have spies everywhere. You're an important Hollywood wife – you're news. So am I right now. We shouldn't even be seen together like this."

"I know," she said. "But for once I don't want to do the right thing. I want to do what makes me happy."

Freddie's wife was on a roll. *Jesus!* What had he done to deserve *this*?

"Diana," he said, attempting a serious voice, "I have too much regard and respect for you to allow you to jeopardize your future."

"What do you mean?"

"We all know Freddie has a vindictive streak. If he even suspected you had eyes for another man . . ."

"I don't care," she said stubbornly.

"*I* do. I'm trying to protect you here."

"When I'm with you, Max, I don't need protecting."

This kind of response was exactly what he *didn't* need. "You might *think* you don't," he said sternly. "But trust me, you do."

He imagined Freddie's face if Diana went to him and informed her husband she was running off with Max Steele. The shit wouldn't just hit the fan, it would explode all the way from Beverly Hills to Bel Air. Christ! How to get out of this one?

Then it came to him. The perfect solution. "Diana," he said, with a perfectly straight face, "I think you should be the first to know. Last night I got engaged."

# CHAPTER SIX

FREDDIE LEON thought of himself as an in-control and reasonable man, but in view of what had happened over the last twenty-four hours, he could not remain calm. His faithful partner Max Steele had betrayed him, and it infuriated Freddie that Max had manipulated him in such a way. The disloyal sonofabitch.

Freddie stood under the powerful jets of his shower, soaking his body. After a night away from home he felt the need to thoroughly cleanse himself. Hotel rooms disgusted him – however luxurious. The late Howard Hughes had had the right idea, covering his shoes with Kleenex and walking around with a hospital mask over half his face.

Last night Freddie had known he had to get out of the house. He had no desire to lie in bed beside Diana, listening to her nag about how he had ruined her dinner party.

271

Through the noise of the shower he heard the phone ring. To his annoyance no one picked up, so he stepped out of the shower and answered it himself. "Yes?" he snapped.

"Mr Leon," Ria said, "are you aware there's a woman from *Manhattan Style* magazine in town? She's been sent out here from New York to write a piece on you. In fact, she fully expects you to grant her an interview."

"Excuse me?" Freddie said irritably, annoyed that Ria was bothering him on a Sunday.

"Madison Castelli. She's here to conduct an exclusive interview with you."

"Why me?" Freddie said, frowning.

"You're very high profile, Mr Leon," Ria said. As if she had to explain it to him, she thought. He knows exactly how important and powerful he is. "So I'm to presume you don't know anything about this?" she continued.

"No, I don't," he said, annoyed she'd seen fit to disturb him at home. "How do *you* know?"

"Miss Castelli called me herself."

"Where did she get your number?"

"I didn't ask. I merely informed her you would not be interested."

"Right. She'll get no co-operation from me. So if she's smart, she'd better quit now."

"With all due respect, Mr Leon, you cannot tell the press what they can and can't do."

"I can tell them what I like," Freddie snapped, and put the phone down. "Diana," he yelled. "Diana!" There was no response, so wrapping a towel around his waist, he walked from his bathroom into the bedroom. Then he remembered, Diana had gone out. "Damn!" he mumbled under his breath. He hated it when his wife exhibited attitude and wasn't around to attend to his needs. He sat on the edge of the bed and decided to give Ariel Shore a call.

When Ariel came to the phone she was suitably cool, which annoyed him even more. He had a good relationship with Ariel and did not want anything spoiling it.

"I guess we're the last to know," Ariel said, her tone icy.

"What do you mean?" Freddie asked.

"Didn't you see the *L.A. Times* this morning?"

"I haven't read the papers yet."

"Take a look. Your partner made an announcement, or somebody made an announcement for him."

"How could that happen?"

"*Exactly*, Freddie," Ariel said triumphantly, as if she'd caught him cheating at poker. "How *could* it happen without either of us knowing about it? *We're* supposed to be Hollywood insiders. *We're* supposed to know everything weeks before anything takes place."

"Ariel, I—"

"Anyway," she rudely interrupted, "I went to see Billy this morning."

"You did?"

"I thought it was time I settled this nonsense."

"What happened?"

"I told Billy he could not hire *anyone* without asking me. And if you're as clever as I *know* you are, when Max comes crawling back, you'll immediately terminate your partnership."

"You don't have to tell me what to do, Ariel," Freddie

said, pissed that she would even try. "That was already my plan."

"Good, because my studio does not care to conduct business with anyone who has anything at all to do with Max Steele."

"Point taken, Ariel," Freddie said. And as far as he was concerned, that was the end of Max Steele.

L.A.
Connections
3

# CHAPTER SEVEN

MADISON HAD finished writing her piece on Salli T. Turner. She didn't consider it up to her usual standard, but she knew that she was too emotionally involved to be able to do any better. She faxed a copy of the article to Victor in New York, then immediately wished she hadn't. Victor responded quickly. He phoned and told her it was good.

"Not good enough," she answered, an expert at putting herself down. "Do I have time to do a re-write?"

"No," Victor said firmly. "The piece is excellent. Stop being so critical."

When Cole returned from his hike, he suggested to Madison that he take her out for lunch. "We'll grab a Neil McCarthy salad at the Beverly Hills Hotel," he said persuasively.

"I don't know," she demurred, feeling guilty at the

thought of going out to lunch while Salli lay brutally murdered. "I'm not in the mood."

"C'mon," Cole urged. "It'd make *me* feel better to get out of here. An' if Natalie's around I'll even take her."

She stood up and stretched. "Natalie's having lunch with Luther."

"Who's Luther?"

"An ex-football player she met at Jimmy's house last night."

"Straight?"

"Of course."

Cole grinned. "Shame!"

Madison couldn't help laughing. "Okay," she said, deciding it might be good to get out after all. "We're on for lunch. You talked me into it."

"Didn't have to do much talkin'," Cole said with a friendly wink.

*

"So what did you do?" Jimmy Sica asked his brother, who had just gotten through telling him what had happened between him and Kristin the night before.

"I left," Jake said. "What would *you* have done under those circumstances?"

"Jesus!" Jimmy said, shaking his head. "It would've shocked the crap outta me. And she seemed so . . . gorgeous."

"She was gorgeous all right," Jake said grimly. "Five-thousand-a-night gorgeous."

They were standing in the middle of their father's bungalow at the Beverly Hills Hotel, waiting for him to emerge from the bedroom so they could escort him to his wedding ceremony, which was to take place in the lavish gardens.

"What a scam!" Jimmy exclaimed. "D'you think she was planning on charging *you*?"

"Of course not," Jake said sharply, already regretting telling his brother. "We had a good thing going."

"So you think if the phone deal hadn't happened, you wouldn't have found out?"

"That's exactly right."

"Did you use a—"

"Nope."

"Well, buddy, *you* had better get yourself tested pronto."

"I plan to."

Jimmy flopped down on the couch, legs splayed. "There's no way you could've known. The hookers in L.A. are the best-looking broads in town."

"How would *you* know?"

"I get around, little bro."

Jake couldn't stop pacing up and down. "She seemed such a sweetheart," he said. "Innocent . . . clean cut . . ."

"Where exactly did you meet her?"

"In the men's department at Neiman Marcus."

"Ha!" Jimmy exclaimed. "That should've given you a clue. What was she doing *there*?"

"Sitting at the martini bar. *I* picked *her* up, it wasn't as if *she* was coming on to *me*."

"That's what *you* thought," Jimmy muttered darkly.

"D'you think I over-reacted?" Jake asked.

"Are you shitting me?" Jimmy said, making a face. "She's a *hooker* for Chrissake."

"I hope you're not speaking about my future bride," their father, Cosmos, said, emerging from the bedroom clad in a John Travolta *Saturday Night Fever* white three-piece suit and a screaming bright red tie. He was a handsome man, but at least sixty pounds overweight, which caused his suit to bulge in all the wrong places.

"No way, Dad," Jimmy said, attempting to conceal his amusement at his father's outrageous outfit.

Cosmos Sica was sixty-two years old with a shock of silver hair, matching moustache and a wily grin. The woman he was about to marry was a twenty-year-old manicurist from San Diego who was to be his fourth wife. Jimmy and Jake were used to their high-living dad. As far as they were concerned the old guy could do what he liked – and typically he did. Cosmos was smart enough in business that it was okay for him to be stupid about women. And if he could afford them, why not?

"You look good, Dad," Jake lied, knowing his father craved compliments.

"An' you don't look so bad yourself, son," Cosmos said, admiring his reflection in a wall mirror. "Isn't it about time you found yourself a regular girl?"

"He did," Jimmy said with a slight smirk.

"Good," Cosmos said loudly. "It's not healthy for a man to be by himself. You need a warm body to snuggle up to at night."

"She's not exactly someone I'm planning on spending the rest of my life with," Jake said, throwing Jimmy a warning look.

"Shall I tell him?" Jimmy said, starting to laugh.

"No way," Jake objected.

"Tell me what?" Cosmos asked, brushing the edge of his moustache with his fingers. "This is my wedding day – you can tell me anything."

"He fell in love with a hooker," Jimmy announced, unable to stop himself.

"He did *what*?" Cosmos yelled.

"He thought she was a nice girl," Jimmy said. "It turned out she was a nice girl all right – the kinda nice girl you *pay*."

Cosmos roared with hearty laughter. "Nothing wrong with a pretty girl making an honest living. That's what I say."

Jake glared at his brother. "Quit making my business public knowledge."

"I'm your father, for Chrissake," Cosmos boomed. "What's with the public knowledge? You know you can trust me; it'll go no further."

*Sure*, Jake thought glumly, *knowing Dad, everyone will be in on the joke by the end of the wedding. Damn Jimmy and his big mouth.*

Jimmy hauled himself off the couch. "We ready?" he said.

Cosmos nodded vigorously. "You bet!" he said, almost popping a button on his vest. "Fourth time lucky, huh?

Come on, boys, I'm impatient to get to my wedding night!"

*

In spite of a huge and expensive face-lift there was something about the lobby of the Beverly Hills Hotel that screamed old Hollywood. "I keep on expecting to bump into Clark Gable or Lana Turner," Madison joked, glancing around.

"I know what you mean," Cole said. "This place has history."

"It sure does," she agreed.

"C'mon," he said, taking her arm. "We're eating on the terrace of the Polo Lounge. You ever had a Neil McCarthy salad?"

"Sounds vaguely communistic."

"The best chopped salad you'll ever have."

"You're so knowledgeable," she teased. "And to think Natalie and I were both under the impression you'd end up being a gang member."

"Right," Cole drawled. "Instead, I'm a politically incorrect gay guy who knows everyone's secrets."

"You do?"

"I sure do."

"Are there any more secrets about Salli?"

"Maybe," he said mysteriously.

Madison let it drop; she knew when to push and when not to. "So, Cole," she said lightly, "what's *your* love life like? You seeing anyone special?"

"Haven't gotten that lucky – yet," he said ruefully. "So

I keep playing the field. Course it drives Natalie insane. She's convinced I'll get AIDS and then she'll have to look after me. And you know how *that* would piss her off."

"She's always adored you, Cole. When we were at college together she was forever talking about you and worrying that you were okay."

"Yeah." He laughed. "I know, I know. She sure loves her baby brother."

"How did she take it when you told her you were gay?"

"She was kinda cool. It was my parents who freaked. An' it was Nat who talked 'em around."

As they continued walking through the lobby, Madison spotted two vaguely familiar faces coming towards her. She thought about taking evasive action, but it was too late. Jimmy Sica had seen her.

"Madison!" he said, flashing his anchorman smile. "What are *you* doing here?"

"I could ask *you* the same question."

"It's our dad's wedding," Jimmy explained, gesturing toward Cosmos. "Allow me to introduce you to the man himself. We're on our way to his execution – his fourth one."

Cosmos took her hand, squeezing it tightly. "Delighted to meet such a lovely woman," he said, oozing charm before turning to Jake and enquiring *sotto voce*, "Is this the young lady you were telling us about?"

"No," Jake said quickly. "Madison's a journalist from New York."

"I love it when I get billing," Madison said, with a nod in his direction. "Do you all know Cole, Natalie's brother?"

"So *you're* the famous fitness guru," Jimmy said, shaking Cole's hand. "Natalie keeps on telling me you're the best in town."

"The best what?" Cole said, grinning cheekily.

"The best guy to get my pathetic abs in shape," Jimmy said, grinning back.

"I can do that," Cole said.

"Stop flirting," Madison scolded. "They're both straight, or at least I *think* they are." Her eyes met Jake's. "How was your date last night?"

"Casual," he answered. "Nothing serious."

"Why don't you two drop by the wedding?" Jimmy suggested.

"We're on our way to lunch," Madison explained. "Besides, we're not exactly dressed for a wedding."

"You look great to me," Jake said.

Jimmy's attention was taken by a woman in a blue jogging outfit who wanted his autograph. He loved being recognized, especially in front of his father, who was duly impressed.

"Hey, I'm sorry last night kind of, uh . . . ended abruptly," Jake said.

"That's all right," Madison answered, thinking that her first impression from last night had not been wrong, he was very attractive in a sexy laid-back way. "It was abrupt for all of us."

"Bad news about Salli. You knew her, didn't you?"

"Yes, it's so sad. She was a sweet person. You might not realize it from her public image, but she was."

"You wouldn't be free for dinner tonight, would you?" Jake asked impulsively.

"Uh . . ." She tried to think of an excuse, but none came to mind.

"She's free," Cole said, answering for her.

"Well, yes, I guess I am," she said, shooting Cole a mind-your-own-business look.

"Pick you up at seven?" Jake said.

"Let's go," Cosmos boomed. "I got a wedding to attend. An' a bride to make happy!"

"Lots of luck, Mr Sica," Madison said.

"It's not luck I need, pretty lady," Cosmos said, roaring with laughter again. "It's stamina. An' plenty of it!"

The three of them walked off.

"That's *you* settled for tonight," Cole said, pleased with himself for interfering.

"What made you think I *wanted* to go out with him?" she asked irritably.

"He seems like a cool dude. Go for it."

"*What?*"

"Hey, if I can't have him, why shouldn't you?"

"Cole," she said sternly, "you railroaded me into that."

"No way."

"You did," she said accusingly. "I'm not sure he even *wanted* to ask me out."

"Then how come he did?"

"Oh, God! How do I know?"

"Maddy," Cole interrupted, "*you* are *totally* fine. So go, have yourself a good time, an' stop worryin'."

"Now you sound like Natalie."

He arched an amused eyebrow. "Somethin' wrong with that?"

She took his arm. "Okay, matchmaker, let's go get lunch. I'm starving!"

lectured her the next day. "*Never* turn down a client," Darlene had said, practically tut-tutting her annoyance. "It's bad for business."

"He's a tattooed freak," Kristin had replied. "And I don't ever have to do anything I don't want to."

Unable to stomach the details of Salli T. Turner's parcularly brutal murder, she switched stations. A newscaster as speaking about President Clinton, Kenneth Starr, and the goings-on in Washington.

Hollywood and Washington – the men in both cities beyond horny. Kristin was well aware it was all about r and control. Politicians and movie stars – these men o much, that sometimes the only way they could get relinquishing both.

switched stations again. A news reporter droned on nother murder.

body of a young woman was washed up on the hore this morning, identity unknown. The only n so far is that the victim was Caucasian and etectives are investigating."

urders. Two blondes.

normal Sunday in L.A.

*

arrived at the nursing home, she was greeted nurses at the desk. "How's Cherie doing?" ling over a large bag filled with candy, all the es, and a couple of bestselling novels. It was e nurses happy – that way they'd be sure to l attention.

# CHAPTER EIGHT

AT EXACTLY NOON Kristin picked up the phone and called Max.

He answered immediately. "Perfect timing," he said, sounding excessively cheery. "You're an engaged woman."

"Excuse me?" she said, wondering what he was up to now.

"Don't worry," he said. "It's a paying job. You'll be my fiancée for a while. What do you think of *that*?"

"I think you're crazy, Max," she said with a sigh. "But then that's nothing new."

"Don't you like my idea?"

"I'll repeat what I just said. You're crazy."

"Can you come over?"

She'd never been to his house, and yet, if he wanted her to move in, she certainly had to check it out. "Where do you live?"

"I'll give you the address. Be here in an hour."

"I can't do that," she said quickly. "I have somewhere to go first. I could be there around four."

"Where are you going?"

"We haven't done the deal yet, Max," she said sharply. "So don't question me."

"Okay, okay," he answered, soothing her with his voice. "But, honey, believe me, this is gonna be a cool situation."

She was resigned to her fate – whatever it might be. "If you say so."

"I *know* so," he assured her, and then he gave her his address in Bel Air. She replaced the receiver and sighed deeply, wondering if she was making the right move. What did she really know about Max Steele? He was just another client, that's all. Why was she even considering such a radical move?

All she could think about was Jake. They'd had such a strong connection, or so she'd thought. And then her stupid answering machine and Darlene's message had ruined everything.

She had known she would get screwed by Mr X, one way or another.

She went to her closet and picked out the simplest clothes she possessed. Then she pulled her long blonde hair back into a ponytail and did not bother putting on makeup.

It was time to visit her sister.

*

The drive to the nursing home took about an hour. Kristin liked to play books on tape, usually biographies; it gave her

something to talk about with clients who were into conversation. Right now she was listening to Robert Evans's *Kid Stays in the Picture*. He had led a fascinating businessman, movie star, studio head, grand prod the great Hollywood tradition. Recently she'd he'd had a stroke, and then a few weeks later h married for the fourth time. Shortly after he marriage annulled! Hollywood survivors – themselves!

She wondered what Jake was doing. his father's wedding by now, wearing th out and having such a good time that gotten all about her. She couldn't h final words: *I wish you'd told me . condom.*

How could he say something s ever have put him at risk.

She found it impossible to c she put on the radio instead. A the murder of Salli T. Turn although she'd had several band, Bobby Skorch. Bo who loved call-girls. She he'd performed quite p he had a famous wife off, and he had plent endowed men Kris fact, that several Kristin being on

She rememb

"Same as ever," Mariah, the fat, black, friendly nurse replied. "No change."

"You never know," Kristin said hopefully. "One of these days she might open her eyes, like Sleeping Beauty."

"Yeah, baby, keep on thinking that way," Mariah said, squeezing her large frame out from behind the desk.

"That's why I come here every week," Kristin said. "My voice gets through to her, I know it does. She has to realize *someone* cares."

"You're lookin' pale today," Mariah said, crinkling her eyes. "Everything okay with you, hon?"

"I'm fine," she said quickly. "Too many patients this week." Early on she had told all the nurses that she worked as a dental assistant.

"Ugh! Dunno how you do it," Mariah said. "Staring into all those sloppy mouths. It'd drive *me* loco."

"Somebody's got to do it," Kristin said, anxious to see Cherie.

"Bet all your patients fall in love with you," Mariah said with a saucy wink. "You sure are pretty 'nuff."

"I'm there to do a job, that's all," Kristin said, thinking, *Ain't that the truth*.

"Yeah, yeah," Mariah said disbelievingly. "Didja catch *Lethal Weapon Four* yet? What a movie! I'm hot for that Chris Rock. Skinny an' sexy! Wouldn't mind spendin' a night in *his* company."

Kristin summoned up a laugh. "Yes, he is cute," she said. Actually she had no idea who Chris Rock was.

"Cute?" Mariah exclaimed. "Honey bun, he's a *horny* hound-dog!"

Kristin followed Mariah into her sister's private room and stared down at Cherie, a shadow of the beauty she'd once been, kept alive on a machine. It broke Kristin's heart every time she saw her.

"Hi, baby," she said, sitting on the edge of the hospital bed and taking her sister's hand, which was ice cold. "It's Kristin. How are you today?"

No response. There was never any response. But she'd stay for an hour and keep talking.

Maybe one day she would get a reaction. She had to keep trying.

If she gave up, all hope would be lost.

L.A.
Connections
3

# CHAPTER NINE

MARTY STEINER emerged from Bobby Skorch's bedroom at noon, made his way downstairs and confronted the two detectives in the front hall.

"We're ready to ask Mr Skorch a few questions," Detective Tucci said, asserting himself.

"I'm sure," Marty Steiner replied, smooth as a one-eyed snake. "Fact is, he's too upset to talk to you right now. I'm requesting that you vacate the premises."

"We still have things to do here," Tucci pointed out. "This *is* a crime scene."

"I think you've had enough time to collect all the evidence you need," Marty Steiner said. "Mr Skorch would like you and your partner to leave immediately. This is an extremely difficult time, and Mr Skorch does not need to deal with having his house invaded."

"I'll remind you again, this *is* a crime scene," Tucci said, hating the sleek lawyer and everything he represented.

"Yeah," Lee said, joining in. "It's a goddamn crime scene, for Chrissake. You think we *wanna* be here?"

Marty Steiner's face gave not a flicker of recognition in Lee's direction. "If you wish to stay, you'll need a warrant," he said calmly. "The bodies have been removed. As I said before, you've had ample time to collect your evidence. Now I want you people out of here."

"Are you telling me that Mr Skorch has nothing to say to us?" Lee said, belligerent as ever.

"That's correct, Detective."

"Where was he last night?" Lee asked, getting right in the lawyer's face.

"On his way back from Vegas."

"He didn't arrive here 'til three," Lee said accusingly.

"I'm sure you're aware that it's a four- to five-hour drive."

"His *wife* was murdered," Tucci said. "Doesn't he have any questions for *us*?"

"Mr Skorch has a funeral to prepare for," Marty Steiner said, his voice hardening. "Now unless you have a warrant, I insist you vacate at once."

Tucci and Lee exchanged glances. "I knew he was an asshole," Lee mumbled under his breath.

"Nothing we can do," Tucci said.

"Why *wouldn't* Skorch talk to us?" Lee muttered. "I'm gonna check on his alibi. I wanna know exactly what time he left the hotel in Vegas, an' who was in the car with him.

He probably got back here early, found his wife with a guy an' lost it."

"If that was the case," Tucci said, ever the voice of reason, "where's the other man? Why hasn't he come forward?"

"Would *you* under these circumstances? The jerk must've run for his life."

"We'd better go," Tucci said, thinking to himself that maybe on the way back to the station he could stop by a diner and grab a bite to eat.

Lee shrugged. "Fine with me. I came to this case late. If *I'd* gotten to the prick when he arrived back from Vegas, I'd have questioned him then and there."

"He knew his rights," Tucci said, choosing to ignore the fact that Lee was criticizing him. "He was aware he didn't have to talk to me."

"The asshole's guilty," Lee muttered angrily. "Fuckin' guilty."

On his way back to the station, Tucci stopped at Fatburger and devoured a couple of hamburgers with everything. Then he indulged himself with a side order of French fries and onions. There was no way he would confess to Faye that he ate all that food – she'd be too angry. He'd lie, tell her he grabbed a salad.

Back at the station he remembered Madison Castelli's tape, and decided to give it a listen. He found it most informative hearing Salli T. Turner tell about her life. She had a lovely voice – young and vibrant.

Tucci's thoughts kept flashing to her dead body, the

vicious cuts and lacerations, the sheer fury the killer had wreaked upon his victim.

Ah, the price of fame, he thought. Was it worth it? Not for Salli T. Turner.

Later in the day he went down to the morgue to inspect the body of the "Mystery Malibu blonde" as the media were calling the latest victim. The media were having a field day. First the celebrated Salli T. Turner, and now an unknown beautiful blonde washed up on the Malibu shore. Movie star territory. Two murders in as many days. Ratings were zooming.

The mystery blonde was young and lovely. Probably no more than nineteen or twenty, Tucci figured. What had happened to her?

"We're tracking her dental records," Lee informed him. "Should have something by tomorrow."

Tucci shook his head. There was so much violence in the world, so much anger. He picked up the phone and called Faye. "I'll be home late tonight, sweetheart," he said.

"I'm not surprised," she said. "Salli T. Turner is all over the television. What a terrible tragedy. They're comparing her death to the Nicole Simpson murder."

"They would."

"Don't think about it," Faye said. "Solve it."

"I plan to," Tucci answered.

"Did you enjoy the sandwich?"

He didn't have the heart to tell her that the maid had eaten it. "Delicious," he lied.

"How about the coleslaw?"

"Even more delicious. Almost as delicious as you."

"You're such a flatterer," she said, chuckling happily. "Did you meet with that woman from *Manhattan Style* – Madison Castelli?"

"Yes. She brought me an audiotape of her interview with Salli."

"Have you played it?"

"I'm listening to it now."

"Anything useful?"

"It sounds to me like Salli had a real problem with her ex. I'll question him shortly."

"Has he been arrested?"

"Yes. We brought him in on parking violations."

"I miss you," Faye said wistfully.

"Miss you, too," Tucci replied.

"I could make you your favourite pasta tonight," she said, playing the temptress. "Special treat 'cause you've been so good."

The two burgers had made him uncomfortably full, not to mention totally guilty. "That'd be nice," he said, not quite as enthusiastic as she expected him to be. "I'll call you later."

Lee appeared, eating a jelly doughnut, the jam dribbling down his pointed chin. "The Captain wants to see us," he said, wiping his sugary hands on his pants. "Like, pronto."

Tucci got up from behind his desk and followed Lee into their captain's office.

Captain Marsh was exceptionally tall, black and bad-tempered. He smoked cheap cigars, sported a half-hearted Afro, and needed immediate dental work. "Just heard from the Chief of Police who had a call from the Mayor's office," he said, getting straight to the point. "This Salli Turner murder. They need an arrest, an' they need it *now*. Forget about everything else an' work this case hard. I promised the Chief we'd have someone in custody within twenty-four hours. If you need extra help, let me know. I'm expectin' immediate results."

*There goes dinner*, Tucci thought. *Nothing like a little pressure to get you through the day.*

L.A.
Connections
3

# CHAPTER TEN

I CAN'T BELIEVE you're going out with that Jake guy," Natalie said, rolling her eyes in a disapproving fashion.

"Last night you thought he was cute," Madison pointed out.

"I also thought he was *available*," Natalie said crisply. "Available and cute is one thing. Available and taken is another."

"Who *says* he's taken?"

"Come *on*, girl!" Natalie said. "Did you *see* the way he hustled that blonde out of sight last night. He was hot for her. I mean *steamin'*."

"Apparently not *that* hot," Madison retorted. "Anyway, wasn't it you who said I should get out and have fun? Do something to take my mind off David the jerk?"

"Yeah, but not if you're jumpin' from one jerk to another," Natalie replied. "That'd be too sad."

"It's a date," Madison said patiently. "I'm not moving in with him."

"Praise the Lord!"

"Don't go getting religious on me."

"If Jake's anything like his brother . . ."

"I thought you *liked* his brother, you dragged me over there for dinner last night."

"That's only 'cause Jimmy and I work together."

"Anyway, I'm seeing him. Big deal. One lousy date."

Natalie threw up her hands. "Okay, okay. I'm only trying to watch out for you."

"How was your lunch with Luther?"

Natalie's pretty face broke into a wide grin. "Now that man is *some* hunk."

"You like him, huh?"

"Understatement, girl. He's big and *damn* sexy. Makes me feel protected."

"My turn to wave a warning flag in your face. You, too, are coming out of a lousy relationship – Denzl, remember? So don't get carried away."

Natalie giggled. "This is *such* a buzz!" she said. "I feel like we're back in college, sitting around talking about guys. I mean, aren't we a little *old* for this crap?"

"Yes," Madison agreed, smiling.

"One of these days," Natalie said, "I'd like to be married with a couple of kids, live in a nice little house by the sea, have a great husband who comes home every night at the same time, *and* watch Oprah!"

"Dream world, Nat," Madison said. "You'd *hate* missing out on the action. You *love* what you do."

"True. But I want to do more than cover the entertainment beat. I am *so* sick of talking about Salli T. Turner. Yeah, she was a big TV star, and great looking, if you like silicone. But the girl got herself murdered, and now *I* gotta go on and on eulogizing her. It's enough already. I want to report real news, not sensational Hollywood murders."

"I understand," Madison said. "But remember, it wasn't Salli's fault she got killed."

"Yeah, I know, it's a tragedy. Truth is, it brings back too many bad memories for me."

Madison nodded sympathetically, remembering the night in college when Natalie had been attacked and raped by a man who turned out to be a serial killer. They caught the guy, but it had taken Natalie a year to get over it and stop shaking.

"What're you gonna wear tonight?" Natalie asked, hurriedly changing the subject. "Something sexy, I hope."

"I don't do sexy," Madison said, straight-faced.

"You know what would be *really* good for you?"

"What brilliant idea have you come up with now?"

"Use *him* like guys are always using *us*. Throw some condoms in your bag and have a night of wild sex."

"What're you *talking* about?" Madison asked, perplexed.

"Guys do it all the time," Natalie said matter of factly. "And my personal opinion is you need one night of mind-blowing sex. Kind of like a revenge fuck."

"Revenge for what?" Madison asked patiently.

"For the way David treated you."

"He did what made him happy. Besides, one-nighters are not my style."

"*Make* it your style. And you're *not* wearing one of your laid-back outfits. Have I got a dress for you!"

"Don't do dresses either," Madison objected.

Natalie wasn't listening. "It's red, short, and *veree* sexy. I was saving it for your birthday – but since you're here, it's perfect! Oh yeah, an' you gotta wear your hair down."

"Why are you trying to make me something I'm not?" Madison asked, exasperated.

"Treat tonight like an adventure. What's to lose?"

Later, both Cole and Natalie sat around watching Madison get ready for her date. She tried to argue, but couldn't help dissolving into laughter as they instructed her. Cole was a whiz with the makeup brushes; he worked on her eyes and lips, then stood back to admire his handy-work. "Kevyn Aucoin – drop dead!" he crowed.

"It's the Madison makeover!" Natalie yelled. "You're like one of those secretaries with the bun and glasses."

"I don't wear glasses."

"You know what I'm saying. Remove the glasses, let the hair down, and *voila* – you're Sharon Stone!"

"I'm not even blonde, Natalie. And I feel ridiculous in this dress."

"The point is, you *look* hot, girl!"

Cole handed her a packet of condoms. "No, thank you," Madison said, shoving them back at him.

"Just in case," Natalie urged. "Maybe Jake'll take you dancing, and you'll be in his arms, then all of a sudden there's that wild moment of no return. If that happens you'll be so damn sorry you don't have them with you. 'Cause no glove, no love."

"Now I *really* feel like I'm back in college," Madison said, breaking up. "You two are unbelievable!"

"Yeah, we're a fun couple, aren't we," Natalie said, impulsively hugging Cole. "Get used to us, 'cause, girl, we're takin' our act on the road!"

"What's *your* plan tonight, Cole?" Madison asked.

"Got a *hot* date."

"Who with?" Natalie demanded.

"Your favourite," Cole said. "Mr Mogul."

"Oh, God," Natalie groaned. "Don't you *get* it yet? All those power guys are into is using and abusing buff young things like you. They're worse than playboys who try to get one over on women."

"I wish you'd meet him. He's a nice guy."

"Nice guy, my ass," Natalie snorted. "He's a billionaire gay *caballero* who'll use you big time."

"You're prejudiced," Cole said, narrowing his eyes. "You'd sooner see me settle in with a nice, boring accountant."

"I don't care what you do. Your lifestyle doesn't bother me."

"Liar! You wish I was straight."

"Can you two quit fighting," Madison said, placing her hands on slender hips, wishing she could get out of tonight's date with Jake.

Too late. The doorbell rang, and both Cole and Natalie began shoving her towards the door.

No backing out now.

L.A.
Connections
3

# CHAPTER ELEVEN

"WHAT ARE *you* in such a bad mood about?" Freddie asked irritably.

"I'm not," Diana replied, although she obviously was.

"And where *were* you this morning?" he added, annoyed that she hadn't been around to tend to his every need.

"Why do you care?" Diana said, her face flushed. "I didn't ask where *you* were last night."

He threw her a warning look. "Don't get pissy with me, Diana."

"Why *did* you leave?" she continued, determined not to be intimidated. "You know I'm not happy alone in the house."

"You weren't alone. You had dozens of caterers around."

"Oh, *please*."

"Do you have any idea how much these dinner parties of yours cost me?"

"As if you care," Diana said, exasperated. "It's all tax deductible." She stalked into the kitchen and poured herself a cup of coffee. It was difficult for her to get over the shock of Max's engagement. Unbearable timing, yet she *still* couldn't stop thinking about him.

Freddie followed her into the kitchen. She turned and faced him. "What are you doing about Max?" she demanded.

"Breaking all ties with him as soon as possible," Freddie answered, as unemotional as ever. "I'll buy him out."

"You can't do that. He's your partner," she said, reminding him of something he knew only too well.

"True. However, I have fifty-one percent, he has forty-nine. He's history."

"You might be making a mistake."

"How many times have I told you not to interfere in my business?"

"You're so insulting," she said, her face reddening. "Who was right beside you when you were building the business? Who went out with boring movie stars and temperamental directors, and made them feel like a million dollars so they'd sign with you? I was with you every step of the way, Freddie, and don't you forget it."

"What the hell's gotten into you today?" he asked, his voice rising.

She took a gulp of coffee and let her frustration rip. "When was the last time you touched me?"

"God!" he groaned. "Not that again."

"You don't care, do you?"

"Of course I do."

"No, Freddie, you never liked sex much anyway, and now in the last few years . . ." She trailed off.

"Enough of this nonsense," Freddie said harshly. "I have more important matters to deal with."

Diana's anger and frustration continued to surface. "I want a man who loves me," she blurted, "in every way."

Freddie's response was completely devoid of emotion. "What are you after, a divorce?" he asked coldly.

She shook her head, frightened to tell him that yes, that's exactly what she wanted. "I . . . I don't know," she stammered.

"Pull yourself together, Diana," he said, leaving the kitchen.

She trailed him into the library. "Are you aware that Max got engaged?"

"What are you going on about now?"

"He's engaged."

"To the model who stood him up last night?"

"No, to someone called Kristin – I have no idea who she is."

"How do you know?"

"Max phoned this morning."

"Oh, did he? Abject with apology no doubt. Dying to slither back into my good graces."

"He merely told me he was engaged."

"Why didn't he announce it last night?"

"He hardly had an opportunity the way you and Ariel ganged up on him."

"I don't intend to keep repeating myself, Diana. Stay out of my business."

She glared at him. "If that's the way you want it. And by the way, if I *do* decide to divorce you, Freddie, how *would* you feel?"

He looked at her in astonishment that she would consider such a rash move. "Don't even think about it," he said warningly. "We're perfectly happy. Everyone knows that."

She stomped out of the room. Freddie shook his head. What the hell was going on with her? She must be going through the change of life early. God! Poor hard-done-by Diana. Didn't she realize how lucky she was? After all, she was married to one of the most important men in town.

L.A.
Connections
3

# CHAPTER TWELVE

MAX PROWLED AROUND his house with plenty of time to spare before Kristin arrived. He didn't want to waste it doing nothing, so he called Howie to see if he was around. Howie's service picked up. Max left his name, and then decided to take a swim in his luxurious pool and maybe work on his tan for an hour or so. May as well catch some rays, he thought, grimly acknowledging that he had nothing else to do.

Tomorrow he would face Freddie; no way was he dealing with that little problem today. He knew Freddie so well. In fact, he knew him better than anyone which, he realized, wasn't saying a lot because nobody really knew Freddie. He was a man of mystery – impossible to bond with on a man-to-man level. He wasn't into ball games, poker, horses *or* women. Only work.

Max wandered outside, stripped off his shirt and pants, and dropped into a lounge chair. He was happy in his brief white Calvins – the snug style – which emphasized his considerable assets.

As he stretched out, his mind drifted briefly to Inga Cruelle. Supermodel bitch! How dare she dump him to go on a date with Howie Powers? How dumb could a girl get? Howie was his friend, but everyone knew the man was an idiot, a rich playboy with nothing going for him except his father's money.

Yes, Inga had really blown it. No way would he help her with her so-called movie career now, she could find herself another agent.

When he'd had enough sun, he jumped in the pool and swam, overdoing it as usual. Max never did things by halves, he always had to excel – probably because when he was a kid his father used to beat the crap out of him if he wasn't the best at everything.

After swimming, he decided he had an appetite. Lunch at the Ivy didn't seem like a bad idea, the only problem was that eating alone was not on his agenda – too loser-like.

Maybe he'd give Inga one last chance.

No, he decided. Screw her! Nobody dumped on Max Steele and got away with it.

Of course, there was a long list of other lovelies he could call, but he wasn't in the mood to make conversation, and all most of them talked about was their career.

Actresses. He'd had it with actresses. How nice it would be to have Kristin in his life. A natural beauty with no ambitions. And no more clients except him.

Idly he wondered how much it would cost a week to keep her. Hmm . . . she probably didn't come cheap. But what did he care? He owned half of IAA and whatever happened between him and Freddie, he'd still end up with a bundle of money.

Instead of lunch he decided to go to Jhama Juice and grab a health drink. Jumping in his Maserati, he set off. The sun was shining, things weren't so bad, tomorrow he'd make everything okay with Freddie.

As he drove along San Vicente he thought about Diana Leon, and how bizarre it was that she had come on to him. If Freddie ever found out, he'd choke on his own surprise.

Depending on what happened between him and Freddie, he wondered if maybe he *should* have an affair with Diana, simply to keep her on his side.

No, she was too old. He couldn't remember the last time he'd had a girl over thirty. Did they even exist in L.A.? Not in *his* mind.

He parked in the underground structure below the health juice bar, locked his car, and began walking out of the tunnel-like structure.

"Gimme your fuckin' money, mothafucker."

*Oh, Jesus!* Before he could spin around he felt a gun sticking in his back. *Oh, Jesus!*

"An' take that fuckin' Rolex off, prick, or I'll blow your motherfuckin' head right off."

L.A. Connections 3

# CHAPTER THIRTEEN

VAN MORRISON was singing "Have I Told You Lately That I Love You". As Kristin listened to the touching lyrics she felt like bursting into tears. Whenever she left Cherie, she was always in a highly emotional state. The doctor who looked in on Cherie a couple of times a week had long ago told her she should pull the plug, but she couldn't bring herself to do it. While her sister was still breathing, there was always the possibility of a miracle.

Deep down, however, she knew it wasn't realistic. Deep down she knew her precious sister was already dead.

The heartfelt lyrics enveloped her as she raced her car along the freeway. Should she tell Max about Cherie? That was the question. Maybe if he knew, he wouldn't want her. Too bad. She had a new policy: the truth above all else. If she'd been truthful with Jake she wouldn't be so miserable now.

What was Max up to anyway? She was anxious to find out. First she had to go home, change clothes, and return Darlene's call. Darlene was probably mad that she hadn't responded to last night's message. What did she care? She was through worrying what other people thought.

Her apartment was delightfully cool and welcoming. She'd left the air conditioning on full blast because it was one of those muggy days that L.A. denizens always said screamed earthquake weather. She'd never experienced an earthquake herself, having arrived in L.A. after the big Northridge one of '94. It seemed impossible that it could be as bad as people said, but all the same she kept a special earthquake cupboard filled with canned goods, bottled water and flashlights. If there was ever another major quake, she'd get in her car and drive straight to the nursing home. It worried her that they probably wouldn't look after Cherie properly in an emergency. That's why she visited every week, taking the nurses presents and candy, making sure they paid attention.

The first thing she did when she walked through the door was check her answering machine to see if Jake had called. Not that she expected him to, of course, and quite frankly, she didn't care if she ever heard from him again.

So why was her heart beating so fast as she approached her machine? Why was she willing the red message light to be flashing?

The red light *was* flashing. One flash. One message.

Probably Darlene wanting to know why she hadn't responded regarding Mr X.

She pressed down the rewind button. "Kristin," said a

muffled male voice, not Jake's, "why didn't you come last night? I do not appreciate being ignored. It is not good for either of us. Tonight. Eight. The end of Santa Monica Pier. I'll pay you double. Be there."

She was shocked. How had Mr X gotten her home number? Had Darlene given it to him? This was absolutely unacceptable.

In a fury, she picked up the phone to complain to Darlene, but Darlene's housekeeper informed her she was out. Kristin left a message for a call back, and hung up, still outraged. Mr X being in possession of her home number made her feel totally vulnerable and uneasy. Having her number was only one step away from getting her address. She shivered at the thought.

Maybe Max's timing was right on target. At least if she was living with him she'd be protected. The more she thought about it, the more she knew it was the only sensible move.

Hurrying to her closet, she changed into a simple yellow sundress and high-heeled sandals. Then she applied some makeup and set off to close the deal with Max.

L.A. Connections 3

# CHAPTER FOURTEEN

As HE DROVE his truck to pick up Madison, Jake had a strong urge to call Kristin. He'd had a few drinks at his father's wedding, and also time to think things over. Why *hadn't* he demanded to know what was going on? It was a puzzle he couldn't quite solve. What was Kristin doing in bed with him anyway? It wasn't like she'd asked him for money. What was her motive? And how long had she planned on keeping her profession a secret from him?

He had seriously thought they had something together, so when he heard that woman's voice on her answering machine, he'd gone into shock. As for Kristin, she'd lain there, not saying a word in her defence. God, she must've thought he was a gullible fool.

Now he was depressed and a little bit drunk, and sorry that he'd asked Madison out to dinner. She was an attractive woman, but she wasn't Kristin. Was he supposed to stop caring about somebody simply because she turned out to be a hooker?

*But how can I care for someone I don't even know?* he asked himself glumly. He'd seen her three times and fallen in love. How dumb was *that*?

He parked his truck outside Natalie's house, got out and walked slowly to the front door. Jimmy had booked him a table at the Palm. "Take her there, order the steak and lobster, get her drunk, fuck her, and forget about Kristin," his brother had told him.

"Is that all you think about with women? Getting laid?"

"If *you* were married to Bunny, that's all *you'd* think about. She nags me to death."

"She always did. You knew that before you married her."

"I've been meaning to tell you," Jimmy had confided. "You do know that I see other women on the side?"

Jake had no desire to listen to Jimmy's sexcapades. "What is this, confession time?" he'd said abruptly. "I don't want to hear about it."

"I'm your brother," Jimmy had said indignantly. "If I can't tell *you*, who can I tell?"

"Dad – he's the philanderer in the family. At least he marries *his* conquests."

Jake had not wanted to hear any more about his brother's extracurricular love life. Bunny might be a pain, but it didn't seem fair that Jimmy used that as an excuse to be unfaithful.

He rang the doorbell of Natalie's house.

Cole answered. "Hey, man," he said. "How was the wedding?"

"Predictable," Jake answered, entering the small house. "My dad's sixty-two, his bride's twenty. I guess that says it all."

"You gonna call her Mommy?" Cole joked, leading him into the living room.

"I'm not going to call her, period," Jake said dryly. "I went to the wedding, I've done my duty for the year."

"You and your dad tight?"

"Is Madison around?" Jake asked, not comfortable with Cole firing questions at him.

"Yeah, I'll call her. Hey, Maddy!" Cole yelled. "Your knight in tarnished armour is here."

"Very funny," Jake said. "Can I get some water?"

"Sure." Cole left the room, returning moments later with a bottle of Evian, which he handed over.

"Thanks," Jake said, swigging from the bottle.

A few moments later Madison walked in. Jake did a slow double-take. He'd known she was an attractive woman, but he hadn't realized she had such a great body and was actually devastatingly beautiful. Her oval face was surrounded by a cloud of dark hair, which up until this time he'd only seen pulled back. Her seductive lips were emphasized with a brownish-gold lipstick, matching the subtle shadow above her elongated eyes. She wore a red dress which took his breath away – low-cut, short, with little spaghetti straps. She looked amazing.

"Hi," she said, unaware of the effect she was having on him.

He'd gone back to his hotel after the wedding and changed out of his one and only suit into khaki pants and a denim shirt with no tie. "I feel under-dressed," he said, and then he realized he'd said almost the same thing to Kristin on their first date.

"Shall I go change?" Madison asked. "I feel half naked."

"You *look* sensational, and if you're comfortable like that . . ."

"No," she said, delighted to see he hadn't bothered to dress up. "I'm certainly *not*. Getting all done up was Cole and Natalie's idea. They were in a makeover mood, and I went along with it. Do you *mind* if I go change?"

"Whatever makes you happy."

She smiled. "That'll make me happy."

\*

Two hours later they were engrossed in deep conversation. Madison had put on a loose sweater, black jeans and a casual jacket. She'd left her hair down and not removed her makeup. Men's heads turned. She was a striking woman.

Jake found her fascinating because he could talk to her in a way he couldn't talk to most women. She was sharp and savvy and aware of everything that was going on. Yet she wasn't a know-it-all, she listened intently to what he had to say, and had a throaty laugh he found quite enticing. They'd already discussed politics, religion, the state of the movie industry, publishing, pornography on the Internet, and his favourite subject – photography. Madison was a stimulating conversationalist.

"Where are you from originally?" he asked, taking a bite of one of the best steaks he'd ever tasted.

"I'm a true New Yorker," she said. "My parents still live there. Well actually, they don't – they moved to Connecticut."

"What does your dad do?"

She was silent for a moment. "Uh . . . he's in commodities."

"Commodities," Jake said. "The stock market?"

"Kind of."

"I don't get the stock market," Jake said. "It's like legalized gambling to me."

"Have you ever been to Vegas?"

"Haven't been. Don't want to go."

"Damn!" Madison said with a low sexy laugh. "There goes my plan of taking you there for a long weekend of unbridled lust."

Jake sat up very straight. "Huh?"

"Just joking," she said with a tantalizing smile.

He was confused. Under any other circumstances he would have found this woman completely irresistible. But he had to be honest with himself and admit that his mind was still on Kristin. All night he'd been wondering what she was doing and if she was thinking about him.

"Why don't you tell me about her?" Madison said, leaning forward, her eyes bright with genuine interest. "I'm an excellent listener. In fact, it's part of my job."

"Tell you about whom?"

"Listen," she said, matter-of-factly, "three months ago I

broke up with my boyfriend. Or rather *he* broke up with *me*. Now believe me, I *know* it takes time to get over something like that. I'm almost there; you're obviously just starting."

He considered denying it, then thought, Why not be honest? She was too smart and too nice to try and fake it. So he began telling her his story.

She listened attentively, interjecting an occasional wise comment.

"That's it," he said when he'd finished his sorry tale. "And like an idiot, I told my asshole brother, who announced it to everyone at our dad's wedding. Now I feel like the world's biggest jerk."

"Don't," she said, shaking her head. "Your reaction was perfectly understandable. You felt out of control and betrayed."

"That's exactly it!" he said excitedly. "Hey, were you ever a shrink?"

"No, but I write stories, so I know people. My father taught me how to analyse situations and sum up the players. My dad's a brilliant guy."

"So . . . what's my next move?"

"You call her up, apologize for bolting like a frightened rabbit, and make a date for lunch on neutral territory."

"Are you sure?"

"Yes. You have to give her a chance to explain why she didn't tell you."

"Good," he said, relieved. "I can't wait to hear what she has to say."

"Remember," Madison said sternly, "no accusations. Simply hear her out."

"I'll do it," he said, finishing off his steak.

"You won't be sorry," she said, taking a quick peek at her watch. "Now, do you mind if we leave? I want to catch the ten o'clock news, see if there's anything new on Salli's murder."

"No problem," he said, calling for the check. Then he looked at her long and hard. "Y'know, if this was another time, another place—"

"I know," she said softly. "You don't have to say a word. We'll get together again when we're both feeling a little less vulnerable. How's that?"

He grinned. "You're a great lady."

She grinned back. "And you're a great guy. So let's get the hell out of here!"

# CHAPTER FIFTEEN

SINCE CAPTAIN MARSH was demanding an arrest concerning the murder of Salli T. Turner within twenty-four hours, Detective Tucci knew that he had to put the remainder of the day to good use. The fact that Bobby Skorch had summoned his lawyer and refused to talk to them had aroused Tucci's suspicions. If Bobby had nothing to hide, then why wouldn't he allow himself to be questioned? And why wasn't he anxious to find out the details of his wife's brutal murder?

After their meeting with Captain Marsh, Lee had decided he should get on the next plane to Vegas so he could thoroughly check up on Bobby Skorch's every move from the previous day.

While Lee was taking care of things in Vegas, Tucci interviewed Eddie Stoner, Salli's ex.

The good news was that Eddie's lawyer had not arrived to bail him out.

The bad news was that Eddie was in a vile mood.

"What the fuck am I bein' held for?" Eddie demanded, wild bloodshot eyes bulging with fury as he sat at the interview table.

"Parking tickets," Tucci said, pulling up a chair. "Too many of 'em."

"Where the *fuck* is my lawyer?"

"You had your phone call, Eddie."

"Well," Eddie said truculently, "guess what? I want another goddamn phone call."

"You know the rules: one call."

"This is a joke," Eddie snarled. "I'm tellin' my fuckin' union 'bout this shit."

"What union?"

"The Screen Actors Guild, that's who. No way they'll let their members be treated like this."

"Where were you last night, Eddie?"

"I want a lawyer present before I answer any questions."

"Why? You got something to hide?"

"I need a cigarette."

"Sure, Eddie. Let me get you one."

Tucci got up and left the room. He could see that Eddie Stoner was a nervous wreck, and it wasn't just for the want of a cigarette – he was obviously hooked on something stronger than nicotine, and he was starting to miss it badly.

Tucci bummed a cigarette from the desk sergeant and re-entered the interview room. "Here you go."

"Thanks," Eddie said, grabbing the cigarette and lighting up.

Tucci took a moment to study him. Eddie was good-looking in a dissolute way. Although only thirty, he had bags under his eyes that you could take on a trip, a long mane of dirty blond hair, flat blue eyes, and a mean scowl. He was wearing an old Nike T-shirt, jeans that had seen better days, and scuffed sneakers.

"I'd like to see you go home today," Tucci said. "So let's make this easy on everybody and you tell me where you were last night."

"Let me ask you somethin'," Eddie said, dragging hungrily on his cigarette. "What's so important about where I was last night? You hauled me in on parking tickets, not a fuckin' murder."

Tucci studied him. From that remark, it would appear that he didn't know about Salli T. Turner's murder. Or maybe he was playing it smart. "What's preventing you from answering?" the detective asked.

"'Cause I don't 'preciate bein' dragged outta bed in the middle of the night. You guys have fuckin' balls of steel."

"Just doing our job."

"Yeah, well, when I do *my* fuckin' job, I don't hassle people in the middle of the night."

"Y'know," Tucci said, "unrelated to this little mess, you're a very good actor. I've seen you in a couple of movies. Shame you never got that big break."

"You bet your ass it's a shame," Eddie said excitedly. "I look at the assholes who make it, an' I gotta say to myself,

Why the *hell* isn't it me? Jean-Claude Van Damme: what the fuck's *he* got that I haven't? I'm better lookin', an' I'm *certainly* a better actor."

"Right, Eddie," Tucci agreed. "You're also an American."

"You bet your ass."

"So, I'll tell you what I'll do, Eddie. Since your lawyer hasn't responded, I'll allow you to make another call if you tell me where you were last night."

Eddie ran a hand through his long hair. "Let me see," he said. "I picked up a coupla chicks at a club on Sunset. Went back to their place round midnight, got crazy outta my skull. I musta got home around three."

"Who were the girls?"

Eddie laughed dryly. "You think I asked their names?"

"You mean you spent the night with two women, and you don't know who they are?" Tucci asked, knowing he must sound like some out-of-touch old fogy.

"This is Hollywood, man – chicks are everywhere. Who gives a shit what they're called?"

"Try to remember, Eddie."

"Hey, you're not *listenin'* to me," Eddie said irritably. "I dunno who they were. Picked 'em up in a club. *They* were horny, *I* was horny. We all got off."

"Do you remember what club it was?"

"I was in the Viper Room earlier. Maybe it was a place called the Boss."

"Does the Boss have a doorman?"

"They got a bouncer."

"Would he know who the girls are?"

"Hey, man, he's not lookin' to identify no one. All he's lookin' for is a big, fat tip."

"Okay, Eddie."

"Do I get my call?"

"Yes. Only I don't want you leaving town. Oh, and by the way—"

"What?"

"Your ex-wife—"

"Salli?"

"She was murdered last night."

"Oh, *fuck*!" Eddie said, his upper body slumping on to the table. "Oh, fuck! Now you're gonna tell me you think I have somethin' t'do with it?"

"I'm not saying anything," Tucci said. "But don't leave the city. Is that clear?"

"How'd it happen?" Eddie asked, sitting up. "Was it that moron she married? I warned her he was trouble."

"When did you last see her?" Tucci asked.

"Hey, man," Eddie said, throwing up his hands, "I may *look* stupid but I know when it's time for no more questions. I need a lawyer."

Tucci got up and headed for the door, where he stopped for a brief moment studying Eddie's expression. "She was stabbed to death," he said, "multiple times. I'll make sure you get your phone call."

L.A. Connections 3

# CHAPTER SIXTEEN

As SHE DROVE TO Max's house in Bel Air, Kristin made another attempt to listen to the Bob Evans biography on tape. Once again she couldn't concentrate and turned it off. She tried to steer her thoughts away from Jake, thinking instead of Cherie and the nursing home. Her sister had looked paler than usual today. Dr Raine, the physician who took care of Cherie, had left a message with one of the nurses that he wished to speak with Kristin. Since Dr Raine was never at the nursing home on Sundays, her only real day off, she knew she had to call him, but she kept delaying it, because whatever he had to say she was certain it would not be good. Dr Raine was a nice man, but he didn't understand about miracles.

She often thought about the day she and Cherie had gotten in their battered old car and set off for Los Angeles. Cherie had been so excited, in fact, it was she who had instigated the trip. "We're going to be famous actresses," Cherie had promised, her pretty face glowing with anticipation. "Both of us. And we'll *never* be jealous of each other. We'll *never* have any of that stupid sibling rivalry."

Three months after they left home, their parents were killed in a train wreck, so there was no going back. The tragedy had drawn them even closer, they had no one except each other – at least until Howie Powers entered their lives.

Kristin often wondered what Cherie would think of how she made her living. There was no doubt that her sister would disapprove, but what choice did she have? The nursing home bills had to be paid, and she couldn't make it as an actress – too tough a profession by far. Besides, she'd never studied acting, nor ever had any ambition in that direction. Cherie had been the ambitious one. Cherie had envisioned stardom for both of them.

The gates to Max's house were closed. Strange, Kristin thought, how in the affluent neighbourhoods of L.A. everyone surrounded themselves with iron gates, guard dogs and elaborate alarm systems. People lived in fortresses. Who did they expect was coming to get them?

She got out of her car and rang the outside buzzer. No reply. She rang it again, then glanced at her watch. It was almost five o'clock, and she'd told him she would be here at four. Had he not bothered to wait?

She rang again and again. Nothing.

After ten minutes of trying, she realized nobody was home. Had Max Steele changed his mind? Was that what had happened? He'd invited a hooker to move in, and then reconsidered?

Angrily she got back into her car. Why was it that every man she met let her down? How come they were all a bunch of selfish, sex-crazed, perverted bastards?

Then it occurred to her. If she was going to deal with bastards, she may as well get paid for it.

Mr X's words ran through her head. *I'll pay you double.*

Double was good. In Mr X's case, double meant a great deal of money.

*Who needs you, Max Steele? You couldn't even leave a note for me. Whatever happened to common courtesy?*

Backing her car out of the driveway and into the winding street, she drove home.

\*

When the bullet hit Max it was like a sharp blinding jolt from hell. He felt as if his shoulder was being torn away from his body, and he screamed out in pure agony. This wasn't a movie. This was the real thing. And he could not believe it was happening to him.

He had given the bastard his Rolex, much as he hated doing so. He had handed over his money as well – all twenty bucks of it – which was every dollar he had on him.

The meagre sum clearly made the guy mad. "You're drivin' a freakin' Maserati," the robber snarled, a woollen ski mask concealing his face. "A cocksuckin' Maserati, an' you're walkin' around with twenty pissin' bucks. Don't jack me off, mothafucker."

"That's all I have," Max responded with a shrug.

"Fuck you, you rich bastard!" the robber screamed. And then he'd fired a shot. Just like that.

Max fell to the ground. The robber didn't seem to care whether he died or not. He kicked him in the groin with the sharp tip of his cowboy boot before he grabbed the keys of the Maserati and drove off, leaving Max lying there in a pool of his own blood.

He lost consciousness almost immediately, until somewhere in the distance he heard a child's voice yelling, "Mommy! Mommy! There's a man lying down. Mommy! Mommy!"

And the worried mother's voice answering, "Don't look, darling. Stay away from him. Get in the car and lock your door."

Jesus! What did they think he was, some falling-down-drunk bum? He tried to speak, his voice weak as he managed to croak, "Somebody . . . gotta help me."

The woman said, "You should be ashamed of yourself!" Then she must have noticed the ever-widening pool of blood, because she suddenly gasped, "Oh, my God! You've been shot!"

"Get . . . the . . . police . . ." he mumbled. "Go for help . . ." And he slumped back, wondering if he was dying.

The woman jumped in her car and phoned the police on her cellphone. She even waited until they arrived.

The next thing Max remembered was lying in an ambulance as it raced him to an emergency room, sirens screaming.

He couldn't believe it. He, Max Steele, had gotten himself shot.

Then everything went black.

L.A.
Connections
3

# CHAPTER SEVENTEEN

LUCINDA'S CALL caught Freddie by surprise. He was in his study, contemplating Diana's foul mood and Max's unconscionable behaviour when she phoned. "Darling," she drawled, as only a superstar of Lucinda's calibre could, "I desperately need a favour."

"What?" he asked, suspicious as always of movie stars courting favours.

"*Manhattan Style* is doing a cover story on me," she informed him. "The editor, Victor Simons, is an old friend, so I know it'll be a positive piece. However, Victor has asked me to do him a personal favour which involves you." A dramatic pause. "Darling, the magazine is desperate to profile *you*."

"Lucinda, you know I don't do publicity," he said, keeping his voice pleasant and even.

"Yes, Freddie, darling, I *do* know that. But if you did this for me they'd give you full copy approval, so what's to lose?"

"My privacy," he said grimly.

"*What* privacy?" she retorted, as if it was the most amusing thing she'd ever heard. "You're acknowledged to be the most famous agent in Hollywood. You *should* do it, Freddie. After all, Sumner Redstone is in all the media, so is Michael Eisner."

"Sumner owns the world, Michael runs a studio," Freddie pointed out.

"Who knows," Lucinda said. "Perhaps that's what *you'll* do one of these days."

"Mike Ovitz already made that mistake," he said, annoyed because he knew he was going to have to say yes on account of Lucinda's twelve-million-dollar deal – which meant a two-million-dollar commission for the agency. How *could* he turn her down?

"Well, anyway," Lucinda said, bored with the conversation, "I *would* like to tell Victor yes, that you'll meet his reporter tomorrow at eleven. Can you accommodate me, Freddie, please? I hardly *ever* ask favours. Please?"

"What's the name of the reporter?" he said resignedly.

"Madison something or other. Apparently she's very good."

"Is she aware I get copy approval?"

"It doesn't matter whether she knows or not. Victor Simons is the editor. He has the last word."

"Only for you, Lucinda," Freddie said, sighing. "Have

Victor send me a fax confirming copy *and* headline approval."

"Thank you, darling," she cooed. "I knew you wouldn't let me down."

When she hung up, it occurred to him that the woman she'd mentioned must be the same journalist Ria had told him about. That's all he needed: an interview with some nosy journalist prying into his life.

The phone rang again. "Yes?" he said impatiently.

"Mr Leon?"

"Who's this?"

"I'm phoning from Cedars Sinai."

Freddie felt his stomach turn. Why was he getting a phone call from a hospital? "What is it?" he asked tersely.

"Max Steele was recently admitted. We thought you should be informed immediately."

"Admitted for what?"

"Mr Steele was shot during a robbery."

Freddie was silent. He didn't know how to digest this piece of information, it seemed so unreal. "How bad is he?" he asked at last.

"It's critical. We have him in intensive care."

"I'll be right there," Freddie said, slamming down the phone and jumping up from his desk. "Diana!" he yelled. "Diana!"

She was sitting in the living room reading a book on Oriental art, studiously pretending to ignore him.

"You won't believe this one," he said. "We have to get over to Cedars immediately. Max has been shot."

Diana leaped out of her chair. "What!" she exclaimed, the colour draining from her face. "How? Where?"

"Apparently it was a robbery."

"How serious is it?" she asked.

"I don't know. Let's go."

"Oh, my God!" she said, her face crumpling. "Oh, my God!" And suddenly she burst into tears.

"Pull yourself together," Freddie said abruptly. "Hysterics won't help anyone."

And even though he was mad at his partner, and felt he'd been betrayed, Freddie was panicked at the thought of anything happening to Max.

He rushed from the house, Diana close behind him.

L.A.
Connections
3

# CHAPTER EIGHTEEN

"How was it?" Cole asked the moment Madison walked in.

"What are *you* doing here?" she said, surprised to see him. "I thought you had a hot date."

"Got cancelled," he answered.

"That must've pleased Natalie," she said, shrugging off her jacket.

"You could say she's thrilled. There's no way she approves of me seein' Mr Mogul." He indicated his dinner laid out on the coffee table: pizza, a carton of French fries and a large diet Coke. "Hey, wanna piece of pizza?"

"What happened to your health foods?"

He grimaced, patting his finely muscled stomach. "Sometimes you gotta give it up."

"What was his reason for cancelling?" she asked, settling on the couch and stealing a French fry.

Cole made a how-would-I-know gesture. "Dunno. Don't care," he said vaguely.

She could see he was hurt. "I'm sure it was a good one."

"Who knows," he said, picking up another piece of pizza. "By the way, some dude called Victor wants you to call him."

"My editor," she said, reaching for the phone and waking Victor up in New York – which seemed to be becoming a habit. "What's going on, Victor?" she asked.

"You have your interview with Freddie Leon," he said, sounding pleased with himself. "Tomorrow, eleven o'clock, his office. *Be* there!"

"I'm impressed," she said, delighted that he'd finally delivered on his promise. "How did you arrange it?"

"Let's just say my connection came through."

"How long will he give me?"

"Use your charm, Madison. I'm sure you'll get as long as you want."

"Thanks, Victor. I love it when you deliver."

"Good news?" Cole asked when she hung up.

"Excellent," she said. "I've got my interview with the elusive Mr Leon."

"So, c'mon," Cole said. "Tell me all about your date."

"Actually, it was very nice," she said, curling her legs under her. "Jake's a terrific guy. He's also completely en-amoured with someone else, but that doesn't make him a bad guy. We had a great time, talked about everything.

Then I gave him advice on his love life and he brought me home. How's that?"

"Doesn't sound too romantic to me."

"It's not supposed to," she said. "Can we switch channels and watch the news?"

"They identified the blonde those two surfers pulled out of the ocean today."

"They did? Who is she?"

"Some girl from Idaho."

"Really?"

"They're saying she was drowned in a swimming-pool *then* dumped in the ocean. How about *that*?"

"God, there's some sickos out there," Madison said, shivering. "Anything new on Salli?"

"The same old crap. One moment she's the Virgin Mary, the next she's the biggest slut who ever walked, depending on what channel you're watching."

Madison really wanted to get into bed and watch TV there, but she had a suspicion that Cole felt like having company. "Is Natalie back?" she asked.

"If I know my sister, she will *not* be comin' home tonight," Cole said. "I took a look at Luther when he came to pick her up. Boy, he's a big one."

"Yeah, just the way Natalie likes 'em."

They both giggled. "Hey, Maddy," Cole said. "It's cool you had a good time."

"Jake's an interesting man," she said. "However, I can promise you this: I am *not* in the frame of mind to get involved with anybody right now. And since he's already involved, no problem."

"Not into one-nighters, huh?" Cole said teasingly.

"No," she answered firmly. "And you shouldn't be either – too dangerous."

"I often wonder what it must've been like in the sixties, when sex wasn't gonna get you zapped. When you could do anything, an' not have to pay with your life."

"Yeah," she said. "It must have been pretty nice then. That's when my mom and dad got together."

"You talk about your dad a lot. You're real tight with him, huh?"

"I certainly am. He's a wonderful man."

"And your mom?"

"She's great, too, but I've always been closer to Michael. He taught me how to go out in the world and chase after what I wanted. He taught me to be fair. And, most of all, he taught me to follow my dreams."

"Michael sounds like quite a guy."

"He is."

\*

Luther was a romantic. He took Natalie to a small restaurant in Santa Monica overlooking the ocean. It happened to be located in the hotel he was staying at – "Shutters on the Beach". Of course, he omitted to tell her this vital piece of information as he plied her with red wine and compliments.

"Y'know, baby," he crooned in a low-down, smoky voice, "I feel like you an' I, well, like we was an accident waitin' to happen."

Natalie leaned across the table. It wasn't exactly how she

would've put it, but he had a point. And she was quite ready to jump into bed with him and start what she was sure would be a more than satisfying sexual relationship. Even though Luther lived in Chicago, he could visit on a regular basis, and that would make seeing him all the more exciting.

He reached for her hand, pressing his strong fingers up against hers. She felt the heat and smiled to herself. Oh, baby, this was going to be finger-licking good!

And then her cellphone went off. "Damn!" she exclaimed, scrambling in her purse to answer the stupid thing. It was Garth, her station manager.

"We need you here immediately," Garth said tersely. "We got a lead on the Malibu blonde. Turns out she might be part of a high-priced call-girl ring. I want you to come in right now and put together a story on her."

"Now?" Natalie objected. "I'm in the middle of a date."

"You can get laid any time," Garth said rudely. "This is important."

"How important?"

"You're always whining that you want to get into real news. If you do a good job, this could be the start of a whole other direction for you."

"News anchor?" she questioned breathlessly.

"Don't get carried away."

"I'll be there," she said, clicking off her phone. Suddenly Luther's lustre dimmed. He was big and sexy, but he was, after all, only a guy.

"Uh . . . Luther," she began.

"Yes, baby?"

"I know you're a real understanding guy, so if I told you I had to go to work . . . could we pick this up where we left off, say, tomorrow night?"

"But baby—"

"I know, I know," she said softly. "It's a real bummer, an' I'll miss you like crazy—"

He shook his head as if he couldn't quite believe this was happening to him. He was a man *definitely* not used to a woman putting work before him.

"Go with me on this, Luther," she murmured sweetly. "And I promise, tomorrow we'll make it a night to remember."

Before he could object, she was on her feet and out the door.

L.A. Connections 3

# CHAPTER NINETEEN

ANGELA MUSCONNI, the hot young movie star with the bad drug habit, was in bed with Kevin Page, the hot young movie star with *no* bad drug habit, when the phone rang.

They'd been in bed all day since they'd partied all night and had not gotten to sleep until five in the morning.

Angela stretched out a long naked arm, wearily groping for the receiver. "Yes," she mumbled. "Who's wakin' me up?"

"Angelina," said a voice from her past.

"Who's this?" she asked suspiciously, although a familiar gnawing in the pit of her stomach told her exactly who it was.

"You know I'm the only one who calls you Angelina."

"Eddie?" she questioned sharply. "Is that you?"

"Yep, it's the man himself."

"Whaddya want?"

"I want you to bail me outta jail."

"What *are* you talking about?" she said, struggling to sit up.

"I'm in deep shit, Angie. Can't reach my lawyer, an' I dunno who else to call who'd have the money to bail me. I gotta get outta here *now*. The cops told me Salli's bin murdered, an' they got their eye on me."

"I haven't spoken to you in three freakin' years," she said accusingly, finally becoming fully alert. "Ever since you ran out on me and married Salli."

"I know, babe, but if old friendships mean anythin', you gotta come and get me. I can't take it here."

"Jeez!" Angie said, completely amazed that he had the nerve to call her. "Is *that* why they've arrested you? *Did* you do it, you bastard?"

"No fuckin' way," he said indignantly. "I'm here 'cause of some crap about unpaid parking tickets."

"You were always threatening us, Eddie," she said, remembering the past. "Me *and* her."

Kevin rolled over in his sleep. "Whoisit?"

"Nobody."

"You gonna come?" Eddie demanded.

"Why should I?"

"Oh Christ! I need you, Angelina."

Angie was torn. On one hand she was outraged that after all this time Eddie had called her, and on the other her natural curiosity was fast getting the better of her. "Maybe," she said grudgingly.

"What does maybe mean?" Eddie blustered. "You comin' or not?"

"I'll see," she said, putting the phone down and breaking the connection. She stared at Kevin, who didn't stir. Carefully she edged her way out of bed.

Kevin grabbed her bare leg, startling her. "Where you goin'?" he mumbled.

"I gotta go out," she said briskly. "Emergency."

"Bring food," he said, as he rolled over and promptly went back to sleep.

She ran to the bathroom, pulled on a pair of tight jeans and a midriff-baring sweater. She knew Kevin always kept a stack of bills stashed beneath his pile of T-shirts, so she raided his dresser drawer and helped herself to a bundle.

*Why am I doing this?* she asked herself. *Sure, I loved Eddie once, but the asshole dumped on me big time. Now he's probably hacked up Salli, and I'm the one springing him from jail. What's* wrong *with me?*

But Angie always *had* gotten off on excitement, and this was the most exciting thing to have happened to her in a long time. Being a movie star was way too safe and predictable. Living on the edge – that's the way she liked it.

And there was nobody better than Eddie Stoner for taking you on a trip to the wild side, and then right to the very edge.

# CHAPTER TWENTY

FROM HER CHIC, upswept, dark blonde hair to the tips of her finely manicured, blood-red, inch-long nails, Darlene La Porte was one of the best-groomed women in Beverly Hills. It took a lot of money to look like Darlene – plenty of big bucks, considering she kept a team of professionals always on call to attend to her grooming needs. She had a hairdresser who came to her house every morning. Then there was her manicurist, dietician, makeup artist, clothes stylist, yoga instructor and personal trainer. They were all on Darlene's payroll. She was no movie star, but she took better care of herself than most of them did.

The pay-off was worth it. She looked thirty. She was actually forty-one.

A youthful appearance was extremely important to Darlene. She needed to interact with and relate to the young girls who worked for her. Every month there was a new batch of pretty girls who arrived in Hollywood hoping to become actresses or models. When their dreams faded – which invariably happened fast – Darlene was there to lead them on to another path. She offered them glamour and excitement and big money. She offered them movie stars and moguls and intimacy with all the men they'd have no chance of getting anywhere near in real life. Once they were thoroughly initiated, she then had them service the rest of her client list – those men with unspoken demands and demented perversions. Men such as Mr X.

Darlene had no idea who Mr X was. She only knew that he grossly overpaid, and that was enough to keep her perfectly happy. The only interaction she'd ever had with him was over the phone. Last night he had called to book a repeat performance with Kristin. When he phoned back an hour later, she had to tell him that she had been unable to reach Kristin. He'd sounded angry. She had asked him if he wanted another girl. He said no. Then five minutes later he called back and said yes – but only if she had someone fresh and new. Darlene immediately thought of Hildie, a pretty blonde from the Midwest who'd only been a working girl for two months. She and Mr X had arranged a meeting place, and Darlene had called to tell Hildie. "This guy's a tiny bit weird," she'd warned her, thinking of Kristin's complaints. "But he's not dangerous, and here's the good news: he pays *really big*!"

"Sounds like fun!" Hildie had said with all the confidence of youth.

Now Darlene sat in front of her television set staring at a picture of Hildie on the news, taken at her high-school prom. Hildie at sixteen with braces on her teeth and brown, frizzy hair. Hardly the same girl Darlene had sent out on a date with death. The Hildie that she knew was blonde and sleek. Hollywood and four years of experience had given her a totally new image.

Now she was dead.

Drowned.

Not in the ocean where she was found. In a swimming pool.

And Darlene remembered another of her girls who'd ended up fished out of the ocean. A year ago. Kimberly. By the time Kimberly's body was discovered there was not much left to identify.

Three weeks prior to her body washing up on the beach, Kimberly had also gone on a date with Mr X.

Darlene had chosen not to connect the two events. Kimberly had been a wild party girl – into coke and heroin. Darlene imagined that she'd died under unfortunate circumstances – maybe partying with friends after her appointment with Mr X. Darlene had not called the police.

Now Hildie.

And Darlene knew that if she went to the police this time, the publicity would be so overwhelming that she'd soon become public property like Heidi Fleiss. After that, her lucrative call-girl business would be over.

There was only one way to deal with such a terrible event. Never send any of her girls out with Mr X again.

Yes, she decided, even though it meant giving up a healthy amount of commission, that's exactly what she would do.

Conscience assuaged, she began switching channels until she found an old Ava Gardner movie.

*Ah* . . . she thought. *Whatever happened to Hollywood glamour?*

Darlene settled comfortably into her couch, and within minutes was totally engrossed in the movie.

# Revenge

### L.A. Connections 4

# PROLOGUE

SINCE MR X had not stipulated that she wear any particular outfit or colour, Kristin chose to go with scarlet. She felt bold and bad and vengeful – while deep inside she felt hurt and abandoned and useless.

Jake didn't want her.

Even Max Steele had rejected her.

And Cherie lay in the nursing home – never showing any improvement – wasting away, waiting for her to pull the plug.

Once in a while Kristin did a little cocaine to take away the pain. Tonight she indulged, snorting the insidious white powder, all the while hating herself for doing so. And yet she knew it would make her feel better, set her up for her date with Mr X. After all, he deserved the best, didn't he? Because her mystery man was the only one who seemed to care about her.

Two sharp, final snorts and she was done.

Every time she did cocaine she vowed it would be the last. Yet when her supply ran out she'd always call Darlene and set up another delivery.

She stared at her reflection in the mirror. *Kristin. Call-girl supreme. Worthless whore.*

The scarlet dress looked sensational on her. Her blonde hair swirled around her fresh gorgeous face.

She took a deep breath, grabbed her purse and left her apartment.

*Mr X . . . here I come . . .*

*And I promise – you will <u>not</u> be disappointed.*

L.A.
Connections
4

# CHAPTER ONE

THE GIRL was barely more than sixteen. The pupils of her large hazel eyes were enormous. So was her sexual appetite.

Bobby Skorch had picked her up on Sunset as soon as he'd been able to get out of the house, which had been a hassle due to all the fuss over his wife, who'd gotten herself murdered the night before.

*That Salli,* Bobby thought, his mind mired in a drugged-out haze, *you never knew what she was going to do next, always full of surprises.*

Finally he'd managed to sneak out of the house by lying on the floor in the back of his maid's car. She'd dropped him off at a hotel where he kept a permanent penthouse suite in his manager's name.

Later he'd taken a cruise along Sunset in the black Ferrari he kept in the basement parking area of the hotel – also registered in his manager's name. The girl had been hanging around outside a club, and she'd willingly accompanied him back to his hotel. Now she was riding his dick like she was competing in some kind of equestrian event. He didn't have to do a thing except lie back and tolerate the ride, because he certainly wasn't enjoying it. This girl wasn't Salli. *Nobody* was Salli. Salli was one of a kind. The others were all slags and sluts and whores. He had no idea what the girl's name was, or whether she had AIDS or the clap – he didn't care.

Bobby was into taking risks. He'd taken a big risk marrying Salli, whom many people had considered a joke with her large fake tits and cascades of dyed platinum hair.

But hey, a lot of *her* friends had considered *him* a risk. Bobby Skorch, the original danger man, with tattoos from here to Cuba, including one on his famous dick.

All he knew was that together they were an awesome sight. *S'long, Pammy and Tommy, Heather and Richie. The Skorches ruled.*

He'd loved her with a burning passion. Now she was gone.

The girl spread her legs even wider, practically balancing her moth-like weight on his dick. Then she moaned – a prelude to ecstasy.

He wasn't there. Not even close. He was hard and angry and stoned and in the worst pain of his life.

When the girl's moans turned to orgasmic cries and he felt her coming, he screamed his anguish so loud that two maids working on the penthouse floor came running to hover outside the door of suite 206, their eyes bulging with fear and curiosity.

Satisfied and more than a tiny bit alarmed, the young girl rolled off him, quickly scurrying to get into her clothes. When she reached the door, she looked back at the man, still spread-eagled on the bed, still erect.

There *was* no release for Bobby Skorch. He was in hell.

And there was absolutely nothing he could do about it.

L.A. Connections 4

# CHAPTER TWO

"THE GUY has pussy for breakfast," Detective Lee Eccles said, chewing on a ragged toothpick.

"What?" said Detective Tucci, distracted as he pored over his copious notes on the Salli T. Turner murder.

"Salli's old man, Bobby Skorch. His cock is bigger than the Empire State Building – an' every broad in Vegas has had herself a slice."

Tucci removed his glasses, glanced up at his partner and nodded. "I know. He has quite a reputation."

Faye had informed him last night – when he'd gotten home after midnight – that Bobby Skorch was the king of the tabloids. "Not that I read those rags," she'd quickly assured him. "Only sometimes I can't help it when I'm waiting in the check-out line at the market."

*Sure, Faye*, he'd thought affectionately. *Why don't you*

*admit that it's your secret vice? You're like a teenage boy hiding his* Playboy *magazines.*

But then he had his secret vices too, food being one of them. Especially since Faye had put him on the diet. No fats. No sugars. Life was hardly worth living.

He'd already checked out Bobby Skorch. It turned out that Salli's husband had quite a rap sheet. Two arrests for drunken driving; assault with a deadly weapon – the weapon being a broken vodka bottle with which he'd made an unprovoked attack on a photographer; unlawful possession of a firearm; driving with a suspended licence; and sexual battery of a teenage girl. The usual celebrity list of misdemeanours.

Tucci sighed and looked up at Lee, who was now perched on the edge of his desk, cleaning his dirty fingernails with the wooden toothpick. "What else did you find out in Vegas?" he asked.

"Plenty," Lee said, digging deep. "Saturday afternoon our boy performed a motorcycle stunt, jumpin' over, like, a hundred and three cars – some kind of crazy shit. Came out of it without a scratch. After that, he took himself to a lap dancin' joint, where he picked up three strippers an' ferried 'em back to his hotel. Then I guess he partied for a coupla hours, an' when he finally left, the doorman told me he still had two of the girls with him."

"You mean he brought them back to L.A.?" Tucci asked, considering the possibilities.

"They were in his limo when he left the hotel." Lee paused for dramatic effect. "But here's the kicker. Bobby didn't *drive* back to L.A. like Marty Steiner said. He took a private plane. So *why* is his asshole lawyer tellin' us he was in the car for five hours? The fucker *flew* back. I already questioned the pilot. He told me they arrived in L.A. at eight, which just *might* have given him time to get to the house, kill his wife, an' who knows what else."

"The strippers were on the plane?"

"Yeah."

"Who met them at the airport?"

"A limo. I'm tryin' to locate the driver. The jerk's taken off on vacation. Limo company's trackin' him for me."

"And the strippers?"

"I'm on it."

*I bet you are*, Tucci thought. When it came to women, Lee was a disrespectful dog. It was one of the reasons Tucci couldn't stand him. That and the fact that Lee had once had a date with Tucci's wife – long before they'd met but it still bothered him – especially since Faye refused to discuss it.

"Any action on the lab reports?" Lee asked.

"She had consensual sex shortly before her death. Put up quite a struggle when the stabbing frenzy began. The lab is analysing the skin under her fingernails and fibres found on her body. There's also blood that isn't hers."

Lee nodded, hitched himself off Tucci's desk and strolled over to the coffee machine. Tucci watched him go. All day long he'd had a weird feeling. He'd investigated twenty-six murders and this one was giving him the most trouble. He couldn't help picturing Salli's hacked-up body, lying in a pool of blood. Salli T. Turner. So young and vibrant and pretty. So horribly butchered.

The public wanted answers. So did Tucci's captain – not to mention the Mayor. And Tucci wouldn't mind knowing himself. Who'd killed her in such a vicious and unconscionable way? Skorch, or her recent ex, Eddie Stoner? Both men had a proclivity toward violent behaviour – especially concerning women.

Eddie had his own rap sheet, which included getting busted for possession of cocaine, assaulting a police officer, and several domestic abuse arrests.

Salli had certainly picked herself a couple of charmers.

Tucci bent over his desk, concentrating on his closely written notes. He had always found that when investigating a murder, it was of major importance to write down even the smallest detail while the evidence was still fresh. Not that he had much evidence to work with: no fingerprints, no witnesses, no murder weapon.

Where was he supposed to start? Ah yes, the bullet extracted from the wall near the houseman's residence. The unfortunate Froo had been in the wrong place at the wrong time. Probably alarmed by the loud music and the frantic barking of Salli's two small dogs, he'd gone to investigate. Maybe he'd even heard her screams, although none of the neighbours had mentioned hearing screaming – only the music and the dogs. Of course, in Salli's neighbourhood the houses were so goddamn big he was surprised they'd heard anything at all.

The bullet that had obliterated Froo's face had embedded itself in the wall. Tucci was checking on any guns registered to Bobby or Eddie.

He'd already decided to interview the neighbours again.

# REVENGE

Sometimes a twenty-four-hour break gave people time to remember things they hadn't considered important.

Details, that's what solving a murder case was all about. Details.

Detective Tucci was known for his detail work.

# CHAPTER THREE

THE OFFICE BUILDING that housed IAA was impressive.
Designed by the premier modern architect, Richard Meier,
the man who was also responsible for the splendid new
Getty Museum, the clean lines were superb. Acres of Italian
marble and pristine white walls with just the right amount
of glass block. Dominating everything was a huge David
Hockney painting of a swimming pool hanging in the
massive lobby.

Madison took all of this in as she approached the front
desk. "I'm here to see Mr Leon," she announced.

The Asian woman at reception glanced up. "Do you
have an appointment?"

"I certainly do," Madison replied.

"Please take a seat," the woman said.

Instead of going straight to the seating area, Madison

strolled across the lobby and stood under the Hockney painting, gazing up at the impressive work of art. As a journalist she loved observing visual images. Capture those and you had your reader hooked. She found Hockney's work arresting and very Californian – which was interesting considering he was from England.

*Well, here I am in the lobby of IAA*, she thought, her mind working overtime. She glanced at her watch, noting that it was exactly eleven o'clock, the time of her appointment. She wondered how much time Freddie would grant her, and if he was as intimidating as his reputation.

She was intrigued at the prospect of meeting him, also anxious to get on with it. She wanted to get out of there in time to attend Salli T. Turner's funeral this afternoon.

This wasn't the way she'd planned her trip, but if she'd learned one lesson in life, it was that there was always something around the corner to surprise you.

She thought about her date with Jake. She decided that if he ever got over Kristin, they'd get together again, because he was a genuinely nice guy – unlike his brother Jimmy, who appeared to be a major lech.

She glanced over at the reception desk. The Asian woman was busy on the phone. Hmm . . . It was her experience that the more important the subject, the less they kept you waiting. She made a mental bet with herself that Freddie would summon her to his office within five minutes, and she was right. "Miss Castelli," the woman called out less than two minutes later. "Somebody's on their way down to fetch you."

"Thanks," Madison said.

Moments later a young black man in a spiffy suit and expensive horn-rimmed glasses appeared at her side. "Miss Castelli?" he asked politely.

"That's right."

"Please come with me."

She followed him to a glass-enclosed elevator. They travelled up three floors, then walked down a long corridor flanked with many open-door offices. Finally they reached the desk of Ria Santiago, Freddie Leon's loyal sentinel.

"Good morning, Miss Castelli," Ria said.

"Good morning, Ms Santiago," Madison responded. "I'm sorry I disturbed you by calling you at home yesterday. I was under the impression that everyone knew about my visit here."

"Apparently they do now," Ria said, with a thin smile. "Mr Leon's expecting you. Please come with me."

Madison followed her into a spacious office with an incredible view of Century City. The room was decorated more like a library than a working office; there were several large couches, many shelves of leather-bound books, and expensive art on the walls. In the middle of the room sat the great Freddie Leon, ensconced behind a magnificent steel and glass desk, poring over papers. He did not look up when she entered.

"Take a seat," Ria Santiago said, indicating a Biedermeier chair to the side of his desk. "Mr Leon," Ria said, all business, "your eleven-thirty called to say they'll be five minutes late. I'll alert you three minutes before they're due."

*Hmm* . . . Madison thought. *Does he really think I'll be satisfied with half an hour? No way.*

367

Ria left the office. Freddie continued to study the papers on his desk.

Madison had a feeling that if she didn't exert herself immediately she would be hustled out within fifteen minutes. "Good morning, Mr Leon," she said, determined to make her presence felt. "I'm delighted you agreed to see me."

Freddie put down his pen and looked up at her for the first time. He saw a beautiful, slender woman in her twenties, with jet hair pulled back, large eyes and full lips.

She stared right back at him, taking in *his* appearance. She saw a poker-faced man in his forties, with cordial features, straight brown hair and a quick bland smile, which she noticed was not reflected in his eyes.

"Good morning, Miss Castelli," he said. "As I'm sure you've been told, I'm seeing you as a favour. I don't normally give interviews."

"I understand, Mr Leon. I've sat down with a lot of people who don't normally give interviews. Sometimes my subjects find it an enjoyable experience, sometimes they hate it." She smiled. "Let's hope you find it enjoyable."

He smiled back – once again the smile did not quite reach his eyes. "I'm really extremely boring and very dull," he said, tapping his index finger on his chin.

"Isn't that for *me* to say?" she said, slightly amused.

"It depends. What kind of a journalist are you?"

"Maybe you should ask some of my other subjects," she answered evenly. "Henry Kissinger, Fidel Castro, Margaret Thatcher, Sean Connery. Take your pick."

"Quite an eclectic group," he said. "I'm duly impressed."

"Perhaps you wouldn't be if you read the pieces."

"I'd like to read them."

"Then I'll make sure they're faxed to you this afternoon."

He was summing her up, trying to decide what he thought of her. "Now," he said, "before you start bombarding me with questions, I should tell you that I do *not* discuss the money my clients make. In fact, I do *not* discuss my clients, period. I don't talk about my family, politics, sex, *or* my personal opinions on anything."

Madison laughed politely. "Wow! This is going to be some story!"

He liked the fact that she didn't seem to be in awe of him, it made a refreshing change. "You don't seem to understand, Miss Castelli, I do not *want* to *be* a story in your magazine."

"Mr Leon," she said patiently, "there's a great amount of public interest in what goes on in Hollywood, and you are the absolute power broker. People have heard about you, you have a famous name. Sometimes, when we achieve greatness in our lives, we have to give up our privacy."

"I don't *have* to give up anything, Miss Castelli."

"I wish you'd call me Madison."

There was something in her eyes that drew him in. She was not the normal pushy journalist he was used to encountering at openings and parties. This was an intelligent woman who knew what she wanted and had no fear of pursuing it. For a moment he forgot she was the enemy. "Can I offer you a drink? Apple juice, Diet Coke . . ."

"How about I buy *you* a coffee somewhere other than your office?"

He raised his eyebrows. "Excuse me?"

"Oh, please," she said lightly, playing with him. "We all know it's a game. Your eleven-thirty is running five minutes late – I don't think so. Why don't we get out of here, drive somewhere, enjoy a leisurely coffee and talk about how you got into this business? People would kill to know how you got started."

"Now let's not get dramatic."

"I promise I won't pry into your personal life. I merely wish to portray you as an ordinary human being who has achieved great power. Not as some ice-cold Hollywood mogul, which is the impression everyone has of you."

He couldn't help laughing, which was a relief after the stress of the last twenty-four hours. "You're very persuasive . . . Madison. To tell the truth, I wouldn't mind getting out, it's been one of those mornings."

"*Can* I buy you a coffee then?" she asked, fixing him with a strong gaze.

She was a beautiful, smart woman, and smartness had always intrigued him. "Why not?" he said, surprising himself. "I suppose I can live dangerously for once."

He got up from behind his desk, and together they walked out of his office.

Ria gave him a stony stare. "Mr Leon," she said, her voice full of disapproval, "What about your eleven-thirty?"

"Postpone it," he said easily. "I'll be back in an hour. Miss Castelli has persuaded me to play hookey."

Ria frowned. It was unlike Freddie Leon to be so light-hearted. "Very well," she said, tight-lipped. "If you're absolutely sure."

"Yes, Ria, I'm sure."

"And if the hospital calls—"

"You have my numbers."

# CHAPTER FOUR

KRISTIN COULDN'T STOP shivering. She was naked and alone, locked in some funky little beach house where she'd been held captive all night.

She was not afraid. She refused to be afraid. This was another one of Mr X's sick sex games, and now that it was light outside, she was confident he would soon come back to release her.

Last night she'd met him at the end of the Santa Monica Pier as arranged. As usual he was dressed as a chauffeur: all in black with a baseball cap pulled down low over his forehead, and oblique wraparound shades hiding his eyes.

"Where are we going?" she asked, as he gripped her arm and led her back to his car – a limo.

"You'll know when we get there," he said.

Mr X was a man of mystery, and for her sins she was getting used to his odd ways.

So she'd climbed into the back of the limo, thinking that, however bad her life was, at least she was luckier than Cherie.

"Put on the blindfold," Mr X commanded.

She'd done as he asked, covering her eyes with the soft velvet mask that was lying on the back seat. As she did it, she told herself, *I'm a paid whore; I deserve everything I get.*

Mr X had then driven along the Pacific Coast Highway at great speed for about twenty minutes, turning off on to what felt like a bumpy dirt road. When the car had finally come to a halt he'd thrown open the rear door and almost dragged her out.

She could hear the roar of the sea and smell the cold night air, and for a moment she'd felt fear. "Can I take off the blindfold?"

"No," he replied, roughly gripping her arm and proceeding to take her on a trip down perilous steps to what she assumed was a house. Several times she nearly fell, but he yanked her up. Finally they entered the house, which smelled musty and damp. He led her to a bed, pushed her on to it and said, "Strip."

"What?"

"You heard me."

This was her worst experience with him yet. The man was a true pervert – getting his kicks from frightening people.

"First I want my money," she said, berating herself for not asking earlier.

"Spoken like a true whore," he said, shoving an envelope stuffed with cash at her. She felt the stack of bills with her hands and was instantly reassured. This much money would pay Cherie's nursing home bills for months.

"Strip," he repeated in a flat monotone. "Slowly."

She stood up and did as he asked. Hating him. Hating herself.

Standing there naked, she felt vulnerable and exposed. This man who had asked her to do a variety of perverted deeds had never once touched her sexually. Was he finally going to make love to her?

Suddenly she heard the door slam, followed by the click of a heavy lock. Next she heard wild laughter from outside. Then silence.

She waited a few minutes before ripping off the blindfold. The room was pitch black. She couldn't see a thing, there was no light coming in at all.

It was then she realized she was totally alone.

She didn't panic. This was only another way Mr X had of getting his sick kicks.

After a while she began groping around for her clothes, only to discover the perverted freak had taken them.

She edged her way slowly around the small room, feeling ahead of her with her hands. First she tried the door, it was firmly locked. Next to it was a window, which on examination appeared to be boarded up. No getting out of there until he chose to come back, so she settled on the narrow bed, covered herself with the one thin sheet and attempted to sleep.

Now it was morning, light was creeping through the

small gaps in the sturdy boards covering the window, and soon Mr X would be back to release her.

No matter how much money he offered in the future, this encounter was definitely the final one. She would *never* do business with him again.

L.A. Connections 4

# CHAPTER FIVE

ANGELA MUSCONNI knew she was doing the wrong thing, but then Angie had not gotten where she was today by doing the right thing. So, against her better judgement, she bailed out Eddie Stoner, who might or might not be a suspect in the violent murder of his ex-wife.

Eddie was delighted to see her, and so he *should* be. It had been three years since he'd left her, and in those three years she'd become a bankable movie star, bigger than either of them had ever imagined.

Obviously she still harboured feelings for Eddie, even though she lived with Kevin, otherwise she never would have agreed to bail him out.

"You look amazin', Angelina," Eddie said, seated in her Ferrari as she drove him to his apartment.

"I *should* look great," she boasted, thinking that he

377

didn't look as hot as she remembered. "Like I'm a big movie star now."

"Glad it happened for one of us," he said, scratching his stubbled chin.

"It could still happen for you," she said, driving recklessly. "You're not too old. What are you – twenty-nine?"

"Thirty," he said grimly. "Thirty and fucked."

"Can't be all bad," she said lightly.

"Get *this* shit," he said, outraged. "Those filthy pigs dragged me out of bed in the middle of the night an' threw me in jail. They freakin' think *I* did it."

"Did what?" she asked innocently.

"Killed Salli."

"*Did* you?" she asked, throwing him a sly sideways glance.

"No freakin' way," he said vehemently. "How could you even *think* I'd do somethin' like that?"

"You used to beat the shit out of us, Eddie," she reminded him. "Me *and* Salli. You can't deny it."

"So once in a while I got a little carried away," he said with a careless shrug.

Angie remembered him getting more than a little carried away. Eddie in a rage with his eyes bulging was not a pretty sight. Before Salli had stolen him from her, he'd been a violent bastard, prone to beating her up whenever he felt like it.

"Did you get carried away with Salli on Saturday night?" she asked boldly, secure that now she was famous he wouldn't dare touch her.

"What're *you*?" he said, scowling. "A freakin' cop?"

378

"Just askin'. No need to go nuts."

"I'm gonna tell you who did it," Eddie said, nodding his head. "Her moron husband, Bobby, *that's* who."

"How do *you* know?" Angie questioned him. "It was probably some crazy stalker. I've got a ton of 'em. I'm sure Salli did, too."

"It was Bobby," Eddie repeated. "He's a stoned psycho – I've seen him in action."

"Doing what?"

"Anythin' he can," Eddie said ominously. "Drive faster," he added. "I wanna get to the TV, see what's goin' on. The cops told me she was hacked to death. What else are they sayin'?"

"Not a lot."

When they reached his apartment one thing led to another, and before she knew it, Angie found herself back in his bed.

Sex with Eddie was everything she remembered – and more. Eddie might not be a star on the screen, but he was certainly an above-the-line performer between the sheets. A sexual box-office hit.

When they were finished, she knew she should dress and go home to Kevin. But Eddie was back in her life, and Eddie was her addiction – an addiction she'd thought she was over.

Apparently not.

"Why'd you dump me and marry Salli?" she asked, leaning on one elbow and staring at him accusingly as they lay in bed. "I was only a baby. *You* treated me like I was nothin'."

"You're *still* a baby," Eddie said with a self-satisfied smirk, because he was well aware he was the greatest cocksman that ever lived. Women were so damn easy, give 'em head for ten minutes and they were his for ever. "An' rich, too, I bet."

"You got *that* right," she said, giggling.

"What're you doin' with all your loot?" he asked, reaching for a cigarette on the bedside table.

"Whatever I want," she answered cheekily.

"You goin' with anybody?" he asked, keeping his tone deliberately casual.

"Don't you read the fan magazines?"

"Oh, yeah," he said sarcastically. "Like I'm freakin' *glued* to the fan magazines."

"I'm living with Kevin Page."

"Kevin Page?" he snorted. "*That* fairy."

"He's not a fairy," she said defensively.

"Get a life, sweetheart," Eddie said, blowing smoke in her face. "He's gay as a two-cent piece."

"Kevin is *not* gay."

"Yeah?" he said, tweaking her left breast. "I bet he doesn't do it to you like *I* do."

This was true. Kevin might be on the cover of every teenage girl's fan magazines, but as a lover, he had a lot to learn.

"You're *sooo* conceited," she said with a sigh, longing for his hands all over her, not to mention his tongue where it would do her the most good.

Eddie laughed confidently. "So what else is new?"

380

L.A.
Connections
4

# CHAPTER SIX

"WHAT WAS that about a hospital?" Madison asked, as she settled next to Freddie Leon in the passenger seat of his gleaming maroon Rolls-Royce.

"Off the record?" he said briskly.

"Of course."

"My partner was shot last night."

"Max Steele?"

"You know him?"

"Yes, we went jogging together a couple of days ago."

"You get around."

"Is he okay?"

"It hasn't hit the news yet," Freddie said, gazing straight ahead as he drove along Santa Monica Boulevard. "Right now he's in intensive care. My wife is sitting vigil at his bedside."

"This is terrible news."

"It's the reason I agreed to get out of the office today; couldn't concentrate. You see, as of last week . . . well, Max and I were not exactly on good terms."

"God! I hope he'll be okay."

"So do I," Freddie said dryly. "Because if Max dies, everyone will say I put a hit on him. That would go nicely with my reputation. Right?"

"How can you be so cynical?" she said, wondering why he would even say such a thing.

"Let's make a deal, Madison. Unless I signal that you can put your tape on, *anything* I say is completely off the record. Agreed?"

"I'll go with that."

"Excellent decision."

She shook her head. "This is a very violent town."

"Where are *you* from?"

"New York."

"And I suppose New York isn't violent?"

"I've been here three days, and already Salli T. Turner's been murdered, and now Max Steele has been shot."

"Read the papers, something happens every day."

"Was he at home?"

"No, the police say it was a robbery in a parking lot. Apparently somebody wanted his Rolex." Freddie sighed. "Do you *know* how many times I've warned him not to walk around with a seventeen-thousand-dollar gold watch on his wrist?"

Madison wanted to respond, "How about you in your two-hundred-and-fifty-thousand-dollar car?" But she did the prudent thing and resisted. "Will you be able to *keep* it out of the news?" she asked.

"I doubt it."

"And you say your wife is at the hospital with him?"

"Diana took it badly. I never realized they were so close."

*Hmm*, Madison thought, *there's a telling remark.*

"You'll have to excuse me," Freddie continued. "My head's not in a good place right now. When I left the hospital last night I took a ride to the beach. We have a small house there which nobody ever uses. It's the only place I can relax. I enjoy solitude."

"So do I."

"I'll lend you the keys one day."

"I'll take you up on that," Madison said, thinking that Freddie Leon was not at all like his reputation. This titan of the big deal seemed lonely and almost vulnerable.

They rode in silence for a while.

"Y'know," Madison said, "the last thing I want is to hassle you. So if this isn't a good time, we don't *have* to talk today – we can get together next week."

"I like you," Freddie said, ignoring her offer. "I knew that the moment you walked into my office. Believe me, I don't say that to many people."

"I'm flattered."

"Madison – interesting name."

"My parents met on Madison Avenue," she said lightly. "My mother was shopping, and I guess my father was looking."

"Your parents still alive?"

"They live in Connecticut, moved out of the city last year."

"Smart. That's exactly what I plan on doing eventually. I'm going to buy myself an old farmhouse in France and give all this up."

"You'd relinquish all your power and leave L.A.?"

"In a moment," he said, making a sharp turn on to Melrose.

"Where are we going?" she asked, peering out of the window.

"My secret place," he said. "Only it's not so secret with the tourists. It's somewhere I don't have other agents and producers begging for favours. Also, they serve the best Danish in the city."

"Where's that?"

"Farmer's Market on Fairfax."

Her eyebrows rose. "Farmer's Market?"

"You'll love it," he assured her.

"I will?"

"Yes, Madison, you will."

She settled back in the passenger seat. This meeting was turning out to be much more interesting than she'd expected.

L.A.
Connections
4

# CHAPTER SEVEN

DIANA SAT BESIDE Max Steele's hospital bed. He was still unconscious and in intensive care, but the doctors had told her he had a good chance of making it. She hoped and prayed it was true, because if he survived, she had decided to definitely tell Freddie she was leaving him.

Of course, there was one small snag. When she and Max had met for breakfast, he'd revealed that he had just gotten engaged, and she – like a fool – had later shared the news with Freddie. When Freddie left the hospital last night, he'd instructed her to contact Max's fiancée immediately.

She had not done so. Why should she? It seemed unnecessary. She was perfectly happy sitting next to Max, watching over him. The last thing she needed was a stupid fiancée getting in her way. For a brief moment she'd considered calling Max's secretary at home to get the girl's number, but then it had seemed more sensible to wait until the next day.

Now it was Monday morning and she finally realized she'd better call the girl or Freddie would throw a fit. He was a stickler for getting his own way. It irked her, but there seemed to be no other choice.

She called Max's secretary, Meg, who sounded completely devastated. "When can I come to the hospital?" Meg asked, choking back tears.

"Not yet, dear," Diana responded.

"Everyone at the office is so concerned," Meg continued. "Mr Leon called a staff meeting this morning and told us all. Oh, Mrs Leon, it's such a shock. What can I do?"

"I need the number of a friend of Mr Steele's," Diana said crisply, unable to bring herself to say fiancée.

"Of course, Mrs Leon. Who would that be?"

"Her name's Kristin something. I don't have a last name."

"Hold on a moment, I'll look in the book."

Diana held on impatiently. It was obvious Meg knew nothing about a fiancée. Good.

Finally Meg returned. "I can't seem to find a listing in the business book for a Kristin. However, his personal phone book is on his desk. Would you like me to take a look in that?"

For a moment Diana was tempted to say no. If she was unable to get the girl's number she couldn't inform her. "Very well," she said at last.

Meg left her hanging again and returned a moment later. "Since we have no last name I'll look under the K's," she said. "Ah yes, there *is* a Kristin listed. Kristin, and in brackets, Darlene, then there's a number."

"Give it to me," Diana said impatiently.

"Yes, Mrs Leon. Is there anything else I can do? Maybe bring some of his clothes to the hospital? Or drop by his house?"

"Good idea, Meg. Go to his house and warn the house-keeper that if anyone comes to the door, not to say a word. We're trying to keep this quiet."

"There're spies in all the hospitals, Mrs Leon," Meg said. She was an avid reader of the tabloids and knew these things.

"I know, dear. Which is exactly why we've hired security."

Diana did not call immediately, but waited another half-hour before reluctantly dialling the number Meg had given her.

An uptight sounding woman answered.

"Is this Kristin?" Diana said, equally uptight.

"Who *is* this?" the woman demanded, her voice shrill and angry.

"Mrs Freddie Leon," Diana said haughtily.

"There's no Kristin here."

"Is this Darlene?"

"Are you from the media?"

"Ex*cuse* me?"

"Don't bother me at home again," the woman shrieked.

"Call my lawyer. I'm suing every one of you. You people make me *sick*."

And with that the woman slammed the phone down, leaving Diana stunned.

L.A.
Connections
4

# CHAPTER EIGHT

NOW THAT his father was safely married for the fourth time, Jake decided he'd done his duty by attending the wedding, and now it was time to start getting *his* life together. Since arriving in L.A. so much had happened, and he'd been so preoccupied that he'd done nothing about finding an apartment, let alone checking in with the magazine he was about to start taking pictures for. Which was kind of stupid, because until he let them know he was in L.A. and ready to work, there would be no weekly paycheck coming his way. And although he was an award-winning photographer, he was not exactly rolling in bucks. Which is one of the reasons he'd decided to take the highly paid magazine job.

He sat in a coffee shop on Sunset toying with a late breakfast of bacon and eggs, ruminating his fate, and wondering why it was his luck to have met a gorgeous delectable woman – with whom he'd fallen instantly in love, not to mention lust – who then turned out to be an extremely highly paid call-girl. Goddamn it! The whole scenario was like a bad movie.

Madison had advised him to call Kristin and hear her side of things. He'd done so, but Kristin was out, so he'd left a long message on her answering machine. So far she hadn't responded.

He had a feeling she might have been sitting beside her machine listening to him and hating him because he'd walked out on her when he'd found out the shattering truth.

Fuck! He'd blown it. He should at least have stayed around long enough to listen to what she had to say. Instead he'd marched out like an insulted virgin, yelling something like, "Why didn't you tell me? I would've worn a condom."

Jesus! Talk about bad behaviour.

After brooding over his coffee, he finally went to a pay phone and tried again to reach Kristin.

This time a female voice answered, only it wasn't Kristin – it sounded more like a foreign maid. "Kristin?" he asked hopefully, even though he knew it wasn't her.

"No, this Chiew. I take message?"

"Uh . . . I need to talk to the lady you work for. Will she be back soon?"

"Don't know. Madam not come home last night."

Oh, that was great. She was probably out with a big-bucks client having wild, paid-for sex.

"What time *will* she be home?"

"No, sorry."

He gave her his number at the hotel, impressing upon her that it was urgent Kristin call him the moment she came in. He didn't know what else to do, but he *did* know it was imperative that he talk to her as soon as possible so that he could try to straighten things out.

He went back to his table, finished his coffee, paid the check and strode out into the hot noon sun.

\*

In her office at the TV station, Natalie was busy working on what could turn out to be the biggest story of her career, and it wasn't about Salli T. Turner. The lead had been handed to her by Garth, who had a loyal spy in the police department. She'd taken the small amount of information he'd given her and run with it.

Natalie was well aware that this was her big opportunity to get out of boring show-business gossip and into hard news. This was her chance to shine with a *real* story. She, Natalie De Barge, was about to become famous.

She'd been working on her story all night, and now she had it together in time for the noon news.

As she sat at her computer finishing up, Jimmy wandered over and stood behind her. "I hear you got a hot deal goin', babe," he said, rubbing her shoulders.

"That's right, Jimmy," she replied, shrugging his hands off her back.

"Y'know," he said casually, "Garth and I were talking,

and although your story's kind of showbiz related, he thought *I* should be the one to break it."

She turned around and stared up at him. "You've *gotta* be kidding. This is *my* story, Jimmy. *Mine*. I worked on this all damn night and all morning, and I am *not* giving it up to *anyone*."

"But it'll be stronger coming from me," Jimmy pointed out.

"What's *wrong* with Garth?" Natalie snapped, her eyes flashing major danger signals. "He didn't have the balls to tell me himself?"

"Guess he knew you'd be mad," Jimmy said weakly.

"Fuck him and fuck you, Jimmy," she said furiously. "I'm on air with this. Don't mess with me."

"No need to get nasty," he said, backing off, a hurt expression on his handsome face.

"If *you* had a great exclusive, wouldn't *you* be angry?"

"I'm only trying to be helpful."

She narrowed her eyes. "In what way?"

"You're not used to presenting hard news. You do the trivia – who's sleeping with whom – the Leonardo DiCaprio and Gwyneth Paltrow shit."

"Yes. And that's *exactly* what I'm trying to get away from. *This* is my opportunity."

"Okay, okay, don't get your panties caught up your butt," Jimmy said, rapidly backing off. "I'll tell Garth."

"Yeah, and while you're doing that, tell him the *next* time he has something to say to me, he can do it himself."

Jimmy mock-saluted. "Got it."

Natalie was fuming. She should've known that Garth

wanted *her* to do the work, while Jimmy took all the glory. It was always that way.

But they weren't getting away with it this time. This story was *definitely* hers.

# CHAPTER NINE

"I'M COMPLETELY disarmed," Madison said, brushing a lock of dark hair out of her eyes.

They were sitting outside at Farmer's Market, eating Danish and sipping iced tea.

Freddie leaned across the small table. "What was that?"

She laughed. "I *said*, I'm completely disarmed by you. You're nothing at all like your public image."

"Yes, but we'll keep that between us, won't we?"

"In everything I've read about you, you come across as a cold power broker with a heart of stone. A man who's only interested in mega deals. Are you aware that everybody's scared of you? Yet here *I* am, a journalist of all people, sitting here with you having an exceptionally pleasant time."

"Glad to hear it," he said, sipping his iced tea. "As I told you before, you caught me on a strange day." For a moment he paused, staring reflectively into the distance. "You see, yesterday I thought I wanted nothing more to do with Max Steele. And today I keep thinking about how we both started out together, our close friendship, the way we built our agency from nothing. Max was the personality, I was the brains. Not that I'm saying Max doesn't have brains. He's a hard worker and street smart – qualities I admire."

"I only met him briefly," Madison said, remembering Max climbing into his pristine red Maserati with a big smile on his face. "However, I must say I liked him. He's a complete egomaniac, but an unabashed one, which gives him a certain amount of charm."

"How did you meet him?" Freddie asked curiously.

"My girlfriend's brother, Cole, arranged it so that we bumped into each other jogging. He knew I wanted to ask Max about you."

"And how does Cole know Max?"

"Cole's a personal trainer. In fact, I think he's worked *you* out a couple of times. Black guy, very good looking."

"Diana hires the trainers."

"I get the picture. Your wife runs your personal life. You run the business."

He threw her one of his cold looks. "I can assure you, Madison, my personal life is all mine."

*Hmm*, she thought, *mustn't go too far; this is an interesting, complex man, and I should hold back.*

"So far you haven't allowed me to put on my tape recorder," she said, hoping he might acquiesce. "Which means I have no interview."

"That's all right," Freddie said, taking another sip of iced tea. "As I told you before, we must get to know each other first before I subject myself."

"But this would be so perfect to write about," she said enthusiastically. "The real Freddie Leon. The man who actually bleeds if he's cut."

"Maybe it's the perfect interview for *you*," he said evenly. "However, it is not quite the image *I* wish to present to the world."

She fixed him with a long look. "When *do* I get to put on my tape?"

"Maybe later in the week I'll take you to lunch and give you the official interview, the one I've never given before."

"Sounds good to me."

He offered a glimmer of a smile. "I'll tell you how Max and I started out, all about our first clients, the people we've dealt with over the years. I'll give you a good interview. But today I feel like forgetting about everything. You can understand that, can't you?"

"As a matter of fact, I *do* know how you feel," she said, nodding vigorously. "When Salli Turner got murdered I was in shock, and it's only been a couple of days."

"Was she a friend of yours?"

"An acquaintance. I'm going to her funeral later. Did *you* know her?"

He shook his head. "No."

She remembered Salli telling her about how she'd met Freddie in the underground garage of his building. Probably he was stalked by so many would-be actresses that he genuinely didn't remember.

"Where's the funeral?" he asked.

"Westwood," she replied. "Cole's taking me, he knew Salli pretty well."

"It seems Cole knows everyone."

"He does. And all their secrets, too. Sort of like you, although on a different level." She took a big bite of Danish. Freddie was right, it was delicious. "Who do *you* think murdered Salli?"

Freddie paused before answering. "Difficult to know with these girls," he said slowly. "They arrive in town with nothing but their looks and a whole lot of ambition. Then, if they're lucky, they make a little money, get a touch of fame, and that's when they all pick the wrong man. They're incapable of dating anyone with substance. I've seen it happen a thousand times. We have a girl at our agency, Angela Musconni. She's a talented young actress, yet there's something about her – something I know will eventually destroy her, one way or the other."

"Must be tough for you to watch. Can we talk about that?"

"Don't push it, Madison," he said shortly.

She pushed it anyway. "I was thinking of interviewing your secretary, maybe your wife, and some of your friends. Would that bother you?"

"When I'm ready, I'll give you the list of who you can talk to," he said abruptly.

"You're very controlling, Freddie."

"The secret of my success, Madison."

"Okay," she said, sighing. "The rules are yours, so I guess I'll have to play the game your way."

"Good. Because otherwise you'd be out of the ball park."

An hour later he dropped her off in the underground parking garage at his building. "Call me tomorrow," he said.

"Will I get past the dreaded Ria?"

"If you're persistent."

"Gee, thanks."

She collected her car from the valet and drove home.

"Am I glad you're here," Cole said, greeting her at the door. "Natalie called – she's breakin' a big story on the noon news, wants me to tape it. You got any idea how to work this goddamn machine?"

"Put in a tape, and press record."

"I don't have to set it?"

"C'mon, Cole, of course not. When you play it back, you merely fast forward to where you want to go."

"Hey, very smart."

"What's Nat's story about?" she asked, opening the fridge and taking out a bottle of Evian.

"The Malibu blonde deal. She's been working it all night."

"What happened with Luther?"

"She gave him up for her story."

"Natalie putting work before a guy? Now *that*'s progress." They both laughed. "What time should we leave for Salli's funeral?" she asked, swigging from the bottle.

"Soon as we've watched big sis. We should get there early."

"Good."

"How'd it go with Freddie?"

"He's an amazing man," Madison said thoughtfully. "With a great deal of personal integrity."

Cole raised an eyebrow. "Never heard *that* about Freddie Leon. Y'know around town they call him the Snake – he'll bite you soon as look at you."

"You're a cynic, Cole."

"Takes one to know one," he said, turning on the TV and fiddling with the tape machine.

"I have bad news," she said, flopping down on the couch. "The story hasn't broken yet, but Max Steele was shot in a robbery yesterday."

*"Whaaat?"*

"He's in intensive care. *Don't* spread the news; I was told in confidence."

"Anythin' we can do?"

"Guess not."

Cole shook his head and turned the TV sound up as Jimmy Sica appeared on screen and began reading the current news.

"Jimmy sure is one good-lookin' dude," he commented.

"And straight, too," Madison murmured dryly.

"A guy can fantasize, can't he?"

"Personally I think his brother's more attractive. Jake doesn't realize how sexy and handsome he is. Jimmy *does*. He probably spends most of his time admiring himself in front of a mirror."

"That's 'cause he's on TV," Cole pointed out. "The dude *has* t'look good."

"Jake would get *my* vote any day."

"Gotta feelin' you're into him, huh?" Cole teased.

"We're friends, that's all," Madison said defensively. "As I told you last night, the man is taken."

"That, sugar pie, would *never* stop me," Cole said with a wicked grin.

"Hey, if a guy is bagged, it's okay with me – I can walk away."

Natalie appeared on screen. "The sister's lookin' fine!" Cole exclaimed proudly.

"She sure is," Madison agreed, impressed with Natalie's businesslike image: a black Armani suit with a white silk shirt, and no outrageous jewellery – Natalie's usual trademark.

"Good evening," Natalie said, poised and in control. "Natalie De Barge reporting." A short dramatic pause. "Hollywood. Land of dreams. A fantasy paradise where anything can happen, and sometimes does. Yesterday a young girl's body washed up on the Malibu shore. We were all quick to christen her the Malibu Mystery Blonde, after all, this *is* L.A., land of the instant sound bite, and we – the media – go with it every time. What could be better? A beautiful young blonde female to titillate our thirst for the latest headline. But *our* Mystery Malibu Blonde has a name. She was nineteen-year-old Hildie Jane Livins from Idaho. Hildie came to L.A. three years ago, just like thousands of other young hopefuls with starry eyes and Hollywood dreams."

The camera cut to a medium shot of a plain-faced woman in a print dress standing outside a remote farmhouse. "Hildie was a good girl," the woman said. "I lived next door to her family going on thirteen years. She was a pretty little thing. Never gave no one no trouble. Minded her own business an' helped her mom around the house."

The camera cut back to Natalie. "In Hollywood Hildie tried to make it in show-business. She got a job working as a check-out girl in a supermarket, attended acting class, and hung out with her friends who were also trying to make it. Mavis Ann Fenwick was Hildie's roommate for two years."

Cut to shot of a skinny brunette with a big ass. She was standing on a Hollywood street, dressed in shorts and a T-shirt. "Hildie was the coolest," Mavis Ann said, blinking nervously. "We always had fun, and when things weren't going good, she *never* complained." A manic giggle. "Once we lived on Campbell's soup for three solid weeks 'cause we couldn't afford nothin' else."

The camera switched back to Natalie in the studio. "Eventually the temptations of Hollywood lured Hildie into a life of decadence," Natalie continued. "This innocent young girl met a sophisticated worldly-wise woman who goes by the name of Darlene La Porte. Darlene's real name is Pat Smithins – a former convicted prostitute who has also been arrested several times for pandering. According to Mavis Ann and other friends of Hildie's, Darlene promised Hildie money and acting opportunities if she agreed to sleep with movie stars and rich men. Darlene, in fact, became Hildie's madam." A long pause. "Now Hildie is dead, murdered by drowning and dumped in the ocean to make it look like an accident. When we tried to reach Darlene La Porte for her comments, we were informed she had nothing to say. Tell *that* to Hildie's grieving parents."

"*Jesus!*" Cole exclaimed, leaping up. "Whaddya think?"

"I think it's damn good investigative reporting," Madison said. "I only hope she has plenty of hard facts to back up her story, because Darlene whatever-her-name-is will have her lawyers crawling all over everyone."

Cole grabbed his jacket. "Come on," he said. "We got a funeral to attend."

# CHAPTER TEN

KRISTIN WAS desperately trying to keep it together, but it was getting difficult. She was naked and alone, locked in a boarded-up room with no bathroom. She had no food or water, and although she was desperately trying not to panic, it had already occurred to her that maybe Mr X might *not* return.

The thought sent tingles of fear up and down her spine. Nobody knew where she was or with whom she'd had a date. Mr X had booked her dircctly, and like a fool – because she was upset and disappointed about the Jake situation and Max not keeping their appointment – she'd gone.

*Stupid little whore. You're getting what you deserve.*

She attempted to shut off the inner voice that constantly screamed in her head. The voice that always spoke the painful truth.

The light seeping through the boarded-up window was stronger now. It must be at least noon, she thought, and still there was no Mr X.

The sick degenerate sonofabitch. Her greed had led her to him. Her greed would be her downfall. And yet all she'd really wanted to do was make sure Cherie was taken care of. Was that so terrible?

Cherie. What would happen to her if there was no Kristin to pay the bills? They'd switch off the machines keeping her alive. Oh God!

With a sudden burst of strength she hurled herself against the door like she'd seen heroes do in movies. It didn't budge. She wasn't a hero. She wasn't even a heroine. She was just a lonely whore locked in a room with an envelope filled with cash.

*I'm going to die in this room.* The thought seemed to hover over her like a black shroud.

She slumped to the floor. And then she screamed – a long, piercing wail of a scream.

But there was no one around to hear.

# CHAPTER ELEVEN

CAPTAIN MARSH was yelling about the news story on the Mystery Malibu Blonde. "Where'd they get their information?" he shouted. "We only just identified the girl. How come they're on air with a full story before we gave out an official statement?"

Tucci shrugged. "I got a funeral to go to, Captain. Can we get into this when I come back?"

"No!" Marsh snarled. "Where's this Darlene woman? I want her questioned pronto."

"We've already contacted her lawyer. He's agreed to bring her in later to answer some questions. We had to put on the pressure. She apparently has . . . connections."

"Fuck this shit!" Marsh stormed. "Salli T. Turner. Now this. I need some fuckin' arrests around here."

Tucci stifled a yawn. "Yes, sir."

"Where's Eccles?"

"Questioning the lap dancers who flew back with Bobby Skorch."

"He would be," Captain Marsh growled.

Tucci glanced at his watch. "I don't want to be late—"

"Get the fuck outta here."

Tucci was only too glad to leave. He felt like crap. Hungry. Tired. Overworked. There'd been a spate of murders over the last month. He'd been lucky enough not to have pulled duty on any of them, now this.

Faye said it was a good thing. "You'll solve them," she'd told him in a quietly confident voice. "You're the best."

It was nice to have a woman who believed in him. On his way to Salli T. Turner's funeral, he stopped at a Winchell's and bought three glazed chocolate doughnuts. Faye's disapproving face flashed before his eyes. Jesus! It wasn't as if he'd had time for lunch. The doughnuts were in *place* of lunch – a poor substitute, but certainly better than nothing.

He utterly refused to feel guilty.

\*

Meanwhile, in a luxury hotel on Sunset, Lee Eccles knocked on the door of Suite 300 and prepared to interview the two lap dancers/strippers who'd flown to L.A. with Bobby. He'd tracked the limo driver, who told him where he'd deposited Bobby and the girls.

The two women answered the door together. Lee flashed his badge and informed them he was there on official business. They mentioned they were about to take off on a shopping spree, but at his insistence they reluctantly allowed him into the untidy suite.

Their names were Gospel and Tuscany, both blondes, both stacked. Gospel, who was clad in a red catsuit with several gold crosses hanging round her neck and two giant crosses hanging from her ears, had long, straight hair down to her waist. She was stoned.

Tuscany, pneumatic body poured into a crotch-skimming leopardskin dress and hooker heels, had short bubble-cut hair.

"This won't take long," Lee said, checking out the spacious suite which was costing *somebody* a buck or two. "I only have a few questions."

"Don't you need a warrant t'do this?" Tuscany asked, obviously the brighter of the two.

"Want me to get one?" Lee countered, shooting her his best I'm-a-cop-so-get-outta-my-face look.

"If it's about that old guy in Vegas," Gospel interrupted, feigning outrage, "wasn't *my* fault he had a heart attack. Dunno *why* his old cow of a wife is suing me. You from the insurance company?"

"No, he's not from the insurance company," Tuscany said irritably. "He's a cop. Didn't you see his badge?"

"Cop, insurance company, all the same to me," Gospel said, absentmindedly stroking her left nipple through the thin material of her catsuit.

"What do you want anyway?" Tuscany demanded, staring him in the eye.

Lee didn't answer for a moment. He was fantasizing

about how they'd be, girl on girl. Pretty raunchy if he knew his women. Yes, this was definitely a dynamic duo. "You flew into L.A. Saturday night with Bobby Skorch, is that right?" he asked, eyeballing Gospel's ample cleavage.

"Who told you that?" Tuscany said suspiciously, tugging down her leopard skirt.

"The Secret Service," Lee drawled sarcastically.

"Bobby said we weren't supposed to tell anybody," Gospel whined.

"Why you wanna know?" Tuscany demanded.

"Routine," Lee said. "Did Bobby give you money?"

"Whaddya think we are – hookers?" Gospel said, clearly insulted.

"Not at all," Lee said with a smirk. "I know you're two nice young ladies who simply happen to strip for a living. Right? You make a buck here, a buck there. Why not? If you've got it, show it."

"We're good at what we do," Gospel said defensively. "That's why Bobby chose to fly *us* to L.A. with him, not any of those other bitches."

"After you got off the plane Saturday night, what happened?" Lee asked. The limo driver had already told him he'd driven all three of them to the hotel, but Lee wanted to hear their version.

Gospel giggled. "What *didn't* happen?"

"You came directly to the hotel?"

"Yeah, we came straight here," Tuscany said. "So what?"

"Can you recall what time you arrived?"

"Dunno," Gospel said with a careless shrug. "Maybe

seven or eight. We had a coupla shots, then Bobby hadda go out."

Tuscany shot her a warning look.

"He told us not to tell anybody that either," Gospel added lamely. "Said we was to say we were with him all night."

"Aren't you supposed to give us a warning or something?" Tuscany said. "You know, like one of those anything-you-say-may-be-used-as-evidence-against-you kind of deals. That's what cops do in the movies."

"Only if I'm planning on arresting you," Lee said. "Which I'm not."

"Ooh, good, I'm so relieved," Tuscany said sarcastically.

It was as if neither of them knew what was going on. "You *do* know about the murder?" he said, exasperated.

"What murder?" Gospel said, her eyes widening.

"Salli T. Turner."

"Horrible!" Tuscany squeaked. "We watched some of the coverage stuff on TV."

"And you *do* know that Salli was Bobby Skorch's wife?"

Both girls went into dumb overdrive.

"Didn't know that," Tuscany said.

"Me neither," Gospel said.

"Didn't even know he was married," Tuscany added.

These girls were plain stupid, but then he hadn't expected a couple of Einsteins. "So, ladies," he said, "you'd better think *very* carefully about what you're about to tell me and be completely honest about it. Because otherwise, you girls could find yourself in a shitload of trouble. Get it?"

L.A. Connections 4

# CHAPTER TWELVE

OUTSIDE PIERCE BROTHERS cemetery in Westwood there was a line of limos and cars stretching for blocks. It was always that way at a celebrity funeral. In Hollywood, celebrity funerals were regarded as an event – people attended them to be seen, it validated their very existence.

Tucci bypassed the line, flashing his badge at security, who waved him by. He'd devoured all three doughnuts on the way there, and now he felt bloated and guilty. If Faye knew what he was doing she'd kill him. *Maybe death's better than deprivation*, he thought with the shadow of a smile.

He fell in with the other guests entering the already overcrowded chapel. Although he was early, there were only a few places left. He recognized the journalist who had brought him the audiotape of Salli. She was sitting near the back, so he quickly slid in beside her.

"Good afternoon, Detective Tucci," Madison said, turning to give him a quick once-over.

He acknowledged her with a nod, unable to recall her name, which infuriated him because he was good at remembering names, although in the last few months this had happened to him several times. A couple of weeks ago he'd complained to Faye. His wife had prodded him gently in the stomach and said teasingly – or so he'd thought – "Alzheimer's. You're nearly fifty, you know."

Screw nearly fifty. He was forty-nine years old, he had another ten months to go before he was fifty. Sometimes Faye exhibited an uncharacteristic mean streak.

"Miss Castelli – Madison," he almost shouted, so happy was he to suddenly remember her name.

"Yes?" she said, startled.

"Uh . . . how did the piece you were writing about Salli turn out?"

"I've done better," she said wryly.

"I'm sure it was excellent," he responded. "My wife raves about your work. Reads your magazine every month."

"Thank you," she said with a pleasant smile.

Tucci considered Madison Castelli to be a very beautiful woman with her dark hair and almond-shaped eyes – not to mention her lips, which gave seductive a whole new meaning. Not that he was interested in other women, but he could look and admire, couldn't he? He leaned forward to see who she was with.

"Hey, man," Cole said, noticing he was getting checked out, "how ya doin'?"

Tucci nodded briefly and leaned back. Then he began

surveying the room, noting one famous face after the other. Faye would have a great time here; she loved stars and gossip, her one failing.

"This is so very sad," Madison sighed, shaking her head. "I still can't believe it."

"I know," he agreed.

"Do you have any leads?"

"We'll be making a statement soon."

"Was my tape helpful?"

"Yes, ma'am."

All of a sudden, raucous old-fashioned rock and roll began blaring through the speakers, silencing any further conversation. Mick Jagger. Metallica. Rod Stewart. Kiss.

Tucci thought his eardrums might burst. Funerals today – you couldn't trust 'em.

*

Eddie Stoner insisted they attend Salli's funeral, and Angie didn't argue. After all, she was in his bed again, why shouldn't she go along with what he wanted to do? If she'd been working it might have saved her from falling back into his life, but her new movie didn't start principal photography for six weeks, so she had plenty of time to play.

Her immediate problem was what to do about Kevin. By this time he must have realized something was amiss since she'd run out in the middle of the night. She knew she had to call him, so finally she did so in the car on the way to the funeral.

"Uh . . . listen, Kev," she said when he answered, "somethin' came up."

"Where the *fuck* have you been?" Kevin exploded; he sounded like he'd been waiting by the phone.

"I bumped into an old friend, and uh . . . here's the thing, I won't be back 'til later."

"Later when?"

"Dunno," she said evasively.

"Hey," he responded furiously, "how about not bothering to come back at all?"

"Go screw yourself," she said, her temper rising. "It's *my* house, too. *I* paid half the money."

"Y'know, Angie, this isn't working for me," he said, his voice grim.

"Not working for *you*," she said indignantly. "*I'm* the one who's checking out."

"Oh, *you're* leaving? Good. *I'll* keep the house."

"No freakin' way," she objected, her tone getting shriller by the minute. "We bought the house together, remember?"

"Tell you what," Kevin said, relieved to have this sudden escape hatch. "I'll call *my* lawyer, you call *yours* – let *them* work it out. Right now I don't want to see you here."

"You asshole!" Angie yelled. "*I* don't want to see *you* there. Anyway," she added, lowering her voice, suddenly remembering that Eddie was sitting right beside her, "I can't talk about it now. I'm on my way to Salli's funeral."

"Oh, your good friend Salli," Kevin jeered. "Isn't that the girl you used to trash all the time?"

"Can't you speak well of the dead?" Angie said contemptuously.

"Goodbye, Angie," Kevin said, and abruptly hung up.

Eddie, who was pretending to concentrate on driving her Ferrari, stared straight ahead. "Problems?" he said, casually patting her on the knee.

"I was plannin' on dumpin' him anyway," Angie muttered. "His ego's bustin' out all over. The moron's startin' to believe his own publicity. Jerk! Some people can't handle stardom."

"Not like you, huh?" Eddie said, tossing back his luxuriant mane of dirty blond hair.

"I handled it ace," Angie boasted. "All these sex-crazed producers tryin' to jump me. Ha! Dumb old cockers – they pop Viagra with their morning coffee to see if they can still get it up. Think gettin' a boner makes 'em more of a man."

"Now, now," Eddie said, laughing. "Don't go gettin' bitter on me."

He turned the car off Wilshire Boulevard, immediately noticing a long line of limos ahead of them. "We should've taken a limo," he moaned. "This is gonna be a rat fuck."

"Thought you *wanted* to drive the Ferrari," Angie retorted, her mind still half focused on Kevin.

"I did," he said, opening the window, leaning out, and attracting the attention of a young Hispanic traffic cop. "Hey, excuse me, friend. I've got Angela Musconni in the car. She's tryin' to avoid gettin' mobbed or set upon by the photographers. Anything you can do for us?"

"Sure, man," the cop said, attempting to peer into the passenger seat and take a good look at Angie, whom he'd recently seen in a movie where she'd strutted around half naked. "Leave your car. I'll get a parking valet to take it. You can sneak her in through the back."

"'Preciate it," Eddie said.

"Very smooth," Angie said, jumping out of the car.

"Yeah, well, don't see why my darling should wait around," said Eddie. Then he leaned over and gave her a long, slow French kiss.

Angie surfaced with a stupid grin on her face.

It was great being back with Eddie, especially now that *she* was in the boss position.

L.A.
Connections
4

# CHAPTER THIRTEEN

"I'M SUING every single stinking one of them. I'm suing that black bitch, *and* the TV station, and anyone else who dares cross me."

"Calm down," said Darlene La Porte's lawyer, Linden Masters, a tall man with piercing blue eyes and a distinguished white beard. Linden had an air of respectability about him, which went down well with judges, considering he represented some of the most notorious people in Hollywood, including Darlene, who'd come to him when she'd grown tired of using cut-price lawyers, and had realized that paying for the best got her the services she required.

"That bitch practically accused me of *killing* Hildie," Darlene fumed. "I know *nothing* about it."

"Which is exactly why we're visiting the police station later today," Linden said in an irritatingly calm voice. "You'll tell them you don't know anything, after which they'll leave you alone. Co-operation is the key. If you avoid speaking to them, Darlene, they'll think you have something to hide."

"What do you mean?" she asked crossly.

Linden pulled on his beard. "*Did* you send Hildie out to meet a client?"

"No," Darlene said, pacing up and down the thick pile carpet in her luxurious living room.

"You're sure? Because if you did, you'd better tell *me*. As your lawyer I'm here to protect you. And if you're concealing any evidence at all . . ."

"Oh, God, Linden," she said, collapsing into an over-stuffed armchair. "Of course I'm not." What she really wanted to say was, "Yes, I sent her out with the one client I know nothing about. He calls himself Mr X. I hear from him only occasionally. He pays big bucks. All cash. The girls think he's weird, but he's never done any of them harm." But, of course, she said no such thing.

"Good," Linden said.

Darlene jumped up and walked over to the large picture window overlooking Wilshire Boulevard. She gazed out, watching the cars down below race by at great speed. For a moment her mind drifted back to a year ago and Kimberly. She'd fixed Kimberly up with a client. That client was Mr X. A week later the girl's body was fished out of the ocean.

In her mind Darlene had always refused to connect the two, imagining Kimberly had gone off with her friends *after* her appointment with Mr X, and died or been murdered at one of the drug parties she always hung out at. Now this.

"I *help* these girls," she said, speaking rapidly. "If I

wasn't around to supervise their lives they'd be out on the street or mud-wrestling in some seedy place by the freeway. *I* save them from themselves. Thanks to me they live in nice apartments, wear beautiful clothes. I'm *good* for them."

"You don't have to tell me," Linden said, sure that Darlene believed her own lies. But as long as she paid his exorbitant bills, what did *he* care?

"What will this do to my reputation?" she wailed, turning towards him. "*Can* I sue? I have no desire to become another Heidi Fleiss."

"There's not much chance of that," Linden said. "They nailed Heidi on alleged tax evasion. You *pay* your taxes."

"Yes, yes, I'm a good citizen," Darlene said, convincing herself that she was. "I own a successful flower shop, which is where my income comes from. And I pay plenty of taxes. *Plenty*. Now my reputation has been besmirched and I want retribution."

"Don't worry," Linden said. "We'll get it. But you've got to remember, Darlene, you *do* have a record, and that's *not* in your favour."

"Dammit, Linden," she snapped, "I pay you a lot of money to keep my reputation clean."

"I'll be back to fetch you in two hours," Linden said, anxious to escape her bad mood. "In the meantime, don't speak to anyone. No public comments. Tell your service to handle all calls."

"Very well."

Darlene saw Linden to the door and went into her bedroom. Hildie had been such a sweet, fun-loving girl, almost innocent in a way. *Why* had she sent her out with Mr

X? She knew the man was a pervert. Why hadn't she chosen one of her more sophisticated girls? Then she remembered, it was Kristin he'd wanted.

Impulsively she went to the phone and dialled Kristin's number. The maid informed her she was out. "I need to speak to her urgently, Chiew," Darlene said.

"I sorry," Chiew replied. "Miss Kristin no come home last night. I worried. No message, nothing."

"Didn't come home?" Darlene said, panic suddenly rising. It wasn't like Kristin to vanish without leaving word where she was – she always made sure she was reachable in case there was an emergency concerning her sister. "Do you know where she went?" Darlene asked, attempting to remain unruffled.

"No, ma'am. A gentleman called. Jake Sica. When she come back, he want her to phone him at hotel."

"Give me his number," Darlene said abruptly. "And when she does come home, have her call me immediately."

Darlene looked at the number as she put down the phone. She had a bad feeling, a very bad feeling. Who was Jake Sica? Kristin didn't go out unless it was business. She'd confided to Darlene that she had no need of a personal life, all that concerned her was making enough money to take care of her sister.

Picking up the phone, Darlene called the number. It was a hotel. "Jake Sica," she said, trying to get her mind around the name which sounded vaguely familiar.

He answered on the first ring.

"I understand you're looking for Kristin," Darlene said.

Jake recognized the woman's distinctive voice from Kristin's answering machine. "Who's this?" he asked anyway.

"It doesn't matter who I am. Do you know where Kristin is?"

"You're her madam, aren't you?" he said accusingly.

"*Excuse* me?"

"I was there when you left a message on her answering machine. You wanted her to meet a Mr X. You said he'd pay her a lot of money."

"Who the hell are you?" Darlene screeched, blowing her usual cool.

"Somebody who cares about her."

"If you care about her so much, how come you don't know where she spent last night?"

"Not that it's any of your business, but we got into a fight because of your message. Now I'm looking for her, too."

Darlene slammed the phone down. She wasn't about to get involved. Getting involved could only lead to big trouble.

\*

Lurking outside the bedroom, Junia Ladd, Darlene's significant other, had been listening to the conversation with her ear pressed close to the door. Junia, a pointy-faced girl of eighteen, with delicate ivory skin and wispy fair hair, had been Darlene's live-in lover for eighteen months, ever since Darlene had rescued her from a juvenile detention centre.

Junia enjoyed the luxury of living with Darlene, but

sometimes she had to break free, and when she did, she needed extra money. Making something on the side was most desirable, because although Darlene was generous, she always had to know exactly how Junia spent her money. Junia could go into Sak's or Neiman's and charge whatever she wished, but if Darlene suspected she was out spending her money on grass or coke, she threw a nasty fit.

Sometimes Junia stole the odd hundred from Darlene's Prada purse when she thought she could get away with it. Other times she tried to do people favours in return for cash. Giving Mr X Kristin's number was a favour for which she'd gotten paid five hundred bucks. Luckily Darlene had been in the bathroom when she'd answered the phone. It was Mr X tracking Kristin. He must have sensed Junia was someone he could manipulate, because the first thing he'd said was, "Give me Kristin's home number and I'll pay *you* five hundred bucks."

"How do I know you'll do that?" Junia had said, glancing at the bathroom door, making sure that Darlene was not about to emerge.

"Go downstairs in an hour. The hall porter will have an envelope with your name on it. The money will be there. Leave another envelope with Kristin's number for me. Mark it Mr Smith."

"Okay," Junia had said. "Only don't you *dare* tell Darlene."

The deal had taken place on Saturday. Now with all this stuff going on about Hildie getting murdered and Mr X being involved and Kristin not coming home all night, Junia had the shakes. She wondered if she should confess to Darlene what she'd done.

No, she couldn't. She was too scared. Darlene had a vicious temper, and Junia didn't want to get thrown out. She liked her set-up. She even liked the dyke action, although that wasn't to say she was totally gay. Junia swung both ways, she considered it prudent to keep her options open.

She thought again about Kristin, whom she really liked, because Kristin was a genuinely nice person, unlike Darlene's other girls, who were mostly stuck-up pieces of work Junia didn't get along with at all.

She could hear Darlene banging about in the bedroom. This was probably not a good time to tell her about Mr X's phone call, but she realized she'd better do something.

She ventured into the bedroom.

"Goddamn it!" Darlene screeched. "How *dare* the cunt drag me into this murder investigation. I'm suing her black ass right off television. You'll *never* see *her* again."

Darlene was on one of her rants. Once she got going there was no stopping her until she'd gotten satisfaction one way or another. Darlene, who presented a calm and sophisticated public image, was actually a raving bitch. However, over the eighteen months they'd been together, Junia had learned how to handle her moods.

"I am *not* happy," Darlene said ominously. "And I look like shit. I'm going to change." She stalked into her dressing room.

Junia hurried over to the notepad next to the phone.

Darlene had a habit of writing everything down, and sure enough, there was the name of the guy she'd been talking to about Kristin – Jake Sica – and a number.

Junia didn't know what to do. It wasn't like she was a good Samaritan or anything, but how could she sit back and do nothing? Hildie had been murdered, and indirectly it was probably Darlene's fault. She was sure Darlene didn't remember, but one night about six months ago she'd gotten drunk on a bottle of Cristal, and under the covers she'd confided to Junia the story of Kimberly and her connection to Mr X.

Junia had listened and said nothing. The next morning Darlene seemed completely oblivious to her ramblings of the previous night, and it was never mentioned again.

If Darlene went to jail, did that mean that she, Junia, would be left in the apartment with all of Darlene's money and clothes and stuff?

Yes! She would be the official custodian while Darlene was locked away. Wow! Not too bad a job.

Then reality hit. That's not the way it would work. No, she'd be thrown out. She'd end up with nothing.

Surreptitiously she copied down Jake's phone number on a scrap of paper and slid it into the pocket of her jeans.

"Hey, Darl," she yelled through to the dressing room, "want me to go to the cop station with you?"

"Are you *serious*?" Darlene said, marching back into the bedroom wearing a La Perla bronze lace slip on her well-toned body. "*You*, my dear, will stay out of this. Let us not forget where I found you. So I suggest for the next few weeks you keep a very low profile indeed. In fact, I don't even want you answering the phone. Let the service pick up."

"It's not like I have anybody calling me," Junia grumbled. "You don't allow me any friends."

"That's not fair," Darlene said sharply. "We live a different kind of lifestyle than other people. You're happy just to be with me, aren't you?"

Junia wanted to say, *No, you're twenty-three years older than me, and we've got nothing in common*.

But she didn't. She knew she was living a cushy life, and she wasn't about to blow it.

At least not until she was good and ready.

# CHAPTER FOURTEEN

THE FAMILY entered from a private room in the back and filed into the first pew. They were led by the bereaved husband, Bobby Skorch, who was heavily sedated or maybe stoned. Bobby, clad in an ankle-length black leather coat and dark shades, his long, greasy, black hair pulled back in a tight ponytail, could barely keep his balance. A cigarette dangled from his thin lips.

Behind him came Salli's father, a short stout man with a carrot-colour crew cut and a nervous tic. And then followed two very young, fair-haired girls – pretty in an unsophisticated way. They were Salli's half-sisters. Their mother, an overweight woman wearing too much makeup and an unsuitable shiny blue satin cocktail dress, trailed closely behind them. And finally Grandpa, an old man with a wily gait, wearing a shabby, ill-fitting brown suit.

Tucci's attention was on Bobby, the grieving husband, who'd been spotted last night picking up a girl on Sunset and taking her to a hotel. *Some grieving husband*, he thought. Hmm . . . he couldn't wait to hear Lee's report on the two strippers.

The more he thought about it, the more he was beginning to target Bobby Skorch as his prime suspect.

\*

"That's Angela Musconni with Salli's ex," Cole whispered, nudging Madison.

She took a peek at the exquisite young woman who was walking in from the side door accompanied by a wild-looking guy with a mass of dirty blond hair. Salli had obviously harboured a penchant for guys who resembled out-of-control rock 'n' rollers.

"So that's Eddie," Madison said in a low voice. "Salli talked about him on the tape, said he used to beat her."

"I told you that," Cole said. "Hadda make the hospital run a coupla times myself. In fact, Eddie and I duked it out one day."

"You did?"

"Yeah. I kinda got on him 'bout the way he was treatin' Salli, an' he called me a fag. So I beat the crap outta him." Cole laughed at the memory. "The dude deserved it. Treats women like shit."

"Do you think he could've murdered her?" Madison asked.

"Wouldn't surprise me."

She watched as Eddie and Angela sat down, noticing

**430**

that as soon as they were settled, Angie began running her hands through the back of Eddie's hair and cooing in his ear. Obviously they were a couple.

Then Madison's attention was drawn to talk-show host Bo Deacon, whom she'd met on the flight to L.A. It was only a few days ago, but it seemed like months had passed. Bo made a noisy entrance, demanding seats in front. He was with a zoftig redhead in her forties, who clung to his arm as if she expected him to make a daring escape at any moment.

"Bo was coming on to Salli on the plane – or trying to," she whispered to Cole. "Only Salli wasn't buying his bullshit."

"Another slimeball," Cole remarked.

"You know everybody."

"In my job – sure. I'm kinda like a shrink or a barman, my clients spill the goods."

"You trained Bo?"

"For about three months. He's a lazy sonofabitch. Didn't wanna work it, then blamed me 'cause he continued to put on the pounds. So he fired me. *That* was the luckiest day of my life. He had hot and cold running women *and* a wife, a very jealous wife."

"Charming."

"I used to work him out in his dressing room at the studio. There were all these little interns running in and out. His deal was to fuck 'em an' fire 'em."

Madison sighed. "Aren't there *any* nice guys in Hollywood?"

"Me."

"I mean nice *straight* guys."

"Hey, didn't you know?" Cole said with a big grin. "Straight guys are a dying breed."

"Thanks!"

\*

"Why are we here?" Mrs Bo Deacon demanded. Her name was Olive, and she was a former showgirl.

"Out of respect," Bo growled, wishing his wife would shut up. She was drunk as usual; he'd caught her slurping straight Scotch behind the bar at their house before they'd left for the funeral. "If I *wasn't* here, people would talk. Salli was on my show countless times."

*And that wasn't all she was on,* Olive thought with a hidden scowl. Did her cheating no-good husband think she didn't know what he was up to? If it wasn't for the children, and the glory of being married to a famous man, she would have left him years ago.

"I hope you don't expect me to go to the reception," Olive said, her overly glossed lips turning down at the corners. "Salli T. Turner was nothing more than a cheap tramp."

"How can you say that at her funeral for Chrissake?" Bo objected, glancing around to make sure no one had heard.

"Because it's true," Olive hissed. "And I for one am not turning her into a saint now that she's dead."

"You're a real bitch, Olive," he said, getting a strong whiff of the Scotch on her breath.

"Yes, and don't you love it. *That*'s why you married me."

*No*, he thought, *I married you because you had big tits*

*and you were sexy as all get out, and like a dumb schmuck I thought you'd stay that way.*

Unfortunately, Olive was now about as sexy as a sack of old beans. Plus she was a true lush, and however many times she promised him she'd stop drinking, it never happened. Two stays at the Betty Ford clinic and it *still* hadn't happened.

She muttered something to him. He wasn't listening, he was too busy waving at everyone in sight. He'd found, over the fifteen years that he and Olive had been married, that the only way to deal with her when she'd been drinking was to ignore her. Sometimes it actually worked.

*

By the time Natalie arrived in Westwood the crowds were so large that it was too late for her to get anywhere near the funeral. She located her camera crew, taking up a position with them behind the ropes. The trick was to catch the celebrities on their way back to their cars. Some would speak to her. Some wouldn't. After all, this wasn't exactly a big movie premiere. This was a funeral – albeit a hot funeral.

Natalie was on a high. Her story had gone over big; even Garth was pleased. This could be the start of a whole new direction for her, and it was about time. She was ready. She'd been ready since college.

*

The widower in the black leather coat leaned back on the hard wooden bench and let his tears flow as he listened to Mick Jagger screaming out "Satisfaction". He'd personally

**433**

picked every track of music to be played at the funeral. They were not Salli's favourite songs, they were his. *He* was the one who'd been left behind. *He* was the goddamn survivor, so *he* could choose the music.

Nobody could see his tears, because heavy black Raybans concealed the action.

He swiped a hand across his cheeks, destroying any evidence of vulnerability. On the back of his hand there were two words tattooed through a blazing heart. *Salli Forever.*

And while Mick Jagger continued to yell out "Satis-faction", Bobby continued to wail his silent scream of unbearable pain.

# CHAPTER FIFTEEN

STRUGGLING TO keep it together, Kristin decided that lying on the floor and feeling sorry for herself was not going to help her situation. She was trapped, that much was obvious. She was naked, which made her even more vulnerable. And she was determined to survive this ordeal. She had to, for Cherie's sake.

She got up and took a long, deep breath. Then she went over to the small bed and frantically ripped off the one sheet. Holding it taut, she punched a hole in it with her fist, and then forced her head through the opening. Next she punched out two more holes for her arms and ripped off the bottom. Now she was wearing some kind of tent-like poncho, but at least she wasn't naked.

Next she inspected the wooden bed, dragging the sagging mattress on to the ground. The bed frame stood several inches off the floor, supported by four sturdy legs. Using all her strength she managed to tip the frame sideways. She inspected the legs closely. Yes! They screwed into the base. If she could dismantle the legs, she would have several formidable weapons to use on Mr X when he came back.

She needed a screwdriver, but where was she going to get *that*?

Easy. She still had her jewellery. A ring. Small stud earrings. A St Christopher medal that she never took off.

Unclasping the chain on her pendant, she worked with the small gold circle, slowly but surely loosening the first leg.

The feeling of triumph when it finally came off was intoxicating.

After a few minutes of rest, she armed herself with the small lethal weapon and made a pass at the window, giving it a hearty whack. The glass shattered, which really got her adrenalin going – so much so that she hardly felt the shard of glass that cut across her arm. The pain meant nothing. Determination meant everything.

Brushing the broken glass out of her way, she went to work on the boards covering the window. Using the wooden leg as a battering ram, she attacked the middle board, using every ounce of strength she could muster. For a while she thought it wasn't going to give, but after half an hour of solid slamming the board finally began to sag in the middle, causing her to strengthen her attack, even though she was dripping with perspiration and quite exhausted.

The small room was like a sweat box with very little air.

Outside she could hear the pounding of the ocean. Where was she?

And where was Mr X?

What was his devious plan? Was it murder?

Because if it was, he'd chosen the wrong victim.

L.A. Connections 4

# CHAPTER SIXTEEN

THE FUNERAL service seemed never-ending. Many people insisted on speaking, including Salli's agent, her manager, her publicist, her female and male co-stars from the television series, and finally her father, who mumbled a few almost incoherent words so intense was his grief.

Bobby Skorch said nothing.

After the ceremony there was an air of frenzy. Everyone was up and socializing. The crowds outside were enormous, and as the celebrities filed out of the chapel, screams from nearby fans filled the air. Three or four helicopters hovered overhead, photographers were balanced in trees with telephoto lenses, while the cops went crazy trying to get everyone safely into their cars and limos and out of there.

Madison stood outside with Cole, getting jostled on all

sides. "This is quite a scene," she commented, looking around in amazement.

"It sure is," Cole agreed. "And I want out."

That was easier said than done since they were caught in human gridlock as everyone vied to get their cars first.

Somebody accidentally shoved Madison in the back. She turned around to object and came face to face with Bo Deacon. He looked at her as if he knew her, but couldn't quite remember from where.

"Mr Deacon," she reminded him. "Madison Castelli – remember? We met on the plane a few days ago. You, me and Salli."

"What's that?" he said, attempting to back away, which was impossible because of the mass of people.

"On the plane, flying in from New York."

He moved backward, his wife moved forward. "I'm Mrs Deacon," Olive announced coldly. "Who did you say you are, dear?"

"Madison Castelli. Your husband and I flew in from New York together. He wanted to sit next to Salli, so I changed seats. It's such a terrible tragedy, isn't it?"

Olive shot her husband a filthy look. "You wanted to sit next to Salli, huh?" she sneered as if she'd caught him jerking off in Times Square.

"For five minutes," Bo blustered. "I had some business to discuss with her."

"What kind of business?"

"Nothing important."

"You make me *sick*."

"Be quiet, Olive," Bo said, desperately gesturing to the

valet. "Bring me my damn car at once. Don't you know who I am?"

Madison wondered what was going on with Bo and his wife. He appeared to be extremely agitated. And she was quite obviously drunk. A delightful couple.

Before she could wonder any further, Bobby emerged, surrounded by Salli's family. People fell back, making a path for him through the crowds. Salli's two little stepsisters were crying, overcome with emotion. Their mother kept on urging them to be quiet.

"They shouldn't bring kids to something like this," Cole muttered. "Look at 'em, they're all confused. Probably never been out of Idaho before."

Salli's father was openly sobbing, tears rolling down his crumpled face.

A lone photographer managed to dart through security and started snapping pictures of the family.

Two guards leaped forward and grabbed him by the shoulder, smashing his camera to the ground. "You fuckers!" the photographer shouted. "I'm only doing my job."

Madison turned away in time to see Eddie Stoner pushing his way through the mob, dragging Angela Musconni behind him. Eddie was heading directly for Bobby, a purposeful look in his eye. "You did it, didn't you?" he yelled belligerently as he drew closer. "You . . . freakin' . . . did it."

Bobby refused to acknowledge him, but everyone else turned to gape unashamedly.

"C'mon, admit it! You motherfuckin' hypocrite," Eddie screeched. "You killed my Salli."

Bobby finally focused. "You talking to me?" he snapped. "You cowardly piece of dog shit."

"Yeah, it's *you* I'm talkin' to," Eddie responded, thrusting out his jaw.

The two little girls clung to their mother, terrified by the two angry men.

"Don't do this," Salli's father begged, tears streaming down his weathered cheeks. "Please don't make a scene."

"Make a scene?" Eddie shouted bitterly. "I'm gonna bash his freakin' face in."

Angie grabbed his arm. "Let's get out of here, Eddie," she urged. "This isn't doing you any good."

Eddie was on a roll. He shrugged her off, almost causing her to lose her balance. Then he threw a wild punch, cutting Bobby above the eye with his pinkie ring, knocking off Bobby's dark glasses, which fell to the ground and shattered.

Bobby let out a roar of pain and fury and swung back. Before anyone could intervene the two of them were embroiled in a vicious fist fight.

Paparazzi sprung out from everywhere, flashing away with their cameras, elbowing each other for the best position. The helicopters overhead hovered even lower. Several security guards leaped forward, intent on separating the two men – so intent that they forgot about controlling the media.

"God! I can't stand it. This is turning into a circus," Madison gasped.

"Let's get our asses outta here," Cole responded, taking her by the arm. "We'll pick up the car later."

Half of her wanted to go, and the other half wanted to stay. There was a big story taking place right in front of her and she knew she should cover it. "No," she said. "I have to see what happens."

"Somebody's gonna get hurt, that's what's gonna happen," Cole said, still attempting to pull her away.

Two of the guards had Eddie in a lock, both his arms twisted behind his back.

Bobby took the opportunity to smash his fist into Eddie's face. There followed the sound of teeth breaking and then blood began spurting.

"Leave him alone, you crazoid freak!" Angie screamed, jumping on Bobby and pummelling him with her fists. Bobby hauled back, shaking her off and then hitting her on the jaw. She dropped like a stone.

"Jesus!" Cole groaned. "Now *I* gotta get into it." And he went for Bobby, wrestling him to the ground.

Pandemonium reigned. Women were screaming. Men shouting and swearing. Like a swarm of mosquitoes the photographers were everywhere. And the TV news crews, sensing blood, broke ranks and added to the chaos.

In his struggle to get out of the way, Bo Deacon was accidentally hit in the face by a security guard. "My nose," he yelled. "You idiot! You've broken my fucking nose."

"Serves you right for coming here," Olive muttered.

"Get me to a fucking plastic surgeon," Bo screamed. "And shut the fuck up!"

There was not enough security to control what was

going on. The entire aftermath of the funeral was turning into some kind of crazed celebrity riot.

And there was absolutely nothing anyone could do.

*

By the time Detective Tucci made it to the scene, everybody was involved. Quickly taking the situation in, he shoved his way through the crowds, grabbing Cole off Bobby, who now had a bloody nose as well as a gash over his left eye. Tucci summoned the help of a couple of cops.

Angie staggered to her feet. "I want that man arrested!" she screamed, pointing an accusing finger at Bobby. "The prick assaulted me. I want him arrested."

"Go fuck yourself, cunt!" Bobby responded.

"You *dumb* asshole!" Angie screamed. "Look what you've done to Eddie. Look at him!"

Eddie could hardly talk. He was sitting on the ground with blood gushing from his mouth, missing two front teeth.

Tucci took control of the situation. "You'd all better come to the station," he said. "We'll sort it out there."

"You bet!" Angie yelled, pointing at Bobby. "I'm suing his ass! We're pressing charges."

Meanwhile the cameras captured every exquisite, celebrity moment.

# CHAPTER SEVENTEEN

"ARE YOU JAKE?" Junia said.

"Who wants to know?" Jake asked, cradling the phone.

"You interested in hearing about Kristin?"

"Where is she?" he asked, jumping to attention.

"You got money?"

"What is this – a shakedown?"

"I know stuff about Kristin you'll want to hear. But I gotta get paid for my information, 'cause if I give it up, I'll have to scoot outta town."

"How *much* money?"

"How much you got?"

"This conversation is dumb – I don't even know who you are."

"Your girlfriend could be in danger."

"What kind of danger?"

"You read about that blonde found dead in the ocean? It could've been Kristin."

"Who *are* you?"

"If you've got ten thousand dollars, we can meet. If you don't, forget it."

"Where am *I* going to come up with ten thousand dollars?"

"Not my problem."

"You sound like a crazy person."

"Insults make me want to hang up."

"Okay, okay, I'll meet you," he said, deciding that the smart thing to do was to find out what this was about. After all, if Kristin was in trouble, he wanted to help.

"And you'll bring cash?"

"Yes," he lied impatiently. "Where do we meet?"

"There's a restaurant, Chin Chin, on Sunset Plaza. I'll be at a table outside. Be there in an hour."

"How will I know you?"

"I'm wearing an orange sweater. And don't blow it. If you want Kristin safe, you'd better bring the money."

Jake put down the phone, his mind in turmoil. What was going on here? And what could *he* do?

First of all, he'd hardly brought any money to L.A. with him – six or seven hundred dollars at the most. His bank was in Arizona, and there was no way he could make a withdrawal that size today. And who was the mystery person on the phone? It certainly wasn't the woman who'd called Kristin's answering machine, this woman sounded much younger.

Realizing he needed help, he called his brother at the

TV station. Jimmy wasn't there, so he tried him at home and got Bunny.

"Jakie, we miss you," Bunny cooed. "When are you coming to dinner again?" She'd obviously forgotten the petulant fit she'd thrown the last time he was there.

"Tell Jimmy to call me as soon as possible," he said, hanging up and pacing furiously around the room. What next? he wondered. Suddenly he thought of Madison. She was an intelligent woman and a journalist. She was also the only friend he had in L.A. Hoping that she'd have some ideas, he called her.

"Hi, Jake," Madison said breathlessly. "I just walked in. You're not going to *believe* what happened at Salli's funeral. Put on your TV, I'm sure it'll be all over the four o'clock news."

"There's something urgent I have to discuss with you," he said. "Can I come by?"

"Of course."

"See you in a minute," he said, grabbing his leather jacket and racing downstairs, stopping at the desk to tell them where he'd be. Then he jumped in his truck and drove over.

Madison greeted him at the door. "You sounded like it's something important."

"It is," he said grimly.

"Come in and tell me everything. You remember Cole, don't you?"

"Yeah. Hi, Cole," he said. "Uh . . . Madison, this is kind of private. Can we talk somewhere quiet?"

"Hey, man, you caught me on my way out," Cole said.

"I got appointments backed up, an' they're all gettin' pissed at me, 'cause since *this* lady hit town I never get anythin' done. It's more of a kick hangin' with her."

"Didn't mean to be rude," Jake said.

"No sweat," Cole said, kissing Madison on the cheek. "She'll tell you all about our insane funeral experience. It's a story, man."

"Can I get you anything to drink?" Madison asked as soon as Cole left. "Seven-Up? Evian? Pellegrino? We've got it all."

He shook his head and sat down. Madison looked great as usual, and best of all, she seemed to be free of complications. Why couldn't he have met *her* first?

"Remember I told you about a woman I was seeing?" he began.

"Kristin, wasn't that her name?"

"Yeah, well . . . I did what you suggested and tried calling her. She wasn't there, and according to her maid she didn't come home last night. Which I guess, considering the business she's in, is not unusual. However, she *still* hasn't gotten home, and a short while ago I got a weird call from some girl who informs me Kristin's in danger, and if I meet her and hand over ten thousand bucks, she'll fill me in."

"You're kidding?"

He shrugged. "No, although I thought *she* was. I mean, I know L.A.'s got a crazy reputation, but this has to be a bad joke, right?"

"Let me get this straight," Madison said, frowning. "Kristin didn't come home last night. You haven't spoken to her since you walked out. Now you've got this person calling, demanding money."

"That's about it. The woman on the phone mumbled something about a dead blonde in the ocean."

"Oh, God!"

"What?"

"Did you happen to watch Natalie on the news today?"

"No."

"She had a story on the blonde. Apparently she was a call-girl who worked for a madam called Darlene. Does that name mean anything to you?"

"Darlene? No."

"Wait a minute," Madison said, thinking fast. "Do you have Kristin's number?"

"Yeah."

"Give it to me, I've got an idea."

"Hey, listen, we don't have time. I told my mystery caller I'd meet her at Chin Chin in an hour, which," he said, glancing at his watch, "is now in about half an hour."

"Let me try this first," Madison said, punching out the number. Chiew answered the phone. "I'm looking for Kristin," Madison said.

"Madam not here," Chiew said.

"Is she at Darlene's?"

"No," Chiew said. "Don't know where."

"Damn!" Madison said. "I owe her money. What's Darlene's number? I'm in my car and don't have it with me."

Chiew gave her the number.

Madison hung up. "I want you to take a look at something," she said to Jake.

"I gotta get going," he said impatiently.

Madison pushed the tape of Natalie's news-cast into the VCR and began playing it for him. "I think Darlene could be your girlfriend's madam, too," she said. "And I have a feeling that whoever you're supposed to meet is right. Kristin might be in trouble."

"Shit!"

Madison jumped up. "C'mon, Jake. I'll go with you. Between us, we're going to find out *exactly* what's going on."

L.A.
Connections
4

# CHAPTER EIGHTEEN

LATER IN THE DAY, when Max showed definite signs of improvement, Diana had him moved out of intensive care and into a private suite. He was conscious and well aware of the fact that she was sitting beside him holding his hand.

"How are you feeling?" she asked anxiously.

"Like I had a battle with a rhinoceros," he groaned. "What happened to me?"

"You got shot."

"Shot?" he said, managing a laugh. "Who did it – a dissatisfied actress?"

"The police would like you to try and identify some mugshots when you're ready."

He sighed. "Oh, yeah, yeah, I *really* feel like doin' that. Y'know, identify some gang member who's gonna come back and cream my ass. I think not." He struggled to sit up, wincing with pain. "Hey, how come *you're* here?"

"I came as soon as I heard. I stayed with you all night."

"That's nice of you."

"It's more than nice, Max. I think you must know how I—"

Before she could finish her sentence, the door opened and Freddie strode in. "Well," Freddie said, "what kind of a situation did you get yourself into this time?"

"I've done worse, haven't I?" Max said, grinning weakly.

Freddie gave a dry laugh. "A lot worse. The good thing is that you're okay. Has Diana been looking after you?"

"She's the best," Max said. "Thanks for the loan."

"With my compliments," Freddie said, his attitude infuriating Diana.

An attractive black nurse entered the room. "Everything all right, Mr Steele?" she asked.

"Perfect."

"Ring if you need me."

"Not bad," Max said, as the pretty nurse retreated.

"Congratulations," Freddie said. "Diana told me you're engaged. Who's the unlucky lady?"

Max struggled to figure out what Freddie was talking about, then it started to come back to him. Kristin. Hadn't he told her to come to his house? Oh man, was she going to laugh when she heard *this* one. Maybe an engagement wasn't such a good idea after all, although it might stop Diana, who'd been about to say something intimate when Freddie arrived. Yes, he'd be wise to keep the story going.

"I'm engaged to a beautiful girl called Kristin," he said. "You haven't met her, but you will."

"Where is she?" Freddie said, turning to Diana with a questioning expression.

"I tried phoning her," Diana explained. "The phone was answered by someone called Darlene who was extremely rude."

Max knew exactly what must have happened, Diana had connected with Kristin's madam. He choked back a laugh. Thank God she hadn't put it together. "Oh, yeah," he mumbled. "Darlene's her cousin. Sometimes she stays there."

"Give me Kristin's number and I'll phone her personally," Freddie said. "Can't wait to see the woman who's hooked *you*."

"Don't want to worry her," Max said.

"She must be worried anyway," Freddie said. "Not hearing from you."

"To tell you the truth," Max lied, "she was so happy we got engaged that she went to visit her family in San Diego. I guess that's why you couldn't reach her, Diana. She'll be back in a few days, so let's not worry her for now."

"If that's the way you want it," Freddie said.

"That's the way . . ." Max said, feeling sleep creeping up on him.

"Is there anything I can do?" Freddie asked.

"Yeah," Max said, grimacing. "Tell me all is forgiven. I was a schmuck."

"I think we've both realized we're a team," Freddie said

gravely. "I'm taking the rest of the day off. If you need anything, Ria can reach me."

"Where are you going?" Diana asked.

"I need to be alone for a while," Freddie said. "I'm driving to the beach house."

"What time will you be home?"

"Maybe I'll stay overnight," he said abruptly. "I'll call you later."

"Whyn't you take Diana with you?" Max mumbled. "I'm sure there's a bunch of gorgeous nurses on call, an' your wife's been here all night, she needs a break."

"No," Diana said stubbornly. "I want to stay."

"You look tired, Diana," Freddie said. "Max is well taken care of. I'll drop you home."

Diana realized this was neither the time nor the place to take a stand. First she'd better deal with the fiancée situation. Then, when Max was out of the hospital, they'd talk about their future together. "Very well," she said, deeply disappointed. "I'll come back later if you like, Max."

"Don't like," he slurred, almost out. "You've been great, but, please, I gotta sleep."

"Then I'll be here first thing in the morning."

"Whatever."

"Can I bring you anything?"

"Yeah, a stack of *Playboys* to cheer me up." Her mouth slid into a tight, disapproving line. "Only kidding," he said. "What's the problem? You don't approve of *Playboy*?"

"The name says it all," Diana said primly. "You're not a boy and you don't play."

"C'*mon*," Max said. "Lighten up." He gave them both

a weak wave, waited until they were out of the room, then rang for the nurse and requested a phone.

"You're not allowed any calls, Mr Steele," the nurse said. "Don't forget, you're only just out of intensive care. Rest and sleep, that's all you're supposed to do."

"Anybody ever told you you've got a great—" He yawned and settled back on the pillow. "Nah – forget it."

"A great what, Mr Steele?"

"I'm changing my ways," he mumbled, and immediately fell asleep.

# CHAPTER NINETEEN

LEE ECCLES stopped Tucci as soon as he entered the station. "What in hell's going on?" he asked, falling into step beside him.

"Big brawl at the funeral," Tucci said, hitching up his pants. "I've got 'em all coming in. Everyone wants to press charges."

"Who're you talkin' about?"

"Bobby Skorch, Eddie Stoner – those are ~~l~~ questions that matter. If we mov~~e~~ fast ~~we~~ ~~S~~obby."

~~strippers?~~"

at 'em bef~~ore~~ the~~ir~~ ~~B~~obby. He checked 'em into a hotel,
~~upla~~ times – which gives him the oppor-
~~the~~ alibi they're less than zero."

"The more I see him, the more I think he could've done it," Tucci said. "I got a blood sample, one from Eddie, too."

"How'd you manage that?"

"They're both bleeding. I did a little mopping up with my handkerchief and jacket: Bobby's the handkerchief, Eddie's the jacket. Faye'll kill me when she sees I've ruined her favourite jacket."

"Oh yeah, Faye," Lee said with a knowing smirk. "Mustn't piss *her* off."

Tucci shot him a look. He didn't want to hear Faye's name coming out of Lee's mouth. If there wasn't so much going on he would've gotten into exactly what Lee meant every time he mentioned his wife.

As it was, there was no time for anything. Eddie and Angie came rolling into the station, Angie still screaming about assault charges. They were followed closely by Bobby, who wanted Eddie arrested. And then came Bo Deacon with his wife.

Trailing closely behind them were hordes of media, who were forced to stay outside, jockeying for position, waiting for when the principals emerged.

Captain Marsh poked his head out of his office. "What It was on here?" he demanded.

in the chose to arrive. moment that Darlene and her lawyer

"Why'd you do it, Bobby?"
Slouched on a chair in the in

458

to get Eddie Stoner's ass slung in jail, upset from the funeral, depressed and suicidal about Salli, Bobby Skorch stared blankly at the tall, stoop-shouldered detective with the weather-beaten face and exceptionally large hands.

"What?" he said, his eyes blank and red-rimmed, with no shades to hide his pain or his worsening black eye from the world.

"Why'd you kill her?" Lee Eccles demanded, leaning over the table and eyeballing Bobby with a ferocious glare.

Bobby's head snapped back. "Who the fuck d'you think you're *talkin'* to?" he said in a low, angry voice. "What the fuck is *this* shit?"

"Your two little scum-buckets from Vegas blew your alibi out the window," Lee said, scrambling for a used toothpick in his jacket pocket.

"Hey," Bobby said, reality hitting home through his conflicted haze of self-hatred and drug-induced euphoria, "get me my fucking lawyer."

"Your fucking lawyer ain't here," Lee said, not trying to hide his loathing for the famous person sitting before him. Loathing him because he had everything Lee didn't – including a sex-symbol wife who any red-blooded American

*Dead wife,*

male would... harshly. "I came here to ... Bobby. Thought you might wanna

... you can't accuse me of shit."

... fuck yourself in the ass. You wanna know who killed

Salli? It was Eddie Stoner, an' you got him here now, so whyn't you do somethin' about it?"

"Where *did* you go Saturday night when you got back. Didja go to your house an' catch Salli with another guy? Was that what happened?"

"Jesus!" Bobby screamed. "Don't you understand English? *Eddie Stoner murdered my wife*, and I want him in jail. Got it, moron?"

\*

Oblivious to the scene going on in the next room, Tucci was attempting to calm Angela Musconni. Eddie Stoner was slumped in a chair beside her, clutching a blood-soaked wad of Kleenex to his mouth. It was almost as if he'd lost his balls along with his two front teeth.

Angie, however, more than made up for his silence. She was acting like a wild-cat, jumping up and down, pummelling the air with her small fists to make her point. "You gotta arrest the prick," she yelled. "Eddie said Bobby did it, an' Eddie knows what he's talkin' about. An' if you *can't* arrest him for the murder, you can sure as crap arrest him me ersonal assault. He knocked Eddie's *teeth* out and hit charges.

"If we ar on the ground *unconscious*! I'm pressin' "it won't look go on the ground dozens of witnesses who said it!" wife's funeral. He wa lawyer will bail him immediately,

said candidly,

**460**

drawn-out court battle with all the attendant publicity. Are you sure you want that?"

"No!" Eddie managed to say, spitting out more blood.

"Yes!" Angie insisted.

Tucci regarded the two of them, trying to decide who had the power in the relationship. Right now it was probably Angie – she was certainly the most vocal. But if she pressed charges against Bobby at this particular moment, it would complicate things. When the time came, they'd nail Bobby Skorch, but it would be for murder, not this petty stuff.

"Can I be frank with you both?" Tucci said. "Can I trust you?"

"Huh?" Angie said, suspicion narrowing her eyes.

"Mr Skorch is indeed a suspect in the murder of Salli T. Turner, so an arrest at this time for assault would do nothing but hamper our investigation."

"Why?" Angie demanded.

"Because if we arrest him on a minor charge, it would not help us." He watched her carefully; she seemed to be listening, which was a good thing. "This is what I'd like you to do," he said.

"What?"

"I'd like you to go home, think about it, and if you still wish to press charges you can do so tomorrow. Is that fair?"

Eddie nodded vigorously. Angie was still not convinced.

"Miss Musconni," Tucci said in his most persuasive voice, "do the smart thing. I promise, you won't regret it."

\*

"Get me to a plastic surgeon," Bo Deacon whimpered as Olive drove their Rolls erratically down Wilshire Boulevard.

"I'm taking you to the Emergency Room," Olive said, not at all upset at her famous husband's predicament.

"Don't wanna go to Emergency," he groaned. "I want a plastic surgeon."

"Shame your little sweetie is dead," Olive said, weaving erratically from one lane to the other. "I'm sure she was an expert when it comes to plastic surgeons. Let's see, she had silicone tits, pumped-up lips, false cheekbones, a new chin, probably a brand new pussy after all the action the old one got."

"Jesus, you're a bitch," Bo said, wishing he was anywhere else. "She was twenty-two years old, for God's sake. And she's dead."

"Good," Olive said.

"Good?" Bo repeated, not quite able to believe she'd said such a thing.

"Did you fuck her?" Olive enquired, tossing back her red hair.

"*What*!?"

"*Did* you?"

"You're crazy," he said, disgusted.

"Did you do her on the plane, Bo Bo, *did* you?"

"Jesus, Olive, I can't even listen to you talk anymore."

"You went to her house, I know you did."

"Are you *insane*?"

"Oh, yes. Saturday. You were there, sniffing around while her husband was away."

"You've lost it."

**462**

"Have I?"

"For God's sake, Olive, I'm in pain."

"I don't care," she slurred, nearly smashing his precious Rolls into the back of a truck.

"You're drunk," he said, stating the obvious. "Stop the car and let me drive."

"I'm drunk," she sing-songed. "And you've been fucking around on me. Who's the baddest, Bo Bo?"

"Come on, Olive, not now."

"When?" she demanded, taking her eyes off the road and giving him a long, pained look. "When's *my* time?"

"My nose is broken!" he screamed. "I'm warning you, Olive, don't get into this now!"

"I hate you!" she bellowed, her face contorted with drunken fury as she hit the gas even harder. "Hate you! Hate you! HATE YOU!"

"For God's sake!"

And before he could do anything to stop her, she swung the wheel of the powerful car into the oncoming traffic, and smashed head-on into a gold Mercedes.

# CHAPTER TWENTY

# CHAPTER TWENTY

IT HAD TAKEN her hours, but Kristin had finally managed to remove the middle board in the window. Unfortunately the space was only four inches high and two feet across, not big enough for her to squeeze through, but at least she could get some idea of where she was. As far as she could tell she was in some kind of guard house halfway down a cliff. The undergrowth on the cliff was unkempt and wild, which made her think that nobody ever came to this building. Several hundred feet below her was the ocean, and there seemed to be no other properties in sight.

She'd tried desperately to pry the rest of the window boards loose, but after a while she'd given up. It was impossible. Her hands were cut and bleeding, and there was a gash on her arm. She was lucky to have gotten the middle board out of there without breaking anything.

Being able to look out and get some idea of where she was struck her as a major triumph.

What she couldn't figure out was *why* she'd allowed herself to be led down a dangerous cliff side blindfolded. She must have been crazy. One false step and she could've fallen hundreds of feet to her death.

*Little lamb goes quietly to the slaughter.*

What kind of a monster was Mr X anyway? she asked herself. Did he get a sexual kick out of this? Whatever. Clearly his motives were evil. *He* was evil.

The good thing was that she no longer felt like a victim. She had a plan and a weapon, and even though she was hungry and thirsty, she was determined to remain strong.

Now that she had some light, she could explore the room properly. Not that there was much to explore: bare floorboards, the bed, one sheet that she was now wearing, and nothing else.

She'd thought long and hard about what she would do if and when Mr X returned, and she'd finally decided her only move was to take him by surprise, try to knock him out, and escape. If she could do that and make it to the highway, she'd be able to summon help.

The thought of Cherie depending on her gave her strength.

Her inner voice had stopped screaming vile things in her head. Now it urged her to be strong.

*Don't be frightened. You can do it. You're a survivor.*

Yes. She was. And she *would* survive.

Of that she was sure.

L.A.
Connections
4

# CHAPTER TWENTY-ONE

"THAT'S HER," Madison said, striding confidently towards the open-air restaurant.

"How do you know?" Jake said, squinting at the fair-haired girl sitting at a table by herself leafing through a copy of *Movieline*.

"One, she's alone. Two, she's wearing an orange sweater. Pretty easy to be smart under these circumstances. Did you get her name?"

"Nope."

"Well, okay, let's go over."

Jake put his hand on her arm, stopping her. "She's expecting me to be by myself. She's also expecting ten grand, which I don't have."

"We'll suss the situation out," Madison said. "Let *me* do the talking."

He wasn't sure if he liked Madison's new take-charge attitude. "You can be incredibly bossy," he remarked.

"You wanted help, didn't you?" she fired back. "Come on, let's do it."

Together they approached the girl in the orange sweater. She was busy reading an article on Vince Vaughn, and did not look up until Madison said, "Hi."

"Yes?" Junia said, her eyes darting this way and that.

"Meet Jake Sica," Madison said. "I'm his sister."

"Sister?"

"We're twins. We do everything together."

Junia wrinkled her forehead. What kind of a kinky scene was *this*? "Where's my money?" she said, putting down the magazine.

"Safe," Madison said matter of factly. "But of course, as I'm sure you're aware, we can't hand it over without knowing what we're paying for."

"I *told* him to bring the money," Junia said stubbornly, slamming her delicate fist on the table.

"He did," Madison said calmly, pulling out a chair and sitting down, gesturing for Jake to do the same. "Here's the deal. Why settle for ten grand when you can make a lot more?"

"How?" Junia asked suspiciously.

"Did you ever hear of Watergate?"

"What's that, a bridge?"

"No. Watergate was an event in history. People with the right information made plenty of money out of Watergate."

"I don't get it," Junia said, intrigued in spite of herself, and starting to feel quite important.

"Do you work for Darlene?" Madison asked, thinking that this waif of a girl was the least likely looking call-girl she'd ever seen.

"Work for her?" Junia snorted as if it was the most ridiculous thing she'd ever heard. "No way! 'S matter of fact, I live with her." As soon as she'd said it, she regretted her words. She wasn't supposed to tell them anything about *her*. No way. Her plan was to get the money and take off.

"You mean you're her girlfriend?"

"'S right," Junia said, nodding vigorously.

"Platonic or otherwise?"

"What d'*you* think?" Junia said with a sly smile.

"Where's Kristin?" Jake asked, getting impatient.

Junia ignored him, more interested in what the woman had to say. "What do you mean I can make more money?" she questioned.

"I'm sure you have a very interesting story to tell," Madison said. "And if you're prepared to reveal details about Darlene and exactly how she runs her business, well, I think we could be talking about a *lot* of money."

Junia's eyes popped. "A lotta money, huh?"

"Right," Madison continued, silencing Jake with a warning look. "I work for *Manhattan Style* magazine. If you agree to give us an exclusive, I'm sure I can get my editor to pay you twenty thousand dollars."

"Wow!" Junia exclaimed reverently. "Twenty thousand bucks!"

"Here's my card," Madison said, fishing in her purse.

Junia took the engraved card and studied it. "How do I know this isn't a fake?"

"Why would I go to that kind of trouble?" Madison replied. "You see, we've been planning on writing an exposé on the call-girl industry for quite some time. My brother's a photographer, that's his involvement. He was about to take some photos of Kristin for the magazine."

"Was she co-operating with you?" Junia asked.

"She certainly was," Jake said, getting Madison's drift and joining in. "Which is why it's so disturbing that she's vanished."

"I'm glad you're smart enough to get out now," Madison said, speaking fast. "We can put you in a hotel for your own protection. I'll have a contract from the magazine Fed-exed here immediately. Only thing is, you *have* to tell us how to find Kristin."

"Dunno where she is," Junia said. "But I *do* know that Mr X got her home number, and *he's* the client who had a date with Hildie. And—" She stopped, realizing she might be saying too much. "There's more about him, but I need t'see money first."

"Who's Mr X?" Jake asked with a distinct note of urgency.

Junia shrugged. "Nobody knows, not even Darlene. He calls every so often, whenever he wants a girl."

"The phone company," Jake said. "If he called Kristin, maybe they'll have a record of his number."

"I don't think it works that way," Madison said.

"We can give it a shot. It's better than doing nothing."

Madison turned to Junia. "Listen," she said, "you shouldn't go home. We'll check you into a hotel, all expenses paid."

"Why *can't* I go home?" Junia whined. "Darlene doesn't know I'm meeting you."

"Darlene's in trouble," Madison said. "She's all over the TV. You'll be better off in hiding until we get your story. And remember, it's exclusive, or no big check."

"Well, okay," Junia said reluctantly. "But I'd better get paid tomorrow, otherwise the deal's off."

"Done," Madison said.

There was nothing that excited her more than a hot story. And she could tell this was going to be a good one.

# CHAPTER TWENTY-TWO

"I'VE BEEN kept waiting for forty-five minutes," Darlene said, although Linden had warned her it was not smart to complain. "Forty-five minutes," she repeated icily, not particularly caring whether it was smart or not.

"Sorry, ma'am," Tucci said politely, sitting down across from the well-groomed, extremely attractive woman and her Beverly Hills lawyer. "Emergency situation arose."

"I was forced to rush my lunch to be here on time," Darlene said, pushing her point home.

Christ! *She* was complaining. All *he'd* had to eat all day was three lousy doughnuts, and the way things were going he'd be working straight through dinner. Hopefully Faye would save him something. Lately he'd been daydreaming about her pot roast. The good thing was that over the last few days he must have lost at least ten pounds. *Goodbye diet. Hello food.*

"We understand you have some questions you'd like to ask Ms La Porte," Linden said. "Can we kindly proceed."

"Certainly," Tucci said. It had taken him a while, but he'd finally convinced Angela Musconni not to press charges against Bobby Skorch. She'd left with Eddie, reluctantly.

Meanwhile, Lee had managed to upset Bobby, who'd stalked out of the station just as his lawyer arrived. Marty Steiner was not a happy camper, furious that they'd had Bobby to themselves for an hour. Marty would be even more furious if he knew that even now the lab was running blood sample tests which could possibly connect his client to Salli's murder.

Tucci was in no mood to conduct an interview with some Hollywood madam, who probably had more connections than a multi-purpose vacuum. He knew the way these things worked. These women always had clients in high places who eventually put on the pressure to get the charges dropped. Not that they had anything to charge Darlene La Porte with. She was a known madam, but right now they had no concrete proof. Her girls wouldn't talk, nor would her rich and famous clients. To nail Darlene they'd have to put some kind of entrapment plan in the works. And now was not the time.

"We appreciate you coming in," Tucci said.

"Appreciate away," Darlene said, shooting him a haughty look. "The sooner I'm out of here, the better."

"Yes, ma'am."

"And *don't* call me ma'am."

\*

Madison was on a roll. In her mind she visualized the story she was going to write about L.A. and it had her adrenaline pumping. For the time being she forgot about Freddie Leon, because right now she was into investigating the call-girl business. It had all the ingredients for a killer story. Power. Obsession. Murder. Revenge. Her kind of deal.

And Junia, Darlene La Porte's almost underage lesbian lover, was set to spill everything.

They'd stashed Junia in a room in Jake's hotel, made sure she had cable and room service, then they'd gone to Jake's room where Madison sat on his bed and called Victor.

"Have I got a story for you!" she bragged.

"Freddie Leon was *that* interesting?" Victor boomed in his annoyingly loud voice.

"Not Freddie," she said excitedly. "Bigger and better. Only you've got to come up with a check for twenty grand pronto."

"Excuse me?"

"I have a songbird from the inside of an exclusive call-girl operation. And she's ready to Whitney Houston it."

"You know, sometimes I don't understand a word you say."

"That's okay," she said breezily. "Make the check out to cash and Fed-ex it to me at once. We'll have a story that'll blow the magazine off the stands."

"Now wait a minute—"

"No waiting, Victor. And I want to work with a great photographer who just *might* be available." She winked at Jake, who couldn't believe this was the same Madison he'd gotten used to. "He's expensive, but you should definitely consider signing him. His name's Jake Sica. I'll let you know if we can get him."

"Madison—"

"Bye, Victor." She hung up and turned to Jake. "Why work for some popular crap mag when I can get you a gig on *Manhattan Style*?"

"What happened to you?" he said, shaking his head at her metamorphosis. "You're all fired up."

She beamed. "I feel good. In fact, I feel *great*. I'm back in action. This story's going to be *sensational*. Let's go tell Junia the good news."

"I need to find Kristin," he said. "That's the only important thing to me."

For a moment she felt a shiver of disappointment. Just when she'd thought she and Jake were a great team . . .

"Sorry," she said quickly. "You're right, and I have an idea."

"What?"

"We should go by her apartment, see what we can find."

"The maid'll never let us in."

"Jake," she bragged, "doncha know? You're working with *me* now, and when I'm into it, *I* can do anything."

L.A.
Connections
4

# CHAPTER TWENTY-THREE

PROPPED UP in bed, watching the unbelievable goings-on at Salli T. Turner's funeral on the TV news, Max Steele was completely comfortable and out of pain thanks to the miracle of modern drugs. The nurses were all fans. Well, how often was it that they got their hands on a genuine eligible Bel Air bachelor? They kept on popping into his room, two at a time, to take a peek at him and ask a question or two, such as did he know Matt Damon? And was Ann Heche really gay or was she just going with Ellen for the publicity? Normal questions the general public liked to ask.

Max got off on being the centre of attention. He had his eye on the pretty black nurse – she had a Halle Berry quality about her, and he liked her personality, not to mention her perky tits.

Yes, all in all, it wasn't *that* bad getting shot. And now

that Freddie wasn't mad at him anymore, which was a good thing, as soon as he recovered and recuperated at, say, the Four Seasons in Maui, it would be back to business as usual.

He kept on drifting in and out of sleep, which was quite pleasant. *Gotta call Kristin*, he thought. *She must've wondered what happened to me. Gotta call her . . .*

Boom. His eyes closed. He was asleep again, which is how Inga Cruelle and Howie Powers found him when they burst into his room.

"Jesus, man," Howie exclaimed, waking him up. "You frightened the shit outta us."

Us? Did that mean the delectable Inga and his erstwhile friend – the brain-dead playboy – were an "us"?

"How'd you find out?" he mumbled.

"Your maid told me when I dropped by your house," Howie said, picking at a bunch of grapes on the bedstand. "What a bummer!"

"When was that?"

"'Bout an hour ago, soon as we got back from Vegas."

"Didja win?"

Howie beamed, and put his arm around Inga's waist, pulling the exquisite Swedish supermodel close. "I won the prize of all time. Inga did me the honour of becoming my wife."

*"Whaaat?"* Max said, trying to sit up. Sharp stabs of pain prevented him from doing so. "You got *married*?"

Inga gave a supermodel sneer, the one she'd perfected on runways all over the world. "That is right, Max, dear. Howard and I are joined in matrimony."

Max could not believe what he was hearing. Howie

Powers and Inga Cruelle married? Impossible. He, Max Steele, hadn't even fucked her, and she'd married a major jerk like Howie. What was going on in the world? This was insanity.

"Show him the ring, honey," Howie urged.

Inga waved her hand under his nose. On her engagement finger was an enormous diamond, at least ten carats.

"Congratulations," Max managed, the words almost sticking in his throat. "What happened to your fiancé, Inga? The Swedish guy you told me you've been with since high school?"

She shrugged. "Howie is very sweet," she said. "And persuasive. He came to see me last night at midnight. So touching."

"With the ring?"

"Naturally."

"Yup," Howie said happily. "I got to thinkin', I've been a bachelor long enough. We flew to Vegas this morning, did it, and the first person we came to tell was you, 'cause you're my best friend, buddy."

*Yeah, sure*, Max thought. *You came to show me your prize. Because for once in your life, you rich little fucker, you got a girl before me. Well, good luck, 'cause this one's gonna take you for a lot more than a diamond ring. And you're such a schmuck, I bet you never had her sign a pre-nup.*

"I couldn't be happier for you," Max said, full of insincerity.

"Howard," Inga said, glancing at her Patek Philippe diamond watch – a wedding present Howie had presented to her on the flight home – "I have to go."

"Gotta get my bride to the airport," Howie said. "She's off to Milan for the collections."

"*You're* not going?"

"Havta take care of some business first. I'll join her in a coupla days."

As if Howie, the playboy jerk, had any business to take care of. All Howie did was watch his trust funds grow, that was about it.

"Well . . ." Max said. "Thanks for dropping by."

"Your turn next," Howie said, winking.

*Ha!* Max thought. *Wait until he sees Kristin. She makes Inga look like a skinny version of truly gorgeous. No contest.*

"I'll see you, guys," he said.

Inga blew him a kiss. Nice of her. Howie winked again and mouthed, "Somethin', huh?"

And then they were gone.

Max waited a minute and summoned Halle Berry. Life wasn't all that bad.

L.A.
Connections
4

# CHAPTER TWENTY-FOUR

DETECTIVE TUCCI was sitting at his desk when he got the call that Bo Deacon had been killed in a horrendous car accident on Wilshire. His wife, Olive, who had been driving at the time, had been rushed to Cedars with multiple cuts and bruises, but nothing life threatening.

She was conscious, hysterical and insisting on seeing one of the detectives in charge of the Salli T. Turner murder investigation.

Since Lee had gone off to re-interview several of Salli's neighbours, Tucci guessed he was it. He sighed. What a day this was turning out to be. Bo Deacon killed in a car wreck. Talk about bad karma. You leave a funeral and run right into your own death.

Fate. The twists and turns of life. Never predictable.

Tucci left the station and drove to the hospital,

calling Faye from the car. "Do you miss me?" he asked wistfully.

"Yes, I miss you," she answered. "When will you be home?"

"Not soon enough."

"How was the funeral?"

"Hectic. Did you see the news?"

"I'll turn it on."

"Faye?"

"Yes."

"I don't want to do this diet thing anymore."

"Why?"

"Life's too short." A beat. "Are we too old to have a baby instead?"

She laughed softly. "What's a baby got to do with dieting?"

"Thought we could get fat together."

"Yes."

"Yes?"

"Yes."

"I love you. Can I have pot roast for dinner?"

"You can have anything you want."

By the time he reached the hospital he had a big smile on his face. Sometimes it was nice to goof off, have nonsensical conversations, fall in love with his wife all over again.

There was a uniformed cop stationed outside Olive Deacon's room. "What's going on?" Tucci asked.

The cop spoke out of the side of his mouth like he didn't want anyone to hear. "She's hysterical, Detective, and drunk."

"So?"

"So she's confessing to Salli Turner's murder."

\*

"Hi," said Madison, standing at Kristin's front door. "I spoke with Kristin and she asked me to tell you that she'll be home shortly."

Chiew stared at her blankly, guarding the entrance to her boss's apartment with her sturdy body.

"She also asked me to wait for her here, but if you're not comfortable with me coming inside . . ." Madison shrugged, as if it didn't matter one way or the other.

Chiew stared at her for a few more seconds, then decided that she looked perfectly honest, so surely access to Kristin's apartment was in order? Especially as Chiew needed to take off early to visit her boyfriend in prison.

As soon as the maid left, Madison called Jake in the car and he came right up from the underground garage. The first thing they did was play back Kristin's answering machine. Right away they hit pay dirt, the second recorded message was from Mr X requesting that Kristin meet him at the end of Santa Monica pier on Sunday night.

"Let's go," Jake said.

"Where?" Madison said. "If she *did* meet him, it's highly unlikely they're still there."

"Maybe somebody saw them together."

"Then we need a picture of her. Did you take any?"

"No, but there's one of her with her sister in a frame in the living room."

"Get it," Madison said, still in her bossy mode, but now

just as anxious as Jake to find out what had happened to Kristin. She kept on hoping they wouldn't turn on the TV and hear about another body washed up on the beach.

While he was getting the photo, she took a quick look around. Nothing unusual. No clues. No jotted down notes that might tell them more.

Jake brought her the photo. Kristin was indeed a dazzler – Madison had gotten a brief glimpse of her when she'd stopped by Jimmy's house to meet Jake for their date, but she'd honestly not appreciated how gorgeous the girl was. Fresh and natural with cascades of golden hair and a glowing smile. Nobody in their wildest dreams would tag her as a call-girl.

"Whadda we do now?" Jake asked.

"Call Darlene," Madison said. "Let's see what it'll take to get her to co-operate."

L.A.
Connections
4

# CHAPTER TWENTY-FIVE

*HE'S NOT coming back and there is no way I can escape from this room where I'm being held prisoner.*

The words ran through Kristin's head as she lay on the mattress in the small space, which was now like an oven. She was trying to reserve her strength.

*I'm tired, hungry, thirsty, hot, dispirited, exhausted. And yet, I'm still alive. And so is Cherie. For her sake I have to get out.*

*But if he doesn't come back . . .*

*If he's left me to rot . . .*

How long could a person last without food or water? Was it days, weeks, months? How long?

She wanted to scream and cry out. Yell for help.

But no. She couldn't do that. Had to stay strong for when HE came.

Mr X.

And he *would* come.

She knew he would.

L.A.
Connections
4

# CHAPTER TWENTY-SIX

"BYE, HONEY DOLL."

"Goodbye, Howard."

"Take good care of the ring."

"Of course."

"Give me two days an' I'll be there all ready to fuck your brains out."

"Such a romantic," Inga said with a superior smile, thinking that the only one getting fucked in this relationship was Howie. She'd put her true fiancé on hold while she collected as much jewellery as possible in as short a time as possible. Then she'd have the marriage annulled. Howie was an obvious playboy, she was merely getting revenge for all the women he'd used and abused.

Howie made an attempt to kiss his new wife on the lips. She not so gently shoved him away. "Please, Howard, not in public," she scolded. "People are always watching me."

He lifted up her hand where the ten-carat-diamond ring sparkled. Ten carats of cubic zirconia. When they'd been married a year and she presented him with a child, he'd buy her the real thing. People thought he was Howie Powers, *schmucko* playboy. They were wrong. There was much more to Howie than that.

He left the airport and drove back to town. The traffic was deadly, but Howie didn't care, he had the rest of the day all planned out.

\*

Freddie Leon headed for Malibu, cursing the heavy traffic. He'd dropped Diana home first. There was something going on with her; she wasn't acting like herself. And what was her sudden attachment to Max?

Maybe he should consider giving her more attention. He always put business first and she knew it. And when he wanted to relax . . . well, it wasn't Diana he turned to. No. There was somebody else.

And today he desperately needed to relax.

\*

Olive Deacon clutched Detective Tucci's hand. "I killed him!" she wailed. "He's dead because of me!"

Her alcohol-drenched breath caused him to take a step back. "Who?" he asked.

"My husband, that's who!" she sobbed.

"Mrs Deacon, I'm going to read you your rights. Anything you say may be used in evidence against you. You have the right to a lawyer. If . . ."

As he droned on she disintegrated before his very eyes. Her face crumpled, mascara coursed down her cheeks, lipstick stained her teeth.

"Mrs Deacon," he said quietly, feeling sorry for her, "do you want to contact your lawyer before we talk?"

"No lawyer," she said between sobs. "It's my fault Bo's dead. I've been punished, and I have to tell you everything."

"You wish to make a formal statement?"

"Yes, I do."

"Very well."

And before he could get his pen out, she began talking.

# CHAPTER TWENTY-SEVEN

THE MOMENT she heard the click of the lock, Kristin was ready. She raced to the door, positioning herself behind it, so that when he opened it there would be an element of surprise. Her heart was pounding, but she knew that if she didn't seize the opportunity all would be lost.

She was filled with anger as she crouched in position. Anger would make her strong. Anger would help her gain her freedom.

Mr X pushed open the door.

She braced herself, holding the bed leg poised above her head, ready to smash him with it, ready to run.

Light flooded the dusty little room. He stepped inside.

For a moment she was paralysed, unable to move or think. And then, as if in slow motion, she sprang forward, side-swiping the figure in black with all her might, hitting him as hard as she could with the wooden bed leg.

To her amazement he didn't fall. In movies when you saw someone get hit they always fell. Instead he staggered, letting out a furious cry of surprise.

Before he had a chance to react further, she bashed him again.

This time he almost went down. His baseball cap fell to the ground, and his sunglasses hit the floor and cracked. Seizing her opportunity, she ran past him, through the door, out into the unknown, frantically trying to figure out the best way to freedom.

She found herself on a narrow, overgrown path. To her left, hundreds of feet below, was the ocean. Ahead of her there were steps hewn into the rock leading up to a big house perched high above.

The steps were her only way out. She raced towards them, concentrating on survival, not looking back.

As she reached the first step she could hear him behind her. He grabbed her leg. She kicked out blindly.

"Bitch!" he snarled.

"Leave me alone, you sick bastard!" she screamed, scrambling desperately up the hazardous steps.

He grabbed her again, this time getting hold of her makeshift dress. The sheet tore. Half naked she continued to claw her way up, determined that he was not going to stop her. Nobody was. She was heading for freedom in every way – not just from this man, but this life.

"Don't you get it?" he yelled behind her. "I own you. I

always have. You're *my* whore. My very own personal whore."

There was something about his voice . . . something she almost recognized. It wasn't the Mr X voice, the disguised growl. This was the real man talking, and it was . . . Oh God, SHE KNEW WHO HE WAS!

For a moment she could barely breathe. Then, as if in a trance, she stopped climbing and turned around.

The monster was two steps behind her, baseball cap gone along with the dark glasses. A trickle of blood rolled slowly down the side of his face.

She stared into his eyes.

He knew she recognized him.

They were both still, like two big cats in the wild, watching each other, waiting to see who would pounce first.

"Okay," he said at last. "So now you know. And there's *nothing* you can do." And he laughed, that self-loving cackle she remembered so well. "You and your dumb sister – you're exactly alike," he continued. "She was a whore, too. She didn't deserve to live. Neither do you."

In perfect slow motion she rose from her defensive position, brought her leg back and kicked out with such force that when her foot connected with his chest he had no chance to correct his balance.

He fell back, his hands clutching the air as he tumbled over himself twice, and then disappeared over the edge of the cliff with a long, blood-curdling scream.

Kristin watched him fall, heard the sound of his body as it struck a tree on its way to the rocks and ocean below.

She wasn't sorry. She had finally avenged her sister's death. And it felt completely satisfying, as if it was meant to be.

Howie Powers would *never* laugh at anyone again.

L.A.
Connections
4

# EPILOGUE

## Nine Months Later

DETECTIVE TUCCI agitatedly paced the corridors of Cedars Sinai. Faye was giving birth and although he'd tried to stay in the room holding her hand, the sight of blood, his wife's blood, had sent him running.

His new partner, Wanda O'Donahue, had stopped by to keep him company. She'd also brought a box of doughnuts and a flask of Starbucks coffee. There were many advantages to having a female partner, although Faye didn't seem to think so.

"How's it going in the delivery room?" Wanda asked, biting into a doughnut.

"It's a war zone," he said, grimacing. "A lot of blood and guts and screaming."

"You'll live," Wanda said, giving him a friendly pat on the back.

Yeah, he'd live.

It had been some year. The murder of Salli T. Turner had garnered the most headlines, especially when Mrs Bo Deacon had confessed, right after the terrible car accident that killed her husband.

Tucci had not felt that her confession rang true – although his superiors were in we've-caught-the-murderer heaven, and the press went into headline overdrive. Olive simply didn't have the details the killer would have possessed, although she *was* able to produce the gun used to kill Froo. It was registered to Bo Deacon.

Tucci stayed on the case, establishing that Bobby Skorch had gone to his house earlier in the evening, made love to his wife, fought with her, and left, for ever feeling guilty that he hadn't stayed around.

Bo Deacon had then arrived, unaware that Olive was following him. He'd come on to Salli, who'd told him he had no chance with her. A fight had ensued and he'd killed her in a frenzy of frustration. Then he'd shot the houseman and fled.

Olive had observed everything from her hiding place in the bushes next to the pool.

When Olive had killed Bo in the car wreck, she'd been so overcome with guilt that she'd decided to take the blame for the murders and protect her husband's not-so-spotless reputation. At least in death, he would be her hero.

If it wasn't for Tucci and his concern for detail, she

would have been incarcerated for life. As it was, she was soon back in her Bel Air mansion with a twenty-five-year-old boyfriend, a lucrative book deal, and a new passion for life.

Tucci took a swig of coffee. It tasted fine. For the last six months he'd taken up spinning – an exhausting form of aerobic exercise on a stationary bike. It worked for him, and best of all it meant no more dieting. He'd lost twenty-five pounds.

Faye's doctor approached him, a gentle Asian woman with the most captivating smile. "Your wife would like to see you now, Detective."

"Is it over?"

"Yes, it is."

"And?"

"You're the proud father of a beautiful baby girl."

His grin practically lit up the entire hospital.

\*

The Freddie Leon divorce was one of the most expensive L.A. divorces in recent years. Diana received half of everything – and everything was a lot. Freddie decided it was worth it. He had his freedom and no price was too high to obtain *that*. Besides, business was fine, he could afford to pay Diana off.

A discreet six months after the final decree, Ria Santiago moved into Freddie's beach house – he'd given the Bel Air mausoleum to Diana. After a seven-year affair, he and Ria were finally able to be seen together in public. Freddie felt it was the least he could do for the most loyal woman he'd ever met.

*

Out of the hospital and fitter than ever, Max Steele eschewed a lot of his material possessions. He traded in his Maserati for a Hummer. Sold his house and moved into a Wilshire high-rise. He did not replace his gold Rolex, and after trying to contact Kristin a couple of times and getting no response, he'd fallen in lust with Angela Musconni, even though it was against policy since the agency represented her. Of course, he'd had to persuade Angie to dump the loser she was living with, but that hadn't been too difficult, since shortly after they got together, Eddie Stoner scored a TV series that was shot on location in Hawaii.

It was amazing what could be accomplished when you were one of the most powerful agents in town.

*

Blaming himself for Salli's death, Bobby Skorch lost all sense of concentration. While attempting a record-breaking motorcycle jump between skyscrapers in New York, he faltered and fell to his death.

*

Natalie De Barge got the anchor job she'd been yearning for. Sitting beside Jimmy Sica every night, they made a fine couple. When the cameras weren't rolling, she practically had to beat him off with a stick, but that was just one of the hazards of being an anchorwoman.

She put her love life on hold and enjoyed every second of her new invigorating career.

Her brother, Cole, moved in with Mr Mogul, who so far was treating him like a prince. However, to Natalie's eternal relief, Cole was smart enough not to give up his day job.

\*

Junia took the twenty thousand dollars she received for revealing all of Darlene's dark secrets, and moved to Nashville, where she met a blonde and bubbly country singing star with enormous breasts. They soon became a couple. Junia took up singing. She wasn't half bad.

\*

Darlene was finally nailed on that good old standby – tax evasion. Her lawyer, Linden Masters, was so livid to discover she'd kept things from him, that he refused to represent her anymore. She hired a new lawyer with even more savvy than Linden, and because of her powerful connections she got off with an extremely short jail term.

After she got out, she threw all caution out the window and found a ghost-writer to collaborate on a book, naming names. Her book – dramatically entitled *Madam* – was due out shortly.

Hollywood waited in a state of paranoid fascination.

\*

Kristin took stock of her life, and her sister's too. She met with Cherie's doctor and finally listened to exactly what he had to say. He was a nice man with brown hair and kindly eyes. "There are no miracles, Kristin," he informed her. "Cherie is brain dead. The only reason she's still alive is because you won't allow us to pull the plug."

"Pull it," she said quietly. "I understand."

"You're sure?"

"Yes, I'm sure."

After escaping from the beach house, she'd come home and anonymously called the police – telling them all she knew about Mr X, including his death and where they'd find his body.

Jake had been frantic to see her, so she had agreed to have lunch with him and listen to everything he had to say. It wasn't enough though – there was no going back. He was part of her past now, and she was moving forward.

He told her about the story his friend Madison Castelli was working on.

"Do me this one favour, Jake. Leave my name out of it."

"Done," he assured her.

A week later she moved out of her luxurious apartment into a simpler place.

A few weeks later the doctor called and invited her to dinner. "What are you going to do now that you no longer have to pay your sister's bills?" he asked.

"I'm going back to school," she said. "I want to get my degree in child psychology and maybe – sometime in the future – work with children."

"Sounds like an excellent idea."

# REVENGE

The doctor didn't lead a glamorous life or drive a flashy car. He was a hard-working professional who really cared for people, and he genuinely liked her for herself. Kristin found a great deal of comfort in his presence. So much so that they were married three months later.

*

Jake Sica stayed in L.A. for several months, photographing movie and sports stars, singers and moguls. Working for *Manhattan Style* was an interesting gig, and very highly paid, but after a while he began to yearn for the wide-open spaces of Arizona.

One morning he woke up, looked out his window at the hovering smog, and decided that was it.

By noon he was packed and on his way.

*

Madison wrote the best story of her career, all about the call-girl business in Hollywood. It was so good that Hollywood shelled out, bought the movie rights for an astronomical sum, and asked her to work on the script.

She stayed in touch with her good friend, Jake. He was a great guy, but they never quite connected romantically. Wrong timing.

She took a weekend off with her parents in Connecticut. They were delighted to see her, especially her handsome father, Michael.

Then she flew to Hollywood and met Alex Woods, an edgy, incredibly talented writer/producer/director with a penchant for making powerful Oscar-nominated movies. He wanted to make *her* movie.

So Madison entered the next phase of her life with her eyes open and an appetite for excitement.

Things were looking up.